THE MOON-BLESSED SERIES

THE ETERNAL HUNT

The Eternal Hunt

This book is a work of fiction. Names, characters, places, and incidents are the product of the author's imagination or are used fictitiously. Any resemblance to actual events, locales, or persons, living or dead, is coincidental.

Copyright © 2026 by Hollis Sophia

All rights reserved.

The scanning, uploading, and distribution of this book without permission is a theft of the author's intellectual property. If you would like permission to use material from the book (other than for review purposes), please contact author.hollis.sophia@gmail.com.

NO AI TRAINING: Without in any way limiting the author's exclusive rights under copyright, any use of this publication to "train" generative artificial intelligence (AI) technologies to generate text is expressly prohibited. The author reserves all rights to license uses of this work for generative AI training and development of machine learning language models.

Cover Design: INK Book Designs
Editing: Devon Alexandra
Book Design and Typesetting: Enchanted Ink Publishing

The text type was set in Times New Roman

ISBN: 979-8-218-86466-8 (E-book)
ISBN: 979-8-218-86465-1 (Paperback)

Thank you for your support of the author's rights.

TRINITY PUBLISHING GROUP

To The Trinity—

for helping me climb every mountain.

The Moon-Blessed Series

The Eternal Hunt

Hollis Sophia

CHAPTER 1

THE THUNDERING CRACK OF THE GAVEL'S STRIKE echoes through the air with a ring of finality. Fatality. Within the hollow silence that follows, my fate is sealed.

I am going to die.

Judge Bartlet's words, uttered through those papery thin lips mere moments ago, pound within the confines of my skull until they manage to breach through my haze of disbelief.

Wrenley Hawthe, for the crime of which you have been accused on this day, I hereby sentence you to death by execution tomorrow at dawn. May the Gods have mercy upon your tarnished soul.

If I wasn't so crushed by the weight of the sentence, I might scoff at the word "mercy", for I have never felt the relief and fortune of such a word. And I very much doubt it will favor me in my death.

The only one able to grant any mercy is sitting right before me, an ominous and looming figure in black. Judge Bartlet has always been known to be a fair wielder of impartiality, his scales of justice never tipping in one overly-corrupt or overly-forgiving direction. He has always been considered, as his profession demands, just. But I see now that these rumors are false.

Chest a vice of constricted muscles, heart lodged in my throat, my mouth opens, words a tangled mess on my tongue.

When I manage to sort through them, I croak, "But...it was just a few apples."

And it was. Nothing more. Nothing less. And certainly nothing I haven't stolen before.

My inconsequential thievery has never incited any trouble or animosity within the town of Atherton. As one of very few village vagrants, vendors and shopkeepers have never felt impacted by my occasional but very necessary pilfering. Even less so when they see me for what I am: a young woman who lost everything and has been forced to survive off nothing.

Despite my dishonorable deeds, I've always restricted myself from stealing valuables and coin. Just food and only that which I can't manage to procure through my own paltry means. Sometimes my spoils are bread, other times a piece of meat. And, on that one occasion last year, on my nineteenth birthday, it was a plum tart, the pastry that held so many fond memories within its delicate layers. My father and I often shared them when I was a child. He'd carry me on his sturdy shoulders as we walked home through the market after he finished work. My mother had supper waiting, so the pre-dinner sweet was our little secret. Though I'm fairly certain the lingering jam on our mouths was a tell-tale giveaway.

I'd thought savoring it on my birthday would've been a heartfelt nod to their memories, to our family's memory. But, once I'd taken a bite, the fruit tasted bitterly of melancholy, and the crust crumbled like dry ashes in my mouth, and I ended up choking on my tears. I haven't had one since.

As for the rest of my transgressions like today, it was nothing significant, nothing that would be missed. So consumed with my own wretchedness for what I must do to survive, I try to pick the undesirables: the bruised pear, the burnt loaf, the imperfect rind. Today, it was a small basket of apples containing no more than four or five. It was sat atop crates of dried and cured quality cuts of meats, pastries and confections, jarred jams and preserves, fresh produce, all waiting in an alley to be loaded into a cart and delivered somewhere.

Judge Bartlet's narrowed gaze, magnified by the half-moon lenses of his spectacles, settles on me with shrewd severity. "Lord Cornelius has enacted new laws and made amendments to pre-existing ones. More to the point, these few apples were to be delivered to Lord Cornelius himself and, as he'd already made payment, he is the owner of the purloined goods and holds the right to press these charges. I must say, it is indeed a pity that you were not caught last week, Miss Hawthe, as perhaps then the law might have been more forgiving."

Only one week in power and the new lord has made himself a tyrant of our little town. His predecessor, Lord Eggar, was kind and generous, beloved by our community. When a village has lived in relative harmony, the sovereign presiding over such peace is missed. Yet, it's been but two weeks since his passing and already the town has managed to recover from its grief, installing his replacement. Given that Lord Eggar, who now rests peacefully amidst the soil and earth, bore no children, he had to name a successor in his will. The options had been limited, and until now, Lord Cornelius had done a fair job of concealing his tyrannical tendencies.

I wonder just how long it will take for the rotting infection of corruption to spread throughout his entire system. It's clearly already well on its way what with his new laws and disproportionate punishments, evidence of his transition from leader to oppressor.

My minds spins, gaze blearily running over the small, unfamiliar court room, noting the dour, black painted walls and wooden beams, the empty benches behind me where thankfully no audience is here to witnesses my pitiful demise. I take in the portraits of past judges that line the walls, each one more severe and discerning than the last. When my gaze falls forward again, I study the austere, mahogany wooden desk where Judge Bartlet stiffly sits, his wispy hair and reddened nose shining beneath the lamp overhead.

The air leaves my lungs, pulse thudding beneath my skin, each heavy beat like the tick of a clock. "But...death?" I breathe. I'd had no idea that the food had belonged to Lord Cornelius. That those few apples would sentence me to death. *If only I had known.*

For this question, I receive no response, merely a wave of dismissal gestured to someone over my shoulder. Firm hands clasp around my arms in a steely hold, a guard on each side as though I'm some great threat to society.

The familiar position incites a surge of flashbacks of what transpired not but an hour ago when I was first arrested. Sitting on the small walking bridge near the butcher's shop, staring down into the brook that runs through the edge of town, listening to the babbling water rushing over the rocks, savoring the crisp, sweet taste of the apple's flesh. The next thing I knew, hands were locking around my arms like now, dragging me away without a word.

The guards begin to haul me back, and my heart pounds against my ribs, reality suddenly rushing in as I throw a terrified gaze to the judge. "Please! Please, I didn't know! This is a mistake! *Please! Ple—*"

The door to the courtroom is slammed in my face and, with it, my only chance at being pardoned.

Hot tears sting my cheeks as I'm dragged out of the courthouse, shaking my head in utter disbelief. I squeeze my eyes shut, hoping that by some miracle I'll open them to find this has all been just a wretched nightmare. My legs buckle when I see that the guards are taking me out the prisoners' entrance. Because that's what I am now. A prisoner.

Who will die tomorrow.

The afternoon sun weighs down upon us, heavy as my misery. They march me through the town streets, my shame flaunted for all wandering eyes to see. Because it's Sunday, there aren't many of those, the only small blessing to be had. If one could even call it that.

At some point, I lift my hanging head, gaze latching onto a familiar street as we rush past. My heart aches with a throbbing yearning as bittersweet memories consume.

My family's house was on this street. All that's left on the plot is a desolate ruin. A gaping hole between abandoned soot-stained structures where there once was a home full of love and abundance. Flashes of that night run through my mind; of the roaring blaze, the inferno that breathed against my flesh with an unforgiving appetite, glowing violently like hot coals, the screams and pleas, the swallowing despair. A day I will never forget, no matter how hard I try.

A bitter scoff at the irony settles in my throat. *Of course we had to take this route to the prison. Of course I have to be doubly tormented.* As though my impending death isn't enough to destroy me, I must be struck with the memory of my past, of everything that I've lost, and the sheer nothingness I'm headed toward.

May the Gods have mercy upon your tarnished soul.

No, it seems Judge Bartlet's parting words will not come to fruition. I do not believe the gods will show me any mercy at all.

CHAPTER 2

As a shadow falls over my frame, I dare to look up, finding the looming edifice of Atherton's prison standing before me in all its desolate glory. Color leeching from my complexion, terror eats its way through my body and bones with a ravenous hunger. I fight the urge to be sick, to wait to do so in the privacy of my cell where the racking sobs that simmer within me can take hold. Where the wells of tears within my eyes can finally be unleashed.

Roughly shoved inside, I'm greeted by a burly man in grimy, sweat-stained clothes who eyes me with a raised brow. "What's this one in for?" he grunts to my escorts, a hint of surprise in his tone.

"Thievery," one of them answers coldly. The other hands the warden a folded piece of paper which he opens and reads, no doubt outlining my execution order so that preparations can be made for tomorrow morning. After a quick review of the parchment, he stashes it in his pocket before turning to face a wall of shelves and plucking a pair of the few sets of iron cuffs. I try to swallow my fear, but my frame shakes like a leaf as the warden clasps them around my small wrists. The chilled iron is already rusted, rough and heavy against my delicate skin. Their weight sits upon me everywhere, my entire body inflicted with the shackled sensation.

"Follow me," he grumbles after offering a parting nod to my guards. Both leave without a word as I follow my new captor. His oily skin glistens in the scant light while his body odor wafts behind him with a pungent stench, poisoning my lungs.

As I'm led through the hall of cells, I realize how puny the prison actually is. And completely vacant of any prisoners, though this comes as little surprise given Atherton's low crime rate.

At least I'll have the place to myself, to mourn and grieve in peace, I think. The half-soothing thought is abruptly shattered as we reach the end of the hall making our way toward the last and largest cell...which is anything *but* empty.

A figure stands inside, and I'm immediately unsettled at the prospect of spending my last night alive with another criminal—a *male* criminal. "Am I not allowed my own cell?" I murmur as the warden gathers a ring of keys linked to his belt.

"The other locks are too rusted, can't get a key to work in 'em," he answers, proceeding to unlock the cell before me.

Once again, I'm forcefully shoved inside before the key turns ominously, leaving me to watch the warden's retreating frame. I turn quickly, not wanting to expose my back to a potential predator. But as I give my cell-mate a once over, he's nothing like the common criminal I expect.

An older boy leans against the stone wall, arms folded over his chest, one long, muscular leg crossed over the other. His rich blue eyes appraise me curiously, head tilting to the side. "Have they brought me a gift?" he asks, eyes narrowing in interest.

The deep, rumbling voice washes over me with a swell of surprise. *Not a boy then.* The fiendish grin he wears has my stomach twisting, and I suddenly feel like an innocent lamb cornered by a ravenous wolf.

I don't respond, still too dazed to do anything apart from rub around my already sore and tender wrists, the chain between the cuffs rattling with my movements. His eyes track the motion before he tosses me a knowing look. "Joining me at the chopping block tomorrow?"

My eyes flare when they meet his gaze. *He's been sentenced to die as well? For what?* I wonder.

From another cursory glance, I note that his clothes are clean and unwrinkled, hands and face unmarred. *Certainly not a beggar, and it doesn't seem as though he's been in a brawl.* Yet, despite my wonderings, I have no appreciation for his mockery. Jeering about tomorrow, of what's going to happen to me, to him, treating it like it's a joke. If he wants to be funny, then I too can make a weapon of wit.

"Of course. I've had this in my diary for weeks," I sneer, relishing in the anger that's bubbling within me, a welcome distraction from the consuming numbness.

He chuckles with a shake of his head, wavy, golden locks shifting across his brow. "Really?" he asks with mock interest. "This was a spontaneous turn of events for me." He stashes his hands in his pockets.

I roll my eyes before I begin to pace the cell, my body and mind demanding movement if only to take away from the pain of my ever-tightening chest.

"So, what are you in here for?" His tone is causal, as if we're sitting down for tea and he's making light conversation. "Gambling, swindling, alcoholism, grievous bodily harm—"

"Thieving," I snap, if only to shut him up.

"Thieving? You must've stolen something very valuable to warrant this kind of sentencing," he notes, eyes twinkling with intrigue.

I huff a humorless laugh. "Depends on how much value you place on a few apples," I reply bitterly.

His eyes marginally widen. "You're in here for stealing *apples*?" A hint of incredulity paints his tone, and I can't help the small bit of validation derived from his genuine surprise. Still, I can't meet his gaze to answer. My eyes start to burn again with the madness of it all. *I'm going to die tomorrow—for some apples.*

"Did you steal them directly from the lord's hands or something?"

I throw him a glare. "Why are *you* here?"

"Murder."

The word stops me cold. My blood chills, skin prickling with sudden wariness. His answer was spoken simply, with a small, inconsequential shrug. Even his expression remains neutral, neither pleasure nor guilt etched into the sharp planes of his face. As if he's answering a question as benign as the weather.

Beyond the shock his admittance instills, the first thought that strikes me is, *how do I deserve the same sentencing as him? How is murder on equal footing with apples?* I'd laugh at the absurd injustice if I wasn't so disturbed by his answer.

He's a murderer.

But he's so young, too boyish to be a killer. And to declare it so casually. A million questions run through my mind—who he killed, why he did it, how he did it—all before the realization hits: I have to spend the night with a murderer. Who knows how crazy he is. Quite a bit I'd wager given how calm and unfazed he seems.

The male startles me with a low chuckle. "I should make it clear though that it wasn't some random act of bloodlust. It's my profession," he clarifies, tone polite.

"Your profession?" The question comes out as a hushed whisper, afraid anything I say will set him off. As if he's a trigger awaiting release.

"I'm an assassin."

I find my body instinctively taking a step back. His eyes follow the movement, disapproval in his expression.

"Fair enough. Although, I'd expect a little less judgment from you given how similar our professions are."

"They're nothing alike," I bite, surprised by my boldness in the face of someone so lethal. Even though he looks young, face relatively innocent, I realize how intimidating he actually is. His body, although lean, is packed with muscle, the curves in his arms visible through his jacket. He's unnervingly tall, and the confidence with which he holds himself doubly so. I don't think there's an apprehensive or bashful bone in his body.

"In principle they're the same, taking something from someone. You take belongings, I take lives."

"I hardly think we merit the same sentencing."

He nods in agreement before shrugging. "Maybe they just don't like you here."

I send him a searing glare in return before it suddenly dawns on me as to what our verbal sparring has done. The conversation has helped distract from some of the shock, allowing me to forget my panic, if only temporarily. Whether he's doing it on purpose or not, I decide to let him continue to irritate me. To let his words kindle my ire.

"I guess so. They claim that it's a new law…they wouldn't even hear my defense. Maybe they just wish to make an example of me."

His features shift into amusement. "You can always ask them before they slit our throats."

How can he be so calm about his impending death? Maybe because death is his profession and he's numb to the fear it inflicts. Or maybe he's just really that deranged.

My gaze flits to the confines of our cell, floor laden with rotten straw, a small bucket in the corner to my left which, thankfully, is sealed shut with a lid. My home for the night. My last night.

I hadn't even realized during my escort that the march to the prison was my last time walking the streets of Atherton. I was too consumed by the shock to realize that I should've savored the journey. That I had the chance to see the remains of my childhood home one last time. Another thing to lament, another loss to mourn.

The fading light of sunset from the small window draws my attention to just how quickly the day has passed. A few hours are all I have left. And I'm wasting them squabbling with some assassin who very well might try and end me before sunrise.

I shuffle to the barred window, stepping onto the little stool below it so I can peer out through the tiny square. The cool, evening air brushes across my face, and I close my eyes, letting it attempt to calm me. After a few moments, I turn back around, only to find the male's dark eyes trained on me, expression contemplative.

"What's your name?"

"Wrenley."

"I'm Ryland." He sketches a mocking bow.

"You expect me to believe that's your real name?" I question. The breeze whispers across the back of my neck as I watch him from the stool, offering me a smug grin.

"I don't need to rely on aliases," he returns, tone dripping with arrogance.

I snort. "Pretty confident for someone stuck in a cell waiting for his death. Must not be that skilled if you were caught." As soon as the words slip out of my mouth, I snap it shut. Insulting him is the last thing I should be doing. I know I'm going to die tomorrow, but I'd rather not have it be any sooner.

The prisoner only smirks. "My client sold me out after I finished the job, wanted to tie up loose ends." He shrugs. "Can't blame him though. Lack of strategy is what gets a man killed."

"Clearly," I quip unintentionally. I realize too late that he might mistake my empathic sarcasm as a jibe. In a haste to change subjects, I ask while stepping down from the stool, "You're not mad?"

"It's not the first time it's happened."

Before I can ask what he means, the warden reappears, shoving two bowls of a questionable watery broth through the slot in the door. The metal of the plates grates against the stone with a shrill screeching. "Eat up," he barks before shuffling away.

Neither one of us approaches our supposed dinner. My stomach protests my refusal, but I remain adamant. I'd rather face a blade tomorrow than that grey, oily liquid. I refuse for that to be my last meal. I'll go with the memory of the crisp apple accompanying me to my death.

All the fire and sass from moments ago quickly ebbs from my system. The realization of another hungry night, my last hungry night, consumes me. I slump down on the stool, back pressed against the cold wall, head tipped up to stare at the ceiling. My eyes trace the edges of each stone.

"Do you have family?"

The unexpected question has me lowering my head to meet my companion's gaze. "No." While I don't mind him knowing that it's just me in this world, I don't need him to know the exact details of my orphaning.

Despite residing in the local orphanage, my existence in this town has been a painfully isolated one. It's no home, but I've not parted from its safety since making a deal with the owner two years ago. My first year as an orphan was spent moving from home to home, taken in by acquaintances or clients of my parents. Those stays were always brief, a couple weeks and then an awkward conversation trying to subtly prompt me into offering to leave—which I always did. I never wished to burden anyone and, in that desire, I learned that even generosity has its limits. The people of this town had a threshold as to how much accommodation they were willing to make given my suffering and desperation. But grief doesn't expire, and sometimes, it takes more sustained charity to help an individual overcome the pain and challenges such as those I faced. And yet, the most they could offer was a cot for a week or two or to overlook a missing tart or stale loaf of bread.

So, finding a stable shelter at the orphanage had been a blessing. Unfortunately, food wasn't part of our agreement, hence my periodic transgressions. I'm sure if there was enough to spare, I could've negotiated a few meals, but, at the time, I'd had plans to find work and earn an honest living. Of course, I hadn't realized that work is a privilege and not a right, even for those able and willing. Most especially for those tainted like me.

Atherton is a simple town, smoothly functioning, its residents facing little to no strife. The problem with falling upon hard times is that if things become dire enough, say if one loses their home or family, people have no interest in associating with you and your misfortunes. Here, once a beggar, always a beggar. The label stays with you like ink to skin, and no one is willing to help.

While I'd briefly considered leaving Atherton and my many misfortunes behind, I was overwhelmed at the emotional prospect of leaving my family. True, they were gone, but there was something about walking the same streets of my childhood that kept them close. So, I stayed, taking on the occasional odd-job, earning a few coins that left my pockets as soon as they were placed in them.

My cell-mate nods, registering the information as if it has value. Overwhelmed and antsy, I rise once more to gaze out the window, wanting to savor my last sunset. But I've missed it now. The sky is already dark, moon near fully overhead, radiating its silver glow over the midnight landscape.

I'm reminded of the lore and legends of the gods, the stories my father would share with me at night. It's said that the gods worship the moon, a symbol of their power and majesty. The thought brings to mind a favorite tale from my childhood about how the moon came to be.

The world began with night, a depthless, endless veil of black, with no ray of light to be found. The sun later emerged, breathtaking in its radiance but fleeting with its brightness, fading all too quickly into that onyx abyss. After the gods were born, they grew to dislike the overwhelming ebony haze, so they each bore a token of light, studding them into the darkness. Over time, a cluster of those little lights, stars, formed and accumulated into one great sphere of white light. It's beauty was so astonishing that the primordial beings made it their emblem, reverently worshipping it's glorious magnificence.

It makes me wonder whether I shall soon dance amidst those twinkling jewels, resting in the heavens above and beholding the beauty of the moon from a nearer distance. Perhaps my spirit will be pardoned and allowed to roam freely amidst the stars. *That wouldn't be so bad*, I think.

A tear slides down my cheek, the first of what I know will be many.

Footsteps and the sounds of hay shuffling fill the drafty space. I instinctively turn my head, wanting to keep the assassin in my periphery. The male, Ryland, lowers himself to the floor of our darkened cell, settling himself for the night. He pulls one leg to his chest, the other stretched out. His deep blue eyes meet mine.

"Get some sleep, little thief. You'll need it."

I'll need sleep? I'm about to enter an endless slumber, how could I require more? Perhaps he meant that it's better to sleep than dwell on tomorrow. But if he thinks I'll manage to get any rest, he's delusional.

Ignoring the suggestion, I turn back around and continue to watch the star-flecked sky and the beaming moon, imagining a fate that is not so dark and cruel. One filled with light and hope.

When the breeze is finally too much for my chilled face to bear, I lower myself to the floor, hoping that the male across from me is asleep so that I can finally mourn the loss of my existence. Mourn the beautiful, little pockets of life that I'll miss, the ones that I've come to savor the most in these years of poverty. Like soft, summer rainfall, the cacophony of cricket and forest sounds at night, the first fall of autumn leaves, the drowsy, quiet moments before waking in the morning, spring's first bloom, snowflakes on my winter-kissed skin.

Every yearning, desperate memory flits through my mind, begging to be savored one last time. And I do, parting from each one with a longing farewell.

My light, that inner spark filled with life and my essence, was dimmed long ago. What's been left for me to kindle has been nothing more than a few flickering embers. And now, that little bit of remaining warmth is going to be snuffed out entirely. That last piece of me, Wrenley Hawthe, is going to be erased into darkness.

Chapter 3

As one might expect on the night before their execution, I didn't sleep. Instead, I'd sat against the cell floor, tucked away in my dark corner of the earth and said my farewells. To all the things I'd never see again, the things I'd never do.

I imagined being reunited with my parents. I wondered how they'd feel about me joining them in death so soon. Would they be ashamed of what became of me, of the life I fell into? I know they would've told me to do whatever I needed to do to survive, but would they have felt I hadn't tried hard enough to remove myself from my circumstances? That I was weak for not moving on from their memory?

The tears had streamed silently, forcing me to breathe through my mouth to hide the sounds of my stuffed nose so my cell-mate wouldn't notice. But he slept rather peacefully, neither tossing nor turning. I envied him. Though I didn't sleep, I managed to fall into that place right between waking and resting. The drowsy state where your mind slows yet is still somewhat coherent. The very state I now find myself in, until an unnaturally chipper voice says from above, "Good morning, little thief."

Slowly, I lift my head from where it had been nestled between my propped knees. The male's gaze travels across my face. Although my tears ceased some time ago, I'm sure my eyes remain glassy and red, my nose swollen and blotchy. To my surprise, he extends a hand to help me stand, his own cuffs matching mine.

I eye his hand warily, but ultimately, my stiff and weak joints prompt me to accept. As my fingers skim his palm, a small jolt runs through me. I flinch. It was like a spark of electricity had surged from his flesh to mine. My eyes flash to his, finding his expression neutral, gaze only slightly narrowed.

I wonder if the heightened sensation is due to the subconscious and very morbid realization that this is my last occasion of physical contact with another. I discard the chilling thought and place the rest of my hand in his as he helps me up. Though my senses are dulled from my sorrow, the fact that his hand swallows mine doesn't escape me.

The sound of footsteps and jangling keys prompt a jarring return to reality. My vision instantly blurs, heart straining in my chest.

This is it. No more time to try and prepare myself, no excuse of a breakfast to add a delay. They're getting it over with. Now. And maybe it's for the best. *What would be the point in crying over more of that horrid broth?*

A wall of warmth suddenly hits the side of my face, and I suck in a startled breath as a hushed voice murmurs in my ear, "Don't let them see you cry." The commanding edge in his tone has me shifting to face him. His eyes are firm, holding my gaze until I give a shallow nod, trying to swallow back the lump in my throat.

As much as I wish I could appear unfazed as he's advised, I'm too much of a coward. Too human.

The warden and yesterday's guards stand before the cell door, as foreboding as one might expect. "Out," the warden orders, yanking open the door with a loud and wrenching creak.

I hesitate near the threshold, limbs finding it difficult to obey orders. Sensing this, my cell-mate casually steps in front of me, taking the lead. Outside the cell, he's shoved forward before I'm given the same royal treatment. But the guard who pushes me has a very different, and very unwelcome, hand placement. Low. Too low. And lingering.

I jerk away from his touch, startled and disturbed.

Someone *tsks*, drawing our attention ahead. "That's not how you treat a lady…" Ryland's low tone is nothing compared to the unsettlingly dark expression that mars his features, his gaze locked on the guard who touched me. But his glowering is interrupted as we're both pushed forward again.

I somehow manage to keep an even pace. My thoughts are blurred and slow as we pass cell after cell eventually led down a dank and narrow corridor before approaching an open doorway where dawn's soft light streams in. As soon as I pass the threshold, I inhale the crisp morning air, savoring the lush periwinkle sky.

"Ah." My cell-mate sighs merrily. "Such a glorious morning to perish." The sharp contrast in his tone from a few moments ago leads me to believe he's genuinely insane.

A soft grunt follows his words after the guard nearest him shoves him forward again, clearly disliking his glib tone.

A few more yards crossed, and we enter through another hall, this one much shorter in distance, before stepping into an enclosed, circular space. Despite being walled, there's no roof, allowing the fresh air and sunlight to filter in. But my thoughts are less focused on the view above, gaze instead trained on the wooden platform sat in the middle of the space. Atop it, a man donned in all-black waits with an unsheathed sword in his hand, lank grey hair fluttering in the breeze. He watches us with a cold and vacant stare. My heart tightens like a noose.

Once a few feet from the platform, we're ordered to halt, and the guard who so indecently touched me earlier nods to the male in front of me. "Up you get, boy," he commands.

Though I can only see the broad expanse of his back, Ryland's voice is laced with casual ease instead of the fear or reluctance I expect. "Surely you don't intend for the lady to witness such dreadful gore before her own end," he chides, admonishing a naughty child.

The guard considers this for a brief moment before turning to my trembling frame and gesturing for me to step onto the platform instead. Part of me thinks I should hate the male for sending me to go first. But, deep down, I can't exactly find fault in his logic. I really didn't want to see the aftermath of a headless body collapsing onto the scaffold.

I swallow. Despite feeling the weight of eyes on me, my own gaze remains on the platform, imagining the crimson stains that will soon mar it. In my periphery, I can sense the guard stepping forward to push me in haste, but, he suddenly halts, his gaze locked with my cell-mate's whose expression I can't see from this angle. All I know is that the guard relents, allowing me to mount the platform at my own pace.

I'm grateful. Every spare moment I receive is one extra second to treasure the warmth of the rising morning sun, the soft breeze caressing my face and shaking frame.

I take a stiff step forward, throat dry as I mount the platform, trying to keep my head held high. If I'm going to die, I'll at least do so with some sliver of dignity. I won't cower. Not before these heartless men.

The executioner takes a step closer, towering over me like death himself, waiting to claim my fear-stricken soul. "Kneel," he orders, voice void of sympathy, my impending death meaningless to him.

The lack of empathy spurs some of my bottled panic, my body's trembling morphing to full on quaking as I lower myself to my knees. The executioner shifts to stand behind me which sends a shiver down my spine.

I suddenly wish that my cell-mate had killed me in my sleep. It would've been better to be oblivious to the exact moment of my death rather than counting down each thundering, torturous second. Or, better yet, I should've asked him to do it, begged him to make it quick. He probably knew a million ways that were swifter and painless. Instead, I now must endure the terror clawing in my chest, the sweat and chills warring on my skin, my bladder fighting to keep itself contained.

Holding in the sobs that are desperate to be loosed is a battle I'm about to lose. The tears start to escape, dripping onto my chest and seeping into the fabric of my dress. My gaze lifts to the sky, the glorious, golden sun quickly making its ascent. I look to my right, staring into the deep blue eyes of my cell-mate, the last face I'll ever see, this stranger with whom I spent my final night. I don't know why I hold his stare. Maybe it's because it's the only one that feels human.

A faint smile dances on his lips before he winks at me. My brow creases, trying to decipher the strange gesture when I hear the executioner's blade shift.

I stiffen, lips trembling. I want to close my eyes, to hide in my terror, but since I'll have them closed for an eternity after this moment, I will them to remain open.

"Any final words?" the cold voice asks from above. I want to scoff at the offer. Am I really supposed to recite some profound and inspiring prose, a noble quote that will be recorded in the death logs? *How can I be expected to concoct something even remotely eloquent? Besides, who would I even say them to?* I have no family or friends to mourn my demise.

"None that I would waste on any of your ears," I reply, voice managing to carry some bitterness.

I hear a grunt of amusement to my right, then the sound of the blade being raised. My breath hitches, and my mind, in a panicked and hysterical frenzy, desperately tries to cling to pleasant thoughts like last night. A thousand moments and images flicker in my mind, each one as fleeting as the last.

Summer sun. The babbling of a brook. Willow trees dancing in the wind. Sunday markets and plum tarts. Village dances. My mother's warm embrace. The rush of releasing an arrow from a bowstring. The smell of old books. A crackling fire. My father's rough and sturdy voice.

The pyre that is my life is about to be lit and razed into a wild and unforgiving inferno, leaving no traces of me behind. I open my eyes, not having realized I'd succumbed to closing them.

Nothing's happened.

It's quiet.

Unsettlingly quiet.

I don't shift from my frozen state, too afraid that any sudden movements might bring about the sword's descent.

Why is it taking so long?

Suddenly, there's the distinct sound of another blade being drawn. Before I have a chance to consider the implications, a sharp gasp echoes, followed by another abrupt silence.

Around me, chaos ensues.

Shouts erupt, drawing my attention to the right where I witness my blonde-haired inmate unsheathing a sword—from one of the guard's chests. His body crumples to the ground with a muffled thump. The other guard immediately takes notice, charging my cell-mate.

Stupefied, I watch as the boy swiftly glances from the oncoming attacker to his iron-clad wrists. With little effort, he sharply pulls them apart in a quick and precise tug.

The chain snaps. *Snaps.*

As if he merely broke a twig and not *iron*.

With his wrists now free, he flicks the sword around in an elegant arc, a maneuver only an accomplished swordsman could achieve. As I watch him swiftly parry with the guard, I hear the executioner behind me remove himself from the platform either to flee or solicit help. A glance over my shoulder confirms the latter.

Ryland catches my stare, right after he stabs another guard directly in the stomach, the blade disappearing within the flesh. Even the burly warden attempts to join the fight, already breathless as he rushes our way.

"Go on ahead, little thief. I'll join you shortly." Ryland's voice is only mildly urgent, as if we're running late to a performance, and he can afford to catch up in a minute.

I gape at him for a few seconds before the order fully registers. He's offering me a chance to escape. He doesn't have to tell me twice.

Rising on unsteady legs, I stiffly leap off the platform, knees nearly buckling upon impact. A small amount of guilt settles within me for leaving him behind considering he's currently saving my life, but since I have no skill with a blade and would likely end up getting myself killed in the process, he's probably better off without me.

I race through one of the open doorways directly across from the one we came through. Once out, I don't turn back, chasing my freedom like one chases the tail of a good dream—desperately.

Despite the hope of liberation, doubt begins to creep its way into my thoughts. We'll likely be caught and carried back to finish what was started. *Or, maybe they'll just kill us in a brutal attack on sight.* The visuals make my stomach churn, yet my legs keep moving. My cell-mate bought us this opportunity. I at least have to try.

Sprinting through an enclosed space while trying to keep quiet is an artform I doubt I accomplish with any skill. But I ultimately decide that swiftness is the greater priority. It also helps that the hallway is empty.

I catch sight of a small door up ahead. To my relief, I find that it leads to a vacant alley, likely a back exit meant to dispose of corpses if the dried bloodstains on the floor and walls are any indication.

Pausing in the silent street, I take a beat and contemplate. The better part of me wants to wait, to see if he made it, but the self-serving voice rooted in survival reminds me that he told me to run. And if this is my chance, I can't afford to waste it.

Creeping forward, I stop at the edge of the alley, peeking around the corner. The street beyond is quiet, only a few people milling about.

My imprisonment and execution wouldn't likely have become public news, not yet at least. So no one woul—

A hand lands on my shoulder, and I shriek as I whip around. The hand swiftly strikes out to clamp over my mouth, my body pushed flat against the wall. Heart hammering in my chest, I behold brilliant blue eyes and shiny blonde hair.

He survived.

I can't tell if it's only adrenaline coursing through me or also a bit of relief.

Ryland's entire frame presses flush against mine, and I suddenly realize just how large he is. In my haze of grief last night, it seems my usual level of observation was impaired. In my current state of heightened alarm, I manage to truly take him in.

A towering and lean figure with broad shoulders and muscled arms. *Definitely* not a boy's body. And his face, while boyish looking at times, likely due to the somewhat unruly blonde locks, is a man's. Sapphire eyes are set beneath two strong brows between which is a straight nose, full, pink lips, and a jawline sharp as the blade he just wielded.

His hand practically swallows my entire face, my body completely trapped by his. It dawns on me, a little late, just how lethal he is. Not only through his profession, but his body alone. The firm, imposing frame is primed for violence and, clearly, extremely capable of executing it. He could probably snap me as easily as he did the chain and cuffs and not think twice about it.

He throws me a roguish half-grin, only mildly out of breath. Lowering his hand, I stare at him in bewilderment.

"Shall we?" he asks, stepping back and allowing me a chance to take a breath. My mind spins with a million thoughts, pulse thrumming, heart aching so painfully I'm concerned I may have caused some damage.

He stands there, waiting with that smile of ease on his face as if this whole situation isn't the epitome of stress but rather fun. As if this has all been part of some scheme...some strategy.

His words from last night ring in my head. *Lack of strategy is what gets a man killed.* "You planned this?"

"I'll admit that you were an unexpected adjustment, but yes. I had no intention of dying today."

He was always going to escape, had known it the whole time. It explains why he was so infuriatingly calm and untroubled. Those pieces of the puzzle quickly click into place. But the next question is why. Why didn't he just tell me his plan? Why let me panic?

He seems to sense the string of questions forming in my mind and preempts them. "You can ask me later, but for now, we need to get out of the city." He grins fiendishly. "Our freedom awaits."

The words sound like a tantalizing dream, a wisp of hope dangling in front of my desperate soul. And yet, the sharp sting of reality slices through that hazy fantasy, reminding me of our current predicament. "How? The streets will be crawling with people."

It's a Monday morning after all. Our chances would've been far better had we fled yesterday on the day of rest. The start of the week commences the monotonous routine of countless chores and tasks, putting everyone in an already irritable and irksome mood and making them far less forgiving when happening upon strange occurrences and unusual sightings.

Ryland simply lifts his brows tauntingly. "Not the streets we'll be taking."

Is he daft? I'm very well certain the look on my face captures such a thought as he smirks. "Don't worry. I've got us covered."

I arch a dubious brow, making to fold my arms over my chest when I recall that they're restrained. Lifting my bound wrists, Ryland frowns before reaching behind his back. Miraculously, he pulls out a ring of iron keys and proceeds to unlock the cuffs. I don't want to imagine what he did to acquire them, only relieved that he did. Because as soon as he removes the cuffs, my entire body sings, the burden of their shackling weight instantly vanishing.

Ryland pivots toward the street in front of us, tossing the cuffs and keys to the right, the direction that leads to the town center. With that, he twists back around and begins to stride deeper into the alley.

Into a dead end.

It's as though he's expecting us to waltz through some magical portal within the wall that'll whisk us away to safety. I follow behind hesitantly, wondering if perhaps this male should have been kept behind bars. If I ought to make a break for it on my own. We don't have a sanitorium in Atherton, but I'm beginning to think the prison was doubling as one.

He stops in front of a corroded grate near the alley wall, promptly bending down and wrapping his hands around the iron bars. Without displaying an ounce of taxed exertion, he lifts the rusted grating and sets the manhole cover on the ground before rising to his full height again. His gaze flicks between me and the gaping black hole before us, features expectant. "Ladies first." The words sound completely witless given the situation.

Offering him a patient albeit redundant expression, I utter each word slowly so he can absorb them clearly. "They lead to the sewers."

He has the audacity to mirror my dubious look before a smile pulls at his lips. "Care to make a wager on that?"

Hastily, my gaze flicks over my shoulder to the crossroad of streets, wondering if I should just bolt. Every second I stand here deliberating is another second eating into our head-start. But Ryland interrupts my vacillation. "Trust me, they don't lead to the sewers." His now serious gaze is the final push in my decision.

Carefully, though well-aware that time is of the essence, I approach the opening, staring into the dark hole. Crouching low, I palm the edges of the ground before scooting myself toward the center of the manhole. With a steadying breath, I ease myself downward. Legs dangling helplessly, I realize that my short stature isn't long enough to meet the remaining distance. Mustering the last dregs of my courage, the already shallow well now completely depleted, I let myself fall.

Unsurprisingly, my landing is rough as my feet slam onto the compact ground. Pain radiates up my legs in throbbing tingles as I steady myself, a hand resting on the dampened wall coated in a green, slimy substance. My eyes quickly flit about the space. These are tunnels. Definitely not sewers.

I'm impressed by his craftiness, I'll give him that. We'll be able to walk right through the town, completely undetected. Although, I'm not sure how wise it is for me to traipse through the dark with an unfamiliar assassin at my back. But it's either that or walk through the bustling town streets in broad daylight.

Stepping back, I squint up to the small source of light as my cell-mate makes his descent. He lands smoothly on his feet, so tall that he merely reaches an arm up to grip the grate and pull it back over the opening, sealing us inside, encasing us in darkness.

The lack of light instantly sets me on edge, and I keep blinking in the hopes of adjusting to the pitch black.

Without a word, Ryland grabs hold of my wrist, so small in his grip he could probably crush the bones with hardly any pressure. Leading us deeper into the tunnels, the damp and dank air clogs my nose in an unpleasant, stifling sort of way.

I hadn't even realized this underground network existed, broad and vast secret passages unbeknownst to the public. An entire circuit running beneath the Atherton thoroughfare. I can only wonder how long this maze has existed; a good while if the musty scent is any indication.

Hopefully any remaining guards will be too busy following the staged trail Ryland left with our cuffs to consider our escape below.

Our footsteps softly echo, the rhythmic dripping of water occasionally sounding, my ears on high alert since my eyes are failing me. The unforgiving cold and drafty air assaults my adrenaline-taut frame, and I'm shivering as the male in front guides us though the blinding darkness. I'm amazed he's not awkwardly stumbling along like I am. "Spend much time below ground?" I ask, voice gently carrying.

"If the mood strikes." His smug, low voice swallows my senses like the shadows surrounding us, making it feel as though he's a part of the darkness itself, an extension of its shifty and consuming nature. It seems that along with his swaths of courage, he also has no shortage of arrogance.

I try to imagine where we might be located above ground, what direction we're heading. But as we pass under a new grate, a familiar scent filters through my nose, a welcome and tempting aroma. Sweet cinnamon, honeyed apples, freshly baked bread...

We're near Mr. Limrys's bakery. My stomach claws with a ravenous ferocity at the mouth-watering smell, but I quell my hunger as we move further along. It's a miracle we've made it this far, and I'm not about to lose focus because of my unsated appetite. We've had a lot of luck this morning, and I need to keep a clear head to ensure that doesn't change. Although, *our* luck, isn't exactly accurate. My cell-mate is the one who possesses all the magic. If I had any luck at all, I would've never found myself without a home and on the streets, would never have been arrested and sentenced for execution. But it seems this male regularly walks the line of danger, teasing and taunting it with reckless abandon, somehow never succumbing to its clutches. Edwyl must have blessed him.

My heart stalls in my chest as said male starts to whistle a nameless tune as we wade through the darkness, the clear notes ringing a merry melody through the cavernous halls. "Should you really be doing that?" I whisper, the bite still audible in my tone.

"No one will hear."

"You know what they say, arrogance often makes even the cleverest man a fool," I mutter, peeved by his lack of remiss.

His whistling is interrupted by the sound of a throaty chuckle. "No, I'm afraid I haven't heard that one."

"But—"

"This isn't my first escape, little thief. In fact, it's proven disappointingly easy."

After disregarding the oddity of such a remark, I'm forced to acknowledge that he did make our escape look rather effortless. Granted, Atherton's prison is poorly staffed, but still... we'd been outnumbered, and he managed to free us both in what was probably a record time, all while I'd had a sword hovering above my neck.

As we approach another grate, scant shafts of light filtering in a few feet ahead, my eyes catch on faint markings scratched into the stone walls. Their faded visibility hints that they were written a long time ago. Leaning to the side to better make out their design, my body suddenly lurches forward as my feet trip on something, causing me nearly to stumble into my cellmate's back.

His hold on my wrist tightens to keep me upright at the same time my palm slams into the middle of his spine to steady myself. Apparently, I disrupted a pile of *somethings* for the sounds of their sharp clattering fill the tunnels. I quickly step to the side, only to crunch on more of the same objects beneath my boots. Squinting in the sparse light, I can just make out the distinct pale shapes...

Bones.

I jump forward, this time well and truly stumbling into his back, another chill cresting my already icy skin. I suppose these tunnels have a darker history than I'd first thought, one I'm definitely not interested in learning.

Something dark and furry suddenly rushes past my foot on my other side, squeaking softly. I jump, fingers digging into Ryland's shirt, leeching the warmth seeping from his jacket. There may have been a mouse or two to contend with at the orphanage, but they were small, endearing little creatures that I'd sometimes feed leftover crumbs. Not wily and mangy like the rodent that just ran past, its thick, lumpy tail trailing behind.

A sickened shiver runs through me as I try to pretend I haven't just seen anything remotely disturbing. Ryland's voice sounds, the deep tone only moderately soothing my frayed nerves. "It's okay. They're just rats, and the bones don't bite."

"Oh, well when you put it like that," I retort dryly, mostly because my throat is dry as dust. I can now safely assert that walking through tunnels is not for me, whether alone or with company. I prefer to spend my time above ground.

Ryland's soft grunt reverberates down his spine and into my palms, voice sounding much closer now. "Don't worry, we're almost there."

Thankfully, he isn't lying. In less than a few minutes, after several sharp turns, we reach a dead end, another grate positioned above us. Ryland swiftly lifts the iron disc before pulling himself up and reaching for me. Gripping both wrists, he murmurs, "Up we go," before hauling me out and onto the grass.

It takes more than a minute for my eyes to adjust from pitch black to blinding bright. Finally, I take in my surroundings, greedily inhaling the clean air. Proud standing oaks with their bountiful verdant leaves lay ahead of us as far as the eye can see. And behind me, several yards away are a few small structures—the outskirts of Atherton—which means we've now entered the greenery of Stone Wood.

We really escaped.

My head isn't lying on the dirt ground of that prison, a puddle of blood pooling beneath my severed neck. Guards aren't hauling my limp corpse into a cart where I'd have been hauled off somewhere to be burned, my ashes scattered in some nameless dump. We're free. I'm free.

Suddenly, the sunlight on my skin feels more glorious than ever, the breeze more refreshing. The beauty of life quickly reabsorbs into my soul, and I'm fighting back tears.

After closing the grate, Ryland dusts off his hands, nodding for me to follow him into the foliage. The sounds of swaying trees and birdsong fill my ears, and I've never been so happy. The rush of adrenaline begins to dissipate, replaced with awe and confusion. I break the ongoing silence, the million questions I've had running through my mind rising to the surface.

"How did you know about those tunnels? I've lived here my whole life, and no one has ever mentioned them."

Ryland faces forward as he answers. "The best kept secrets are often lost to time."

"So, you had your escape planned since they locked you in that cell?"

He throws an amused glance my way. "It almost sounds like you wish we owed it all to luck."

Ignoring him, I press, "Well, I'm simply wondering why you didn't mention your escape plan sooner. You let me believe the whole night I was going to die."

"I know, and I'm sorry for it. But it was better for you to remain unaware of my intentions. Had you known, you would've been too tense, looking for any signals or clues as to when I would strike. You needed to appear genuinely distressed."

For a good minute, I see red. I hate him for doing that to me, putting me through the trauma. I hate that I had to suffer an entire night preparing for my execution. I'll probably die young from the amount of stress I endured. And, most of all, I hate that part of me understands his logic. Even though it was at the expense of my crumbling sanity, I can understand his reasoning. Besides, whether he told me of his plans or not, he saved my life and bought me my freedom. It's an undeniable truth. I owe him everything.

Swallowing my anger, I offer a sincere expression. "Thank you…for freeing me."

Ryland smiles broadly and without restraint, his straight teeth glistening in the light. "It was an honor, little thief."

I bristle at the name but continue with my questioning. "So, where are you headed?" Really, I should be asking myself that. I've never been outside of Atherton. Ever. Stone Wood is the farthest I've traveled and, even now, most of its expanse is foreign to me. I have no familiarity with anywhere else. I have no one else. And staying in Atherton is no longer an option.

Ryland nods into the distance. "Right now, just up ahead."

My puzzled look goes unacknowledged as he forges on until he eventually halts in front of a large thicket. They appear to be the same shrubs as the countless multitudes we've already passed, but he crouches down by a particular bush, reaching into its base and pulling out a large leather satchel. He rummages in the foliage once again, this time withdrawing a scabbard and sword.

Oh, he definitely planned his escape.

After a few careful maneuvers and adjustments, he attaches the weapon down the length of his spine before digging through the bag. With how stuffed it is, I presume it's filled with a range of traveling items, including more weapons.

The next object revealed is actually a handful of small shiny trinkets which I soon recognize as rings. I'm fairly certain he already wore one, but as he adorns most of his fingers with gold and silver, I can't be certain. They all shine in the light, some studded with brilliant gemstones. I try not to ogle at the sheer amount of wealth that now sits on his fingers. Clearly, assassins are paid handsomely.

Ryland rises and turns to face me as he places the satchel over his shoulder, suddenly looking more like a cruel prince than a trained killer, an unsettling fact that still hasn't fully resonated.

One of his perfect brows arches. "Do you doubt my talent now?"

I shake my head in silence, too much in awe of his altered appearance to answer verbally.

A smirk tugs at his lips. "Come. We don't need to hurry, but we should keep our pace. Word of our escape will have begun to spread by now, and they'll soon send guards after us. They'll search the outskirts of the wood." The smirk spreads into a full on grin. "We're officially on the run."

"And yet you're smiling," I reply warily, matching his pace as we set off. It's a struggle since his legs are twice as long as mine and eat up twice as much distance.

"It's not a death sentence. We just have to keep moving."

"*We?*"

He gives me a side-eyed look. "I should think the wisest path for you would be to follow me."

He's not wrong. Obviously, he knows what he's doing. And obviously I don't. With no belongings, no coin or food—no *map*—I have no way to get anywhere let alone any idea *how* to get there. My life experiences in Atherton hadn't really prepared me for a life on the run.

"You're not opposed to me joining you?"

He shrugs. "I confess, I typically travel alone, but I'm enjoying your company. Besides, I shudder to think what would happen if you were on your own."

So do I, but I throw a scowl his way nonetheless. "I'm not entirely helpless." If I had a bow and quiver in my hands, I definitely wouldn't be so impotent.

"Oh, I don't doubt that. I can sense there's some fight in you."

At least his senses aren't off. "You should know though that just because I'm joining you doesn't mean that I trust you," I clarify, wondering if I'm making a grave error. Anyone would be cautious when receiving an offer to join a strange man on a journey, most probably wise enough to decline. But I have absolutely nothing other than the clothes on my back and a death sentence to my name. If I could just rely on him for a little while, use his resources to get me someplace safe, then I can move on from him and start fresh.

That's what I tell myself as I come to terms with the new arrangement. I just need his resources. That's all.

My cell-mate nods in agreement. "I'd expect nothing less."

"Where are we heading then?"

"I was thinking about Kingsmar," he answers casually.

Kingsmar. The capital. Where better to blend in, I suppose, than in the most populated city in Osterley. It would be near impossible to find us there. But, from my vague knowledge, Kingsmar is a few days' journey from here at least. "And you think we'll make it there without being caught?"

He raises a single eyebrow, the gesture an enquiry if I really want to ask that question.

While I respect his confidence, I find it a little unsettling. He can't be *so* sure. Nothing is absolute, especially not our fates as I've now learned on many occasions.

He gives me a rueful smile. "You don't have to trust me, little thief, but I suggest having a little faith. It'll make things so much more interesting."

Faith. A rather foreign concept to me. Much like mercy, I haven't had much reason to believe in its workings. No one ever came to my aid. No god ever answered my prayers. Faith got me nowhere. And yet, something…some obscure, unknown flicker of feeling tells me that I can allow myself to allot a little bit in him, this strange and curious man who seems to embrace danger with a fiendish grin on his face.

"And what are the plans once we arrive in Kingsmar?" I probe.

"Are you always so methodical?" he questions, starting to walk in a northernly direction.

"When my life is on the line, yes, I like to have a solid plan in place."

"Leave the planning to me. You're in good hands."

I throw him a look the comment deserves. "I'll be returning to this subject later," I warn.

He chuckles. "Then I shall endeavor to provide you with an answer that disappoints you less when that time comes."

We fall into another comfortable silence for about an hour. I have too many thoughts running through my head to engage in light conversation, so I appreciate the quiet. With every step we take further from Atherton, I feel the pull of my home growing fainter and fainter. As if I'm completely severing ties. And, in a way, I am. I doubt I'll ever be able to return, not at least within the next few decades. There are so few criminals that two escapees who'd been destined for the chopping block will not be forgotten. No, my departure from Atherton will likely be an indefinite one. Strangely, I'm not sure I'm all that bothered about it.

I think the only thing I'll regret about leaving is the fact that I did not have the time to visit my parents' graves, to sit beside their tombstones one last time and remind them how much I still love them, how often they consume my thoughts. Even though there are no remains buried beneath the soil.

To new beginnings, I muse, pulling away from my somber thoughts and forcing myself to focus on the present.

Managing to steal a few glances of my new companion, I estimate him to be somewhere in his mid-twenties. And while I noticed his more masculine appearance in the alley, I hadn't fully realized just how unnervingly handsome he is. Beautiful really. I must have truly been consumed with grief and adrenaline to have been so blind to his looks. His skin is flawless, lightly tanned and smooth with luscious, golden hair that gleams in the sunlight. And those blue eyes, so piercing and bright, I feel as if I might see them from a mile away like two luminous beacons. His mouth itself is like a work of art. Soft and full, yet somehow sharp and firm, the contrast as puzzling as it is entrancing.

He's truly breathtaking. Like an angel from the heavens. Those soft lips, unearthly eyes and angelic curls, all contrasted by his god-like build, full of chiseled and sharp angles. My stomach tightens in knots at the sight of him. That beauty is a weapon, one he's undoubtedly used to his advantage. I just can't let myself be so easily fooled by it.

Upon my more detailed study, I realize that he reminds me of what the Sildhe might have looked like—the legendary ancient and mystical children of the gods, half-deity, half-man. They once ruled the Continent, blessed with magic powerful enough to easily manipulate the mortal race. One might relate them to a sorcerer or sorceress, capable of employing the darkest and most impressive of spells and sorcery.

Yet, their preternatural nature inspired inhuman levels of hubris and greed which consequently led to wars erupting over the centuries with countless battles and countless lives lost. Ultimately, as the legends say, the mortals prevailed due to the one and only Sildhe who offered aid to mankind.

As a child, my father used to read me stories of the immortal creatures and their magic. He'd tell me elaborate tales of the great wars and what became of them. I used to sit in bed, riveted, imagining the vivid scenes he painted with his words.

Sometimes, the fables leaned toward the dark. So much so that my mother would overhear and chide my father, who'd argue that I was his "strong daughter" capable of handling a few scary stories, to which I'd nod in agreement. What I never shared with him is that half the time, those frightening stories would send me into a fit of night terrors that left me so wary, I'd ensure my small toes were tucked tightly under the covers, worried that the creatures might seize hold of my feet and drag me away in the dark of the night.

Of course, I could never tell him about the nightmares or else he would've ceased our story time altogether. Even my mother on occasion mentioned the ancient magic-wielders, warning me that if I behaved naughtily or stayed out too late playing, a Sildhe would snatch me away and use their dark magic on me. It scared me enough to rarely step out of line or cause mischief. Sometimes, she'd even recite me the eerie and irksome little rhyme told to children as a warning not to wander. In a sing-song voice, she'd whisper:

HOLLIS SOPHIA

Beware the Sildhe, for much to fear
should ever you may find,

Within the wind, upon your sins,
they've always a watchful eye,

With crooked tongues, nowhere to run,
vanish you beneath the silver sun.

For what the moon-born have won,
shall not be undone,

Their captive held with your freedom felled,
as you remain under the immortals' spell.

Of course, most of the Sildhe history is a blend of fact and fiction, the lines so blurred it's impossible to discern what once may have been truth. What we do know is that they were ethereal, graceful creatures with unearthly, enchanting beauty, much like how my companion appears. If there wasn't reason enough before, I must be doubly cautious of his lethal weapons—both his blade and his beauty.

Chapter 4

As we pause against a towering oak, I discreetly attempt to catch my breath. Ryland's stamina is seemingly limitless, making a hike look like a leisurely stroll. All the while, I'm practically jogging to keep at his side.

Following his gaze, I look out toward the clearing he'd spotted from a distance I could hardly make out at the time. Apparently, he also possesses superior vision.

In the center of the field sits a modest farmhouse, constructed of dull, graying wood that appears as ancient as the trees surrounding us. We continue to hover at the forest's edge, the house only yards away.

"We'll have to share a horse, I'm afraid," Ryland announces beside me, taking me by surprise.

"We can't steal a horse from them!"

He takes his chin in false contemplation. "Remind me again what charge you were arrested under?" He turns to face me fully. "Look, right now, everything we do is a matter of 'us' versus 'them'. Besides, it's not like we're depriving him of his only horse."

I know he's right, no one will help us. And, there *is* another horse in the stables...

I give a reluctant nod before Ryland saunters off, leading us further along the tree line so that we're situated nearer the stables. Halting once more, he glances over a shoulder, extending a hand in a gesture for me to move ahead of him. "I wouldn't want to be so rude as to intrude into your territory. Would you like the honors?"

My face twists with a mixture of disgust and annoyance, and I'm tempted to flick the smug smile off his face. "Kind of you to offer, but since this is your idea, I'll let you handle it," I reply with false sweetness.

He shrugs nonchalantly before silently dashing off. With a moment alone, I'm finally able to release some of my pent up emotions. I lower myself against the base of a tree, rubbing my temples in small circles as the events of the past twenty-four hours resurface.

I was sentenced to die but escaped with another prisoner. A charming and cunning assassin who claims to enjoy my company enough to offer me to join him on his journey to Kingsmar. It seems like some wild, fantastic tale my father might've told me. Trying to accept that this is my reality is as challenging as it sounds.

The deep, calming breaths I keep taking provide little aid. I'm about to switch tactics, to either begin pacing or muttering to myself aloud when I hear the sounds of rustling leaves and the soft cadence of footsteps.

"Where are you, little thief?"

I exhale my relief and rise, facing the direction of his voice. In his hands are the reins to a saddled brown steed. How he managed to take the extra time to saddle it, I don't know.

I realize now that I should've joined him in absconding the horse that way I could've learned from him—and better assess him. I blame the recent traumas for my impaired logic.

With Ryland's satchel already attached to the saddle, we're ready to depart.

Hesitating beside the creature, I try to figure how I should mount it. Like Ryland, the horse is extremely tall. I doubt my foot could even reach the stirrup. The amount of times I've ridden—more like sat on a horse—can be counted on one hand, minus two fingers. And on every one of those occasions, my father or mother had to lift me atop it. Come to think of it, those were probably ponies. And, just like then, I'm equally apprehensive.

In my periphery, I catch Ryland's amused expression, as if he can hear my internal predicament. Before I can blink, he swiftly grips my waist, hauling me up as if I weigh no more than a kitten. My body jolts from the contact as the warmth of his palms seeps through the fabric of my dress. He sets me atop the saddle which I cling to for dear life before wordlessly joining behind.

If I thought his hands were warm, it's nothing compared to the heat of his entire front pressed against my back. His scent follows after, striking my senses for the first time. Crisp, like autumn wind. Rich and earthy like a pine forest. And notes of something purely masculine I'm unable to name.

His arms reach around me from both sides to collect the reins before he sets us off at a steady pace. We ride in silence for the next several hours. While it surprises me that Ryland doesn't fill the quiet with his quips and comments, I appreciate it. After all that's happened, my body and mind are too fatigued to jest or chatter. In fact, after the second hour, I have to fight the urge not to fall asleep against his shoulder. By the time the sun is nearly out of sight and we stop for the night, I'm beyond exhausted.

Ryland selects our camp in a particularly shrouded area of bushes and trees which offer the allusion of concealment. He dismounts the horse before helping me down. My legs wobble upon impact, and I grip his forearms for stability. He smirks down at me, and I quickly release him, embarrassment warming my face.

While he ties the horse to a tree, I stretch my aching neck and shoulders wondering if I'll ever get used to riding…which seems doubtful at present. The sound of rummaging steals my attention, and I turn to see Ryland fishing through his satchel. "Tomorrow, the plan will be to get some food and to get clean," he announces.

There's no need for me to bother looking down. I already know how dirty I am. My dress was in relatively decent condition when I put it on the other day, but a night in a dirty and dank cell guaranteed its soiled state. Even viridian can't hide the stains of prison. I'm just relieved there's no more daylight so Ryland doesn't have to see just how horrible I look. Although, with his sharp senses he's undoubtedly already noticed. Fighting a grimace, I nod at his suggestion. Just the idea of bathing makes me want to salivate, even if my stomach is painfully empty.

Ryland proceeds to pull out what appears to be a blanket before striding toward me, handing over the folded fabric which I accept with a nod of thanks. He lowers himself to the base of a tree, removing his scabbard and setting it beside him.

I set myself up a few feet away against the trunk of another tree, preparing myself for a rough night's sleep. While my accommodations weren't anything special back home, I haven't slept in the wild before, and I can already tell rough tree bark isn't going to grow on me.

I watch as Ryland stretches out on his back, hands folded under his head, the picture of nonchalance. I suppose this is a regular sleeping arrangement for him.

"Isn't there another blanket for you?"

He raises his head to meet my gaze. "I have my cloak." He'd taken the dark grey garment from his satchel earlier in the day and draped it over his shoulders. But he hasn't moved to place it atop himself as he lays there, and it's fairly cold this evening.

As if he can intuit my skepticism, he smugly quips, "Good night, little thief. Rest well."

With that polite dismissal, I bid him the same before covering myself with the blanket and curling on my side, away from him. It's risky giving him my back, but I need the privacy, unable to rest if I know there's a chance that I'm being watched.

But it's not just Ryland I have to worry about disrupting my sleep. My senses are taut and tense from my exposure. It feels like there are eyes on me, either animals or my companion or both. My discomfort only grows as the breeze picks up, shivers racking my body one after the next. I keep myself huddled in a tight ball, trying to maintain my warmth, but it's of no help. I may be exhausted, but with the combination of the cold, the uncomfortable sleeping arrangements, my unfamiliar companion, and the stress of being on the run, it becomes very apparent that I'm in for another restless night.

Chapter 5

The morning sunlight caresses my face with gentle fingers, a welcome warmth on my skin.

Squinting, I open my bleary eyes. My gaze immediately shifts to the tree Ryland occupied last night. But instead of lying in front of it, he's hanging from one of the branches, using his arms to hoist himself up and down. He continues these ministrations, and I realize that it's an exercise…which is clearly paying off. Even through his tunic, I can see the muscles of his biceps straining and flexing.

His eyes latch onto mine, and he winks as he lifts himself up again. "Ready to go?"

I rise into a sitting position, overtaken by a wave of dizziness as hunger gnaws at my stomach. Once it passes, I reach to remove the blanket when I realize another layer has been added. Ryland's cloak.

There's a quiet thud, and I look up to find him now striding toward the horse. I join him, though much slower, my legs and neck stiffer than yesterday. After folding the blanket, I extend it to him, and he returns it to the satchel. I hand him his cloak next. "Thank you," I say sincerely.

"You're welcome to wear it," he offers. Despite the sunlight, it's brisk this morning, but I feel too uncomfortable accepting, so I politely decline. Silently, he takes his cloak, clasping it around his shoulders before helping me onto the horse.

We ride only for an hour before Ryland declares, "I can hear water nearby. We'll stop to clean up." As usual, he's right. A few yards away sits a small creek. Once both of us dismount, we approach the rushing water flow. Ryland drops to its edge, splashing his face before cleaning his hands and wrists. I watch as he runs them through his hair, raking it back. Noticing my gaze, he looks up, his long lashes now wet making them appear thicker. Water drips from the tip of his nose, brushing across his lips, drawing my attention to his mouth. A dangerous area. He lifts a brow, question clear.

"I-I'll wait until you're finished." I want to clean more than my face and hands, and I intend to do so privately. He nods, understanding my implication, and a moment later, he rises.

"Where there's a water source, there's likely a village nearby. While you bathe, I'll try and get some food for us."

My guard instantly rises. "That seems risky."

He flashes a knowing smile. "There's that doubt again."

"What happens if you don't return?"

He detaches his satchel, throwing it over his shoulder before meeting my stare. "I suppose you'd have a horse and total independence," he tosses casually. Flipping over his hood, he gives me another wink before disappearing into the greenery.

Once I've removed my boots and socks, I move to my dress, leaving on my shift. As suspected, the garment is caked in dirt and grime. I scrub and wash the fabric until it's once again a pristine deep teal before I hang it on a tree branch to dry. Returning to the water, already warming under the sun's rays, I clean myself thoroughly, even taking the time to scrub my hair.

Invigorated and refreshed, I lay myself on the grass to dry beneath the sun as I wait for Ryland to return. Though sleep beckons my weary limbs, the nagging awareness of every minute that passes consumes my thoughts. *He's taking too long.*

Ryland was so quick when he obtained our horse. So swift with our escape that he should've returned by now for a task as simple as this. I sit up as it suddenly occurs to me that he left with his pack filled with his belongings and money. He'd said that if he didn't return, I'd have the horse and my independence. *Was that meant to be a warning? A farewell?* The thought makes my chest squeeze. *Have I just been abandoned?* It was the opportune window; leave me occupied and distracted just long enough to give me the slip.

A wave of hot shame licks my skin. How foolish I was. Of course he never intended to stay with me. He said he travels alone, and what do I offer him? Nothing useful. No skills, no trade, no coin.

Tears prickle my eyes, sliding down my flushed cheeks. I warned myself not to be fooled by him, that I couldn't trust him. And here I am, sitting alone, waiting for him like a lost child. Mingling with the burning humiliation and hurt is pure self-loathing. Why would I have thought he'd stay with me? No one has ever looked out for me since the day I lost my family. Why did I think some stranger would want to saddle himself to me?

I sniffle, forcing the tears to stop running. I *know* I don't need him. I *know* can survive on my own. And, like he said, I have a horse. I *know* I can do this. Still...

It would've been nice to have had someone, even for just a little while longer. It would've been really, really nice.

More tears slip against my will, and I quickly scrub them away. There's no time to wallow in self-pity. I have to keep moving; forget the mysterious male and start to fend for myself again. Approaching the branch where my dress is drying, I reach up to—

"Okay, so I got us enough food to last today and tomorrow morning-*ish*, but we'll need to stop again at some point to restock."

I whirl around at the sound of Ryland's voice, eyes wide with surprise. The flap of his satchel is unlatched, the opening filled with what looks like bread and apples, and my mind attempts to process that he's here. He actually returned.

Quickly recalling the remnant wetness on my cheeks, I hastily turn back around, grabbing my dress and discretely wiping my face with it.

"Wrenley, are you alright?"

The use of my name feels all too personal and instantly shakes me from my state of overwhelm. I answer with a simple "fine".

There's a beat of silence. "I can smell your tears, you know."

My entire body stiffens as I feel his weighted gaze on my back. *How does one* smell *tears?* I know his senses are sharp, but they can't be *that* sharp. "What are you talking about?" I huff casually, priding myself on my neutral tone.

I make to step into my dress when his hand rests on my shoulder, turning me around. He grips my chin between his thumb and forefinger, forcing me to look up at him. His sudden proximity and the intensity of his gaze freezes me in place. Those eyes, a blue so rich and deep, I feel as if I could swim in them. Like two bejeweled oceans. He studies me just as intently, as if he's searching inside me. Staring into my soul. Forget swimming in those eyes. I'm drowning in them.

"Why were you crying?" he asks softly. There's no point in denying it now. No doubt he can see the lingering dampness in my gaze. Besides, I can't think to find the words to lie, the truth on the tip of my tongue. My mouth parts as he slowly draws the answer from me, coaxing it from deep within my chest, just from his stare alone. His gaze drops to my lips, a flash of something churning in his eyes, there and gone in an instant.

Managing to break the spell, I seal my mouth shut, lightly shaking my head. His eyes narrow, as if he's witnessing my internal battle to keep the truth contained and lets out a breath through his nose before releasing my chin and stepping back, at last relenting.

With space enough to breathe, I quickly put on my dress, nearly cringing at the uncomfortable silence. It only grows after we've mounted the horse and set off. Eventually, Ryland reaches into the satchel and offers me an apple before collecting one for himself. I'm reluctant to eat it, recalling just how monumentally this food ruined my life. But, ultimately, it's nutrients, and I can't afford to be picky. We eat in more silence, and I begin to wonder whether he's upset with me. Obviously, he shouldn't be. I've no obligation to admit to him my feelings or thoughts, and he has no right to demand them—we just met. But there's certainly a strain between us. It's a palpable weight that makes my muscles tense.

"Did you steal the food or purchase it?" I broach curiously, trying to relieve some of the stiffness.

"I paid in earnest," he answers before biting into his apple.

"You did?"

"I may be an assassin, but that doesn't mean I'm entirely heartless." The sound of crunching fills my ears.

"You have a heart but no guilty conscience?"

He *tsks* chidingly. "Someone has a sharp tongue this morning."

"You didn't answer my question."

His heavy sigh tickles the back of my neck. "I don't kill innocents, but not all my victims are wholly malevolent either."

"And that doesn't bother you?"

I can feel him shrug his shoulders behind me. "I suppose you could say my moral compass is less…defined than others."

Technically, he isn't lying. He must have some form of a conscience. After all, he didn't abandon me. *Unless, there's something he wants from me…* "And how long have you been doing this?"

"A very long time. If you surround yourself with enough death, you start to become immune to its effects." A logical explanation delivered in a tone both clinical and detached.

"And how does one become a professional assassin exactly?"

"So full of questions," he muses.

Now he's the one trying to deflect, but I won't let up so easily. "Is it a family trade?"

"I don't have a family."

"So it was accidental?"

"Let's just say I elected to become this for personal reasons."

"Where—"

"Ah, ah, ah. I think it's my turn to ask some questions now." My stomach tightens with dread, and I take a bite of my own apple, hoping I'll buy myself some time.

"How did you come into thieving?"

I prickle at the question, immediately going to the defensive. "It's not a profession. It was the odd piece of food or firewood for survival."

"I meant no offense, nor do I make any judgments," he says understandingly. It's then that I decide how honest I want to be with him. Although he's been fairly evasive, it seems he's also been somewhat truthful. I feel I owe him the same.

"It's...a long-story. My parents died a few years ago, and I lost my home and everything we owned. So I moved into the local orphanage, and we came to a settlement. I could live in their attic as long as I fed myself. That's when I began to steal. It wasn't exactly my preferred way of living, but it was either that or starve. And, I never took much. But, apparently, that doesn't matter. Apples are considered high treason now," I conclude with a bitter scoff.

Ryland doesn't say anything for several long moments, and my nerves flutter. "You were dealt a cruel hand," he says finally, voice surprisingly quiet.

If only he knew the rest of it. I laugh without humor. "More than one it would seem."

"I'm sorry, Wrenley." The weighted words catch me off guard, and I look over my shoulder to meet his eyes. They're filled with what seems to be genuine sorrow and sympathy.

"I understand what that feels like. To lose everything you hold dear, to have had it taken from you against your will and be left with nothing. Having to learn to survive without—I know what kind of existence that is, and I'm sorry you've had to endure it."

My eyes begin to glisten as his words strike a chord. I quickly face forward again, refusing to be caught crying twice in one day. "Well, it seems you've given me a second chance. Perhaps I can make a better life for myself this time."

A small chuckle. "Happy to be of service, little thief."

As we finish our apples, Ryland tears off two pieces of bread, one for each of us. Taking a small nibble, a thought comes to mind, and I decide to add, voice soft amidst the breezy forest air, "I go by Wren, by the way."

I don't need to look behind me to know Ryland's smiling for I can hear it in his voice. "Very well, Wren."

As the afternoon sun continues its journey overhead, I begin to notice a shift in our scenery. It hadn't occurred to me to mull over the route we'd be taking. "Are we still in Stone Wood?"

"We're entering Lyrewood Forest now."

My body stiffens. The rumors of this forest are known in every city and town. It's said to be a mythical place with elements of remnant magic leftover from the age of the Sildhe. Some have said the terrain is everchanging, no cartographer able to truly map it's grounds. It's known to be both safe and perilous depending on the traveler and their route. Though I'm not familiar with the extent of the dangers lurking in its expanse, I do know one was better off avoiding it.

"We're going through Lyrewood?" The nerves are evident in my voice.

"We can't take the main roads and risk exposure. It'll cost us a half a day more to go this way, but we've got nothing but time on our hands. Why, are you frightened?" His tone is laced with amusement as opposed to concern.

"Its reputation precedes itself." One of the rumors was of a hunter who was slaughtered viciously by his own prey, said to be a mythical creature with unparalleled strength. The thought gives me a shudder.

Ryland's deep chuckle rumbles down my spine. "Fret not, little thief. You'll have my blade and services at your disposal." The words reassure me a little, but the deeper we venture into the forest, the more unnerved I become. The terrain is different—denser, thick with wild, sprawling foliage. I imagine easily being swallowed by this green abyss, as though I might lose myself and never be found again.

"It seems you've heard more unsavory rumors than nice ones," he notes. "Do you know how it came to be called 'Lyrewood'?" I shake my head in response, waiting with rapt attention for his story. "I presume you know of the Sildhe?"

"A bit."

"Back when they ruled this continent, many of them used to practice their magic and spells within these woods. Legend says that on one such eve, they gathered to celebrate a new moon. Only, there were no musicians and none of them knew how to play any instruments. So one Sildhe enchanted the forest, making the trees their music, the melodies floating through the wild wood on the evening breeze. The magic of the spell somehow endured. Some say the music sounds like a flute, others say a lyre."

The story brings a smile to my lips. I'm relieved to know there is some good about this place. It makes our entry a little less intimidating, filling me with curiosity instead of dread.

I'M BONE-EXHAUSTED BY THE TIME WE STOP AGAIN FOR THE night. I never knew riding could be so draining, yet every muscle aches and throbs. At least it's better than going to bed with an empty stomach. For a pleasant change, mine sits comfortably filled.

Though I'd suggested we ration, Ryland encouraged we eat more of our food supply. When I only nibbled on my other piece of bread, insisting I'd save the rest for later, he asserted that I would finish it then and there. Then he'd mysteriously revealed an extra piece, and when I gave him a questioning look, he simply pushed it into my hands.

Tonight, it's only my lethargy I must contend with. Despite the heaviness of my limbs, I decide to broach him with a subject I've been stewing over our ride. "Can I ask you something?"

Ryland turns his head, giving me his full attention. With his brows lifted, I continue "Would you teach me some self-defense, how to protect myself if I'm ever cornered? You clearly know how to evade an attacker."

He flashes me a puckish smile. "Plan on getting into trouble?"

"It seems to follow me wherever I go. I'd like to be better prepared to face it. Running away won't always be an option."

He nods in understanding. "One lesson won't nearly be enough, but I can go over a few moves that could help you if you're attacked." He stands, dusting off his hands, lips pulling mischievously, and I'm suddenly very wary. "Turn around," he instructs.

Cautiously, I do so, giving him my back and waiting for him to make a move. Even though I'm mindful of his approach, it still takes me by surprise. Ryland swiftly wraps his arm around my throat, pulling my body flush against his, my chin resting in the crook of his arm. His hold isn't air-constricting, but it's tight enough to cause discomfort. Enough for me to want to get out of this position as quickly as possible.

"I've come at you from behind. What I want you to do is step forward with your left foot and then twist your body around to the right before using your right leg to step back."

I try to picture his instructions in my mind, visualizing how it would work. After a moment, I move my left foot forward before I twist to the right, head and body now facing him as I rotate. It seems the opposite direction of what I would want in escaping his hold, but I follow with the rest of his instructions, stepping back with my right leg. The movement provides me the chance to get some distance from him before I manage to step out of his hold completely.

He'd obviously loosened his grip so it was easier for me to move, but at least I understand the general idea.

I give him a small smile which he mirrors. "Now I want you to try twisting to the left and see what happens." He comes behind me again and repeats the hold. As asked, I twist to the left. While my body is able to inch away from his frame, my head remains trapped in the crook of his elbow, leaving me defenseless.

"From this direction, you're just moving closer into my arm's hold. So whichever arm the attacker is holding you with, go that same way. Most will be right-handed, so it should be easy for you to remember," he explains. "Now try the proper way again. I'm going to use more force this time."

I nod as I give him my back, excited that I'm learning something even if it's only one maneuver. Ryland waits a few seconds this time, likely to increase my suspense.

It works.

When he finally attacks, I bump forward, more of my air cut off than before. Despite the surprise, I wait a moment to steady my legs and mind. I step forward, then sharply twist and rotate, stumbling when I try to move back. But, with another sharp tug, I manage to break free.

It was far from graceful but effective nonetheless. I grin with delight, feeling a rush of power and capability. *This is a start.*

"Well done," he says, and I'm too busy preening to notice him stepping closer. His nearness startles me, and I look up beneath my lashes.

Faster than lightening, faster than any person has a right to be, Ryland's hand is on my throat, shoving me back against a tree. My eyes bulge, his sudden roughness shocking as the air is knocked from my lungs.

"Try and get out of this." Despite his unyielding grip, his tone and gaze are soft in encouragement.

Quickly, I think of what his weakness is in this stance. Instinctively, hastily, I aim between his legs, lifting my knee to strike, but Ryland uses his other hand to effortlessly shove my knee aside, throwing me off balance. His hold around my throat tightens, and for a moment, I'm scared that he actually may harm me.

"The groin is too easy to block. Too predictable. Try again."

I scan the rest of his frame, trying to focus on vulnerable points instead of my increasing lack of air. His throat is exposed, but something tells me he'd be just as quick to block it. I look at his arm next, imagining the anatomy. It's locked in place, seemingly immobile. *But the elbow is where we bend our arms...*

I lace my fingers together over his arm, ensuring my hold is firm. Once secured in their grip, I roughly shove my bridged hands down on the crook of his inner elbow. The grip on my throat loosens as his arm drops a little from my yanking. I step aside swiftly, looking for Ryland's approval as I suck in air.

He watches me with widened eyes, lips parted in surprise. "Well, that's certainly another way to do it," he murmurs with a half-smile. "Very clever." I practically beam at the compliment, pleased that I was able to surprise him. "But there's another way you can do it."

I return to the tree where he takes hold of my throat again. I don't think I'll ever adjust to the feeling of a hand wrapped around me like this. It's difficult not to squirm.

"You're going to use your right hand to roughly push away at my wrist. But when you do, pivot with your right foot and turn your body as well."

Once again, I try to envision the act before doing it. When

the time comes to make a move, I work as swiftly as possible. His grip is softer again, giving me the opportunity to easily escape before he returns for another round. But, this time, he stands even closer.

His front is mere inches from mine, face even less. Given how much taller he is, I have to crane my neck to meet his gaze. His breath brushes across my face, expression surprisingly intense. For some reason, this hold feels different.

His thumb brushes across the side of my neck in a featherlight touch, causing me to suck in a startled breath. Chills crest my skin but not from the evening air. His eyes dance with mirth, inviting me to play.

But then his hand squeezes more firmly, reminding me of what I'm supposed to do and distracting me from the gesture entirely. I put all my strength into the shove against his wrist. It breaks the grip, and I dodge to the side, away from him.

Another approving nod. "Good. Now, stand still, and close your eyes. I don't want you to see me coming," he instructs, waving me to step away from the tree.

Reluctantly, I do as asked, feeling vulnerable by the lack of vision. I listen carefully for any movement, but I hear nothing. Even though I know an attack is imminent, I'm unfortunately still very much unprepared for the semi-forceful push against the back of my right knee.

My eyes fly open as I begin to fall forward, the ground swooping closer and closer. Reflexively, my hand reaches back, fingers clutching Ryland's forearm for support. But my grip isn't strong enough, and my body merely rotates until I'm half facing him, the drop unavoidable.

But then Ryland is falling with me, carefully landing atop me, hands and forearms bracing against the earth. Our faces are suddenly inches apart again, his broad frame caging mine, forcing me to stare into that unsettlingly beautiful face.

Somehow, in the back of my mind, I have a growing suspicion that Ryland could've prevented his fall. The realization only worsens the flushing of my face.

We fall into a lapse of heavy silence, and the weight of his gaze settles on mine. It feels as though he's dissecting my eyes, sorting through my soul and digging through every layer in search of my core. I can only imagine the lovely shade of pink my face must be.

"Hopeless, right?" I huff bashfully, a weak attempt to distract from his gaze.

Ryland's face breaks into a soft smile, blues eyes glittering like sunlight over water. "Not entirely."

Seeming to sense my discomfort, his expression shifts, mouth down-turning into a gentle frown, only there a moment before it morphs into a large grin, and he pushes himself onto his knees.

I sit up while he's chuckling. "You're fairly crafty," he admits, playfully tapping the tip of my nose with a finger. Before I can blush, he stands, offering me a hand to join him. "You'll have to use that to your advantage. In most instances, someone untrained such as yourself won't even see an attack coming. So you'll need to react quickly.

"Whatever you do, don't stop fighting." I nod along, branding his instructions in my brain. I appreciate the fact that he's being realistic. The likelihood of me being able to apply any of the maneuvers he's taught me in a split second is slim at best, so this advice is crucial to remember.

"Where did you learn to fight?"

"The Assassin's Guild in Kingsmar. I trained with them for many years."

I hadn't known such a place existed. It's little surprise though that it would be established in Kingsmar, the city where only the finest and most talented crafts- and tradesmen reside.

I open my mouth, questions at the ready, but he cuts me off. "We can practice more tomorrow if you'd like."

I nod eagerly, a small bit of pride blooming in my chest. "Thank you. I know it's not anything special but…it's nice to not feel so helpless."

Ryland strides to the horse as he replies, "You should never have to feel helpless. But, as long as I'm with you, I will ensure your safety."

My pulse jumps at his words, at the sincerity of his tone even though his gaze isn't on me. Like last night, he hands me the blanket before I move to settle under one of the trees. Stretching out on my back, my gaze is directed toward the night above. Through the leafy canopy, I can make out patches of sky, the stars studding the midnight canvas like thousands of twinkling diamonds. It makes sleeping in this forest a little less frightening.

I hear the soft sound of footsteps before Ryland crouches down beside me, cloak in hand. He drapes it over me gently. Though I try to refuse, he shakes his head before lowering himself to the ground, only a few inches separating us. I realize then that he intends to sleep exactly where he's settled himself: right next to me.

My heart's tempo increases. Like me, he's fully stretched out, left hand resting beneath his head as he gazes at the sky. We remain in silence for some time, but I think it's clear that neither one of us is sleeping anytime soon.

"You thought I left, didn't you?" His low voice is carried by the soft breeze that ruffles through the branches.

"What?"

"When I left to get food, you thought I'd left you for good." It's no longer a question. His voice is full of solemn surety. "That's why you were crying."

He knows. And he knew it then.

My skin heats with shame. How obvious I was, how pathetically transparent. Crying over being abandoned by a man I hardly know. He owes me nothing, not after he saved my life. And yet I mourned his absence after hardly knowing him.

It takes several moments for me to find the courage to respond. "The last few days have been...a lot. I think my emotions are more heightened than usual," I explain, which is true enough, but not the actual truth. "But I have better control of them now," I assure him.

"I would never abandon you like that." His voice sounds mildly strained, as though my assumption had actually caused him pain.

"Even if you had, I'd be fine. I don't need to rely on anyone to get by."

"I know that," he says sincerely.

I try to focus on the sky again, bottling the emotions trying to resurface. Those familiar feelings that have sat upon my shoulders like old companions for the past several years. Since meeting Ryland, his presence has subdued some of those stirrings or at least helped me forget their existence. But, when he left, they returned like autumn's chill after summer's warmth. Part of me had fleetingly forgotten what their haunting felt like, and it struck twice as deeply now that they tried to return.

I suddenly feel the brush of Ryland's littlest finger against mine, and my heart jolts from the contact. The touch is barely there, but I can feel the reassurance behind it. I turn my head to face him, and he does the same. I study his features in the darkness, the shadows on his face, his eyes like two stars brighter than any of the ones above us. Instinctively, my finger brushes his in return.

Entranced in each other's gazes, time escapes me. It could be seconds that pass or minutes. But our horse suddenly whickers and snorts, and both our expressions shift into startlement, my upper frame lurching upright.

Ryland breaks into laughter, and I can't help but join him. His grin widens as I laugh, the sound refreshing to my soul like water to a parched plant. Some of the tightness in my chest loosens, and I feel as light as a breeze. Weightless and unburdened, that is if I don't stop long enough to dwell on my current circumstances and the reason I'm with the strange man chuckling beside me.

"I can't remember the last time I laughed," I admit softly.

THE ETERNAL HUNT

He quirks a brow at me. "Your standard for humor must be very low if you find a horse snorting so amusing." His words and incredulous tone only incite more laughter from me.

"Well, at least you now know the standard."

"Is that a challenge, little thief? Because I accept." His eyes sparkle.

"There's no prize though."

"Your laughter is. And it's a prize I intend to win."

His words make my stomach flutter, and my face warms beneath his stare which is far less full of jest and more of intention. Lowering myself back down, I return my gaze to the sky, focusing on trying to sleep instead of his promise.

"Good night, Ryland," I say after a minute.

"Good night, little thief."

As I lie amidst the wild of this wood, just as in Ryland's story, I hear it…faint like the flapping of a butterfly's wings, soft and delicate. But there all the same. The trees, they seem to sing. A gentle hum with neither a rhythm nor melody, ever-changing and ever-pleasant. The nameless tune flits amidst the branches and dances with the wind, skittering over my senses and lulling me into a peaceful slumber. Just before I fall into that blissful oblivion, a dawning realization hazily forms in my dozing mind.

Neither one of us has broken the contact of our fingers.

Chapter 6

Much like yesterday morning, I rise to find Ryland already up and hanging from a tree, completing the same exercise as before. And, just like then, I blatantly stare.

"Are those very difficult to do?" I enquire, rubbing the side of my neck as I approach.

He smiles down at me before releasing the branch and landing softly. "Would you like to try?"

Though I'm sure I'll regret it, I nod, moving to stand beneath the same branch before lifting my arms. There's still a gap between my hands and the limb, and I make to jump when a smirking Ryland clutches my waist and lifts me effortlessly.

My grip is a near stranglehold of the branch, arms already burning with exertion. I take a deep breath before attempting to pull myself upward, instantly regretting my decision. Shaking like a leaf, I manage to complete a grand total of one pull-up. My arms scream in protest, but I can't stop now. It'd be absolutely mortifying to give up after only one.

Ryland watches me with knowing eyes, amused by my obvious struggle. I narrow my gaze at him, gritting my teeth as I attempt to hoist myself up again—and fail. Ryland made the pull-ups look so effortless, but here I hang in utter mortification. Undoubtedly, the malnutrition is to blame, but I'm not sure I'd have fared much better even in my healthiest state.

"Tired?" he asks with an arched brow, our gazes now eye-level.

"Not at all," I reply coolly. "I just didn't want to embarrass you by doing more."

He chuckles as he reaches for me. As I'm lowered, Ryland slides my body down the front of his, slowly, his eyes trained on me the entire time. Beneath my hands, I can feel the muscles in his arms working, firm and solid. My skin tingles in response. In a pitiful attempt to divert his attention, I break away, stepping toward the pile of my blanket and his cloak and folding them up.

"So…" I begin, trying to sound casual.

"So…?" he returns, mimicking my tone.

"Are you ever going to explain how you were able to break an iron chain with your bare hands?"

"My, the weather is lovely this morning, isn't it?"

I throw him an unamused look. "How did you do it? That would've taken impossible strength."

"I appreciate the compliment," he replies with a smug grin.

"It wasn't one," I retort, dismayed by another one of his deflections.

"Your assumption isn't entirely off. My strength and agility are greater than the average male."

"And no one has tried to make a study of you?"

"Most haven't witnessed that particular skillset. Most aren't around after."

My heart stalls in my chest. "Because you've killed them."

"Not necessarily," he answers. "Let's just say I don't like to parade those qualities." "Right, because you're so terribly modest."

A breath of laughter. "Exactly. I only use them when it's absolutely necessary."

I laugh with him, storing the information to ponder later. I already knew he was different, but I'm beginning to realize his differences is erring on the side of abnormality. Not that I'm in a position to complain; it's nice to have a companion. I've gone from total independence to constantly having someone around. And I happen to like that certain someone very much. Despite the sometimes ill-placed humor, his good spirits are rather infectious; his sense of adventure and excitement for the unknown mildly catching. In fact, it was his contrasting energy that made my parting with the only home I've ever known a far less sorrow-filled affair than it might've been without him.

Yet, I can't help but wonder how much things are bound to change. If I'm already growing used to waking every morning to his face, to the sound of his deep voice that tickles my senses, to the warmth and ease his aura instills in me, how painful will it be when we go our separate ways? I don't even know him, and already I'm anxious for our impending farewells. I can make no more sense of the contradiction than I can of him and his mysterious abilities. I just hope I'll gain more clarity on the two matters in time.

IT'S APPROACHING SUNSET, AND IT FEELS LIKE THE BOUNDS of Lyrewood Forest are endless. I sometimes wonder if we'll ever make it to Kingsmar, but Ryland seems to know exactly where we're going, calmly leading us onward.

The dappled sunlight filters between the tree branches and warms my skin. We might as well be the only two people in the world, surrounded as we are by this seemingly boundless forest. A couple hours ago, we ventured into new terrain, the ground underfoot laden with moss and lush with evermore vibrant greenery.

Despite the painful hunger gnawing at my stomach and the fatigue in my legs—we've spent most of the day walking on foot as our horse seemed to have injured a hoof in the morning—I relish the last precious minutes of buttery sunlight, the golden yellow blurring into burnt shades of orange and ruby. My attention suddenly catches on an unusual pattern along one of the trees, my neck craning to study it as we pass. "Was that a—"

"Oculum tree," Ryland confirms from beside me.

I glance once more at the mythical trunk, admiring the smooth white bark interspersed with a dark pattern resembling eyes. "My father told me about them, that they're sentient. That they watch and listen to passing travelers." The animate trees are as old as time itself, rumored to have existed even before the Sildhe. It's a truly humbling experience, when a myth becomes reality. "Do you believe they can really see us?" I ask aloud, wondering if those eerie eyes truly possess the gift of sight and are beholding my awestruck form as I pass by them.

Ryland shrugs. "Probably. Legends are always based on some form of truth." Perhaps I'm wrong, but his voice seems to have taken on an edge. "You'll find others along the way if you look closely. I'd say in an hour we should stop for the night."

Just as I nod, our horse suddenly rears back. With a shrill whinny, it bucks its front hooves, Ryland pushing me back whilst trying to calm the beast. Despite his soothing, the horse continues to spur and jolt.

"What's happening?"

"Something's spooked it," he says with a furrowed brow just before our horse takes off, darting away in the direction we came from, the faint thudding of its galloping the only sound between us. Thankfully, Ryland managed to grab the satchel before it ran off, so at least we have our supplies.

We share a flummoxed look, but it's interrupted when Ryland sharply turns forward. His eyes narrow, trying to assess what kind of danger we've just landed ourselves in.

And then, we hear it. Soft jabbering noises, like a herd of animals moving in unison, communicating amongst each other.

Ryland softly curses. "Bantilos."

HOLLIS SOPHIA

The name conjures nothing familiar in my mind, though the unsavory way with which he said it confirms my suspicion that what we're about to face will be entirely unpleasant. I open my mouth to enquire when Ryland's gaze cuts to mine.

"We need to run."

I follow after Ryland as he takes off, sharply veering left. "What are they?" I ask urgently, my imagination going to the worst. The chattering becomes fainter. I can only hope it's a good sign, that we're outracing them.

"You'll see," is all he says, making my stomach lurch in dread. "They must've caught your scent."

The question of what exactly he means by "my scent" sits precariously on my tongue. I'm not sure if I really want to know the answer.

My feet hammer against the damp, mossy earth, legs heavy like weights, heart lodged in my throat. I continue panting out shallow breaths as my lungs seize, sweat coating my brow. The exhaustion and adrenaline of the past few days, not to mention we've been hiking since morning with few breaks, my malnourished body isn't exactly capable of handling a full on sprint that has no expected end.

Glancing over his shoulder, Ryland catches me lagging, the distance between us growing further and further despite my best efforts. He quickly turns back, aiming for me. I'm about to pant out that I'll catch up when the words expel from my lungs with a soft whoosh.

Ryland's arm bands around my waist as I'm suddenly airborne, and he sets off again. It takes me a few solid seconds to get my bearings since everything in sight is now tilted completely off axis.

He carries me at his side as I lie horizontally like a plank, arm wrapped tightly around my middle where his large hand grips me at my ribcage. Effortlessly lifting me onto our horse was one thing, but supporting my weight in this position is staggering. He barely emits a fatigued breath as he races on, the forest-scape blurring in my vision. I try to think all things light-weight, but it seems to make no difference to him. He travels swiftly without slowing pace.

The volume of the chattering suddenly increases tenfold, and the green carpet of the forest is interrupted by a wave of brown as a pack of creatures emerges into view on my left.

The Bantilos.

They're each the size of a small feline, facial features reminding me of a bat's. Their fur is light brown and ragged, and they possess beady eyes and vicious little mouths lined with rows of razor-sharp teeth. Instead of claws, they have rounded paws, nothing capable of slicing visible to the eye.

"Their bite is poisonous," Ryland mutters from above me, sensing the direction of my thoughts. *Of course it is.*

Another wave of the animals comes from the opposite side, and Ryland curses. He may be impossibly fast, but I guess these creatures are too. He abruptly halts, righting me to my feet at his side.

Somehow, *I'm* the one who's breathless.

The creatures continue to chatter, eyes lit with excitement as they crowd around in an ever-narrowing circle. While I don't speak their language, the general message is easy enough to grasp: they've just stumbled upon supper. What they lack in stature I assume is made up for in their ability to overwhelm us.

I glance to Ryland, panicked by the odds, but he hasn't even unsheathed his sword.

"Have you climbed trees before?" His voice measured yet focused, eyes trained on the Bantilos.

"When I was younger," I answer uncertainly.

"Then I suggest reacquainting yourself with the practice straight away." Catching his meaning, I look to the nearest oak and gauge the swiftest route to climb.

Ryland widens his stance, preparing to fight despite still not having reached for a weapon. *I shouldn't leave him to fend them off on his own.*

"But what about y—"

"I appreciate the concern, little thief, but this is nothing I haven't handled before," he returns casually. And, indeed, while his stance is guarded, his aura seems fairly relaxed. Much like when he was fighting the guards at the prison. As if this isn't any real danger, merely a complication in his schedule. With that, I bolt for the tree, hauling myself up its base as though my life depends on it. Which, technically, it does.

I can hear the creatures below, their humming and chatter like a chant for their meal growing more frantic as they close in. Soft grunts and violent little screeches erupt, and I know they've commenced their attack against Ryland. I don't look down, not until I'm high enough in the tree, breathless and shaking.

Thankfully, I can accomplish one thing without his help.

Limbs shaking, I lay on my stomach over one of the thicker branches, arms and legs wrapped around its body as I drop my head and peer through the leaves to try and glimpse Ryland. Standing a few feet from the trunk, he's swarmed by the furry little things. I'd almost consider them cute if it weren't for the beady eyes and the fact that they keep trying to take a bite out of Ryland's flesh.

He's much closer to my tree now as he kicks and flings the creatures away while they try to crawl up his tall form. Apparently, he decided to take out a dagger at some point, but he only uses the handle to knock them away, forgoing the blade entirely. *Strange that he had no problem skewering the prison guards but has a conscience for these creatures...*

Horror squeezes my throat in a vice-like grip when my eyes latch onto one of the little beasts as it lands a swift bite to Ryland's neck. I nearly launch myself from the tree, but Ryland is quick, seamlessly dislodging the animal's hold. I watch as pinpricks of blood start to form.

He's been bitten. My heart stutters as my stomach sinks. We have no resources out here, no aid.

When his body is momentarily free of the Bantilos, he steals the opportunity to scale the tree within lightning speed, landing on the branch next to mine with a soft thud. My gaze traverses his athletic frame, tanned skin glowing in the dappled twilight. He grins, hardly out of breath, with an excited spark in his eyes as he takes in the view. "Well, this is nice."

I surge toward his branch to assess his wound. In my haste, my foot slips on the bark, and Ryland whips out a hand to hold me steady, eyes watching me in pure confusion as I crowd in front of him, fear clogging my throat. With his hand still gripping my hip, my own take hold of the sides of his face which I sharply turn to the side. Urgently, I scan the column of his neck, looking for those tiny serrations. Only…there's nothing there. Just smooth, unmarred skin.

"You were hurt," I murmur in bewilderment, pulling back to study his face.

Ryland quirks a brow, eyes churning with both surprise and humor. As though my concern is as unexpected as it is unnecessary. "I'm perfectly fine," he assures me.

"But I saw—"

"Me rather skillfully fending off their attack?" he offers with a half-grin.

I can only gape. I *saw* one of them bite him. Saw the blood well. And yet, his flesh is entirely unmarked. Not a blotch of redness or irritation in sight. *He said that he's fine, but he didn't flat out deny being bitten either…*

A screech from one of the creatures below has my gaze shifting downward. "Won't they follow?" I ask, suddenly wishing I'd opted for a taller tree.

In my periphery, I see Ryland shake his head. "They don't have nails to climb."

After closer inspection, I can see the creatures struggling to get purchase on the tree bark, many falling in their attempts with an angry hiss.

"We're safe up here. But I'm afraid we'll have to stay the night like this."

"But, couldn't you have…killed them?" I hate asking this given that I'm not fond of unnecessary death, but sitting like open prey in this tree all night doesn't seem like the wisest option either.

"I could've, but killing these *particular* creatures has a rather unpleasant result." My scrunched brow is question enough. "When a Bantilo is killed, the pack will screech in unison for hours. It's so loud and shrill, it can make ears bleed. I thought I'd spare us the torment.

"Besides, they're nocturnal. They would've chased us until dawn, and we would've had to relocate to these heights at some point anyway. They'll be gone by sunrise, and we'll leave then."

I glance down once more at the frantic animals, taking into consideration that this is the first legendary creature I've ever come across.

"And what about the horse?" I ask, wondering what we'll do now that our main source of swift transportation is gone.

Again, Ryland offers an unfazed smile. "We've got two days left. Going by foot won't slow us down much." His lack of worry is reassuring. Although the thought of more hiking on an empty stomach sours my mood.

The incessant chattering below keeps my nerves tense. I'm ready to flee at a moment's notice. When the sun finishes setting, nightfall creeps over Lyrewood, and I force myself to settle in for the night. A glance at Ryland reveals that I'm on the bigger branch with enough space for me to stretch out my legs and lean against the trunk. His, on the other hand, is narrow enough that he can only perch on it, legs having to hang while one hand remains on the trunk for balance, the other, grasping the branch itself.

Sensing my stare, he looks my way and offers a cheerful smile. But he's not fooling me. "That can't be comfortable."

"Believe me, I've suffered far worse accommodations."

I don't doubt it, but it doesn't mean tonight has to be a terrible one too. Carefully, I crawl further up the branch, allowing enough space for him to settle against the crook of it. Looking over my shoulder, I find him watching me with a raised brow. "Come on, there's no need to make that branch suffer," I say pointedly.

A grunt of amusement reaches my ears before he shifts over toward me. His spine presses against the trunk while his legs straddle the thick branch. Once he gives me a nod that he's settled, I slowly ease myself backward, trying not to tense as I rest my back against his chest, settling my legs between his.

Immediately, I'm enveloped by Ryland's heat, his woodsy scent filling my nose. My body conforms to the rigid lines and planes of his chest, finding the position surprisingly comfortable. Yet, my senses remain on high alert as I feel his every breath softly tickling my cheek, the steady beat of his heart against my back. The side of my face warms, and I know his gaze is on me.

Not surprisingly, sleep doesn't come easily when one's several feet off the ground. But the ceaseless jabbering of the Bantilos would've made it impossible anyway. If their squabbling is maddening, then I'd really hate to hear the screeching Ryland saved us from. Their cries are the equivalent of nails scratching stone, grating and raucous.

"What did your parents do?"

The question catches me completely off-guard. For one thing, we've been sitting in complete silence for almost an hour. I'd thought Ryland was asleep, he'd been so still. For another, it's an entirely random query.

My heart aches at the mentioning of my parents, and I debate answering when I realize why he's asked—to distract me. Much like our verbal sparring in the prison cell the night before our execution, Ryland is using the same tactic. Conversation to pull me from my thoughts.

"My mother was a local healer." While Atherton possesses a village doctor, my mother tended to those who couldn't afford his services, or weren't seen quickly enough. She used various herbs and poultices to cure her patients, taking very little coin oftentimes in exchange for saving their lives.

There's always a wash of pride in my tone whenever I tell people about her work.

I feel Ryland nod against me. "And, my father..." My throat constricts, but I force the words out. "He was a craftsman. A coffin-maker." Woodwork had always been my father's specialty. He'd built every piece of furniture in our house, from our dining room table to my bedframe which he'd carved horses and dragons into the posts, the creatures meant to keep me company at night.

"He started off by making one for a family acquaintance and did such a fine job that others began to hire him. He would personalized them, make each coffin unique to the person who was being buried. He'd use different wood and carve special designs and patterns."

I can remember sitting with him while he chopped trees in Stone Wood, the forest populated by a rare species of tree whose timber was sturdier than stone. He'd tell me about all the varying types of trees that grew in the wood and what they meant, how he tried to match them to the deceased's personality and traits.

I used to find the profession itself so strange and morbid. But, the older I grew, the more I appreciated the artform my father made it. He was an artist in many ways.

One of his commissions was for a young couple who'd lost their baby just a year after her birth. I remember hearing the mother's sobs from outside his workshop where I usually played. The couple's grief was so palpable that my father's own eyes were misty while he worked on the project. He'd explained to me that he'd chosen the wood from a willow tree which symbolized grief and the endurance of love after death. He'd carved blooms of flowers around the lid's border with a stork to represent the mother's love. The final piece was so beautiful that I remember feeling so saddened that it was going to be buried in the earth.

My father had poured his heart and soul into every coffin that he made. And my mother did the same with her work.

They were instinctive givers, generous and thoughtful, passing on many of their traits to me including my father's rich brown hair and my mother's pale green eyes. And, while my parents hadn't been wealthy by any means, we were rich in love and joy. They'd given me a perfect childhood.

"They were good people," I finish, voice a mixture of longing and nostalgia. My eyes start to burn, and I contemplate whether to further cross the line of vulnerability with this traveling companion who still remains a mystery.

Ryland gently wraps his arms around my waist, setting his hands over mine resting in my lap. A wash of relief settles over me, reassured by his kindness and sturdy presence at my back. Whether he was bitten or not, though I *know* I saw it happen, I'm happy to have him with me, alive and well. I'm not sure what I would've done had he been afflicted with the poisonous venom. I'm uncertain that I would've been able to handle the ensuing trauma of his suffering. Despite barely knowing this male, we've bonded in some inexplicable, indiscernible way.

"They died from a Aephus outbreak." My voice breaks on the last word. The outbreak had come from the north, trickling down from village to village. My mother had been nursing an elderly woman who'd contracted the illness. She'd known the risk of exposure, and even though there'd been no hope for her patient, my mother insisted on offering her comfort and company. Her fierce compassion ultimately led to my family's ruin.

Like so many others, she'd fallen ill as did my father soon after. Both were bed-ridden within a few days, leaving only me to care for them. Desperate to help, I'd taken all our valuables and as much money as I could gather and brought them to the town physician, pleading for his help. But he'd refused me at the door, claiming he didn't have the time to see them, that his practice was already filled with other patients demanding his attention. At the time there were so many people on their deathbeds with Aephus that treatment became a matter of luck as to how high one was on the physician's list.

The outbreak had spiraled so out of control that Lord Eggar, for the first time in his long reign, made a grave and terrible ruling that polarized our village for some time. Any and all patients who had no chances of being cured were to be quarantined, including any loved ones who chose to stay. Those who had already passed were to have their homes burned, avoiding any risk of the disease spreading further.

I'd sat with my parents day and night, nursing them to the best of my ability—which wasn't very much. Sleep deprived, I'd passed out in the chair beside their bed one night, rising the next morning to find them both still as stones. Peaceful. Too peaceful. Their expressions serene, hands entwined, my mother's other hand extended in my direction. I'd wailed loud enough for the neighbors to hear.

Word of their deaths spread to the local government, and I was soon after dragged from our home before it was promptly burned to the ground.

I was neither allowed to say my goodbyes nor take any belongings with me. All I could do was watch the flames swallow my parents and my childhood, my entire past and present, knowing that nothing would ever be the same again.

A few tears spill as I recount the story to Ryland, as I recall the pile of ashes left in the fire's wake the following morning. How they'd drifted in the autumn breeze as I'd tried to process how my life had changed overnight.

"And the saddest part is that there were no remains of my parents to be buried, no special coffin for my father to rest in."

Ryland's arms tighten around me, and it's in this moment I desperately wish I could see his face. "I'm so sorry, Wren." His voice is raw, unable to provide much more of a response. I think I've surprised him. I've honestly surprised myself, not having expected to share the truth with him. At least not so soon.

"Atherton gave me very little. In many ways, I'm glad to have left it behind. I think it's better for me if I start over someplace new," I admit quietly.

"They didn't deserve you. I should've burned the place before we left, left them with nothing but ashes."

The notion draws a soft laugh from me even though his tone is deadly serious.

As we fall into another silence, I can't help but feel as though a weight has been lifted. I'd never truly allowed myself to wallow, not after the first few months of my grieving. Never let myself dwell on how I'd been so neglected and forgotten by the place I called home. My mother had always taught me to be self-reliant, and I've followed her guidance every day since. But, to have had someone listen to my misfortunes, to acknowledge the magnitude of my losses, was a first. And it felt so nice. Nice enough for me to settle into my fatigue, settle further into Ryland's chest.

Unable to hear the melody of the forest tonight, the chattering of Bantilos too loud, the steady beat of Ryland's heart is the rhythm that lulls me into sleep.

And, once again, Ryland was right.

By sunrise, the creatures are gone.

CHAPTER 7

IN ANOTHER UNFAVORABLE TURN OF EVENTS, WE WOKE to a silver sky. The rain held out for barely an hour after we began the day's trek, quickly transitioning from a light sprinkle to a full on downpour. It attacks in a ceaseless torrent, pelting us in hammering, icy sheets. I've never been more drenched in my life. Buckets of water pour into my eyes and mouth, enough to make me feel fully submerged and drowning.

Carefully, we weave through the towering trees, a dense and heavy fog clouding our sight and clinging to our sodden forms. As deafening claps of thunder start to rumble through the earth, I know our day is only going to get much worse. Honestly, I might've preferred the Bantilos' chattering to these conditions. Ideally, we'd have been riding, but since our horse fled yesterday, we're left to trudge through these unbearable elements as fast as my pace allows, which, unfortunately, is not that fast.

I'm not sure if it's more of Lyrewood's magic, but it's colder in this part of the forest, the foliage more akin to an autumnal landscape. Our path has been lined with a carpet of toasted copper and ebony leaves, their rotting corpses matted into the earth with the forming mud and water.

"Lovely weather isn't it?" Ryland asks from beside me, voice carrying more loudly given the rainfall blaring in our ears. I turn my head to roll my eyes at his obnoxious grin.

Only he could try and make this situation seem pleasant. Anyone else would recognize how absolutely miserable this is.

The skies have become forebodingly dark overhead as if nightfall is near, signaling that the storm isn't about to let up anytime soon. I can't help but occasionally grumble to myself. Any form of shelter would be a blessed gift right now.

My white-tipped fingers tug the hood of Ryland's cloak tighter around my face, a useless attempt to shield myself. He'd insisted I put it on when the rain commenced, claiming that he wasn't cold, though I very much doubt it now given that we've been lumbering through this downpour for hours.

The cloak did provide some insulation…at first. The moment it became completely soaked, it did very little to prevent my temperature dropping. I'm not sure lips can actually turn blue, but I imagine mine are heading toward the unhealthy shade. Then, of course, there's the headache that's been plaguing me all morning. Sleeping in a tree didn't seem to agree with my muscles.

But my misery is marginally eclipsed by my excitement to arrive in Kingsmar and start building my new life. I'm contemplating just how much money—if I had any—I'd give to hurry us along through this wretched forest when Ryland halts beside me, frame going completely rigid. He places a hand in front of me to ensure I do the same.

Squinting up at him through the rain, I make out his taut features and the impossible wisps of steam wafting from his skin. His jaw is locked, eyes narrowed as he scans the forest. My heartbeat quickens, wondering if it's the Bantilos again, but something tells me this is a greater threat he's sensing.

Then, my own skin prickles with awareness as I face ahead once more, sighting four large men approaching. There's a predatory glint in each of their gazes, trained on us like a hawk studying a field mouse before swooping in for the kill.

Each of them has a drawn sword, their stances tense and primed for violence. One of them carries a pair of iron shackles similar to the ones we wore in the prison. Only, these are less rusted and have markings on them, but it's too hazy to make out the indistinct design.

My first thought is that they've found us. Atherton's small village militia finally caught up with us. But something about these men...their dirty, roughened appearances, their array of worn weapons...*I don't think they're from Atherton.* The militia would've been in uniform and traveled by horse. And they would've come from our direction, behind us, not ahead. These men...they seem more like ruffians than soldiers or guards.

My stomach sinks with dread, realizing that this is somehow a far, far worse situation. And, perhaps, worse for Ryland than for me, because I notice that their gazes seem to be trained especially on him. In fact, none of them have even given me a second glance after first registering my presence. One man from the middle, who stands slightly ahead of the pack, grins at Ryland, exposing rotted, discolored teeth. As if he knows him.

We're caught in a thicket of trouble. And I have no idea how we'll disentangle ourselves from it.

"Little thief, I need you to run," Ryland utters from beside me, tone low and severe, barely loud enough for me to make out over the rain.

Run...without him...

Ryland unsheathes his sword, and I panic. This is going to turn into an ugly fight, and there's no way out of it. No negotiating, no fleeing. Just pure, brutal battle. And, once again, I'm weaponless.

"*Now.*" The word is a guttural growl ripped from deep within Ryland's chest, the sharp menace of it taking me by surprise. He sounds like an entirely different person from the one I've known; harsh and unforgiving compared to the man who was just joking about the weather mere minutes ago. But the command in his words is so forceful, so primal, that I bolt.

Veering left, my hood is torn back from my head as the sharp gusts of wind cut through my drenched clothes, straight into my flesh and bones. I don't think climbing a tree is the best tactic this time, so I race as fast as I can despite the mud clinging to my boots and slowing me down.

The sounds of a skirmish faintly reach my ears as I charge ahead. Sparing a glance over my shoulder, wet hair slicing across my face, a hazy figure follows after me, difficult to discern through the thickened fog. With a frantic whimper, I whip my head back around just in time to note how the once flat-footed, level path has morphed into a precarious slope as a steep ravine emerges on my left side. With the slippery mud, I try to keep to the right, but my follower has crept up faster than anticipated, coming at me from the same side and forcing me to run along the treacherous edge.

My heart falters in my chest as a flash of lightening illuminates the darkened forest, the brilliant white light a shock to my senses. It's long enough to distract me for a single moment, just before a figure suddenly lands in front of me, dropping from a tree branch. A startled scream rips from my throat as I stumble backward. Wondering where my first chaser has positioned himself, I glance in my periphery, finding no one in sight.

"W-what do you want?" I ask, hoping I can buy myself time to scramble together some sort of plan. The man eyes me up and down, gaze narrowed from the rain.

Then, his hand is wrapped around my throat.

My muscles constrict as he lifts me from the ground until we're eye-level. Clawing desperately at his hand, my body twitches and shudders, feet flailing as my air supply is harshly cut off.

I try to think quickly, forcing myself to remember what Ryland taught me, the techniques we've further practiced since that first night. Allowing myself to let instinct take over, my right hand slams against his wrist with every ounce of strength I can muster. Either the rainwater had already slackened his grasp or the gods are watching out for me, but his hold breaks. The shock and sheer glee of my success has me forgetting the glaring fact that I'd just been airborne while he'd been gripping me, forcing gravity to pull me down.

I drop to the ground, harshly colliding with the muddy earth. Keeping an eye on my attacker as I prepare to scurry away, I notice that his attention seems to be diverted. I follow his gaze over my shoulder.

Ryland's shadowy form emerges from the billowing fog like a dark knight, blade stained red, blonde waves plastered to his brow. I'm not sure how he found us so quickly, but I'm certainly glad he did. The brute who'd been chasing me earlier immediately starts to spar with Ryland.

His gaze briefly finds mine through his dueling, but my attention quickly reverts to the fifth attacker before me who's now lost interest in Ryland's dramatic arrival and returned his sights to me. I scramble upright, making to flee, but quicker than I can react, he strikes a blow to my stomach, knocking me back. This time, when I collide with the ground, it's at a sharp angle, and my stunned frame starts to tumble down the ravine. Somehow, I manage to act quickly enough, latching onto the first solid object my hands can grab purchase of. I cling to the fallen, rotted tree, digging my fingers into the roughened bark slick in places with moss and lichen, while my body reorients itself.

My head throbs, stomach groaning in agony. All the breath remains stolen from my lungs and attempting to suck in air is made twice as difficult with the pelting rain.

The remainder of the drop is startlingly far. I seem to have only fallen a third of the way. *If I could just haul myself up to the top, use the tree as a step...*

The attacker who landed the breathtaking blow stands at the ravine's edge, exposing a sadistic smile. Just when I lose all hope of an escape, he suddenly jolts, eyes flaring before blood begins to bubble from his mouth.

My eyes take in the gory sight of the dagger that is now lodged in his neck. He collapses at the ledge, thankfully not over it, leaving only a trickle of crimson sliding down the muddy slope.

Shifting my stunned gaze, I find Ryland's torso twisted in the direction of where my attacker had just been standing, his arm slightly extended as if mid-throw. But it's not his swiftness or perfect aim that roots me frozen in place.

It's his eyes.

Once a deep, rich sapphire, his irises are now glacial blue, glowing vividly like the moon's luminescence.

My body and mind still as I behold the other worldly sight. I've never seen eyes like this. I don't think *anyone* has. It's like they've been possessed by an icy fire, blazing and burning with cold, undiluted wrath.

Ryland steps toward the edge of the ravine, toward me, hand extended. My body instinctively shudders in revulsion, the last bit of strain the branch can handle before it snaps.

Everything in sight becomes a cyclone of blurs as I careen down the steep drop. My body succumbs to the earth's mercy, twigs and brush scratching my exposed skin, rocks and stones seeming to hit every sensitive place, limbs brutally colliding with the ground at awkward and contrary angles. Mud collects beneath my nails as I claw at the surface until finally, I hit the bottom.

If I thought the punch had been brutal, this collision is far worse. Everything screams in pain, my entire frame taut and slack all at once, cloak tangled around my body. My vision alludes me for several immeasurable moments, smudges of grey and black flickering in and out of focus, images of that haunting glowing shade making my stomach twist with fear. When clarity finally returns, I try to move my leaden, mud-stained limbs, managing to prop myself on my elbows, only to find that the skirmish has moved down here as well.

Ryland has just reached the bottom while two of the men who must've followed after him carefully slide down the remaining distance.

Automatically, my gaze latches onto Ryland's. *I didn't imagine it.* His stare is searing bright like a living flame has consumed the irises. My gaze tears from his to take in the rest of his frame vibrating furiously with tremors. Not from the cold. No, his very figure looks heated. That soft steam hazes around him, making him appear as if he was blessed by Ilvhal himself, a soldier of the God of Darkness and Shadows, ready to devour any and all light in his path, ready to eviscerate his enemies with a merciless will.

His attention returns to the two men, whirling just in time as they charge him. Like a master painter with his brush, Ryland makes a work of art with his weapon. His strokes are wild yet precise, each made with sharp purpose and raining chaos in their effect.

I watch in sheer horror as limbs and organs begin to fly from bodies, blood spurting in short bursts and long streams. Wails of agony combat the hammering of the rain, all while Ryland remains silent and swift as the wind.

What is he?

The question sounds in my mind like the toll of a church bell, its alarm reverberating throughout my body. Shivers cascade down my skin. The sight of him like this, so primal and unearthly, has me completely immobilized until I jolt back when a string of bloody entrails lands near my hand, skimming my fingertips. The palpable warmth has me heaving, body shriveling in sickness.

This isn't normal. The eyes, his sudden shift in temperament, the unparalleled violence...

I'm so distracted by the sight of Ryland that I don't even notice one of the men approaching me from my front. It isn't until a shadow casts over my frame that I look up. With my body still overwhelmed from the substantial fall, I'm only able to sluggishly scuttle backward with my arms.

Without having to exert much effort, he pounces atop me, pinning me in place with his weight. His knees cage my sides as he presses a dagger to my throat. Rain drips along his scraggly beard, eyes studying me with violent intent.

"Hello, there," he croons, breath reeking of ale and decay.

The blade tips into my skin, and I wince, waiting for him to plunge it deeper. The irony that I escaped the chopping block, chasing a chance at freedom, only to have death reclaim me, doesn't escape my thoughts in these fleeting, final moments. *Though, perhaps it's for the best.* Witnessing all this violence and savagery from men, and, perhaps now monsters, is a reminder of all the rot and fear this world has to offer. *Maybe I should just stop fighting.*

I thank the gods and spirits for allowing me these few extra days amidst the raw and beautiful wild, to savor the sensation of liberation and hope. Then, I send a quick prayer to Hyreth, God of Death and the Afterlife, hoping that by some small chance I might be pardoned for my sins. Spared a painful end and allowed entry into his realm for the pure and benevolent souls.

Just as my eyes are about to fall closed to blind myself to whatever gory end I'm about to meet, a sword spears through the back of the man's neck and reappears through his throat.

The blade is sharply removed, and a fountain of blood pours down on me. The warm, viscous substance soaks my face and slips into my mouth before I have time to close it, leaving me to choke on the metallic-tasting matter.

The body of the man is roughly yanked back, revealing Ryland, eyes still glowing with such icy malice that my heart painfully constricts in horror. Swinging his sword in a sharp, clean arc, it slices into the male's neck.

Again.

And again.

And again.

With every swing, I flinch, the sounds of muscle and bone being hacked to bits drowning me in sickening alarm. I twist over to retch, only to spit out blood.

After confirming that my stomach has nothing else to produce, my gaze returns to Ryland who continues his ruthless butchery. Blood is splattered on his face like warpaint. He doesn't cease his strikes until the man's head is completely detached from his body. Though something tells me that, had he wanted the head severed in one blow, he could've easily done it. An unwelcome part of me thinks he wanted this to be a slow process, the manic look in his eyes telling.

Ryland's heaving breaths cloud in the air as he turns to face me after a long, stifling moment. I can't move, can't breathe, my entire frame locked with crippling fear. A few more seconds pass, and he lowers his bloodied sword, wiping it on the attacker's jacket before sliding it into the sheath at his back. The gesture signals that we are out of danger. Or, at least, he is. I'm not sure about myself anymore.

Somehow finding the ability to haul myself upright despite my quivering legs, I notice that my hands are covered in red. The coppery taste of blood coats my mouth in a warm, sickening film, and I stifle another gag.

"Are you hurt?"

My eyes slowly drift to the sound of the deep, determined voice. Ryland's eyes remain aglow but somewhat dimmed. I'm not sure if I actually shake my head, too overcome to process my thoughts and movements. I can hardly comprehend what just happened. The events occurred in such rapid succession… How did such a mundane trek turn into a massacre? I have no reason to explain it, no idea as to who those men were or what they wanted.

But, what Ryland did…what he became… Menacing. Lethal. Unlike anything I'd ever seen. The blinding speed, the almost gleeful look that sliced through his gaze…he'd been nothing short of unhinged.

He'd been inhuman.

To know what he's capable of, to have been so oblivious all this time, treating him like a new-found acquaintance. I'd known that he could be violent and kill, and yet I'd still let my guard down. I thought I'd begun to form a picture of who he was. Clearly, I knew nothing. I hadn't trusted him before, knew that I couldn't. But I *did* start to feel at ease with him—which is almost worse.

He's an assassin. Beyond that really. The kind of violence he displayed isn't normal by any means. Not with those glowing eyes and that palpable rage.

My eyes lower to the wet, muddied ground, watching as swirls of crimson blur with the murky puddles. Entranced by the sight, too stunned to process much else, I hardly register the movement around me, am barely conscious when arms lift me onto their back before they begin to climb up the ravine's steep slope. My mind must be in complete shock because I don't really feel the warm body pressing against my front or the hands clasped under my knees as we move through the rain. I don't even fully register when we stop sometime later in front of a wooden edifice. Don't quite feel it when my hood is pulled over my head to shield my face or when I'm led into the structure. But, once inside, warmth immediately rushes into me. Like frost melting on a window-pane, I can feel some of my stupor dissolve.

I catch glimpses of things, like the scent of ale, the deep baritone of Ryland's voice, a glint of gold, and the discrete shaking of hands. My gaze finally sharpens into full focus as I take in the set of narrow stairs we seem to be climbing. Ryland leads us down a short hallway to the last door on the left before we step into a sparsely furnished room that hosts only a bed, nightstand and wooden chair in the corner.

An inn, I realize. We must be near the main roads if there's an inn. Which means Ryland deviated from his plans to keep off them; a decision I know was made for my benefit.

It's the first time I've been in an enclosed space in days. The familiarity soothes, albeit a fraction of my fraying nerves.

The small window reveals the ceaseless pouring rain and even darker skies as evening now settles in. Only the few candles on the nightstand and windowsill light the small space.

"Wait here. I'll be right back," Ryland cautions before leaving the room, softly shutting the door behind him.

Left alone in the cold, drafty space, I'm once again dazed and unfocused. My settings blur around me as shivers rack my body. Flashes of the events from earlier whirl through my mind, each as haunting as the last. My eyes drift to my muddied and blood soaked hands, the dry coating heavy on my skin. Those hands travel to my face where I can feel more blood crusted on my chin and lips.

The rain didn't wash it off.

My stomach lurches, and I force my gaze to look anywhere besides my body.

The sound of dripping catches my attention, and I realize my clothes are dribbling on the floor.

The trembling in my body doesn't cease, my eyes watering with unshed tears, fear still wrapped tight around my chest.

The door suddenly opens, and Ryland steps into the room, a large bucket filled with water in his hands. Towels and clothing hang from his arms. He sets the bucket down by the worn, wooden chair. I notice that he's removed his jacket. His sword and satchel sit by the door, and I wonder when he left them there.

Rising to his full height, he steps toward me so suddenly that I flinch, the memory of the terrifying violence he'd inflicted surfacing.

He immediately halts, hands raised, palms facing me in supplication. "I'm not going to hurt you, Wren," he states carefully, imploringly.

My heart aches. I have to remind myself that Ryland has never harmed me in all the time that I've been with him. Much the opposite really. But if his personality was able to shift so quickly, so drastically, who's to say it wouldn't happen again—and, this time, be directed at *me*.

Interrupting my thoughts, Ryland repeats my name. "You're soaking wet and covered in…" Another glance at myself reminds me the exact substances that are staining me.

"You need to get clean. If I believed you were capable of doing it yourself right now, I wouldn't insist. But you can't stay in those clothes, you'll get sick," he explains softly. His steady gaze holds mine, blue eyes cautious. Waiting.

I try to conduct a swift assessment of my faculties, coming to the grim conclusion that they're not fully intact at present. The biggest indication is when I reach for the clasp of Ryland's cloak, my trembling fingers are unable to manage undoing it. He's right, I don't think I'm well enough to think coherently let alone bathe myself.

Ryland takes slow, measured steps toward me, reaching his hands to unbuckle the soiled cape from around my shoulders and lets it fall to the floor. Guiding me to the chair in the corner, he carefully eases me onto its edge, proceeding to kneel.

Methodically, he grabs a cloth and dips it in the water. He raises his hand to mine which is quivering in my lap. It's then that I notice that his own hands are clean—his face too. He must've already washed away the gore that I'd found so disturbing.

Gently, he pushes up the sleeves of my dress to my forearms where the bloodstains end. Then, he starts to wipe the cloth over my chilled skin, slowly rubbing away the crimson. His movements are gentle and soft, and, if I wasn't so tense, I might find it soothing. His eyes narrow on the few shallow scratches along my skin, careful not to irritate the abrasions. They'll likely heal in a day or two. It's the internal damage I'm more concerned about.

"It's a miracle you didn't break any bones," he mutters to himself. *A miracle indeed.*

Ryland is thorough as he washes me, even taking the time to remove the dirt from underneath my nails. After my hands are clean, he takes a fresh, damp cloth, raising it to my face. When I flinch, he pauses, meeting my gaze.

"Are you afraid of me?" he asks, eyes shifting to my lap as if he doesn't want to read the answer on my face.

It'd be foolish to lie given how it's fairly obvious that I am. So I nod my head, and his eyes strain with...anguish, sorrow? I find myself suddenly explaining, voice barely above a whisper. "I wasn't so much before, but...what you did back there..." My voice is rough and hoarse, the first time I've spoken since we left the forest.

"They were going to hurt you," he replies, an explanation he deems sufficient to justify the unyielding violence he'd displayed. "I'd *never* hurt you, Wren." The intensity of his tone, the hint of pain in his eyes—I...believe him. Despite all that I witnessed, what I now know he's capable of, I believe what he says. Since I've been with him, Ryland has only ever protected me, looked after my well-being. If he wanted to hurt me, he'd have done it by now. He told me before that I had his sword and services at my disposal. I suppose the scene of carnage we left behind had been him making good on his word.

But I can't let myself be blind to the fact that there's always the chance that his compassion could change. People are unpredictable. They're always full of surprises. And Ryland is probably one of the most unpredictable people I've ever met. Someone who knows about secret tunnels and ancient folklore; who effortlessly breaks iron and can turn a simple skirmish into a savage blood bath; who just eviscerated four men into nothing but limbs and organs. Someone who so carefully cleans me now, removing any traces of carnage, all so I don't have to suffer and risk catching a cold.

Those men *were* going to hurt me, whether they were there for Ryland or not. I'd been in the line of fire, and Ryland had protected me.

Gaze maintained on mine, he waits for me to acknowledge his words. So I nod, and his face relaxes in relief. He waits a moment before pressing the cloth to my cheek, its coolness refreshing despite my body still feeling chilled to the bone. My gaze fixates on his dark blue eyes, watching as he so carefully cleans my features, his expression set with focus. Once he's worked all the way down to my neck, he says, "I need you to kneel with me so I can wash your hair." I hadn't even realized there was blood in my hair, but the sudden reminder has me itching to wash it out, practically feeling the mud and ichor stiffly coating the strands.

Slowly, I ease myself to the floor with him, bending over the bucket and stifling a wince. My stomach remains tender from the blow the first attacker landed, but I try to hide the pain. I must not be doing a very good job though as I can feel Ryland's body tense beside me.

He soaks my hair in the water, fingers gentle as they brush across my scalp. When he's satisfied, he squeezes the remnant water from my hair, guiding me to sit up. My eyes glance into the bucket, startled to find the water tinted a vibrant, ruby red.

Ryland rises, reaching into his satchel and removing a tightly folded piece of fabric before handing it to me as I stand with him. "To sleep in tonight. I'll find you some more clothes tomorrow, but this should do for now."

I take the white shirt from his hand, realizing it's one of his. At least it will be large enough to cover most of me.

After collecting the dirty rags and bucket, he looks to me and says, "I'll put this away while you change," before leaving the room.

I do my best to move quickly and change out of my soiled dress and shift—there's no way they're salvageable. The fabric of Ryland's shirt is soft, the scent clean and crisp, and I instantly feel a sense of ease. My wet hair hangs loose in a dark sheet down my back, causing my skin to prickle with cold.

Ryland knocks on the door in warning before stepping back into the room. His eyes flick to mine before doing a double-take as they rake over my body. There's something stirring in his gaze, but he smothers it quickly as he extends a hand holding a glass of water. I step forward to take it, not having realized how parched I was. I drain it to the dregs, the coolness immediately revitalizing.

I can feel myself starting to gain a sense of normalcy again. No longer soaked in blood, frozen with terror. And I realize it's all because of him. As much as Ryland may have been the source of my terror, he's coaxed me out of it.

With a clearer mind, I'm now able to wonder if perhaps my fear of him was slightly misplaced. "Thank you," I say softly.

He nods once, a little stiff. "We should get some sleep."

I nod in return before turning toward the bed. It feels strange to be surrounded by furnishings and objects again. I was beginning to accustom myself with the forest, being engulfed by the foreign greenery and wildlife of Lyrewood. I almost feel out of place in this room, as though I too am now a part of the wild. *I most certainly looked it upon arrival.*

I set the empty glass on the nightstand before crawling onto the bed and tucking myself under the ice-cold sheets. Bone-tired, my body is racked with shivers as I huddle into a tight ball, trying to stave off the freezing chill. My eyes want to drift closed, to submit to the intense fatigue. Instead, I watch in puzzlement as Ryland blows out the candle on the windowsill before making for the chair in the corner and sitting down, legs outstretched. It dawns on me what he's doing, and a wave of guilt washes over me. After what he did to save me, to take care of me, after hiking that entire journey to this inn with me on his *back*, I can't let him spend his night so uncomfortably.

"You can sleep here. There's enough room."

Ryland's eyes snap to mine, flaring in evident surprise. "I don't want to make you uncomfortable. I'll be fine here," he replies after a moment, tone gentle.

"I want you to," I answer, voice quiet with admittance. I don't want him to sleep in that chair. I want him in this bed, his warmth and safety surrounding me like last night.

He studies my face for a long moment, gauging. When he seems sure that the offer is genuine, he slowly rises and approaches the bed, removing his boots before easing himself down, eyes never leaving mine. I don't fail to notice that he picks the side closest to the door, his instinct to protect visible even in the smallest of gestures. When he's fully stretched out, he leans over and blows out the remaining candle, encasing us in complete darkness.

Though I'm barely able to see anymore, I can feel his eyes on me. Unnerved by the weight of his gaze, I turn onto my side, back facing him, relieved to be hidden from view. My teeth chattering in time with the pounding rain against the roof are the only sounds. Limbs stiff, flesh pebbled with cold, I realize that sleep is a long-way off. The mattress shifts as Ryland moves, leaving me the opportunity to release the shudder I've been holding in. The room was already drafty, and the cool sheets haven't even begun to warm. My wet hair, of course, isn't helping the situation.

When Ryland stills again, I can tell that he's facing me, body inches from mine. My own body is taut like a bowstring, partly from my freezing temperature and partly from his nearness. We may have slept against one another last night, but this just feels different, the bed more…intimate. It makes me wonder if I'll actually find sleep tonight after all.

"May I hold you?" The whispered words catch me off guard, my body locking up. But his voice is soft as he adds, "You're shivering."

I am. Even though our skin isn't touching, his body emits heat like a fire, warm and inviting. And, after today's events, to feel safe like that, to be held by someone, by him…I could let myself be curious, just this once.

I nod, hopeful he'll hear the movement so I won't have to say the words aloud. A moment later, I hear the sounds of his arms shifting. One snakes under my neck, supporting me like a pillow. The other wraps around my waist, hand resting on my middle, large enough to cover my entire abdomen. His grip is gentle, as if he remembers that I was struck there. He pulls me back until I'm pressed flush against his front. The arm under my neck bends to wrap across the top of my chest to my other shoulder, and he tangles our legs together until our bodies are fully entwined with no beginning or end.

His warmth seeps into me immediately, causing a shudder from the much needed heat. With both arms banded around my torso, it doesn't take long until I'm warmed from head to toe.

I can feel the steady beat of Ryland's heart against my back, and I wonder if he can feel the thundering pace of my own. To be held by someone…I never realized how nice, how fulfilling it is. How protected I feel.

I think of all my lonely nights in that dusty, cramped, little attic. My small cot and thin blanket. How I'd barely survived the cold nights of Atherton's harsh winters, shivering much like tonight, trying to savor any bit of warmth. How nice it would've been, to have known Ryland and to have had his arms wrapped around me during all those freezing, forsaken nights where only the howling, snowy winds kept me company.

For the first time in so many years, safety doesn't seem like such an allusive concept, not with his warmth filling my soul, melting a frost I hadn't realized existed.

"Are you still afraid of me?" he asks quietly, the question filling the heavy silence between us.

"Yes," I whisper. "But, it's the fear of what I don't yet know about you." I'm surprised that I find the right words to voice my thoughts. Clearly, a bath and change of clothes can do wonders for an addled mind.

Ryland sighs, the sound only someone truly exhausted—the type of exhaustion one has from years of struggle and hardship—could produce. It makes me wonder even more about this stranger behind me. The man who wields death like an indomitable god, who mysteriously heals from injuries and easily snaps metal, whose eyes glow with an unparalleled, fiery venom. But I'm not sure "man" is even the right word. If glowing eyes had been a trademark characteristic, I'd think him a Sildhe, mystical and dangerous. Having clarity would either reduce or, I suppose, increase my fear. But at least it would be defined.

"You're not wrong," Ryland agrees. "But, as frustrating as it may be to hear, your ignorance is safer for you. And that takes precedence for me."

How could it be safer for me when I've already been threatened in an attack? How much more danger could knowing his truths put me in? I decide to leave those particular questions for tomorrow when I can read his face and body in the daylight.

The warmth of his breath is suddenly at the shell of my ear, and I can't hold in the shiver that runs through me. "What you need to know is that those men were very bad. And while I may be frightening, I would never harm you, Wren. You've nothing to fear of me."

The rain continues to pour outside, its sound a rhythmic, soothing lullaby. And, yet, a hundred different emotions drown me in restlessness. Ryland's presence is as much a balm as it is a weight. He afflicts such unfamiliar feelings and sensations… and questions…so many questions. And one of them escapes.

"Why take me with you all this time?"

I know his answer is spoken through a smile because I can hear the amusement in his voice. "I happen to very much enjoy the company of my traveling companion."

"But, you'll cut me loose at some point. Assassins always travel alone." I shouldn't be giving him reasons to abandon me, but the words slip out nonetheless. It'd be better for me to prepare myself for the inevitable, and his acknowledgment of what's coming will only help me get there sooner.

Ryland's arms tighten almost imperceptibly. "If you're cut loose, little thief, it would be from your own blade for I have no intention of doing so."

"But how can you—" He silences my persisting questions with a soothing shush and a stroke of his thumb across my abdomen. A movement which makes me suffuse another jolt.

"You're supposed to be resting. We can speak of these matters another time," he says, his thumb continuing to make those gentle yet maddening motions.

With a sigh of my own, I tamp my questions and concerns, planning on holding him to his word. In truth, my fatigue *is* beginning to weigh heavy upon me, and my eyes start to drift close.

Once the darkness settles in, other thoughts prowl into my conscience. Four stalking figures; roughened blades; iron shackles; a hand clasped around my throat; violent grins; a dagger lodged in a neck; an unwelcome body straddling mine; glowing eyes; a shower of blood; bodies with ragged stumps and missing limbs. Each one flashes after the other, a haunting story my mind has chosen to illustrate. I can feel the tension creeping its way back into my body, can feel my muscles straining.

"Have you heard the story about thunder storms?" The unexpected words immediately catch my interest, and I shift myself slightly in his direction as I shake my head.

"It's said that when a storm is born and thunder and lightning strike, it signifies that the gods are in battle."

As if the gods' ears are burning at the sound of their mention, a clap of thunder pierces the night followed by a flash of white illuminating our room for a few moments before fading back into darkness. I know this is a distraction, Ryland somehow sensing my internal distress, and I welcome it, trying to imagine what such a scene might look like—the gods gloriously riding into a siege in their golden chariots, haloed by bolts of lightning gilding their otherworldly complexions, the beats of thunder echoing with their cries of battle.

"Well, that's reassuring," I say flatly, causing Ryland to huff a breath of amusement. "How did you hear that story?"

"Oh, years and years ago. Probably read it somewhere..." He makes it sound like this was ancient history and he's an old, wise man.

"And what other stories can you entertain me with?" I enquire archly. Another brush of his thumb against my stomach makes it do a nervous flip as he thinks.

"I once stole an exotic bird."

I can't fight the smile the blooms on my lips. "Knowing you as I do, I suppose I shouldn't be surprised."

His breath dances across my neck as he chuckles. "I suppose not, but I had a legitimate reason."

"Such as…?"

"I was meeting a client in Kingsmar, a duke who'd just returned from the Southern Continent with a ripening grudge he finally wanted settled and a prized exotic bird. We were in his office discussing the terms of our contract—tedious business and undoubtedly the worst part of my job—and I couldn't help but notice an iron cage in the corner of the room housing this rare bird.

"I'm not sure what kind it was, but it was beautiful. Its feathers were a deep onyx with a bright yellow vertical stripe running the length of its spine. But its eyes were what distinguished its beauty from that of any other creature. They were a golden-orange, darker than honey and brighter than topaz. I'd never seen anything like it. There was no doubt it was worth a small fortune."

I settle myself deeper against Ryland's body, the story stealing me away from my memories. Subtly, I breathe in the evergreen scent from his arm, my nose gently skimming his warm skin.

"But I remember looking at it, trapped in that small prison, knowing it was meant to soar in skies far from here. When I finished the job the next night, I felt…incomplete. So, I waited until my client left the house before returning. I left the sack of coins, my fee, on his desk and a note explaining that I'd changed my price."

"You took the bird? But what did you do with it?" I ask, voice a little drowsier.

"I brought it to the sea. I stood on the docks down in the Merchant's Quarter, cage in hand and set it free, hoping it would remember the way back to its home."

My heart warms at the story's ending, once again recognizing that, despite how little I know of him, there's a bit of good in Ryland. More than a bit.

"So, you received no compensation for the job then?"

I feel Ryland's shrug. "I didn't care about the money. Giving that bird it's freedom was reward enough."

I smile softly, picturing the sight of the golden-eyed bird flying into the horizon over a sparkling blue sea. I hold onto that image, letting it lull me into a peaceful quiet.

Much like the bird in Ryland's story, he rescued me from my own cage, and I hope, maybe one day soon, I'll be able to soar too, high above my past.

"Thank you," I murmur softly. I'm not sure exactly what I'm specifically directing my gratitude towards—for saving me today, from my execution, for cleaning me tonight, for not abandoning me, or for sharing the stories to distract me. Maybe for all of it.

The deep rumble of his voice reverberates against my spine as he returns, "My pleasure, little thief."

Chapter 8

I wake to the cloudy, silver light of morning with a merciful absence of rainfall. The lack of sunlight, however, indicates we may be in for more rain later in the day.

As my heavy eyes open further, I begin to recall the events of yesterday and last night. Ryland's body remains pressed against mine, his arms still banded snugly around me as if he didn't shift from his position once. With our legs still entangled, I realize I'm trapped. There's no way for me to remove myself without waking him. But, the thought of him rising to the sight and feel of our huddled bodies makes me flush with embarrassment. Somehow, lying with him like this is far less bearable in the daylight.

Just as I carefully shift one of my legs, Ryland's arms suddenly tighten around me, and he takes a slow, sleepy inhale. His head tilts down to rest in the crook of my neck, nose pressing into my skin and breathing deep, brushing up and down. Shivers skitter across my flesh.

"Are you awake, little thief?" his rough voice rumbles.

I suck in a nervous breath, debating whether or not to pretend to be asleep. But if he caught me in that lie, it'd be even more humiliating than facing him right now. "Yes," I answer quietly.

"How are you feeling?"

"Better," I reply. "More…alert."

"Why do you say that like it's a warning?" he asks amusedly.

"Because I have several questions for you."

He chuckles. "I'm shocked."

"If I'm to remain traveling with you, it's unavoidable."

He sighs softly. "Fair enough. But at least give me the morning to collect my thoughts. I'm practically still half asleep."

"Convenient," I grumble. But he only pulls me into him more tightly. If there was any part of our bodies that wasn't sealed together, he's made sure of it now.

"You're so small," he observes, voice a sleepy murmur. He's not wrong, his body practically swallows mine. I've always known he was bigger, but in this position, it really puts things into perspective.

"And you're so…large," I reply with a grimace, my brain also apparently still half-asleep.

His rumble of laughter sounds before he muses, "What a pair we make."

I wriggle in his arms, shifting to face him with the main intention of avoiding acknowledging his words.

It was the wrong thing to do.

Our faces are mere inches apart now, and those deep eyes hold mine captive. I can hardly breathe. We remain this way, me breathless and him intent, for an immeasurable amount of time, neither one of us sensible enough to break the contact.

The sudden pounding of a fist rattling our door has me flying upright, eyes wide and startled. "Dawn's up—you're out!" a gruff voice barks.

My chest rises and falls, frantic from the interruption. I look down to Ryland who remains horizontal, a hand still resting on my hip. His jaw is clenched, eyes narrowed with annoyance.

Answering my obvious confusion, he closes his eyes, running a hand through his tousled locks. "I told them we'd leave at dawn. We weren't exactly 'welcome guests' last night."

I hardly blame them. I can only imagine how we must've appeared. Blood and mud drenched, Ryland still half-vibrating with rage and me near catatonic.

I quickly rise, only to recall that my clothes are still soiled with blood, currently lying in a damp heap on the floor. Ryland sits up, his own clothes wrinkled and strewn. He eyes me up and down, his shirt hem grazing my thighs, leaving my legs bare and exposed. He flashes a smile. "Planning on wearing that out?"

I send a glare his way.

"I wouldn't mind if you did," he muses, eyes making another long appraisal. I heat under his stare, watching as he rises from the bed. "I'll go down and find something else for you," he says, putting on his boots before leaving.

I take the opportune time to run my fingers through my hair, combing out any knots that formed during sleep. Rubbing the fatigue from my eyes, I pray I don't look too disheveled.

It doesn't take long before Ryland returns. "It seems you'll be sporting a new look," he announces as he unfolds a pair of pants. From their size, it appears that they're meant for a young boy. "It's all they have," he adds.

I nod, taking the pants and quickly shoving them on. While they fit snugly around my hips, the waist is a bit large—*I still have a lot of eating to do*. Clutching the extra fabric, I lift my gaze to Ryland who simply smirks before striding toward me. Holding my gaze the entire time, he reaches beneath his own shirt to his waistline. Wordlessly, he unbuckles his belt with one hand, slowly pulling it from the loops, that maddening smile engraved on his mouth.

The bastard knows exactly what he's doing. Unwilling to concede a defeat, I fold my arms across my chest and tap my foot in mock impatience. He laughs before settling the belt around my waist and cinching it so that my pants are secure. I can't meet his gaze, not while he's doing this. It feels like something a couple might do, help each other dress. If I do, then he's definitely won.

While Ryland gathers our remaining belongings, I take the bottom fabric of his shirt and tie it in tight knot at my side before rolling up the sleeves. Once my boots are laced, I reach for his cloak. The front of it is soiled, streaks of deep brown dried into the fabric. I cringe away from the sight, meeting Ryland's gaze. "Leave it here. We'll find new clothes in the city."

Once at the main entrance a large man approaches us, probably to settle payment. Ryland's mouth is suddenly by my ear, and I stifle an intake of breath. "I'll take care of things. Go wait outside."

Though apprehensive, I decide to do as he says, not particularly interested in conversing with the intimidating innkeeper. Standing at the front door beneath the weary, wooden sign above me that reads *'The Maida Vale'*, I wait for Ryland to join me. Five minutes later, he finally joins me, hands casually stashed in his pockets. He doesn't hesitate before setting off as I follow closely at his side.

The air is damp from last night's rain, the breeze sharp enough that it has me reconsidering going back for his cloak. I'm contemplating suggesting it when Ryland's hand suddenly appears in front of my face. Though, it's not his hand that surprises me, rather what's in it: a thick slice of bread.

I twist around to face him with an arched brow. "He *gave* you this?"

He shrugs. "Sure, let's go with that."

I roll my eyes before accepting the bread. We both finish our slices within minutes, the trauma of yesterday seeming to have had no impact on my appetite.

"Thank you," I offer once we're done. The food, even if small, eases some of the hunger pains.

"You don't need to thank me for feeding you." He proceeds to reveal an apple with mottled red and green skin from his satchel.

"Well, stealing apples is very high risk apparently, at least, for some of us," I tease, wondering when I became comfortable enough to joke about the act that almost had me executed.

And yet, with Ryland, the memory of it doesn't instill as much sobering fear as I thought it might. It sounds more like an adventure I might've read about in my youth.

Ryland's chuckle rings through the damp forest as we make our way back into Lyrewood. "So I've heard." A knife appears in his second hand as he casually peels the skin off the fruit's flesh.

I smile, feeling surprisingly light this morning. It's a sharp contrast to yesterday. In turn, a memory resurfaces, a particular detail coming to mind, and I decide that it's time for a probing. "Can I ask you my questions now?"

"You may," he replies with a teasing lilt, feigning formality. I hesitate at his jovial mood, nervous to bring up his other-like persona. *What if talking about it stirs that thing inside him?* As if sensing my unease, he turns his head to meet my gaze. "Ask me," he urges softly.

"It's about yesterday." His expression remains neutral, waiting for me to finish. "Wh-what happened...with your eyes? They were glowing."

He doesn't supply any reaction. He's completely neutral as he continues to peel the apple. "The answer to that is rather complicated, little thief." Meaning, he won't tell me. His face softens as he stares down at me. "But I assure you that it's nothing for *you* to be afraid of. It happens when I feel certain extreme emotions. Like rage."

My muscles both relax and tense at the same time. To know that it isn't something I should be afraid of is a relief, yet his emphasis implied that others *should* be is concerning.

"Then why didn't they glow when you were fighting at the prison?"

"I hadn't been upset then." He's certainly not lying. Ryland had looked positively gleeful sparring that day. He'd displayed none of the angry venom of yesterday.

I nod my head, momentarily distracted by the work of his hands with the fruit. I can't help but watch as his long, dexterous fingers hold the weapon, so seamlessly removing the peel. There's something so intricately masculine about the way he does it, I almost forget my next question. "And who were those men?"

It takes him less time to answer. "The lackeys of an old foe." *More vague, clipped replies.*

He hands me a chunk of the apple, and I can't help but sigh. "You do realize that you're barely answering anything, right?"

"You requested answers, and I've complied. The level of their detail was never specified," he returns before taking a bite himself. I shoot him a glare, and he laughs. "That look could wither a flower."

Realizing that I have no intention of indulging his humor, Ryland sighs with a remnant smile as he chews before it disappears altogether, gaze now serious. "My past is very…complex. I'd like to share it with you, and one day I will, but for now, it's just better if things remain buried as they are. But I promise to always tell you what I can, when I can."

Reluctantly, I accept his explanation and where things stand. I suppose if I'm entitled to my secrets, he's entitled to his. And he hasn't tried to pry any of mine. I'd opted to tell him the truth of my parents and their deaths, my shameful circumstances in Atherton, of my own volition. He hadn't demanded the truth from me. Then again, when it came to me, what you see is pretty much what you get. I've no superhuman strength or glowing eyes. But, I suppose Ryland doesn't feel comfortable enough yet to reveal his secrets. Doesn't trust me yet. I can't blame him exactly, but it doesn't mean that I care for the situation either.

"And what can you tell me now?"

Another piece of apple is sent my way. "I can tell you that I have many enemies and very few allies. That I've spent the majority of my years alone. That I've lost count of the people I've killed and the places I've been to. And that you have my word that I shall never harm nor lie to you. I may do so for a living but never with you." I process each and every word, each admittance, noting the sincerity with which they were uttered.

One thing becomes perfectly clear: Ryland is not a good man. And he won't pretend to be. He's committed plenty of wrong and immoral deeds, likely without much remorse or regret. And yet, every bone in my body signals the opposite, that he isn't cruel like those men who attacked us. That he isn't full of festering wickedness, that his heart isn't made of rot and ice. Not when he's displayed so much compassion and care, even if only directed towards me. Someone wholly corrupted wouldn't display such tender human emotions.

"Here's a truth I can tell you; it's been a long time since something's managed to capture my interest. Or some*one*, I should say."

The flush on my cheeks spreads throughout my face, and I'm grateful to be facing forward. "You just said you'd never lie to me," I object.

His fingers are suddenly beneath my chin, stopping us in place as he tips my head to meet his steely gaze. "I'm not lying."

I hold his stare for several moments before I find the strength to break it, recommencing our walk. Another awkward silence ensues, at least for me. Ryland's posture remains relaxed at my side while mine is as rigid as stone. I'm beginning to think that apart from extreme survival situations, nothing actually disturbs him. He's unphased by all. *Lucky him.*

Needing to fill the silence, I ask, "When will we reach Kingsmar?"

"Tomorrow afternoon. And, don't worry, I have a place for us to stay."

"You live in the city?"

"I'm not based anywhere, really. The job keeps me mobile."

"Then where are we staying?"

He *tsks* his tongue chidingly. "We'll leave it a surprise, or does that answer also not meet your standards?"

I lightly jab my elbow into his side. He grunts before chuckling, throwing me a wolfish grin that has my heart skipping a few beats. I breathe a laugh myself before clutching my stomach with a wince. I haven't yet recovered from yesterday's beating.

The weight of Ryland's gaze hits me, and I rear back as a flash of a piercing glow shines through them. His brow quirks before enquiring what's wrong. Shifting my gaze forward once more, I shake my head, murmuring, "Thought I saw something."

The lie tastes as strange on my tongue as what I just witnessed. And from the guarded expression I catch in my periphery, I know he tastes it too.

IN A WELCOME SURPRISE, THE ENDLESS GREEN OF OUR journey is interrupted by a large wheat field, the golden-yellow stalks a refreshing change in scenery. With the miraculous departure of the cloudy skies, the afternoon sun sits high overhead, the light cast upon the crop creating a glowing effect.

Ryland is tall enough that his torso sits well above the straw whereas I'm small enough that it keeps poking my face and getting caught in my hair. I don't miss the occasional snicker from my right.

Despite the barb-like shafts, there's something so peaceful about being lost in this golden field. Above, I catch sight of a hawk flying overhead, soaring through the clear blue, reminding me of the bird from Ryland's story last night. I can't help but wonder if that's going to be me soon. Completely free and unencumbered, thriving in uncharted lands.

During our trek, Ryland decided to take the opportunity to query me. From the inane to the imperative, he peppered me with a million different questions, an unexpected assault. From my favorite season to my greatest fear, he found no limit to his curiosities about me. Even simple questions were followed by further probing as he sought my reasonings and rationales.

And, every question he volleyed, I was sure to return. While I hated the incessant attention, it was worth it to learn more about him.

After well over an hour of talking, I learned that Ryland's favorite season is winter with its brutal, cold and icy snow, pine forests and mountain-terrain, crackling fires and howling winds. He tries to spend most winters in the forest, living amidst the frosty terrain. I discovered he speaks several languages and is well-read, his favorite books related to matters of history and warfare—not much of a surprise. He prefers daggers to blades when it's a one-on-one fight because, to him, it's more fun that way. He enjoys attending musical performances and the occasional social event. He often stargazes or rises early to catch the sun's ascent, savors both the natural world and the finer things in life. He prefers rainy days to sunny ones, camping in the woods as opposed to staying in village inns, and favors solitude over company.

Some questions, however, he dodged, like when I asked about his happiest memory. I'd answered it with the time my mother first taught me to shoot with a bow and arrow, the very bow my father made for me. My mother learned at a young age how to hunt having grown up in a smaller village near Atherton less-inhabited and more primitive. She'd wanted me to have the same skills and so, on my eighth birthday, she took me into Stone Wood where my parents presented me with the bow. It was exquisite, carvings of flowers and swirls along the handle with my initials in the center. It was the greatest present I'd ever been given.

My mother, a patient and kind teacher, took her time instructing me, spending months training me in proper form and technique. At the beginning, I could barely draw the string back, my muscles untrained. But, after years of diligent practice, by age eleven, I was a near-perfect shot. I only ever practiced on wooden targets though, having refused very early on to kill harmless creatures. My father was so proud of my talent, he'd promised to take me to competitions when I came of age. He'd actually planned for us to travel to Snaresbrook for their annual tournament—certain that I'd merit a spot—in the autumn. They'd passed just a few months before. Needless to say, I never made it.

Ryland seemed both surprised and delighted when I'd shared with him this beloved activity. "I was actually a decent shot," I recounted. "But, I haven't practiced since they died. The bow...it was burned in the fire." My eyes stung, but I'd held back my tears, quickly lobbing the question back to him.

He'd simply said, "Some things are better left in the past." Before I could ask anything else, he went on with another question.

Despite Ryland pelting me with queries, they felt unnecessary in a way. As though we'd already connected in an indescribable way, as though our bond ran deeper than a few shallow facts. Still, he was incessant. He hasn't stopped in the following half hour, even now as we near the wheat field's end.

"Favorite color," he prompts, unflagging in his curiosity.

I try to sort an answer, brain fogged from all the thinking I've done. "Um...grey, I suppose."

His face wrinkles, and I might as well have sprouted a second head for the way he looks at me. "*Grey?*"

"It has a nice variety. Some shades are dark like storm clouds and mountain rock, others light and soft like silver or mist." He tilts his head, considering my explanation. "And yours?" I return.

His expression creases in contemplation, lips blooming into a soft smile after a moment. "It used to be blue, but I've recently developed a fondness for green." He glances my way before dipping his head in a nod of confirmation.

I shrug. Green *is* a very pretty color. With the amount of time he spends in the wild, it's no surprise he's grown fond of the shade.

As we pass through the tree line and re-enter the forest, my gaze hooks on one of the trees, noticing an unusual shadow at its base.

I pause, curiosity pulling me in its direction. Upon closer inspection, I realize that it isn't a shadow at all but markings. A strange and unusual script that my brain doesn't recall but feels familiar all the same.

A hushed sense of reverence courses through me as my fingers gently brush across the runes, perhaps not recognizing their meaning but appreciating their significance all the same. Their sacredness. They're undoubtedly very, very old.

"*Guin anath elen ahn Sethel cinar dothyn ~ Ruhnis ineth im alwyr ilvar.*"

I whirl around to face the owner of that deep voice, eyes wide with surprise. His expression is severe as he continues. "'Here lies the border of the Sethel ~ May mortals find refuge within its domain.'"

I may not know the origins of those markings, but I do know the origin of his words, the language he used.

"You speak Talaar?" I question, voice laced with quiet awe.

The word itself means, "Old-tongue", and very old it is, for hardly anyone is able to speak the ancient language of the gods and the Sildhe. The name of the dialect is the extent of my translation abilities, and I only know it from the stories my father used to tell me. Talaar is a dying language and supposedly extremely difficult to learn. So difficult that they don't even teach it formally.

"I know only a little, and I hardly have cause to use it."

It would seem he definitely knows more than a little.

"And how does an assassin come to learn the Old-Tongue?" Out of all the things I've learned about this male, this small fact takes me by the most surprise. I'm not even sure the best scholars in the continent would be able to speak and read it as well as he just did. If I didn't know any better I would think Ryland was one of the gods in mortal form. *He certainly has the aura of one.*

The title of assassin suddenly feels too small for him. Too insignificant. While I understand that he became a vicious killer by choice, I wonder what exactly prompted that decision. Had he come from poor circumstances or lost better ones like me? Regardless, he's clearly been well-educated, which would allude to a wealthier upbringing. *But if he comes from noble stock, why turn to a profession of killing?* He mentioned having lost all that was precious to him, that everything was taken. There's so much more to him that I don't know, want to know—*should* know.

Ryland shrugs with an indifferent expression. "Years of travel." Another vague non-answer. Frustrated, I turn back around to study the markings once more, amazed by their rarity. While I wish I knew how he came to learn the language, at the very least I'm glad he could translate the lines. Otherwise, I would've had no clue as to their significance.

"I wonder if there's more?" I muse before scurrying from tree to tree, appraising each with a thorough scrutiny. But, alas, it seems it was only just the one.

When I return to the original tree, I find Ryland leaning against one opposite, staring pensively at one of the rings on his fingers. From this distance, I can just make out the bronze band that wraps around a rich, topaz stone. Sharp spikes of the bronze crisscross the top and bottom of the stone where the two sides of the band meet. It's beautiful, but the way Ryland looks at it is almost with disgust. Clearly, it holds some sort of unpleasant emotional value to him, but I'm fairly certain that asking would only lead to a refusal to answer.

My gaze once again reviews the writing, that faint feeling of familiarity tugging at my senses. I jump back when it hits me, whirling to face Ryland. "These markings were in the tunnels in Atherton. I saw them on the walls!" I hadn't been able to get a close enough look when we'd been rushing through the dark passageways, fleeing for our lives. But I had been intrigued by the odd writing.

Ryland's expression doesn't seem to share the bafflement of my own. Instead, he plucks out one of his daggers, lazily dragging a finger along the blade's edge, almost looking bored. "I'm sure they were. Many towns and villages built underground routes to hide from the Sildhe."

I try to process the new information. Those tunnels weren't just old—they were from the time of the Sildhe, practically primordial. Erected to protect mortals should there have ever been an attack. It's hard to reconcile Atherton with such a rich history. Those passageways must've been built when the town was known by a different name centuries prior.

All that history tracing back to a time of magic and war was hidden from public knowledge. We possessed actual Sildhe history without even knowing it.

"Sorry," I murmur, shaking my head. "We can keep going." Clearly, I find this subject matter far more interesting than Ryland, and I don't want to bore him.

Sunset slowly drips into the horizon as we continue on our way, scarlet skies settling in. I find myself still mulling over those markings and their counterparts written in Atherton's underground. But it's the words we found today, their translation, that intrigues me the most.

Since the question has nothing to do with Ryland and his past, I decide to ask. "So, does the Sethel actually exist then?"

I only know of the Sethel from what my father told me. Supposedly, it was created during the wars, a barrier said to be invisible to the mortal eye, shielding the city of Kingsmar from the Sildhe. But, like most stories of the magic-wielders, many considered it to be only a myth.

"Yes. But it only keeps the Sildhe out—not their magic. And, for that very reason, many say it was a pointless creation."

So, it only kept their physical bodies out, not their powers. "And who made it?"

"One of the Sildhe."

"A *Sildhe* made it?" I stutter.

Ryland nods. "The one and only that pitied the mortals and their losing battle. It ended up changing the tide of the war."

I guess I shouldn't be all that surprised given that someone with magical abilities would have needed to create it. I was aware that the scales of the wars had shifted due to the solitary aide of one Sildhe, but I'd thought the myth was that one of the gods had created the shield in an effort to level the playing field between the mortals and their immortal children. I hadn't realized a Sildhe had been powerful enough to construct such a force.

I shake my head in quiet awe. Hearing the legends of magic has always been fascinating, but to actually *see* the ruins of it, artifacts that confirm it's truth, is an entirely different experience.

It dawns on me, a little late, that since we passed the tree, we've entered the Sethel's domain. In theory, I'm standing beneath magic. The thought brings an amazed smile to my lips.

THE LAST NIGHT OF OUR JOURNEY STIRS WARRING FEELings of excitement and apprehension. It doesn't help that since passing through the Sethel's border, Ryland's entire demeanor has shifted. It's the most serious I've seen him, and I find it unsettling.

I don't know what to expect tomorrow. I've never been outside of Atherton, and to enter such a large city will undoubtedly be intimidating and overwhelming. But, I have Ryland…for as long as he intends to stay with me that is.

I can hear the steady rhythm of his breathing, feel the even movements of his chest against my back and let them calm my racing thoughts.

When we'd settled in for the night, Ryland didn't hesitate before wrapping himself around me like the previous night. And I didn't hesitate to allow him. The instantaneous ease and safety I feel when he's this close to me is unparalleled. But laying here with him like this…I wonder how much will change once we enter Kingsmar. If this is our beginning or end. I don't know what to expect from him once we arrive. Will we go our separate ways or will we stay together?

As much as I want to believe his words from the inn last night, he won't stay with me indefinitely. He *will* cut me loose at some point. All good things, after all, must come to an end. Nothing lasts forever.

But, as ridiculous as it seems, I find myself wishing that just one thing will.

Chapter 9

The city of Kingsmar is a bustling hub of culture and beauty, an ebb and flow of trade and business that buzzes with life in every corner. The sheer wealth and power of the metropolis is etched into the endless grand facades and stone edifices that line the maze-like streets, the rich history carved into every crack and crevice.

While I'm sure there are more unsavory sections as there are in every town, the standard for wealth and opulence is greater than most other places. Clothes and fabrics are more vibrant and tailored. The markets are better stocked with greater variety, practically overflowing with goods and foods. The smells waft from every street corner, making me salivate as we walk past.

Trying to take everything in is like a plant absorbing too much sunlight. I want to soak up every last glorious bit, but it's all so intense. The amount of people alone is astonishing. And the city goes on for *miles*. I could probably lose myself in this place and never resurface. It's an enticing thought.

As we pass the imposing businesses and charming shops, the quaint apartment buildings and the occasional majestic home often enclosed by ornate iron gates, I find myself fighting a smile. Because I know that if I wanted to, I could start a new life here. Create a new identity, a new past, a new future—and find myself happy.

Hope starts to blossom in my chest, the warm, tingling sensation twining around my soul likes vines on a wall. It grows and grows the deeper we venture, the more I see.

There's an electric energy that hums and crackles in the air, making my skin buzz. The desire to wear a permanent grin on my face, to bounce up and down with giddy delight, is consuming.

"What do you think?" Ryland asks beside me, his gaze near constantly flitting to my face to gauge my reactions since we crossed the city limit and parted with the natural world.

"It's...incredible. I'm at a loss for words really."

"This is just the start of it. I'll likely have a job or two while we're here, but I plan to show you the city. All its glories and sites. A new adventure for us," he says with a soft smile. His words are kindling to that ember of hope inside me, morphing the spark into a full on blaze.

"One without any unexpected ambushes I hope." There's a light tug on the braid I plaited earlier this morning which elicits a giggle from me.

"Now where would be the fun in that, little thief?"

I roll my eyes. "Do you have *any* other endearments?"

"Alright then, little love," he supplies smoothly. Needless to say, my face flushes.

Ryland eventually slows our pace as he leads us into a quiet neighborhood filled with stately homes completed with stylish finishings. The streets are far quieter than the main road we'd been walking through, a peaceful reprieve from the overwhelming noise and crowds.

As we turn right down another residential street, my eyes scan the neat line of compact yet elegant grey-stone edifices. Townhouses. From the pristine exteriors, gated entrances and the few carriages that are stationed outside some, I know this street of houses is no exception to the vast wealth of this affluent neighborhood. My suspicion is confirmed by the people milling about, all clothed in an array of expensive fabrics, from rich silks to jewel-stitched laces.

A glance down at my travel-worn shirt and pants removes any and all hopeful doubt that they must presume me to be some sort of lowly subject.

Ryland leads us to the third townhouse from the left, the golden number *23* nailed into the thick, pine green painted door, glinting in the sunlight.

"Who lives here?" I ask quietly as Ryland casually opens the black iron gate, allowing me to step inside first.

"An old friend of mine. She'll be happy to host us."

I stiffen at the word "she". "And does she know what you do?" I enquire, wondering if I'll be expected to lie.

He tosses me an amused smile as we walk up the steps to the door. "Of course. She's a friend," he replies, as if that were obvious.

It's difficult to imagine us staying in a place like this. Well, Ryland easily could. With his breathtaking looks, effortless charm, princely aura and, of course, his sparkling rings, it isn't a stretch to imagine him moving in these circles. Whereas I, having lived in poverty for so many years, have forgotten what it's like to live in decent circumstances let alone refined ones.

Ryland raps the golden knocker crafted in some sort of feminine, floral design. My nerves start to flare as we wait, and I try to picture what this female friend might look like, who she is to Ryland, how they know each other.

The door swings open, and a middle-aged woman stands in the doorway with a polite expression. I flush with embarrassment when I realize a little too late that it's only a servant. *Even their clothes are nicer than mine.*

"May I help you?" Her manner is courteous yet terse, clearly wary of our travel-worn figures and what they're doing on her lady's doorstep.

"We're here to see the lady of the house. Tell her that it's the 'smug dolt'," Ryland says with a smirk.

The maid nods before gesturing for us to step inside. She closes the door softly before heading up the stairs against the right wall of the foyer where we stand, to find her mistress.

I raise a brow at Ryland who gives me a cheeky grin. "One of her many names for me," he supplies with a wink.

Just from a cursory glance, the home is undeniably exquisite. The walls are painted the same rich shade of green as the front door, paintings of varying sizes and styles studded throughout. It's certainly a residence of wealth and prestige but not so austere as to lose all sense of comfort and homeliness. Perhaps it's the fact that the walls aren't neutral shades of cream or white or the furnishings aren't all sharp angles and sparsely appointed as I might've imagined of such a grand residence. Rather, it's a home that's been carefully curated, each item a unique addition that most certainly has a story behind it. It makes me even more curious to meet the owner.

A loud shriek sounds from one of the floors above, and I nearly jump from the shrill pitch. Ryland's frame rumbles with laughter before racing footsteps emerge down the stairs until a lithe figure comes into view. She bounds toward us at breakneck speed, hurling straight into Ryland's waiting arms, practically knocking him back as their bodies collide.

"I can't believe you're here!" she exclaims as Ryland spins them around, a beaming smile on his own face. The scent of lilac and something crisp and sweet like apples tickles my senses.

Ryland eventually sets her down, and I take the opportunity to study the woman before us. Although she's slightly taller than me, she looks about the same age. I'm not sure what I was expecting, but definitely someone…older.

As I stare, I can't help but wonder if she leapt out of one of the paintings on her walls for her beauty is remarkable. A thin, delicate figure carried supported by graceful posture stands beside Ryland, luminous cinnamon eyes meeting mine. Long tendrils of bright copper curls hang to her waist, framing her complexion of creamy, porcelain skin. A batch of freckles dot her nose and cheeks beneath fans of long lashes.

Her attention returns to Ryland as she shoots him a vexed

look. "You beast!" she chides with a light shove to his chest. "It's been years!"

Ryland offers an impish grin. "You know, you could always come and visit *me* for a change."

She rolls her eyes as though she couldn't be bothered. "You're well aware I hate leaving the city. Besides, where would I even find you? I doubt you've landed on any permanent residence."

Immediately, I sense the warmth between them, the kindred bond of familiarity and memories—something I've mourned and craved to have again. A bond deeper than friendship yet separate from kinship; a union that withstands the tests of time and age; a connection of the souls. It brings a smile to my lips to see Ryland so genuinely joyful.

The girl's gaze shifts back to me, those cinnamon eyes fully taking me in. "And who's this?" Like an eager cat about to spring on a mouse, she watches me with rapt intrigue. Her interest seems curious as opposed to threatening, a small reassurance.

"This is Wren, Atherton's infamous thief."

I sputter. If anyone could personify mortification, it would be me in this moment.

Injecting as much venom into my glare, I open my mouth to try and salvage the first impression he's just spoiled, but Ryland chuckles out, "I'm kidding. Wren has been my traveling companion for the past week. Wren, this is the charming and exceedingly self-indulgent Lady Aurelia Aerin."

After the stellar round of introductions, the female, dutifully ignoring his playful insult, shoots Ryland a perplexed look, which I don't fail to miss, before offering me a friendly smile. "I'm so pleased to meet you, Wren. Ryland never brings friends, so this is a wonderful surprise." Despite her encouraging words, I don't miss the pointed look she shoots Ryland, one with confusion etched into her brows. Ryland either ignores it or doesn't seem to notice. "Where are you from?" she asks, tone warm and inviting.

It occurs to me that I haven't spoken all this time. "Atherton," I clear my dry throat, "and it's a pleasure to meet you too."

"But that's information we're trying to keep quiet. For both of us," he adds with a mischievous look.

"Did he get you into trouble?" Lady Aerin asks me, lacking any sense of surprise. It almost makes me laugh.

I shake my head. "No, he actually saved me from it." In my periphery, I notice Ryland's face soften ever so slightly.

Lady Aerin takes one of my hands in both of hers, stealing my attention. "Well, you're most welcome here. I rarely have guests, so your visit's just made my day. My entire year really," she chirps. "How long will you be staying?"

I look to Ryland whose expression is far less jovial. "I have a few jobs in the city so, I's say about two weeks. If you'll have us, of course."

I want to ask Ryland where he's planning to go after those two weeks, if he has another job elsewhere. If…he'd like me to join him.

"That goes without saying, and you know it." Her eyes suddenly widen with alarm. "You both must be famished! Dinner will be ready soon, and I'll make sure there's plenty." Her voice reminds me of tinkling bells, high-pitched and almost lyrical in cadence. Every word is uttered precisely, the perfect tenor of an aristocrat.

"Dinner would be appreciated. We haven't eaten much on the road."

An understatement.

"If you show Wren to her room so she can freshen up and rest before dinner, I'll wait in the library, and we can catch up on a few matters." The undertone isn't lost on me, but I push aside any curiosities about such gravity.

Lady Aerin nods before pulling me forward up the fern-green carpet that lines the stairs. I manage to steal a glance at Ryland over my shoulder who gives me another reassuring wink before I lose sight of him altogether.

"I'm so pleased to have you here. As I said, Ryland never brings company when he visits." She's practically beaming. "I'm looking forward to getting to know you."

"Likewise," I reply, imitating her formal tone. "This is a very lovely home," I add, voice timid as we climb another flight. Though she couldn't be any friendlier, I find myself a little stiff. I think it's from my general state of overwhelm. Kingsmar, the townhouse, the wealth, Lady Aerin herself... it's a lot to take in. Nothing is as I imagined or expected.

I would've liked to have been able to offer the pleasantry of how Ryland has told me so much about her—but he hadn't. Tight-lipped as ever, he didn't tell me just what good friends they clearly are.

"Thank you. It's been in my family for generations. It was their city residence. Although, I'm always making changes to it for I so easily grow bored with décor. Can you imagine the walls were once marigold?"

Whatever inspired the home's current design and styling, well, she did an exceptional job. The walls upstairs are a rich pomegranate color, the paper an intricate floral design that's both feminine and structured.

Aurelia's face lights up with a sudden idea. "I know exactly which room for you," she announces before leading us down a hallway, pointing to various rooms along the way to help me take in my surroundings.

We reach the last door down the hall, and my breath leaves me as soon as I reach the doorway. The bedroom is larger than any I've ever beheld, with silvery blue fabric wallpaper that immediately catches the eye. The bed, which sits to the left, is covered in a plush, silky bedding and pillows the same shade of pale blue. It has an ivory tufted headboard with a muted gold frame design that's fit for royalty. The wall behind the bed is an actual mirror, a delicate tree painted over it in some frosted looking coating. Birds and butterflies flit near the branches, reminding me of an enchanting illustration from a storybook.

The fireplace across the bed is constructed of marble and gold, equally as intricate as the bedframe. Before it sit two elegant ivory armchairs that match the two wooden night tables placed either side of the bed. A large wardrobe stands against one of the vacant walls and, beside it, a door which I assume leads to the bathroom.

I'm speechless. The entire room looks like some fantastical mirage.

And she means for me to stay here.

"There's a library downstairs, so feel free to take any books you'd like. And the bathroom should have all the linens you may require but, if not, just ring for one of the maids or myself, and we'll be able to assist you."

She turns to give me a curious appraisal, and I nearly cringe at the thought of how dirty I must look. I ensure that there's a good distance between me and nearest piece of furniture. "I'll have to sort you with some clothes," she muses in thought. "That may take some time, but I'll provide you with a few things to change into after you bathe."

"That's all I'll need," I say quickly. "Please don't trouble yourself." Given that I have absolutely no means to pay her, I can't accept anything more. Already, this room is far too generous.

"It's no trouble at all. I *enjoy* these things. You're a friend of Ryland's which means you're a friend of mine and, accordingly, I shall treat you no differently." Her smile is utterly infectious, eyes bright. In fact, her whole aura shines like sunlight, and I suddenly have the intense desire to find friendship with her.

She approaches the closest nightstand, tugging on a golden tassel which is attached to the wall, a golden butterfly ornament dangling at the end. "This will call for the maids. I'll have them draw you a bath. Dinner will be ready when you're finished. If you need anything, I'll be downstairs with Ryland in the library." I nod my head before giving her my sincerest thanks. "Please, call me Aurelia," she insists before departing.

Stepping further into the room, I catch sight of myself in the mirrored wall behind the bed, stifling a grimace. Chalky skin with baggy clothes that sit on my too-thin frame. Sunken eyes adorned with purple shadows complete the appearance, making me more disgusted with myself than ever. *I look*, I grimace, *wild*. A thing born from bushes and brush, not belonging in a house of well-repute.

After a few minutes of me trying to ignore my repulsive reflection, two maids arrive to draw me a steaming bath. Once they leave, I make for the bathroom, gasping at its beauty.

Creamy marble adorn the floors and walls, and a porcelain tub with gilded legs and faucet sits in the center. The maids filled it to the brim, adding scented oils that fragrance the steamy air in a floral perfume. A tray of soaps and lathers sits along the tub's edge, waiting for my use.

*Luxury baths, maids bringing me clothes and dinner being prepared downstairs...*I feel like since stepping into this home, I've entered another world. One of fanciful luxury and splendor. I feel so out of place, like a rat from the gutters that's slipped inside a palace. Part of me wants to pinch myself, wondering if this truly could be real.

The warmth emitted from the bath has me undressing in record time, and I submerge myself until the water reaches my neck, scalding temperature be damned. The calming scent of honeysuckle fills my nose, and I breathe it in greedily.

I want to stay in here for hours, relishing in the silky water and it's blessed warmth, washing off years of grime and filth, years of troubles and sorrows. Cleansing myself of those weighted stains. The measly bucket I used in the orphanage is nothing compared to this.

But, I don't want to keep the others waiting. Once my hair and body have been thoroughly scrubbed, I step out of the tub and into the bedroom. As I'd been told, I find a dress and underthings laid out on the silky spread. Quickly, I don the garments, not neglecting the fact that these are the most luxurious clothes I've ever worn.

The dress is a rich velvet crimson with a portrait neckline and sleeves that end just before my elbows. There are matching slippers which I step into before sitting at the vanity. After brushing out my hair, I braid it into a simple crown atop my head, the result of my transformation revealing someone I hardly recognize.

My skin is now smooth and stainless, the deep color of the dress bringing out the yellow in my green eyes. I straighten my posture, reminding myself that I'm no longer living the life of a street urchin. Right now, I'm staying in the house of a Lady of Kingsmar and must therefore be mindful of how I conduct myself. My mother taught me proper etiquette when I was young—*it shouldn't be so difficult to put to use.*

Once downstairs, I walk along the nearest hall in search of the library. More paintings and decorative pieces line the walls, each catching my attention until soft voices from a few doors down steal my notice. I quiet my footsteps as I approach the half-open door.

"I'll worry about that later." I think I'd know that deep voice anywhere at this point. But Ryland's tone sounds severe, edged with indifference. As if whatever conversation they're discussing isn't one he's interested in having.

"But he may learn that you're here," Aurelia protests, the worry evident in her voice.

"As he very well could if I were somewhere else. The risk is exactly the same."

I wonder if they're speaking about one of Ryland's clients.

"We journeyed far to get here. She's been through a lot. I at least want to take her out, show her the city and its fineries." He hesitates a moment. "I want to please her." The words make my stomach flutter.

"Alright then. I can at least help you with that."

Feeling guilty for eavesdropping, I make my footsteps known as I close the distance to the door, gently rapping my knuckles against it before pushing it fully open.

Aurelia stands in the center of the room facing Ryland who leans against the edge of the mahogany desk in the corner. The walls are lined from top to bottom with books of every color and size. An enormous fireplace sits in the middle of the wall to my far right, harboring two plush chairs and a sofa before it. I can just imagine sitting in one of them with a good book on a cold, winter's night.

Ryland's gaze lands on me, slowly traveling up the length of my body, eyeing every inch. He completes his visual journey with my face, and I notice how his eyes are slightly widened, as if he's surprised by my new appearance. I dip my head in embarrassment and agreement. "I know, I look very different."

"No less beautiful," he asserts. My blush deepens.

"I'm so pleased it fits. I've ordered more clothes for you which should hopefully arrive by tomorrow morning. We can have them tailored as needed, but I'm fairly certain I've judged your measurements correctly."

"You're too generous," I reply hesitantly.

Ryland snorts, folding his arms across his chest. "Please. She'll take more pleasure in this than you ever will. Aurelia delights in spending money. You're actually doing *her* the favor."

Aurelia offers a proud smile. "He's not wrong," she admits to me before turning her head to give Ryland a teasing glare. "But there *are* more polite ways of phrasing it."

Playfully, she bumps her shoulder into his side, and they both grin at each other. The sight produces conflicting feelings. On one hand, it's nice to see the relationship that they have. It's so genuine and effortless. I've never seen Ryland so consistently happy. His eyes are lit with excitement, and it pleases me in turn. And, yet, the nature of their relationship stirs some uneasiness. *Is there something more to their friendship? Perhaps on her side if not Ryland's?* "Friends" has different implications for different people, and I'm suddenly desperate to know the meaning of theirs.

But I discard the thoughts quickly, knowing that envy doesn't suit anyone, least of all me when I'm dealing with people as kind as them. I'm lucky to be staying here with such a generous host, so I won't let potential jealousy spoil my time here.

"We should head to the dining room," she announces before stepping into the hallway, leaving Ryland and me to trail behind.

"How's your room?" he asks.

"It's like I'm in a palace. When you said you knew a place for us to stay, I never imagined this," I answer, wonder coating my tone.

He smiles down at me, hands interlaced behind his back. "I wanted it to be a surprise."

"Well, mission accomplished."

He shifts his attention forward, gaze turning wistful, and I take the opportunity to study his profile. He has on a fresh jacket and shirt, hands and face cleaner than when we'd arrived. He must've taken a moment to freshen up himself. But even with the dirt on him, he still looked like a work of art. I only wish I could've said the same for myself.

"It feels like coming home whenever I visit here. It's a safe haven for me," he explains.

I can't argue with that. How could anyone feel otherwise when surrounded by such a magnanimous host and home? If I had the choice, I'd probably never leave this townhouse.

"If ever in the future you find yourself in need of a place to stay, you're welcome here. Aurelia won't hesitate to open her doors to you. This…could be a home for you, too." Ryland says it so simply, as if he isn't offering me something I haven't had in years. Something I thought I'd never have again. A concept so infinitely precious to me.

A home.

To offer it when we still hardly know each other… I should be unsettled by it, doubt his sincerity. Yet, I don't. I know Ryland means every word. Sometimes you know right away a good person from bad, genuine from superficial, and Ryland is one of them. Somehow I also know that Aurelia would follow through too. Whether because of my association with Ryland or because she's genuinely that compassionate.

"And what if things end poorly between us?" I ask with a weak smile, trying to inject light humor, a mechanism to mask my discomfort. "I very much doubt you'd enjoy coming to your safe haven only to find me here."

Ryland steps aside just before a large archway—which I presume leads into the dining room—allowing me to enter first. As I approach, he gives me a dubious look, stashing his hands in his pockets, rolling his eyes. "I'll chalk this ridiculousness to exhaustion from our travels."

Scowling as I pass the archway, I quickly smoothe my expression when I meet Aurelia inside the new space. The dining room boasts a grand table for six with one chair on each end and two on the sides. The surface is bedecked with the finest china and silverware. More ivory shades cover the table-scape, crystal goblets rimmed in gold. And the food… Each place-setting has a plate of food already prepared, steam wafting in mouthwatering billows. It appears to be some sort of roasted red meat, sliced into thick strips with a rich sauce drizzled on top. Beside it are an array of roasted vegetables, varying in their vibrant colors, lying atop what looks to be creamed potatoes.

My mouth floods with saliva. Literally floods. Tracking my gaze, I hear Ryland chuckle beside me. "We haven't had a decent meal in some time," he explains to Aurelia who then looks to me.

"Well, don't waste another moment. Sit, eat," she encourages.

Ryland swiftly moves to pull out my chair, ever the gentleman. I take my seat, Aurelia at the head of the table to my left and Ryland directly across from me.

A servant comes to fill our glasses with wine a similar color to my dress. Taking a small sip, I savor the heady liquid smoothly traveling down my throat and warming my belly. I've only ever tasted wine twice in the past, but this particular one feels like a delicacy in and of itself.

Despite being utterly famished, I wait for the others to begin eating. Once Aurelia cuts into her food, I follow suit. The first bite I take nearly incites a well of tears. The flavors seep onto my tongue, filling my mouth with so many different tastes and textures. I've lived off of sporadic bits of bread, cheese and bruised fruit for so long, I've forgotten what a hot meal tastes like.

Ryland watches me, expression gentle, as if understanding what this meal means to me. And, though I want to gorge myself and clean my plate, I force myself to take small, measured bites. I wouldn't want to perturb Aurelia by wolfing it down like the starved beast clawing inside me encourages.

"Is it to your liking?" she enquires after a few minutes.

"It's delicious. I haven't had a meal like this in…I can't remember." I catch Ryland's frown which is quickly masked. My stomach clenches with the acute realization that Aurelia, although seemingly tainted with an infectious gaiety that could be related to naivety, isn't blind. She'll have noticed my unkempt state when I arrived, how in awe of everything I seem to be. I'm not like any of the normal guests she hosts, of that I'm sure. And there's no sense pretending. *I may as well come clean now and get it over with.*

I take a sip of wine to steel myself. "I'm sure you've already guessed…my circumstances in Atherton were, well, very modest, to put it delicately. I didn't grow up that way, but, my parents passed away a few years ago, and I lost everything. I've been trying to get by ever since. So, this is all rather unfamiliar to me, at least, most of it is. I-I just thought you should know."

It's nearly painful to get the words out, but I release a breath when I'm finished. At least she knows now, and I hopefully won't have to do any further explaining. Confiding in

Ryland was already a challenge, but to do so to someone as pristine and elegant as Lady Aerin…

Ryland's own expression looks mildly pained, and I quickly look away, unable to stand the sight of it. I'm surprised when Aurelia reaches across the table to take my hand. "I neither judge nor condemn your past, Wren. I'm only sorry to hear what you've endured. But, I'm pleased that I can share with you." Her amber eyes hold my own captive, conveying her sincerity. I nod in thanks before she releases my hand.

"May I ask how you met one another? I'm awfully curious," she begins in a lighter tone, looking between the two of us with intrigue.

I glance at Ryland, wondering how much Aurelia is meant to know. He simply gives me a nod of approval. *I guess full disclosure then.* "We met in a prison cell the night before we were both sentenced to be executed."

Aurelia's eyes bulge, and Ryland breaks into a hearty laugh as he sips his wine.

"What?" the word comes out of Aurelia as a breathless murmur, eyes panicked as she worriedly looks to her close friend.

"You have a real talent for storytelling," Ryland compliments with a toasting gesture of his glass, but I ignore the comment, facing Aurelia.

"He was sold out by his client apparently, and I was arrested for some apples."

Her brow quirks, a gesture that contrasts the delicate features of her face. "You were sentenced to die for stealing *apples*?"

I nod, the absurdity of it still not lost on me. "It had never been that way before, but a new lord was recently installed whose governance is apparently far stricter than most. To be honest, I still don't really understand what happened," I admit, shaking my head. "We shared a cell for the night, and Ryland saved us from the gallows the next morning," I continue.

"So you're on the run?"

I nod, amazed myself at what I'm saying. This past week has been a complete whirlwind of danger and adventure and more than a little madness. "Ryland's been kind enough to let me join him," I explain, shooting him a grateful look, not neglecting the fact that I wouldn't be sitting here right now if it weren't for him.

"It was quite an entertaining journey," he murmurs with a grin.

"When isn't it if you're involved?" Aurelia teases.

"Only you would label getting attacked by ruffians as entertaining," I chime in.

"Yes, I heard about that," Aurelia murmurs, voice warier than before. There's a sudden hardness to her gaze, posture slightly more rigid. I wonder if she knows the full details of that whole event. An image of icy glowing eyes flashes through my mind. Even the memory of it makes my skin chill.

Ryland glances at Aurelia before returning his attention to me. "I wasn't referring to *that* incident when I said entertaining. Believe it or not, you're terribly diverting," he says with a cheeky smile, earning another subtle eye-roll from me.

Wanting to shift from the attention, I swallow my next bite of food before asking, "So how long have you both known each other?"

"Since infancy. Our families were good friends, and we grew up together," Aurelia explains.

"And where's your family now?"

"They died when I was very young. I've been Lady Aerin for some time." *With no husband it would seem.*

My mood dampens in sympathy as I imagine her sitting at this grand dining table, night after night, alone. I'm sure her social calendar is full, but that doesn't compensate for family. *No wonder she's so delighted to have Ryland here. He's all she has.*

"I'm sorry to hear that." It seems both her and Ryland have no living kin. We all share that in common. *Like attracts like.*

"It was a long time ago now. Besides, my father wasn't exactly a very good man. Ryland's all the family I require." Although she seemed honest about her father, I detect the somberness in her tone, the slight vacancy in her gaze, as if she's recalling another time, another life. A similar look that Ryland wears now.

So, they've known each other always. It explains the effortless, playfulness to their interactions. The ease in each other's company. I wonder if she disapproves of Ryland's work. She's so soft and delicate that it seems like the last person she would associate with would be an assassin. But perhaps their history prevents her from forming any true prejudices.

"And what about your family?" I ask Ryland, trying to confirm my suspicions about his isolation and hoping to gain a few more clarifying details.

He shrugs. "It would seem we're all orphans at this table."

I open my mouth to demand more—if Aurelia and I can give multiple-sentence answers, then so can he—but, Aurelia speaks. "There's no use asking him, Wren. Ryland's always been very cryptic."

I sit back in my chair in defeat, trying to suffuse my annoyance. Stewing in irritation, I nearly miss the quick, grateful nod Ryland casts Aurelia. The gesture piques my curiosity, but I tamp it down. If Aurelia's telling me it's a losing battle with him, I shouldn't attempt to fight it. At least for now.

In my eagerness to avoid further attention directed at myself, I spend the rest of the meal sprinkling Aurelia with questions. Besides wanting to deflect, I'm genuinely interested in her life. And, unlike Ryland, she isn't hesitant to provide detailed answers.

For example, I learned that she's extremely educated and cultured—*little surprise*—her passions ranging from history and art to music and dancing. Apparently, her social schedule is as full as any favored socialite's with all kinds of events, palace dinners, parties and theatrical performances.

As I listen to her regale us with the story of how she acquired the grand piano in the music room, I suddenly feel the uncomfortable weight of eyes on the side of my face. Glancing over, I find Ryland's intent gaze trained on me. He's drinking from his goblet, the rings on his fingers glinting in the warm candlelight. He's so focused, I wonder if he's even listening to Aurelia. I can't detect the exact expression on his face, but it's unnerving enough for me to quickly look away. His attention lingers though, leaving me flushed for the rest of the dinner.

Dessert is eventually served, some decadent chocolate confection that looks more like a work of art than food. Aurelia gushes about her intense love of chocolate, mood turning even brighter once she begins to eat. And, I can confirm her excitement is warranted, for when I take my first bite, I nearly hum. The richness of the cocoa, the smooth, silky texture, the indulgent sweetness…I feel like I've gone to the afterlife. In fact, I think I'd be content to die after this dessert.

I'm not even halfway through eating when Ryland suddenly inserts, "Careful not to eat too much, little thief. You don't want to get sick." Steadily, I hold his gaze as I spear another bite with my fork and bring it to my mouth, defiance twinkling in my eyes. He gives me a disapproving look, tilting his head. "I hope you enjoy that bite since it's your last." Swiftly, he reaches across the table and takes my plate.

I throw him a fierce scowl, feeling like a naughty child whose toy has been stolen. *Why is he ruining this dessert for me? I haven't had a sweet since…probably that plum tart.* Even Aurelia tosses him an outraged look.

Like a spell being lifted, as soon as he removes the plate, my stomach seems to acquire a conscience and churns with queasiness. I suppose I'm not used to eating such rich, filling food, and my body is discovering the consequences. Even Ryland hasn't finished his plate—either because he's genuinely full or wishes to refrain in solidarity with me.

"You could've warned me earlier so I might've saved for this," I argue, slightly bitter. *Gods, I sound like a petulant child.* I guess dessert has that kind of affect on a person.

Ryland's face softens. "I'd rather you have eaten the more nourishing food," he explains. His answer melts something inside me, and I set down my fork with less resentment. When I look up, I catch Aurelia staring at Ryland, expression…perplexed. She shakes it away before setting down her own fork.

"I would join you both on your ridiculous campaign against dessert, but it seems I was a bit gluttonous," she says guiltily before glancing at her plate. Indeed, it's scraped clean, hardly a crumb left.

"Your dedication to chocolate is inspiring," Ryland teases. Aurelia, in a most *un*-lady-like fashion, plops a finger into her mouth and licks it clean, forcing us all to break into laughter.

"Perhaps we should retire for the evening. I'm sure you're both exhausted from your travels." She's not wrong. I can feel my fatigue creeping in, the vision of that enchanting bed beckoning. We all adjourn upstairs, but when Ryland and I stop at my hall, I notice Aurelia's frame is turned to head up the third flight. "My room's upstairs," she explains. "If you need anything, don't hesitate to fetch me. Breakfast is at eight, but you're welcome to sleep in."

I nod, providing my thanks once more before she bids us goodnight and slips up the stairs. I turn to face Ryland, wondering why he isn't joining her. "My room's also on this floor," he says, answering my unspoken question. "Beside yours," he adds as we start down the hallway.

I try not to react to his words, even though my heart jumps a little.

"There's a door that connects them, so if you need me at all, you can easily reach me." If Ryland has always had a room here, I wonder if Aurelia purposefully put mine beside his? A question for another time.

When we reach my door, I turn to face him. "Today… it's been like stepping into another world. It's reminded me of my old life—well, with a little less gilding. Still, I can't thank you enough." I'm not sure if it's the wine or sheer will that gives me the courage to lift on my toes and place a soft kiss on his cheek.

Ryland stares down at me, lips parted as if also in a little disbelief. A soft smile blooms on his mouth, and it's the most beautiful thing I've ever seen.

"I'd like to take you out tomorrow and show you the city. Will you join me?"

"I'd like that very much."

He dips his head before turning in the direction of his door. Alone in the hallway, I let out a quiet sigh. If this truly is a dream I've stumbled into, I hope I never wake.

Chapter 10

The wonders of yesterday's bath allow my now loosened muscles and limbs to stretch with ease as I lay in my new bed, the morning light filtering through the windows. If I could lie in here forever, I'd perish a *very* happy woman.

I'd slept so deeply last night, that I hadn't dreamt once. In fact, when I finally sit up, I feel a rush of energy and alertness. Not weighed down by the film of grogginess that usually clings to me most mornings.

Uncertain of the time, I decide to rise for the day, heading to bathing room to freshen myself. It's then that I realize that I don't have any clothes to change into, so I make my way to the tassel to ring for a servant when I hear footsteps coming up the stairs. Assuming it's one of the maids, I dash for my door and step into the hallway, abruptly halting when I spot Ryland starting down the hall. The space fills with tension as his eyes rake over my frame, taking in my nightwear.

The maids had left the nightdress on my bed last night when I'd returned after dinner. I was skeptical myself when I first saw it. I'm used to loose, cotton nightdresses that fall to my ankles or calves. But this garment is an entirely different creation, the fashions of Kingsmar apparently possessing equally detailed and bedazzled nightwear as they do for their daytime attire.

It is a form-fitted bodice with a pale pink and ivory floral pattern. There are thin lace panels stitched down the bodice that lead to a skirt of short layers of ivory lace that graze my thighs. The neckline has scalloped edges with a pale pink bow in the center and thin lace straps.

It took me a bit to adjust to wearing something so form-fitting to sleep, but once I'd laid in that bed, I completely forgot about my discomfort. Until now, under the intensity of Ryland's stare.

Slowly, as lazy and unhurried as summer nights, he drags his gaze from my feet to my face, eyes glazed and jaw flexing.

"I...thought you were a maid," I explain awkwardly.

He nods vacantly, gaze returning to the nightdress, and I take the moment to appraise him myself. He's fully dressed, wearing black pants, a crisp grey shirt and a black sleeveless doublet. The smokey grey makes his sapphire eyes even brighter. His hair is slightly damp, darkening the golden color to a burnt chestnut. My gaze lingers, admiring his sheer beauty. It isn't natural, how flawless he is, especially first thing in the morning.

"I was coming to see if you'd like to eat in you room, in case you were still tired."

My hazy thoughts are interrupted by the deep rumbling of his voice, drawing my attention back to his face. "I-I was going to come down, but I just needed to find something to put on."

"You can wear this downstairs. Aurelia won't mind. I certainly don't," he replies smugly. "But, if you were hoping to wear this out today, I'm afraid I can't allow it. While I've been privy to this exceptional sight, I'm not partial to sharing the honor."

I roll my eyes. "As I recall, you were willing to let me go out wearing just your shirt at the inn."

"True, but that's because it had been *my* shirt." My face warms, and I duck my head bashfully, toes wriggling in the plush rug. "We'll find you something to wear after breakfast. Come on," he says encouragingly, offering a hand. Hesitantly, I place mine in his, and he leads us downstairs and into the dining room where Aurelia already sits, reading a newspaper. She might as well be royalty in that velvet apricot gown, half of her loose curls pulled back with a jeweled comb. A vision of prim and delicate beauty. I wonder if anyone has ever asked to paint her. She would make such a captivating muse.

My gaze eventually drifts to the table which is once again filled with an abundance of food and assortments of pastries, fruits and juices. Eagerly, I take my seat.

"How did you sleep?" Aurelia inquires brightly after our morning greetings have been dispensed.

"Very well, thank you." Ryland takes his seat across from me, and we all begin to fill our plates.

"So, you'll be showing Wren the city today?" Aurelia confirms with Ryland. He nods as I look to her in confusion.

"You won't be joining us?"

She smiles warmly. "I'm afraid I have a prior engagement. Not to mention, your wardrobe will arrive today, and I'll need to manage its unpacking."

It's an effort not to gape at the word "wardrobe". *Just how many clothes did she order for me?*

I try not to let my disappoint show that she doesn't plan to join us today. As much as I enjoy my time with Ryland, I've already grown fond of Aurelia. It's nice to have female company. She's so vivacious and spirited. Her joy is an infectious thing, something I'd happily expose myself to with regularity.

"We'll be back for dinner," Ryland adds, tossing a blueberry into his mouth.

"Well, be sure to see as much as you can today. Wren and I have plans for tomorrow," she announces, folding up her paper and setting it aside.

Ryland and I both share puzzled looks. "The king's hosting a ball in two days' time. Naturally, I've been invited, and I intend to bring you both as my guests."

THE ETERNAL HUNT

I nearly choke on my bite of pastry. *A ball…at the palace…* "The king?" I echo in quiet awe.

Aurelia nods enthusiastically. "Ryland and I both thought that if you're going to get a true tour of Kingsmar, you'll need to see the palace. And what better way to do so then at a royal ball?"

My eyes snap to Ryland who flashes me a proud smile. "You knew?"

"Aurelia shared the idea with me," he answers. "But, what I fail to see," he continues, reverting his attention to Aurelia, mildly annoyed, "is why you must monopolize her for *all* of tomorrow?"

Aurelia merely rolls her eyes. "She'll need a gown, which requires fittings. It's bad enough as it is that it'll be done under such short notice, so it'll take most of the day to undergo. She's yours when we're finished."

I feel like a toy that's possession is being fought over between two demanding children. It dawns on me once again how impossible my life has become in the span of a few days. From being completely on my own, struggling to get through each and every day, to now, living in luxury with two of the most exquisite, impossible-looking people arguing over who will spend their time with me. The absurd thought has me breaking into a bewildered smile.

The two finally settle their squabbling, and we manage to finish our breakfast in peace.

"Come to my room, Wren. We'll get you dressed and ready so this smug dolt can take you out," Aurelia huffs, elegantly folding her napkin before setting it on the table and rising gracefully from her seat.

Ryland gives me a look as if to say: *See, I told you.* And I can't deny that the moniker somewhat suits him.

Aurelia leads me to her chambers on the third floor, and I take in the setting as we step inside. The room is not too dissimilar from mine, the color scheme pale green with accents of gold and rose. It reminds me of a summer meadow, and the small floral arrangements placed on almost every hard surface only enhance the vision.

She guides me to an adjoining room which I realize is her closet. Open-faced ivory wardrobes and shelves showcase a senseless amount of clothing and shoes. Gowns of every color and design, fabrics I've never even seen before. I stand in awe for several moments.

"I have quite a weakness for clothing," she admits with a slightly embarrassed look, twirling a curl between her slender fingers.

"It's beautiful. Have you worn them all?" The question comes out before I can ponder its impertinence, but Aurelia doesn't seem to mind.

"Most of them. But, if I tire of certain pieces, I'll donate them and either commission or purchase new ones."

She begins to scan the dresses, eyeing them with the intent focus and precision a scholar would their books and tomes. "I'm a bit taller than you, so I'm trying to find a dress that has a shorter hem," she explains absently.

A garment is finally selected, Aurelia taking hold of the silk hanger and showing me the piece. The dress is made of white cotton, with long sleeves and a loose skirt. The waist is synched by a strip of lace that wraps around the middle like a belt, more lace scalloped along the square neckline and columns that line the sleeves. Perfect for walking about the city on a summery day.

"Let's try this one."

As she warned, the skirt is on the long side but just short enough to avoid me tripping over it. I keep on my brown boots given that we'll likely be doing a great deal of walking. Once dressed, Aurelia helps braid my hair, the result a far less crude version of what I'd constructed yesterday. The reflection in the mirror isn't as startling as last night. A cleaner, softer version of myself.

It surprises me that we hear no complaints or impatient urgings from Ryland at any point during my dressing. He doesn't disturb us once. When we finally venture downstairs, his expression is patient, stance relaxed. His lips pull into a soft smile as he beholds me. I don't give him too long before walking to his side so that we can bid our farewells to Aurelia. My eagerness for what awaits is a raging sea.

As soon as we step outside, the glorious sunlight warms my skin. A melody of the city's sounds fills my ears, and I'm itching to set off and explore. I feel like a child in a confectionary shop, desperate to taste and experience everything on offer. But I force myself to remain measured, to match my pace to Ryland's leisurely gait.

"So, what do you think of Aurelia?" he asks as we set off, hands stashed in his pockets. His tone is offhand, but I can sense the caution in his expression, seemingly wary of my response.

My answering smile is genuine. "I absolutely love her. She's unlike anyone I've ever met...much like you."

He smiles fondly. "You won't find a more loyal ally."

I don't doubt his words. Her loyalty to Ryland is abundantly evident. Knowing we're on the run, she's offered us safety and the comforts of her home without hesitation, jeopardizing herself in turn, all without a single objection or complaint. And, it's clearly not the first time she's done this for him. "I admire your relationship. To be able to rely on someone like that, knowing that at any time they'll be there for you. It's rare."

"Well, we've known each other a long time. We were close when we were children, of course, but our losses strengthened our bond." The somber edge to his tone makes me want to reach out to him. To do what exactly, I'm not sure. Console him in some way. Return him to his usual grins and light-filled eyes. But memory of my boldness last night keeps me from repeating any foolish errors.

Restraining myself, I ask instead, "Do you ever consider giving up your profession and staying with her, or at least starting a new life here?"

"I've considered it," he admits. "But constantly moving around…it helps me forget things I'd like to not remember. I get bored very easily, and my job keeps things interesting."

"You're hardly old enough to already be bored of life."

There's a short tug on my braid, and I toss him a dirty look at which he simply chuckles. "I hope this won't be your mood for the day. I've such grand plans for us."

I sigh, frustrated that he's trying to change subjects—*again*. But I'm genuinely curious about his plans, and I've noticed that he's leading us in a certain direction…

"Where are we headed?"

"Well, this first stop isn't really part of my agenda for sightseeing. I need to make a quick stop at the bank." It takes us less than ten minutes to reach said bank, and the structure itself is a sight to see. The stone building is massive, nearly taking up the whole block with a glass dome ceiling towering above us, imposing and regal. Stepping inside, the sunlight streams through the glass, forming a perfect circle of light in the building's center. As we breach the light-filled halo, I imagine what it would be like to lie on the floor and watch the rain fall.

The building is bustling with people, their figures growing smaller and smaller with each rising level. I can't even fathom how much money and valuables are stored in this place. It's clearly a bank for the upper-class. There's not a single person who isn't dressed impeccably and walking about with courtly grace.

Ryland must be paid handsomely to keep a vault here. It makes me wonder if his wealth is near Aurelia's level. It wouldn't really surprise me if it was.

He stops before one of the many tall desks, facing a middle-aged gentleman with neatly combed hair and a matching mustache. "Please fill in your details," the man directs, sliding a slip of paper and pen across the shining desktop. Ryland doesn't hesitate before writing and returning the paper to the teller.

THE ETERNAL HUNT

The man steps away from his desk to greet us, eyes perusing the slip as he states, "Thank you, Mr.—"

"Just Ryland," he interjects politely but with enough firmness that the man doesn't protest.

More secrets. I can't even know his last name. I suppose, given his line of work, his identity is more precious than anything. Still, while I've acknowledged the fact that Ryland doesn't technically owe me answers, I've been fairly honest and open about myself and hoped he might return the courtesy. He's taken cryptic to a whole new level.

"Very well, sir. I shall lead you to your vault." But the man remains in place, gaze drifting to me. "Unless she is a spouse or member of kin, I'm afraid she cannot join us."

Ryland looks down at me, and I know exactly what's churning in that calculating mind of his. He's debating whether or not to lie. I know he wouldn't be morally opposed to it, but neither of us have rings to be spouses and our looks are far too distinct to pass as family. Besides, there's no need for me to go with him. It's his money—I don't need to be there.

Ryland frowns, as if coming to the same conclusions. He gives my chin a small, reassuring squeeze with his thumb and forefinger. "I'll be back shortly."

"You're welcome to wait over there," the teller offers, gesturing to a sitting area behind me. I nod, watching them depart before I sit in one of the chairs as suggested. As I wait, I've nothing to do but stew in my skepticism.

He wouldn't even let me hear his surname. Would it mean something to me if I did? Would I recognize it from somewhere? Would Aurelia tell me if I asked?

I'm treading a fine line with Ryland and his secrets. I don't want to betray his trust and try to discover the truths behind his back. But I can't stand being so blind to everything. Not if I'm going to be staying with him for a while. It wouldn't matter if I was moving on my own, but I'm living with him now, and I still barely know anything about him. It's not right.

More than that, it's dangerous. Most of all, it makes me foolish, which is possibly the worst part.

Around twenty minutes later, Ryland returns, but I see no money or valuables on him. No pouches filled with coins or new jewelry. He must've concealed the money in his pockets, though they appear unstuffed. He gives me a bright smile as he approaches, the teller slipping away to his desk.

"Shall we?" he offers, lending me his arm in a gentlemanly gesture.

Apparently, our first stop is not but a five minute walk from the bank. *The Scholar's Library,* an incomprehensibly large building that surely must be Osterley's, and likely the world's, largest collection of written works. Visitors are allowed three days of the week, the rest reserved solely for students and academics.

We peer down from the iron railing, observing the numerous floors spiraling downward, the walkways crisscrossing and cutting through the rings. Stacks and shelves of books flood each floor. Small work spaces with desks and armchairs are studded about, people intently reading or writing. I can't even begin to fathom how many books and volumes this wing of the building holds let alone the entire structure. *All the knowledge that lies within these halls, the bright minds that get to feed their curiosities...* Suddenly, I wish I'd had the chance to be an academic, to have access to such an extensive cache of information. To nourish my mind with the vast expanses of the literary world.

Ryland leads us down the levels, allowing me to stop whenever I wish to scan the shelves. They have books of every genre, in every language. And, I wonder how anyone could ever pick just one. I'd probably leave with cart-fulls.

As we tunnel deeper and deeper, I imagine us losing ourselves from civilization and immersing ourselves in a world of endless knowledge and fantasy. In such a cavernous space, I can't help but wonder if I shouted whether my voice would echo. Which only makes it more impressive with just how quiet it is. Without any windows, there are only small lights mounted on the walls, casting a yellow-orange glow, making the space cozy and inviting.

"Do you like to read?" Ryland asks as I admire one of the countless shelves in the history section. I can see the dust floating in the air, the aroma of ancient paper and dried leather filling my nose.

"Of course. When reality isn't very fulfilling, it's nice to be transported someplace else, if only in your mind." Something occurs to me, and I turn to look at him, a frown tugging at my lips. "Why? Did you think I couldn't?"

Ryland's eyes flare in distress, and he violently shakes his head. "Never," he swears. "Some people enjoy it more than others. I simply wanted to know—"

My fiendish smile cuts off his words as he suddenly realizes my jest, a scowl quickly contorting his features. "Very funny."

"I thought so," I murmur in satisfaction before turning back to the shelves and running my fingertips along the thick spines. "My father read to me often, and I read a lot on my own too, but not so much now. I haven't really had access," I admit. "But I do love books."

Ryland remains quiet, so I gesture for us to continue our tour. There's a soft hum in the air, a subtle cacophony of pages being flipped, the rustle of tomes being pulled from shelves, hushed murmurs, and quills scratching and scribbling on parchment. It's a soothing harmony, one I miss the second we return to the surface and re-enter the city streets. That quiet space is immediately replaced by the buzz of voices, carriages and horses.

"Where are we going next?" I enquire eagerly.

Ryland raises his brows in smug delight. "You'll see."

On this one occasion, his vagueness doesn't offend me. I know whatever he's going to reveal will be wonderful.

He leads us toward another grand structure, the edifice so ancient and sacred it can be nothing other than a church. There are three tiers of steps, so daunting in their height and distance that I pity any elderly that must endure them.

I start off, taking the steps at a quick pace, disappointed to find myself mildly breathless when we reach the first platform with still two tiers to go.

"In a hurry, are we?" Ryland asks amusedly, trailing a few steps behind.

I toss him a doubtful look over my shoulder. "Given your line of work, I would think moving swiftly is second nature for you."

"Are you offering to race?"

"No, but since you just have..."

His eyes spark. "First one to the top?" His readiness suddenly deflates any smugness I might've had. My chances of winning are obviously miniscule. Not when he has the build of a warrior.

"I don't expect to win, but sure," I reply with a shrug, concealing my internal dismay.

"Not with that attitude, little thief."

He counts us down from three, and I ready myself, lifting my skirts and widening my stance. I contemplate a strategy; I can either go for rapid speed or take the steps two at a time. From prior experience, I know I'll burn out more quickly with the latter, so I decide to go with speed.

Upon the countdown's final mark, we dart off, racing side by side. It seems Ryland took the same approach as me, which means that it's a fairly even race. Until, the excess fabric of my skirt starts to gather in between my legs, stifling my movements. I hike the dress higher, but it's useless. *If only I had on pants.*

Ryland, who apparently was holding out all this time, shoots off, reaching the top in a startling time. Despite knowing that I've lost, I don't slow down, meeting him at the final platform a few seconds later.

"I appreciate the effort. You kept me on my toes," he says, barely breathless.

"Glad to have helped," I pant out pathetically, lungs burning, sweat coating my brow. My bitterness sparks at seeing Ryland's puffed chest and proud grin. I give him an indifferent shrug. "Wouldn't want you to start losing your assassin's build."

He arches a brow. "Are you implying that I'm not fit enough for my job?"

"Just conscious of your figure," I reply coolly.

"Are you now?" he muses with arrogant intrigue, manipulating my words for his own amusement. "I suppose I should admit then that I wholeheartedly return the sentiment. I'm very much conscious of yours."

His lowered tone has my stomach twisting in knots, and I feel the need to change the subject. "Perhaps we should race again another time. The results weren't exactly fair."

He folds his arms across his chest, eyes filled with mirth. "*Oh?*"

"Now, I'm not blaming the dress, but it *was* a hindrance. I'd have fared better if I was in pants."

His shoulders shake with laughter. "You're most certainly blaming the dress!"

"Well, it's true! You try running with *this*," I bunch the fabric in my hands, "between your legs!" He gives me a placating nod, eyes crinkled with humor. I glare up at him, his arrogance painfully irritating. "I think you're afraid to race me again because you know I'll have a better chance of winning," I accuse.

Tapping a finger on the tip of my nose, he bears a smug grin. "You paint such pretty fantasies for yourself." I lightly shove his arm, turning away from him toward the church's entrance, his delighted chuckle following behind me.

My annoyance is quickly subdued as I take in the large wooden doors, three times the size of any normal kind, propped open to reveal a sliver of the inside. Already, I can feel the divinity being emitted, the serenity and holiness reaching out like a welcoming embrace. As we cross the threshold, a rush of stillness consumes me. The very air smells historic, as if time stood still in here whilst the world moved on outside these ancient walls. My neck cranes as my gaze drifts to the ceilings, countless intricate murals painted and carved into the surface. I slowly rotate to scan them all, trying to study each unique scene.

Angels and divine beings float in clouds with wings and holy relics. Gods and goddesses ride in their chariots, hands extended as they unleash their unearthly powers. Some of the figures—a cherub's soft curls, a god's painful beauty and stoic figure—remind me of Ryland. His beauty should be immortalized on these walls, depicted for all to see and savor. I watch him in secret as he too looks upward in study. It feels like a privilege just to be in his presence.

Large stained-glass windows line the stone walls, blends of brilliant jewel-tones that captivate one's attention. I make to head in one of the window's direction when I pause at the sound of approaching footsteps. A man of cloth with closely shaved hair and stern features eyes me and Ryland with an expression that appears anything but holy.

"Public prayer has ceased for the day. You'll have to visit another time," he informs us in a clipped tone, as if we're beggars pestering him for scraps. To be fair, the church *is* empty, apart from other members of the cloth. I frown at his words anyway, already so tempted to see the rest of the inside, to behold every inch of its serene beauty.

Ryland's expression, on the other hand, remains unfazed. "Another time then," he says before turning for the doors.

"At least we got to see the inside—" I begin, but Ryland's attention has strayed. He glances over his shoulder briefly before suddenly taking hold of my arm and sharply tugging me to the right. I nearly topple over myself, but Ryland pulls me down to duck behind one of the pews. Pressing a finger to his mouth, his eyes twinkle, a devious smile pulling at his lips.

That face immediately has me wary, and I furrow my brow in confusion. Ryland doesn't reply but rather hurries along the back of the bench while remaining hunched over. I trail closely behind as we cross through a small archway into a narrow corridor. I press myself against the stone wall, waiting for someone to call us out, but no sounds emerge apart from my nervous, shallow breaths. "Ryland," I protest, knowing he has some crafty plan in motion.

"We can't leave yet, there's something I want to show you."

Before us is a stone stairwell, narrow enough to fit only one person at a time. Ryland doesn't hesitate before taking my hand and leading us up the stairs. The staircase coils in a tight spiral, the steps steep and short in depth. My legs protest a little given the racing we did earlier, but I forge on, focusing on the warmth of Ryland's hand.

It feels like we've climbed a thousand steps when we finally reach the top, entering a small upper gallery, one of four in each corner of the church. The view overlooks the entire ground floor. From this vantage, I can see the grand organ players flanking either side of the main dais. In front of each instrument are two smaller platforms onto which several people in cream robes file. Men and women of varying ages and sizes line the small rows while the priest who rather unceremoniously requested our departure stands in the center aisle, directing them. Once everyone is in their places, he steps forward, raising his hands as a reverent hush fills the grand space. He begins to move them with purposeful gestures, sharp and demanding motions. And then, the people begin to sing.

The lofty ceilings create an echo of the voices, each one layering over the other's, blending together like an artist mixing paints. As if their singing has been sourced from the heavens. My skin crests with chills, the harmonizing forming one breathtaking melody. I've never heard singing like this before, and my ears feel utterly spoiled by its perfection.

"They're practicing for the evening worship," Ryland whispers in my ear.

Hand still holding mine, he tugs me to sit down with him on the nearest bench as we watch the choir, our presence completely unnoticed by the others below.

"It's beautiful," I say softly, eyes glued to the choir and their glorious music. Despite my intense focus on the scene below us, I can feel the heavy weight of Ryland's gaze on the side of my face.

"I used to visit the city with my family when I was young. We'd come here sometimes to see the choir. My mother loved listening to them."

I turn to face him, unsure as to whether I heard him properly. *He couldn't be revealing something about himself...*

But, to my utter shock, he continues, a fond smile on his lips. "I remember one time, when we were staying here, I went off during the day to wander the city instead of attending my lessons. When I returned, my parents were furious. They took me to this church and left me up here to sit and reflect on my poor behavior. I sat here from dusk 'til midnight, listening to the choir. It was only after the third hour that I actually began to enjoy the music. It turned out not to be such a horrible punishment." He huffs a small laugh. "And certainly not awful enough to prevent me from getting into trouble in the future."

I smile with him, easily imagining a young Ryland, wide blue eyes and tousled blonde hair, carefree and equally troublesome. He obviously hasn't changed much, still possessing that boyish exuberance and insolence in spades.

My smile falters as his gaze turns vacant, lost to a tale of sorrow and longing I'm not privy to hear. I so badly want to reach out and smooth the crease in his brow, to lift the frown marring his perfect lips. My heart soars that he shared with me this memory, that he finally disclosed something personal. Revealed a crack in his carefully crafted façade, a fissure in his impenetrable front. It may not have been much, but, to me, it means everything.

THE ETERNAL HUNT

I reach out to rest my hand atop his, a gesture to comfort. Ryland meets my gaze, shaking off the memory. "Thank you," I say softly, trying to convey my gratitude and understanding. I know it was difficult for him to share with me. It clearly pains him to recall such memories. A warm wave of guilt rushes through me. I've been trying to pry into his past, a past he's clearly buried for a reason. I decide that I'll try not to push anymore, even if several matters still have me wary. It's his life—I shouldn't force him into sharing it with me after we've barely known each other a full week. I'll just have to take accountability, if the time arrives, for whatever may come to pass between us as a result of his concealments, and my acceptance of them.

Ryland's expression neutralizes, placing a mask over the vulnerability he displayed. My heart gives a painful ache at the sight. He rises from his seat, and I join him. "Come on, there's more to see."

I'm saddened to leave the beauty of the church and the choir, especially when they haven't even concluded their lovely song. There's something about this place that clearly invokes bittersweet remembrances for Ryland. Unlike him, I'd been forced to endure mine every single day. Walking the streets of Atherton was a living, painful reminder of my parents' memories constantly breathing down my neck. I hadn't really noticed until now, but thinking about them since departing that village…it doesn't bring that slicing pang of grief like it used to. There's still sorrow, still that gaping hole of loss within my soul, but it's quieted. Before, it had been like an open window when it's raining. You can feel the harsh winds, the rain drops managing to infiltrate inside. Now that the window's closed, the storm is no longer as tangible. Only just a view.

Once we've snuck outside the church, Ryland closes his eyes and takes a deep breath as if physically cleansing himself of the memories of his resurfaced past. When he opens them, they're filled with light again and his usual amused sparkle. "Hungry?" he asks.

Already, so much has occurred today, so much that I've seen and learned, and it's not even noon. This city is like a life-source, filling my body and soul with joy and wonder, feelings I haven't experienced in years. It's as if Kingsmar has awakened something within me.

I nod my head. Yes, I'm very hungry. Hungry for *more*.

CHAPTER 11

THE KINGSMAR FOOD MARKET SEEMS TO SPAN WITH no end in sight. Countless stalls line the streets selling every food imaginable. The very air is an aromatic blend making my mouth salivate. From savory and rich spices to tart citrus and sugary sweets.

Ryland offers me to select any food I fancy, but I opt to let him decide. I'm too overwhelmed by all the options. I could stop at every stall and try something, so I leave it to him, trusting he knows the best of the best.

He starts us off with a small, savory hand pie. The dough is warm from the frier, the oil glistening in the sunlight. The filling consists of spiced meat and vegetables, the rich flavors coating my tastebuds and warming my belly. We gobble them quickly, Ryland having done so in all of four bites whilst still somehow managing to look refined.

After Ryland had taken my hand in the church stairwell, he keeps finding excuses to hold it again. Even now, as we walk through the crowded street, he grips mine in his as if the act is second nature. I must admit, there *is* a certain ease to it. It's like our hands were molded to fit one another, as if mine was made to be held by his.

My thoughts are interrupted when he abruptly pulls me to the left toward a smaller stand though it's no less populated than the others. The line that extends into the street makes it a challenge for me to see what the vendor is actually selling.

But, when we make enough progress, I'm able to see a woman with graying hair as she takes a thin wooden stick stacked with blackberries and proceeds to brush the fruit with a clear, syrupy substance that sits in a copper pot, the liquid bubbling with heat. She hands the stick to the person in front of us, and I'm suddenly desperate to know what this stuff is.

"What'll it be?" she asks us in a rough, weathered voice as if this is a question she's asked an infinite number of times.

"Pick a fruit." Ryland's mouth is suddenly by my ear, and I flinch. He chuckles as I quickly scan the selection.

"Strawberries," I blurt out, still recovering from the rush of chills that his proximity sets across my skin.

"Peaches for me," he tells the woman before handing her a coin. She quickly prepares our skewers, and I look to Ryland in question as she douses them in that clear, gluey substance.

"It's melted sugar. The texture's like honey," he explains.

Within a few moments, the woman hands us our sticks, and I don't hesitate before biting into one of the strawberries. The sugary syrup is slightly warm, coating my tongue before the juices of the fruit burst in my mouth. A battle ensues, the sharp, tartness of the berry clashing with the sweetness of the syrup; all harmonizing together as beautifully as the voices of that choir. I can't help my small moan.

I notice Ryland hasn't even taken a bite of his yet, gaze pinned on me.

"This is amazing," I murmur, licking my lips of the sugary syrup.

His eyes track the movement. "We got lucky. Usually the line is ten times longer." I don't miss that Ryland's voice has dropped a bit, the sound slightly rougher than usual. When he finally begins to eat, I'm not sure that I'm prepared for the sight.

Ryland bites from a slice of peach, the juice slipping from his mouth and dripping down his chin. The syrup pulls as he lowers the stick to chew his mouthful, the sugar glistening on his lips. His tongue darts out to swipe away the juice and stickiness from the tender flesh, and I think my own mouth parts at the sight, stomach fluttering. I never thought eating sugared fruit could be so...seductive. Ryland makes it look like he gets paid to do this for a living. For people to watch him eat with his sensuous mouth. I know *I'd* pay money for it. The act looks sinful and decadent, and I have the strangest urge to kiss the sweetness from his lips—a thought that makes my stomach do a little tumble.

He catches my stare and lifts a brow. "See something you like, little thief?"

I snap into focus, shutting my mouth and swallowing thickly, realizing I'd forgotten all about my own fruit, having neglected it's temptation for that of Ryland's mouth. Shame heats my face, and I try to compose myself. "As a matter of fact, I do," I reply with false surety.

Ryland's gaze flares in intrigue as I slowly lean in. Fast as an adder, I snatch the stick from his hand, shoving mine in his direction before I take a bite. He laughs heartily before accepting mine for a taste. I pride myself on my quick recovery, hoping he won't give anymore thought to my pathetic ogling.

Gradually, we work our way out of the food market and into a large public square that boasts several fountains and statues to admire. Made of smooth marble and stone, the works of art vary in subjects, from past kings and queens and gods and goddesses to celebrated priests and saints.

One of which is a breathtaking female, long, wavy tresses falling to her thighs as she holds a small harp in one hand and a paintbrush in the other. Khata, the Goddess of Art. From poetry to sculptures, drawing to music, the goddess has symbolized the creative pursuits of all artists and craftsmen. Whenever my father struggled with creating new designs for his work, he'd mention needing to pray to Khata for inspiration.

Bouquets of flowers lie at the statue's base, tributes to the goddess who has stimulated the creation of so much beauty in the world. Staring up into her angelic albeit almost forlorn features, it makes me wonder if she bore any half-breed children of her own. Whether she contributed to our world's suffering all those centuries ago under the reign and oppression of the moon-blessed. If she, after inspiring such great artistry, from great buildings and temples to shrines and monuments to effigies and portraitures, unintentionally facilitated its destruction, erasing the very work she helped prompt. The wars with the Sildhe caused irreparable damage across Osterley. Naturally, much art and memory was lost in the carnage.

My somber reflections shift to the few street performers dispersed across the square, performing dances and songs with instruments while small crowds watch in merry delight. One such performance has attracted a fairly large audience, drawing me and Ryland to its fringe.

It's some sort of play, a homemade backdrop painted to imitate a palace hall, a thespian troupe of actors dressed in costumes that remind me of a bygone era. One such character sits in a less than convincing throne, wearing a fake long, wispy beard, his hair powdered white beneath the artificial crown helping the actor appear old and frail. Beside the throne stands a shadowy figure in an all-black cloak, face concealed from view as the figure whispers into the old royal's ear.

Ryland must note the furrow in my brow as I try to puzzle what story they're performing because he leans down to murmur, "It's the tale of the Puppet King."

Practically every citizen of Osterley knows the story of the Puppet King and his tyrannical rule. Originally, his time was known as the Reign of Revyck, the Mad King. Although he'd inherited the throne at an early age, his reign began as one of stability and prosperity. But, over the decades, the public witnessed a shift. Corruption and malice had a stranglehold on the king. He killed countless citizens, ordering public executions for even the slightest of transgressions, oftentimes against those who hadn't committed any at all. Many were imprisoned for no rhyme or reason, tortured and beaten, their fates left an agonizing mystery to their loved ones. Impossible tariffs and untenable curfews were imposed. His iron fist knew no limits.

Some said it had been the weight of the Sildhe Wars, the burden of so much pressure which led to the erosion of his senses and morals until he was considered well and truly mad. What they didn't know, what they didn't learn until after his death, was that King Revyck had not been king at all.

At some point during his reign, a Sildhe had infiltrated his court disguised as a councilman. Whispering wicked words, the Sildhe controlled him, turning the once fair king into nothing more than a puppet subject to his master's every whim and want. Every ruling, every order, every decree had not been King Revyck's but that of the creature who controlled him. As the Sethel was not yet in existence, the immortals were able to reside in the capital, undetected if they were both inclined and powerful enough.

The actor portraying old King Revyck points a finger toward the engrossed audience, feigning as if they're his real subjects. "Upon my one-hundred-and-nineth year..." the actor starts to croak.

Another wrinkle of my brow has Ryland further explaining, tone hushed in my ear. "Revyck lived far beyond a mortal lifespan. The Sildhe prolonged his life, ensuring he lived long enough so they could maintain hold of the throne. Revyck became a living corpse until his body eventually gave out, and the people discovered the truth."

"What happened to the Sildhe controlling him?" I whisper.

Ryland shrugs. "They say he fled, weakened from the amount of power he'd used keeping Revyck alive."

A frown tugs at my lips for Revyck and his poor fate, imagining a life lived not as your own, watching it pass by with no free will or control. Giving orders you don't abide, unwillingly subjecting your people to harm and receiving their hatred and derision.

"His death had been a blessing, to him and Osterley. They left his body to rot in the streets as the people tried to establish order once again."

I turn to face him. "They didn't bury him in the royal catacombs?"

"The people couldn't forgive his atrocities."

"But, he hadn't been himself." *Surely some of his subjects would've understood his cruel suffering?*

"He murdered his own wife and children. His kill count ran into the thousands."

I attempt to swallow my unsettlement, trying to picture life during a time like that. So much fear and uncertainty. All because a selfish species desired more power than they needed or deserved. Moon-blessed was such a deceiving name for the Sildhe for all they seemed to do with their great blessings was curse mankind.

People in the audience start to heckle and jeer, still bitter toward the characters of this ancient tale, the wound still fresh. It doesn't surprise me that the people of Kingsmar know more about Sildhe history than in the country. This capitol is where much of the atrocities took place. In a town as small as Atherton, the stories and history are more shallow in their retelling. Sildhe culture doesn't often come up in daily conversation.

"In Talaar, he's known as *Alvyr Orith*," Ryland explains with a stony expression before leading us away from the performance. Either he's lost interest in the story or has someplace else in mind for us to venture. But, something about his expression, the sudden stiffness in his features, makes me wonder if the topic troubles him. In an effort to change subjects, I enquire, "So, do you have some sort of a permanent residence?"

Ryland finishes the last bite of fruit, and I heave a sigh of relief, no longer at risk of being distracted by his sinful mouth.

"I have one," he answers, tone clipped.

"Am I allowed to know where?"

"A little over a day's journey from here." Despite the question having absolutely nothing to do with his past, it's still like pulling teeth to get him to answer. I sigh quietly to myself, and he smiles guiltily. "I'm still disappointing you with my answers, aren't I?" There's genuine regret in his tone, and I'm once again struck with a wave of my own wretchedness.

"No, I just...I'm trying to understand what could be *so* awful that I can be told hardly anything," I admit. *Why can he only feed me small tidbits that are enough to count as a basic answer so he doesn't have to reveal anything of more significance?*

I take a breath. "At the same time, I also recognize that I've been prying into upsetting matters, so...I'll try not to do it anymore. It's just hard to know what's off limits."

Ryland stops walking and looks down at me, brow furrowed in conflicted. "No, I want you to ask, Wren. And, I'll always try to answer you." He struggles to find the right words. "I-I don't want to keep things from you. Would it make you feel any better to know that I *very much* want to tell you everything? That I hate being silent?"

"It does," I confirm. I can see it in his midnight-blue eyes. He doesn't want to be so cryptic but, for some inexplicable reason, he must. "Is someone forcing you to remain silent?"

Ryland's lips slightly pull at the corners. "No, it's of my own choice. But, I meant what I said before, it's better if you don't know my past—*safer* if you don't. A lot of it would... shock you, put you at risk, and I don't want either of those things to happen."

Shock me? Almost everything about him elicits a lashing of surprise. All that he's done and displayed has left me stunned and confused. Besides, I already know what he does for a living. *Could there really be something worse than that knowledge? Is whatever he's hiding really that much more startling?* I guess I shouldn't be naive in thinking that it couldn't be.

*Ugh, all this secrecy...*I despise it. Part of me is also just curious. Of course, I can't help but wonder if any of his secrets would explain why his eyes glow that brilliant arctic blue?

"You said that you'd tell me the truth one day. Do you still mean that?"

"I told you I'd never lie to you. So, yes, I meant it and still do. One day, I'll tell you everything. Just hold on until then." There's a promise in his words. A plea. I can hear it, see it in his expression. He *will* tell me. I just have to be patient.

"I can do that."

Ryland's features soften in relief, and we resume our walking. Despite my best efforts, despite attempting to stave it off for the better part of the past hour, a blasted yawn escapes my lips. Even though I attempt to cover the traitorous tell with my hand, Ryland's sharp gaze tracks it. "You're tired."

"No," I say all too quickly.

He gives me a disapproving look. "Aurelia will have my head if you're too tired to come down to dinner. Let's head back. You can rest for a bit."

I stop short, cursing myself for letting the yawn slip. "But, I'm fine! Really! I want to stay out."

"It's nearly dusk. We'll have plenty of time to go out again. I promise."

Although I trust his tempting words, I'm too desperate to prolong this perfect day. Offering him my most convincing pleading look, widening my gaze, furrowing my brow, and jutting out my lower lip ever so slightly, I watch as Ryland hesitates, rubbing the back of his neck. "There *was* an errand I was hoping to do. I suppose we could stop there quickly before heading back…"

"Brilliant!" I interject, taking hold of his arm and putting us back into motion. "Lead the way."

THE ETERNAL HUNT

Tucked away in a small side street in Kingsmar's venerable and quaint Historic District sits a small, two-story wooden structure no larger than a cottage. The sign, which extends above the doorway, reads in a faded, gold script, *Maleck's Artefacts & Oddities.*

I have no earthly guess as to why Ryland has chosen to visit such an obscure place, but I'm instantly brimming with curiosity. As we step inside through the thin, creaking door, I'm quickly assaulted by the antiquated interior. It's a stuffy little shop that smells about as old as some of the items inside with objects and curiosities of every variety, shape and size stored rather haphazardly in every nook and cranny in sight: tomes and volumes whose spines are rather precariously held together, ancient apparatuses whose names and purposes are completely lost on me, and woodland taxidermy whose lifeless, dark eyes seem to observe my every move.

My gaze scans the numerous shelves showcasing arrays of dust-coated stones, shiny and dull foreign coins, weapons both common and not, scrolls and ancient maps with provinces and kingdoms whose names have long since been forgotten, small trinkets, and a myriad of other unfamiliar gadgets. Row upon row of these oddities line the walls, crowding into the already very narrow walkway, leaving one little space to move anywhere but deeper into the shop. Ryland's broad shoulders would make the displays easy victims of being knocked into, but his effortless agility allows him to smoothly adjust his positioning as needed.

A flash of something dark and shining to my left steals my attention, and I pause to study the captivating object stored in a rectangular glass case. My eyes flare in both recognition and shock when I read the label next to it.

A talon from a Sothdar Stallion.
Dug from the ruins of Athlog.

The Sothdar were wild, majestic creatures that thrived during the age of the Sildhe. They were one of the many mythical kind in my father's bedtime tales. His chestnut eyes used to always light up with excitement whenever he described the powerful beasts. Per his stories, the Sildhe used to ride them into battle for they possessed a form very similar to a horse. Only, their builds were more muscular, boasting claws instead of hooves and a black coat so glossy many described the color as leaning more toward a bluish-hue. They'd race into a siege, ramming through hordes of soldiers, their galloping strides faster than any steed.

But, the animals weren't just methods of transportation. They were brutal fighters too, using their talons whenever they reared back to slice their prey into shreds before trampling over them and leaving a bloody mess behind. They've supposedly been extinct for centuries now, which makes the sight of these remains so jolting.

"Do you think this is real?" I ask in unsettled awe, sensing Ryland's presence behind me.

"It's real. No other beast has talons like that," he replies over my shoulder.

The obsidian claw, despite centuries of age, seems just as sharp as it might've been when it was actually attached to the legendary creature. There are bits of dried dirt on the surface, the single nail large enough to span the length of my hand.

"You speak as if you've seen one," I reply, injecting a bit a levity into my bewildered tone.

"I've seen drawings," Ryland answers simply.

"And what was Athlog?" I enquire, sensing he'll have an answer since he's so well-informed of this land's history.

"It was a town in the west."

"*Was?*" I brace myself for the surely tragic answer he's about to supply.

"It no longer exists. It was one of the many unlucky sites of battle during the wars." I don't miss the edge of tension in his voice. "Annihilated in all of two days. Not a single survivor."

THE ETERNAL HUNT

I swallow back the unease lodged in my throat, reminding myself that, while the legends of those creatures tout them as exalted, striking animals, warrior beasts with superior strength and endurance, they ultimately fought on the wrong side. Their allegiance had been firmly with the Sildhe. I can hardly fathom the amount of lives lost to the moon-blessed, let alone the Sothdar. Those creatures wouldn't have hesitated to use their talons to rip me into bloody shreds.

I step back from the glass case, very ready to move on. "It's a wonder we won those wars," I mutter with a shake of my head.

"I think the word "won" gives us too much credit. We survived them, and just barely."

There's a sobering ring of truth to his words. We won because of the mercy of one Sildhe who took pity on our losing fight. Without the Sethel—the magical barrier around Kingsmar—we may have lost all chances.

No longer distracted and quite eager to move on, we venture further into the shop, the papery scent of dust and history strengthening with every step. I have to stifle the urge to sneeze on a few occasions.

The stock of this place is endless, the items crammed absolutely everywhere, that I hardly know where to look. Even behind the wooden countertop we walk beside are more shelves and stands. I open my mouth to ask Ryland what he means to find here when a figure pops up from behind the counter, and I jump back in response. Ryland, who remains completely unfazed, turns toward the figure, and I wonder if he sensed his presence all along.

The old man that greets us reminds me of the objects within this place—somewhere between old and ancient, dusty, and a little out of place. His gaze bounces between me and Ryland as though we're the ones who startled him. Milky blue eyes set beneath bushy white brows carefully appraise us behind rounded spectacles. Despite his spooked reaction to our arrival, I immediately feel a wash of comfort in his presence, sensing a docile and solitary nature. With a warm smile, I offer, "We're sorry to have frightened you."

The old man shakes his head, wiping his weathered and age-spotted hands on his brown apron, almost like the gesture is more of a habit than anything else. "Not at all, not at all," he murmurs, voice both high-pitched and raspy. "I misplace many an object in here, but I'm often the one who's lost."

I widen my smile, hoping it might soothe some of his jitters, and it seems to work for he offers me one in return. Any affability, however, dissolves entirely when his gaze shifts to Ryland, taking in the male's tall and imposing form. His wrinkled eyes narrow in scrutiny while Ryland remains impassive. "I know your face," he mutters, head tilting in study. "I never forget one who's walked through these doors. You've been here before…" His gaze widens ever so slightly. "*Many* years ago."

Eyes darting between the two men, I puzzle over what's happening as both fall into a stony silence. I'm not sure what the significance of the man's recognition is given that, if Ryland has traveled to this city many times before, it wouldn't be so odd for him to visit the same shop on more than one occasion.

Ryland breaks the silence between them, voice polite yet firm. "And I remember you, Errol Maleck. I only hope this visit is as fruitful as the last."

Errol's eyes once again spark with recognition, gaze curiously flitting to Ryland's hands before returning to his face. I may not understand their interaction, but I certainly catch the look of unnerved awe on the old man's features. "Er, yes. I will be happy to assist if I can. What is it you and the young lady require?"

"I require a private word with you, if possible," Ryland answers.

THE ETERNAL HUNT

The shop owner nods before stepping out from behind the counter. With a small smile directed at me, he gestures his head toward the back where Ryland follows him until both men are lost to the boundless and chaotic depths of *Maleck's Artefacts & Oddities*.

It's a natural assumption that being left to wait in an oddities shop would leave a person quite entertained. Yet, the mysterious departure of the two males steals all my attention and focus. So much so that my foot begins to excitedly tap against the floor. Forcing myself to find a distraction, I swivel around and face the nearest shelf, gaze latching onto the first object in sight, an iron pole with an attachment at the end in the shape of a strange symbol. I notice the small placard beside the object and take a moment to read it:

> *A branding iron used on mortal slaves by the Sildhe during the Sildhe Wars. The Talaar symbol was used to signify the indentured enslavement of those mortals whom were owned by the moon-blessed creatures.*

I can feel the color leeching from my face, stomach twisting as I discover such a dark part of our history. While it's common knowledge that the Sildhe were considered a cruel and vicious race, many still relate them to divine and revered beings who possessed unearthly beauty and magic. Long since lost to legend, several of the horrible truths such as this have been blended with lore characterized by mysticism and wonder with the effect of diminishing some of the harsher realities of their nature. Seeing such a wicked object in the flesh brings that reality into full focus. Cringing away, I imagine the searing burn of my skin being melted as my life is stolen and bound to another's. A shiver racks through my body before my attention shifts to the faint whisper of voices sounding from deep within the shop.

"As you already know, they're extraordinarily rare. I have not heard of one being in another's possession. Yours is the only I've ever beheld." *Mr. Maleck.*

Instinctively, my body twists in the direction of the voices, and I take a quiet step forward. The rest comes out a muffled murmuring, and I find myself tip-toeing deeper inside, weaving through the aisles as I scarcely breathe, ears straining to hear.

"...need to find another way.........cannot be the only method..." *Ryland*.

"...can have it ordered, but it would take several weeks to arrive......and it will cost..."

"I'll pay whatever—"

As I inch forward through a particularly narrow space in order to catch Ryland's last words, my shoulder bumps into a crystal stone, knocking it off balance. I whirl around just in time to grasp it mid-air, but not fast enough to prevent any of the resulting jostling noises.

Frozen in place, my face contorts in a grimace as I wait to hear if my presence has been detected. When the murmuring continues, I let out a quiet breath of relief. Peeling away from the shelf, I return to where I'd been standing prior, my momentary bout of bravery to eavesdrop having quickly passed.

A few minutes later, both men return to the counter, expressions mild. "Find what you were looking for?" I enquire casually, pretending to look away from an object that might have captured my attention for the duration of their private discussion.

Ryland watches me, eyes crinkled with knowing mirth as he replies, tone equally as casual, "Not quite. But I suspect you did."

I stiffen, neither admitting nor denying my guilt since his words were only an implication and not a full accusation. Even if he's onto me, he doesn't seem upset by it. I feel simultaneously relieved and guilty. *I really shouldn't have snooped.* But, as we say our farewells to the quirky shop owner and make our way back onto the streets, Ryland's warring expression of simmering disappointment and flickering hope only has me wishing I'd heard the full extent of their exchange.

CHAPTER 12

Upon our return to the townhouse, Aurelia practically carried me up the stairs to my room to show me my new, fully stocked wardrobe. It was overflowing with dresses and gowns in a variety of colors and fabrics. Even the dresser was filled with clothes, nightwear and undergarments. She even bought me new shoes and jewelry.

After she'd taken her time going over the haul, I was sure to express my unending gratitude. Though I was a bit perplexed. The stock that she'd acquired was well over what would be needed for a few weeks' stay in Kingsmar. When I'd informed her of said detail, she simply replied that I'd have this all waiting for me whenever I next visited.

Did that mean I was expected to travel with Ryland after this? That I'd one day be returning with him to Aurelia's? Or perhaps she meant I'd visit her one day on my own. What I did know with absolute certainty was that I would forever be indebted to them both.

Dinner is much like it was last night, set at the same table in our usual seats. The only difference is that none of us changed clothing, Aurelia having decided that tonight would be more "informal"—something I'm sure she did for my benefit.

She enquires about our day, and I spare no details. Well, maybe a few, such as Ryland sharing that vulnerable glimpse of his past or my mortifying blunder of nearly getting caught staring at his mouth. Everything else, I share. She seems to approve of his choices, suggesting a few other stops for our next outing. All of them pique my interest, and Ryland often chuckles, claiming my expression of eagerness to be amusing.

"Our last stop was some little artifact shop that Ryland needed to visit. It's run by a nice old man," I add before taking a sip of water.

Aurelia's gaze flashes to Ryland, brow narrowed. "In the Historic District?" she confirms, attention still settled on him.

"You know it as well?"

"I'm...familiar with the establishment," she answers, voice distant as her gaze once again cuts to the male across from me, and I know that I'm missing something. "What were you doing there?"

This time, the question is aimed directly at Ryland, all pretenses apparently dropped. Ryland's expression to any stranger might be deemed neutral. But, having spent so much time in close proximity, I've begun to notice his tells, such as the slight tautness in his mouth or the faint tick of a muscle in his jaw indicating his displeasure.

"Merely browsing," he answers succinctly.

"For what?" Aurelia presses, and I have to admire her persistence. She clearly has no qualms with intruding in his personal affairs.

"Nothing that concerns you."

"I sincerely doubt that." Her voice is as cold as I've ever heard it, and I carefully set down my glass, afraid any sudden noises might disrupt the delicate peace that's about to shatter at any moment.

Ryland's finger taps on the table, and I have the sense he's avoiding my gaze. "If you'd like to probe me, Aurelia, I suggest you find another time," he warns, voice a frosty pairing to her icy expression.

Obviously my presence is the deterrent for his divulging—*surprise, surprise*. But, I promised that I wouldn't pry any further. Desperate to preserve civility between the two, I manage the courage to interrupt. "So, Aurelia, you mentioned plans for tomorrow?"

She reluctantly looks my way and, though her expression softens, I can still sense the hardness in her gaze, one that says that she *will* in fact be returning to the subject later. "Tomorrow, right. We'll have to be up and out early. Dress fittings take quite a while. We might be able to have a quick bite to eat in between, but we'll also need to look for shoes and accessories," she explains.

My body both slumps in exhaustion and hums in excitement just thinking about it. A day of shopping…I don't think I've ever done something like it before. My mother made most of my clothing, each item stitched with her endless love and care. Every piece burned to ash. Reverting from the somber memory, my thoughts shift to the painful reminder that tomorrow's shopping escapade will be costly. A consequential frown tugs at my lips.

"I'm not so sure I should attend to the ball," I say gently.

Both pairs of eyes snap to me, expressions incredulous as if I just told them I want to tour the city's sewers. "Why ever not?" Aurelia asks in quiet shock.

I wonder if my face is visibly reddening. "I…I have no means to pay for the clothing, and I cannot accept anything else from you."

"Money isn't an issue, Wren," Ryland says softly.

I send him a frustrated glower, irritated that he's speaking on Aurelia's behalf. It's *her* money after all, but she just nods in agreement with him. "Ryland's right. Besides, I *never* have guests who I can shop for, and we all know I'm short of family," she insists.

I bow my head, feeling utterly wretched. The tears start to burn, and a few spill onto my plate next to my piece of roast chicken. Guilt and shame war within me, and I'm not sure which of them is winning. I quickly wipe away my tears, but I can feel both their heavy gazes on me which of course makes my embarrassment flare even hotter. It's a losing battle to hold them back.

The harsh screech of a chair being pushed back sounds, although I'm not sure who has decided to rise, because I quickly do the same, stepping out of my seat. "I'm sorry. If you'll excuse me." As I turn to dash away, I catch one last glimpse of the table, Aurelia frowning, napkin extended to me in offer, and Ryland standing upright, expression strained. But, I don't pause to study the scene any further. I scurry up the stairs, unable to hold back the full force of my tears now. They run down my cheeks, hands cupping my face in utter humiliation. Once I make it to my room, I drop into one of the chairs before the sobs start to rack my body.

I've never been so ashamed by my circumstances, so humiliated by my fate. The thought has me almost laughing out loud. *What circumstances?* I mentally snort. I have absolutely nothing. Not a single coin to my name. And now, I've been left to rely on the kindness of Ryland and Aurelia, and it's sickening to continue taking from them. I feel like a leech, sucking them dry of their generosity with nothing of value to share in return.

Another sobs releases from my chest.

I've never let myself succumb to the reality of my cruel circumstances very often. Every now and then do I steep in my misery. But, since arriving in this city and having Aurelia spoil me with her luxuries, it's struck me harder. They keep insisting that it's not a problem, that it's a delight for Aurelia. *How could spending a fortune on a stranger be a true plea-*

sure? Their words only make me feel worse. I can't imagine a more disgusting sentiment than to be at the mercy of other people's pity.

A soft knock on the door interrupts my wallowing, and Aurelia's delicate features appear through the crack before she eases herself inside. "May I come in?"

Hardly capable of a verbal answer, I nod my head, listening to her quiet footsteps before she takes a seat in the chair beside me. "I can't say I wholly understand what you're feeling since I've never been in your position. But, I do think I have a general idea, and I'm so sorry, Wren. I don't want you to feel like we pity you. It's quite the opposite. I admire you greatly. You seem to have endured so much and, not only have come out of it with your head held high, but you're also able to still think kindly of the world. It takes a truly indomitable person to achieve that." I lift my head to meet her gaze, and it's full of gentle sincerity. "The gods are trying to reward you for your suffering. Let them."

"But…it's so humiliating. I can't offer you a single thing in return."

She shakes her head. "But you can. Your friendship, which I would very much like." I know she's trying to be kind, but what she's—*just be gracious and stop your pathetic sniveling!*

"What if I told you that you could pay me back?"

I give her a doubtful look. "I think you wouldn't accept it when the time came." *If* it ever came. I'm not so sure I'll ever find a steady income, at least not enough to pay back the likely staggering sum for what she's spent on me already in one day.

Aurelia smiles guiltily, accepting the truth in my words. "Then settle on accepting to become my friend. I have no shortage of acquaintances, but apart from Ryland, I don't have any *true* friends. I'd like for us to be."

I search for any doubt in her tone and find none. She genuinely means it. I lean in to give her an embrace which she accepts and returns in kind. When I let go, I wipe my eyes and sniffle. "Will you tell Ryland that I'm sorry?"

She nods. "He's out right now, but I'll tell him when he returns."

I furrow my brow. "He left?"

"Went to get some air."

If anyone needed air, it was me. *So, why did he?*

"Come, you and I will finish dinner," she says, taking my hand. "And you can rest assured that *I* won't stop you from finishing dessert."

I release a laugh as we make our way to the dining room. Continuing our meal, I let Aurelia steer the conversation. In the back of my mind, I keep thinking about Ryland. By the time we're done, he still hasn't returned. When I bade her goodnight, as if she sensed my unease, Aurelia assured me that he's fine and insisted I make for bed as opposed to wait up for him, claiming I needed rest for tomorrow's busy day.

I've just begun to doze off when there's a soft knock on my door, drawing me from sleep. I assume it's Aurelia as I pad toward it, the silk of my grey nightdress swishing with my steps.

I startle to find Ryland at my door offering a faint, friendly smile, as if he hadn't been bothered enough by my crying at dinner that he had to leave the table.

"Did I wake you?"

I shake my head, noting the slight apprehension on his face. "If you're not otherwise engaged then, I'd like to take you out." Although his usual teasing tone has made an appearance, it's a little subdued.

I scrunch my brows. "Now?"

He nods.

Go out where? At this hour? I bottle my questions, too relieved that he isn't upset with me anymore, that he wants to spend more time together. "I-I'll have to get dressed," I murmur, recalling what I'm wearing. Or rather what little.

Hooking his thumb and a folded finger under his chin, Ryland studies me carefully, dragging his gaze over my body. "There's no need. We won't really be seen by anyone. Just put on some shoes," he instructs. I'm not sure how we won't be seen if we're going out, but I take his word for it and turn for my boots.

Once laced-up, I meet him back at the door. Looking up beneath my lashes, I whisper, "I'm sorry for how I acted at dinner."

Ryland flinches like he's just been struck, brows slashing over his widened gaze. "You're sorry?" I nod. "You're apologizing for crying?"

"Believe it or not, before I met you, I rarely cried. Yet, it's all I seem to do around you."

"Wren, you've been through so much," he takes a step closer, "and I hate that you've had to suffer. That you have so little, you can't stand the idea of accepting anything from others. That you won't let anyone take care of you. But, I'm here now. Let me take you out."

I follow Ryland upstairs, and as we reach the third floor, I wonder if he intends to invite Aurelia to join us, but he continues up another flight of stairs. *I hadn't even realized there was a fourth floor.*

Once at the top, Ryland takes us through a door which I discover leads to the townhouse's rooftop. I look out at the view, the numerous neighboring rooftops stacked closely together. "What are we doing up here?"

Ryland's lips pull into a mischievous smile, so devious, so devastating, my breathing falters. Several seconds pass before I manage to collect my thoughts.

"Follow me," is all he says before sauntering to the edge and stepping onto the neighboring building's roof. "This is my preferred way of traversing the city," he explains, taking my hand and pulling me to join him.

Hidden from the illumination of the city street lights below, we walk amidst shadows and darkness like two thieves in the night. Strolling alongside the ledges of the rooftops, we venture deeper into the city, admiring the sites below: the people milling about, couples walking arm in arm after leaving a performance from a theater or an intimate meal at a restaurant, taverns filled with revelers and their merry-making, and the occasional street performer and their applauding audiences.

To be down there at ground-level and admire the city's bustle is one thing. But, to remain hidden from view, to watch from above as the world goes about its routine whilst watching from the shadows is an entirely unique experience. It feels secretive and special.

It leads me to contemplate the two contrasting sides of Ryland's life. One that comes out in the daylight, where he sees dear friends and pays visits to his lofty bank and parades the streets with his charming, princely arrogance. The other side belongs to the assassin, a clandestine and allusive life set in a world of silver blades, shadows and midnight. Where his sharp sword and even sharper cunning manifest, though the former seems not in his possession tonight.

No, tonight is a lesser version of the nighttime assassin I'm sure he usually becomes at this hour. He's taming himself for me, I realize.

As we start to distance ourselves from the residential area, I notice the buildings growing more spaced apart, the gaps between the structures spanning wider, the drops steeper. We approach one such gap, and Ryland effortlessly leaps across it, landing on the other side in near silence as stealthily as a cat. I'm about to jump myself but quickly halt when I see just how wide the stretch is. Hesitating on the precipice, I stare into the dark abyss below, the ground of the alley not even visible from this distance. I swallow before taking an apprehensive step back.

"Coming, little thief?" Ryland asks, watching me from across the way.

"Actually, I think I'll just stay here. If you want to go ahead, that's fine," I reply assuredly, settled with my decision. *It's better than falling to my death.*

Ryland flashes me a humored grin. "Don't be afraid. I promise I'll catch you." Despite his sincerity, the words aren't a comfort. *What if he's not quick enough? What if I take too small a jump?* I shake my head, firm on my decision.

"Don't you trust me even a little bit after all this time?" he asks ruefully.

I bite my lower lip, quickly considering. Although secretive, Ryland's always protected me, always been capable. I may not be able to trust him fully, but with my safety, I feel I can. Letting out a nervous breath, I ready myself. "If you let me fall…" I warn.

He chuckles. "I'm sure the rest of that sentence is very colorful."

"Then I won't bother finishing it since you seem to get the gist." A grunt of amusement sounds as I take a step back. Bending my knees, I hike the hem of my nightdress up my thighs to allow better movement. With a final breath, I launch myself into the air. My free arm extends outward in an attempt to maintain balance as I shoot across the formidable drop.

Thankfully, Ryland snatches my waist, pulling me into him then away from the edge. He slides his hands around my back, holding my front against his. I look up to meet his pleased gaze, letting a small smile form in return. "Thanks," I say a little breathlessly. He grins down at me, eyes lit with satisfaction. My own gaze narrows in suspicion. "What's that smile for?"

"I'm making progress with you," he murmurs, the fingers at my back playing with the ends of my hair. Reflexively, my hold on his biceps tightens, and Ryland pulls me infinitesimally closer. If I thought my heart was racing during the jump, it's hammering in my chest now.

Sounds of cheering and music emerge from the distance, and I turn in its direction, unable to see beyond the buildings and homes. "What's that?" I ask, straining to hear what seems to be some kind of celebration. I turn back to face Ryland, curiosity piqued.

He lifts his brows conspiratorially. "Only one way to find out."

I match his grin as he leads us to the edge of the rooftop. A glance below shows a fairly large pipe that travels down the facade of the building. Seamlessly, Ryland lowers himself along it, sliding silently until he's standing on the pavement, gaze lifted upward to me in waiting.

I swallow back another round of nerves as I squat down and reach for the pipe. Holding on for dear life, I slowly ease myself downward. As predicted, my descent is a far less graceful performance than Ryland's. The raw skin of my legs keeps making squeaking noises as it rubs against the metal of the pipe, my boots slipping and clanking as I work my way down.

A peek downward reveals Ryland's gaze on me, and I suddenly remember again that I'm in a nightdress, currently suspended midair above him. Carefully, I reach behind me and try to push the hem of my dress between one of my thighs and the pipe. I'm sure it looks absurd, but at least I'm not exposing myself.

"Did you really just tuck in your skirt?"

The drawling tone has me freezing on the pipe. A flush heats my face, but I keep my tone cool and unabashed as I reply, "I may not be a queen or courtier, but I'm still a lady."

"Are you implying that I'm not a gentlemen who would avert his gaze in such a situation?"

I lower my head, dubious. "You admitted yourself that your morals are less defined than others. I think it's safe to assume that applies to your propriety as well."

"Come now, little thief. I've been nothing but well-behaved." I give him a look the statement deserves.

A few seconds later, I'm on the ground, and Ryland is at my side, taking my hand as he leads us out of the alley. Glancing at our joined hands, he questions, "And do you consider this untoward?"

I roll my eyes at his obvious teasing. "Didn't stop you before," I reply.

"Nor you."

"Fair point," I grumble, which earns me a light laugh.

We make our way to the edge of a small square where the sounds of revelry grow in volume. Crowds of people fill the space, all laughing and clapping and dancing. There's a trio of musicians in one of the corners with fiddles and tambourines playing as if their very souls were attached to their instruments. The music is as vibrant and lively as the crowd, the mutual joy and merriment in the air an infectious, radiating thing.

Ryland and I both watch in rapture as couples twirl and step about, each one adding their unique style to the dance. We join in the exuberant applause when the song reaches its end.

As the trio start a new piece, Ryland suddenly takes my hand again, pulling us into the center of the square. Without a moment to protest, the music picks up, a wild and heady tune. Ryland swiftly puts us into motion, swinging us around with the other couples, all of us moving and weaving around each other in a motion of organized chaos.

Just when I seem to find a rhythm, I'm torn away from Ryland's hold as another man dances with me. I realize that it's a part of the dance for everyone seems to have switched partners. The man doesn't appear bothered that he doesn't know or recognize me. He just smiles happily before I'm cast off to another partner, a female this time, with long raven hair and a booming laugh.

I have no need to worry about knowing the dance since I'm flung between partners every few seconds, twirling and spinning seamlessly around one another. Still, no one takes notice that I'm an outsider. Everyone is too focused on the dancing, drunk on it as I'm quickly becoming.

I've lost sight of Ryland in the whirlwind of motion. I'm breathless and sweating, but it's exhilarating. The music is consuming, something you don't just listen to but *feel*. Thrumming in my veins and humming in my blood and bones. Pulling me by a string, making my willing limbs a puppet to its commanding tune.

THE ETERNAL HUNT

Everyone suddenly scurries back, joining hands until we all form a ring around the square's edges. We fall into motion again, moving 'round and 'round at a rapid pace. I finally spot Ryland across from me, both of us grinning and laughing like all the others. The energy in the air is a blazing and crackling fire. As the music picks up, it's wildness has us all morphing into some sort of frenzy.

A few women break away to meet in the center of the circle, twirling in place. I catch Ryland's gaze as he nods to the girls, encouraging me to join them. On a whim of pure boldness, I do just that. The women smile at me, all of us taking hands and forming a small ring, spinning in the opposite direction of the main circle. One pulls away again to stand in the center and twirl around by herself. Then another girl replaces her. It goes on and on until it's my turn.

I release hands with the women on both sides and leap into the middle, spinning around and around. Spinning until faces blur. Spinning until I'm dizzy and delirious. Spinning until it feels as though I'm flying and my feet are no longer touching the ground.

And then, the music ceases, everyone slowing their movements, hands disentangling as we all applaud and catch our breaths. My heart is thumping in my chest as I pant, searching through the smiling faces for the only one that I know.

We lock gazes, both our eyes bright and chests heaving. Ryland's skin glistens with sweat, the ends of hair on his brow lightly damp, and I want to brush them away for him. The unbidden thought has me schooling my expression as he takes my hand to lead us away.

We return to the rooftops where I'm once again towed along the heights of Kingsmar. I'm not sure how long we spend under the blanket of stars, padding across the city skyline, but I lose myself in it. Lose myself to time and place, only focusing on the moment, the rush of energy and excitement, all while knowing how I'll never forget this night.

At the thought, I stop in place, and Ryland turns to face me, expression curious. We're standing atop another townhouse where, from one of the floors below, we can hear soft music from a stringed-instrument radiating up and into the sky. A milder melody than the one we'd just heard. This song reminds me of warm summer nights, smooth like drizzled honey as it blends into the midnight air, swirling around our shadowed frames.

"Tonight has been...I don't really have the words for it. Thank you, Ryland. I'll treasure it always." It surprises me when he chuckles. "What?"

His amusement dies, features edged with somberness. "You think a night of running on rooftops and dancing in the streets is special."

His words sting a little, and some of the hurt reveals itself in my voice when I ask, "Wasn't it though?"

A sigh. "It was, but..." He shakes his head as his eyes study the floor. "There's so much more I could give you, that I plan to give you."

My stomach flutters, insides feeling warm and syrupy. As his brilliant blue gaze holds mine, I have the sudden urge to kiss him, to taste his lips and feel their softness against mine. "And what if I'd like to give you something in return?"

My feet are practically about to spring upward to reach for him, to seize his golden hair and sturdy shoulders—but I don't.

Ryland may be treating me exceptionally well, but I can't stand the thought of being too bold. Perhaps if he wanted to kiss me too, he'd do it, or already have. I'm not yet brave enough to initiate. It would be like an urchin latching onto the robes of a king and begging for his attention and favor. My insides recoil at the shame. Not to mention the fact that, given all of Ryland's secrecy, I would be the most oblivious of fools to build an even stronger bond between us. No, for now, sensibility must be my course. Although, I'm not sure I can trust myself to follow that path. It's certainly a struggle to restrain myself right now.

A brow arches, intrigue painting his features. "Oh, little thief, you give me something every time you take a breath." Those lips pull. "Then again, I'm greedy when it comes to you. Whatever you might offer, I'd happily accept."

The only thing I end up offering him is an enchanted smile. And, for the way he stares at it, I may as well have offered him the moon in the palm of my hand.

CHAPTER 13

A SUCCESSION OF SHARP RAPS ON MY DOOR PULLS me from a deep slumber. My eyes protest opening, sleep clinging to me like a second skin. Before I have the chance to rise from the bed, the door swings opens, a maid stepping inside. "My apologies, miss, but Lady Aerin has requested for you to be woken and dressed. You're to accompany her to your dress fitting."

Forcing myself to sit up, I glance out the window, noting just how bright it is outside…and just how late it must be.

I fling myself from the bed and dash to the bathing room whilst simultaneously thanking the maid and declining her offer to help me dress. In record time, I wash myself, brush my hair and place it into a messy knot atop my head. Blindly, I reach into my wardrobe and pull out the first dress my fingers latch onto, an off the shoulder, long-sleeved evergreen piece. I take as little time as is required to find matching slippers before dashing downstairs.

Aurelia's waiting in the dining room, standing before a very relaxed Ryland lounging indolently in his seat. He wears brown pants and a loose white shirt, legs propped on the armrest of Aurelia's chair. She glowers at him while he smiles unfazed, tossing a nectarine in the air with casual ease. Neither one looks to me, the two locked in a staring battle.

"I'm so sorry I overslept, Aurelia," I say, hoping to attract her attention. She's clearly mad at Ryland, and I get the sense she knows what happened last night. But, since I chose to join him on our adventure, I can't let him take all the blame. "It's my fault. I should—" I begin, but Aurelia cuts me off.

"Apologies aren't necessary. And, you needn't feel obligated to cover for Ryland, Wren. I know he's responsible for ignoring my *very clear* instructions that you and I were to leave early today," she grumbles, returning her gaze to him.

Ryland's attention, however, has shifted to me. "I appreciate the thoughtfulness, but Aurelia's right. No need to protect me," he explains with a wink, catching the nectarine mid-air before taking a bite.

Aurelia huffs. "If she doesn't acquire a dress for tomorrow, you *will* be taking the blame when she arrives in some plain garment feeling woefully underdressed."

Ryland offers an exaggerated expression of fright. "I'm quivering in my boots." Aurelia folds her arms across her chest, and Ryland snorts. "Still as uptight as when I last visited, Aurelia," he sighs disappointedly before *tsking* his tongue.

Aurelia's upper lip twitches before she takes my arm and leads us to the door, apparently refusing to further engage in their verbal sparring.

The late-morning breeze caresses my face as we make our way to the carriage that awaits us in front of the gate. As I take my seat, I peek out the window to find Ryland following after, strolling toward us at a leisurely jaunt. He stops at the window, face to face with me.

"While you're out today, spare no expense. When I parade you in front of everyone like a queen tomorrow night, I want you to feel like one." The arrogant grin he flashes is nothing short of wicked. "Trust me, my bank account can bleed a little."

Before I can even process his words, he places a quick peck on my cheek as the carriage takes off, leaving me gaping out the window as his laughter chases us. When I finally reel myself back inside, I look to Aurelia who simply sighs, seeming to forgo some of her annoyance. "He's paying for your gown. And..." she hesitates, "he paid for everything else too. Apparently, he went to the bank yesterday and sent money into my account. I received a letter this morning. I insisted he didn't have to, but he *wants* to pay for you. He won't have it any other way."

My heart stalls in my chest as I try and sort through the information. *Ryland has insisted on paying for me.* That was why, or another reason why, he went to the bank yesterday. And he sprung it on me like this, right as we were leaving, so that I couldn't try and argue with him. He knew I'd refuse if he told me he was going to pay. And he's right, I'd be fuming if I wasn't so stunned. But all I can feel is my heart softening and my stomach growing warm.

Aurelia rests her hand atop mine. "I hope you know that I had no issue paying, Wren. I was happy to do so," she says sincerely.

I can feel the frown pulling at her lips, the guilt lurking in her cinnamon eyes. I know she was happy to do it, and a part of me is relieved that she no longer has to. But knowing Ryland has taken her place makes me feel kind of awful. It's like taking the lesser of two evils. But I'm allowed no more time to dwell on it as Aurelia begins to assault me with queries about my fabric and silhouette preferences, and I realize how much she wasn't joking the other night. This really will be a long day.

THE MORNING AND AFTERNOON WAS A WHIRLWIND OF fabrics and fittings, pins and precision, needles and measurements. I think I spent the majority of my time in a dressing room, trying on garment after garment. But, Aurelia insisted my gown had to be original, if not completely hand-made.

We found a sample dress after several hours, one she'd said the seamstress could make into something spectacular. I took her word for it, letting her instruct the seamstress on what to do. Aurelia took care of the bill, providing Ryland's bank details as I was too much of a coward to see the price. Before we departed, I was informed that my dress would be delivered by tomorrow afternoon just in time.

It's been rather nice to spend the day in female company after spending the last week solely surrounded by masculine energy. We chatter about fabrics and frocks with no guilt or worry for the other's boredom. Aurelia even did a little shopping for herself which eased some of my discomfort with all the attention directed at me.

Though we still needed to find shoes and jewels, Aurelia said we had enough time to stop for a quick bite to eat. She took me to her favorite teahouse, a charming albeit extravagant establishment filled with the city's elite, all frosted in colorful, fancy designs like the confectionaries in the shop windows. Nibbling on some finger sandwiches, we pass the time now lobbying each other with various questions.

"So, are you currently…involved with anyone?" I ask mid-conversation. Talking with Aurelia has been so effortless, without any pretenses or facades. I might've wondered if my question was too personal before, but, after spending the day with her, I decide it's okay.

Aurelia sips from her tea, steam wafting around her nose. "Not exactly. Occasionally, I'll go out with someone, but… it's never long-term. I tried in the past, but it always ended in heartbreak. I suppose you could say I'm a contented spinster," she explains before giggling. Despite the laughter, her eyes are shadowed, and I realize that "contented" is anything but how she really feels. She mentioned heartbreak, and I can sense that she's suffered greatly from it—on more than one occasion.

"What about you?" she returns after a moment.

For some inane reason, I hadn't expected her to return the question, and it takes me several seconds to figure out how to respond. "There was never anyone back home. I mean, no one would've been interested in me anyway, so I never really looked. There were the school-girl crushes of course, but after that..."

Her expression is crafted in careful neutrality. "And what about now?"

I have a hunch as to what she's implying, but I decide to feign ignorance on account that I just don't feel comfortable yet speaking aloud what is brewing in my heart. "I haven't really met anyone here yet."

"Well, tomorrow night will be the perfect occasion to meet people. I can introduce you to the city's most eligible men." My throat dries, the prospect unsettling as opposed to exciting. I'm not exactly a social butterfly. Growing up, I was very timid except when in the company of my parents. So, the idea of meeting hordes of new people, especially young men, and being expected to engage in riveting conversation, makes my stomach churn uneasily. "Oh, that's not necessary. I'm—"

"You don't have to engage with them if you don't want to. Actually, I think Ryland would have my head if you did," she mutters to herself, sucking in her bottom lip. I want to ask her to elaborate but reign in the question, opting for another.

"May I ask you something?" She nods eagerly. "What prompted Ryland to become...what he is?" I doubt using the term "assassin" would gain me much favor in a place like this.

It occurred to me earlier as I'd stood in the fitting room, being dressed and positioned like a doll, that while I'd promised to not pester Ryland with more questions, my vow didn't apply to Aurelia.

She frowns, and I add to my inquiry. "I mean, what did he do before? Why did he choose *that* path?"

Her frown only deepens, and I notice that she's fiddling with the linen napkin in her lap, gaze downward. "I-I think those are his stories to tell, Wren. I don't want to overstep," she explains gently.

I can't exactly be disappointed by her answer, not when it was to be expected. But, it was worth a shot. Switching subjects, I ask, "I presume there will be dancing tomorrow night?" She nods, eyes gleaming with excitement. Now I'm the one sporting a frown. "Apart from a few village dances, I'm not really well-versed. Would you be willing to teach me a little?"

Aurelia practically beams, clapping her hands. "Of course I will! We'll go over some dances tonight."

I have no doubt she's proficient in the etiquette of balls and other formal events. And, while I don't exactly have a firm intention of dancing tomorrow night, I decide it might be good to at least have familiarity with one just in case.

After tea and the rest of our errands, we return home in time for dinner positively spent and famished. Ryland enquires about our day, but I'm so hungry, I let Aurelia do most of the talking.

Once finished, we rise from our seats, and Aurelia turns to me. "I'll teach you the dances in the drawing room. There'll be enough space for us in there," she explains as we pass under the archway.

"What happened to 'she's yours when we're finished'?" Ryland drawls from behind us.

We both turn to face him and his skeptical brow, Aurelia visibly ruffled. "Well, I hadn't expected then that we'd need to go over dancing. The plans have changed. You of all people should understand how that could happen. Being adaptable *is* part of your job after all."

"Is it now?" he asks with mock fascination, folding his arms across his broad chest.

I hate that I'm causing a rift between them, so I insert politely, "Perhaps you could teach me tomorrow ins—"

"No, no," Aurelia interjects, placing her arm in front of me to prevent me from crossing to Ryland. "We must commence tonight. Tomorrow will be extremely busy as it is. Believe me, Ryland is *certainly* old enough to have learned some patience," she snipes, eyeing him with distaste.

I'm not sure what I've just started, but I definitely don't wish to be a part of it.

Ryland rolls his eyes. "I know you've been enjoying playing dress up with Wren, but she's not solely yours to occupy."

Aurelia's face pinches in what can only be described as aristocratic offense. "That's hardly fair given that she needed to be dressed!" she exclaims in a manner that still manages to sound ladylike.

I feel bad for Aurelia and the attack Ryland is waging against her. All she's done is provide for me since I arrived here. And without a single compliant. I know she enjoyed organizing my new wardrobe and taking me shopping, but she was under no obligation to do so. I'm sure she'd had events in her schedule that she probably cancelled in order to make time for me. Others most likely wouldn't have bothered, and I can't let her be criticized like this. I step forward. "Aurelia's helped me immeasurably. And I asked her to teach me, so if you're angry, then blame me."

"There's no need for blame here," Aurelia says, and I almost heave a sigh of relief that I'm not the only one seeking peace...until she continues. "Unless Ryland wishes to accept his."

I nearly roll my eyes. It's like the two of them have never had to share a friend before. They're acting like children. I feel as though at any moment they'll each take hold of one of my arms to try and pull me in each direction.

Ryland widens his stance as he appraises the two of us carefully. "I didn't realize it would be so dangerous to have introduced you both. It seems I was naive to the chaos I'd be creating," he murmurs.

I'm very certain the glares Aurelia and I each send him would make any other man squirm, but Ryland merely gives us a disapproving look, disappointed by our reactions. I was trying to remain neutral in their bickering, but after that little quip, I'm starting to pick sides.

Ryland huffs a soft laugh before shaking his head. "I should use you both for one of my assignments sometime," he muses, eyes lighting with interest. "You'd make quite a lethal pair."

"Then perhaps you can be the subject for us to practice our lethality," Aurelia retorts, chin lifted with prim disdain.

Ryland raises his brows in amused surprise before shifting his gaze to me. "Do you also share Aurelia's sentiment?"

"Well, you do make yourself such an easy target with that mouth," I reply coolly, receiving a nod of approval from Aurelia.

This time, only one of Ryland's brows lifts, his lips pulling into an arrogant smirk. "Does my mouth bother you, little love?" he asks, tone low and suggestive.

I startle, all my sass immediately dissolving, mouth parted open. His eyes narrow smugly, as if he knew exactly what his response would do to me. I *walked myself into that trap so easily, falling for it like the most vulnerable of prey.* The very mouth which I insulted was my demise. I lost the battle to his sharp tongue.

Aurelia huffs with irritation. "Only you would resort to crude inuendo to disarm an opponent," she chides.

"It worked, didn't it?" Ryland replies, lifting a shoulder.

Still mortified by my falter, I can't muster the focus to think of a response.

"Don't worry, Wren. It's not the first time he's bested someone with his tasteless guile." Aurelia throws him another stern look before taking my arm and leading us out of the dining room, Ryland's hearty laugh ringing in the air.

W̲E PRACTICE DANCING FOR OVER TWO HOURS, AND, by the end of it, I'm walking on shaky legs. I tried my best, but it's safe to say that I'll be avoiding the dancefloor tomorrow evening. It's not that I'm uncoordinated, as Aurelia explained to me, just that I have a hard time keeping up with remembering the motions and movements of the dances. Which is partly justified given the time constraint to learning.

We reviewed all of two dances, and I barely managed to properly complete one of them. How any society lady memorizes the plethora of dances expected at these balls and parties I'll never understand. It's certainly a skill I don't possess.

The heavy weight of defeat once we're finished shouldn't come as a surprise after having made a complete fool of myself, tripping on my dress and stumbling more often than standing upright. But, more than my shame, I feel a different weight sitting on my shoulders. So, I decide to seek out Ryland as the guilt continues to gnaw at my conscience.

While I don't condone his accusations against Aurelia, I wonder if he's feeling neglected. If that's the case, I don't want to disregard his feelings. Perhaps the tension at last night's dinner bled into today's squabbling. Nevertheless, I feel responsible for their growing divide between my hosts.

I find Ryland in the library at the desk where he appears to be writing a letter. He glances up from the piece of parchment as soon as I step into the room. "I'd offer to take you out again tonight, but it would likely result in Aurelia's wrath which I'd prefer to avoid. She only stays docile for so long," he says as he continues to write, the elegance of his script on the paper visible even at a distance.

"Are you upset with me?" I broach nervously.

He looks up once more, confusion marring his flawless features. "Whatever gave you that impression?"

"I don't wish to cause any tension between you and Aurelia."

He chuckles, somehow amused by what I just said. "That's what you're worried about?" Before I can answer, he continues. "Firstly, you could never so much as be the cause of any form of tension. Secondly, Aurelia and I are like siblings which means we love and fight like them, over both petty and grave matters. But, we never fall out, so don't trouble yourself."

The wash of relief is instantaneous, but before I have enough time to savor it, one of the servants appears in the doorway, drawing our attention. "My lady has requested your presence, sir," she announces.

Ryland gives her a polite nod of dismissal before looking to me, teeth bared in an exaggerated expression of fear, though I see the mirth dancing in his eyes. "A summons," he murmurs with feigned panic. My eyes roll as he rises from his seat to approach the doorway.

He pauses when he reaches my side, staring down at me with a playful smile. "Hopefully, I'll make it back in one piece," he adds with a wink before stepping into the hall.

Letting out the breath I was holding from his dizzying proximity, I retreat deeper into the room, pressing against the back of one of the cushioned sitting chairs. My hands reach behind me to rest on the top of the chair when I flinch at the sharp bite of something hard and cold against my palm.

Whirling around, I peer between the chair's back and the thick vertical cushion, gaze latching onto something that's poking out. Glancing over my shoulder to ensure I have no audience, I reach into the crevice, carefully wrapping my hand around the stinging metal.

My brow knits in puzzlement as I behold the small dagger clasped between my fingers.

Normally, I wouldn't find the sight of such a weapon so vexing, not when I've traveled with Ryland who always carries at least one weapon on him at all times. Not when I've seen the cache of them stored in his bedroom when I stole a glance this morning after he'd left his door open as I'd rushed down our hall. He visits Aurelia often, so it would be of little surprise that he's left a range of weaponry about during his stays. It would be a natural, plausible assumption to make that the dagger belongs to him. And I *would* reach such a conclusion if it weren't for the pink and scarlet floral pattern along the hilt, the creamy ceramic handle and golden blade which all allude to a feminine owner.

I'd never thought Aurelia capable of wielding a weapon let alone possessing one, stashed in such a discrete location as though she might need access to it at the slightest notice. I'm not sure what kind of threats a socialite might receive in our capital, but apparently, there are some grave enough that she feels the need to keep weapons on hand, even in the most obscure of places.

All this time, I'd thought Ryland was the mystery. But, I'm beginning to wonder if there's more to Aurelia than the prim, aristocratic exterior...

Chapter 14

Sleep evaded me the entire night, nerves of excitement consuming any chances of a restful slumber. That, and of course, finding the curious blade in Aurelia's chair cushions. The effects of my sleep deprivation were made worse by the hectic morning we had. Aurelia entered my room before I'd even risen, bustling me about. She apparently had an entire grooming regimen planned for me which took most of the day. From skin scrubs and lotions, to hair creams and nail oils, to face masks and tonics, I was primped from head to toe, every inch of me scrubbed and polished.

My hair took almost two hours alone, curled and styled into braids that were carefully woven into an intricate design at the base of my neck, pinned with fresh flowers that fragrantly perfume my skin. For the final touch, Aurelia applied some cosmetics to my face; dusting rouge on my cheeks, a metallic shimmer on my eyelids and cheekbones, and a rosy pigment on my lips, giving life to my otherwise pale complexion.

My final reflection was someone I barely knew. Aurelia was pleased with her work, nodding at me in approval before leaving to finish getting ready. Soon enough, I was told by one of the maids to make my way downstairs.

"How's it coming along?" I hear Ryland enquire of someone just as I arrive at the second floor landing.

Aurelia's voice carries as she replies, "I was going to surprise you, but I suppose I can show you while you're here. Essentially, it's finished. There are just a few details I need to have finalized, but…I think you'll be pleased."

"I'm sure I will," Ryland replies warmly.

Naturally, I'm curious as to the nature of their conversation, but, when I reach the final flight of stairs, their gazes lift to mine, silence consuming the foyer.

My eyes immediately fall on Ryland who takes my very breath away. He stands regally in a dark grey brocade jacket and matching pants with tall black leather boots, freshly polished. The rich shade makes his blue eyes twice as piercing, his jawline somehow even sharper. His usual silver and gold rings are dispersed across his fingers, blonde hair glossy and shining. It's honestly unfair, how perfect he is. And yet I've never appreciated a greater injustice more.

As he studies me, I notice the slight frown pulling at his lips. I suppose he must find my appearance rather anti-climactic given that my cloak still leaves much to the imagination. My gown will be a surprise for when we arrive at the palace, a "dramatic reveal" as Aurelia had called it. Just then, she, also in her own cloak of rich green, announces, "The carriage is ready."

As we step outside into the brisk night, I find that the butterflies in my stomach have been replaced with bees, nerves buzzing frantically. The most formal events I've ever attended were the village dances in Atherton. While they were jovial, merry affairs, they were undoubtedly a crude comparison to a Kingsmar royal ball, making me feel woefully unprepared for tonight's function.

Ryland helps me into the carriage before taking a seat beside me. As we set off, I can practically feel my body vibrating with energy.

"Tonight is going to be so much fun, Wren. This ball is one of the more social ones, everyone looking to put aside politics for an evening and just enjoy Florynth." Osterley's holiday celebrating the start of summer. Thankfully, we've quite a while until winter bares its frigid face. "I promise, you'll enjoy yourself," Aurelia finishes.

"And, how are we all supposed to know each other? We're your guests, but how are we connected?" I ask.

"It will be the truth—that Aurelia and I are childhood friends, and you're my guest," Ryland answers simply.

"No lies," Aurelia adds with a reassuring smile. "Just say you come from the country. Honestly, no one's going to ask where. It's the music and dancing that draws everyone's attention tonight."

Dancing—something I still plan to avoid. It's easy to imagine myself stumbling through the steps and humiliating both myself and my partner, tripping on their feet and my skirts. No, I'll definitely be avoiding the perilous dangers of a waltz or quadrille. An observer is what I'll be.

Ryland leans his head close to mine. "I can practically hear you thinking, little thief." He rests a hand atop my knee, steadying the jittery bouncing I hadn't even been unaware of. I meet his amused gaze. "Relax, and enjoy this night. Would I steer you wrong?"

His advice is easier said than done, but I make an effort to follow it. I *should* take advantage of this opportunity. Let myself enjoy the luxuries that I could only have ever dreamed of before.

Eventually, the carriage comes to a rolling stop, and Ryland helps both me and Aurelia out. My neck cranes up to admire the palace, an imposing, towering structure comprised of spires of various heights ending in sharp points, the intricate carvings running their lengths giving them a jagged appearance. The highest spire of pale grey stone nearly pierces the moon itself. The palace is nothing and everything I expected it to be. Intimidating, severe, and utterly glorious. Perfectly capturing the essence of a kingdom that is not so easily conquered or corrupted. One that will withstand the tests of time, succumbing to nothing and no one. An emblem of power and endurance. Despite having walked past the impressive structure the other day during our city tour, it's an entirely different beast under nightfall.

Crowds are already gathered outside, guests filing into the main entrance humming with the same crackling energy that runs through me. The three of us fall into the line which moves at a fairly steady pace. As we pass the entrance, our names are crossed off the guestlist, and, soon enough, we're led down a main hall toward a set of open double doors. Music floats down from the ballroom, gracing our ears. Already, I'm entranced.

As we inch up the line, I'm practically bouncing on my feet, stretching on my toes to get a peek of the ballroom. We eventually come to a point in the line where a few attendants are collecting cloaks and overcoats. They help Aurelia with hers first, revealing an ivory tool dress baring her porcelain shoulders and décolletage. The off-the-shoulder silhouette gown is stitched with dozens of green and pink fabric roses and leaves that traverse the entire length. Her hair is curled and left loose with two sections braided and twisted into two roses at the back of her head. She's the embodiment of summer, lush and vibrant with life.

When the attendants come to me, I turn to give them my back as I reach to unhook the clasp, wanting to face Ryland for my grand reveal. He's already waiting, gaze so intense that I can hardly look away. In fact, all I *can* see is the sapphire blue of his bejeweled irises. As the cloak slowly slips from my shoulders, I watch as his eyes slowly travel down the length of my body, beholding Aurelia's handiwork.

The dress is a powdery blue silk with a scooping neckline. The trimming and straps are overlayed with a dusty rose floral lace. A layer of sheer tulle, in the same shade of pink, lays atop the skirt, blending the colors together in a dreamy blur.

My body burns beneath the weight of Ryland's simmering stare. I receive two more full-body appraisals, his eyes out of focus as he subtly bites into the soft flesh of his bottom lip. My stomach clenches as the sight, skin warming.

I turn to Aurelia, giving her a soft smile. "Will I do?"

"You're marvelous!" she exclaims, clasping her hands together.

We're suddenly directed forward, and I can finally see the ballroom interior. The word stunning is an understatement.

Grand crystal chandeliers hang from the ceiling, brilliant and blinding as the sun. The stones are of varying colors, clear, topaz and soft pink, the dazzling orbs casting a warm, multi-colored glow in the room, reminding me of a summer twilight. The floors are a creamy marble which pairs well with the ivory walls and ornate gilding that spans the ceiling. Directly across the floor are tall marble pillars and beyond them the doors to a terrace left open for guests to migrate. To the right along the back wall is a long table lined with a sumptuous array of food and refreshments.

Hundreds upon hundreds of people fill the ballroom, a blend of brilliant colors and glittering jewels, all honoring the theme of Florynth.

Speaking of all things floral, the entire ballroom is filled with countless grand and lush arrangements, their sweet and breezy bouquets perfuming the evening air in their vibrant shades and hues. Apricot dahlias, snow and lavender roses, ice-blue hydrangeas, rosy queen of the prairies, soft plum lilac, sunset zinnias, mauve dried-amaranth, ivory candytuft, tangerine gerberas, blushing peonies, and violet catmint.

I've never beheld something so grand, so extravagant. I want to explore it all. But, before I can even fully enter the space, Ryland takes my arm and wraps it around his, Aurelia situated on his left. As we step further into the room, she immediately guides us toward a young couple, a bright smile of affability on her face. "Edwina, Christoph," she greets merrily before glancing at me and Ryland. "These are my very dear friends, Ryland and Wren."

The four of us each exchange bows and curtsies, and I immediately feel like the impostor that I am, more apt to locate myself in the kitchens or amongst the serving staff.

"It's a pleasure to meet you," the regal lady says to me, her blonde hair perfectly catching the light. Although, the slight edge to her voice hints that meeting me is anything but a pleasure.

"And you," I reply politely, knowing I sound stiff.

She extends her hand to Ryland which, instead of being adorned with a silk glove, is wreathed in thin, twig-like vines that wind up her arm with small fuchsia buds sprouting like the blush of spring. It would seem she took the theme of tonight's celebration *very* seriously.

Ryland distantly accepts her offering, lowering his head toward the back of her hand. I try not to let my relief slip when I notice how he keeps his mouth several inches from her skin.

While the husband chatters to Aurelia about their recent retreat to their estate in the south, I find myself unsuccessfully stifling the ripples of tension that start to course through me. Perhaps it's the overwhelming environment, perhaps it's my lack of social prowess. Or, maybe it's simply because the wife hardly manages to avert her attentive gaze from Ryland, no matter that her *husband* is standing right beside her. She only has eyes for Ryland. And, I have to admit, they would make quite an enthralling pair. With similar complexions, golden-blonde hair and sharp blue eyes, they would be well-suited. The lady certainly seems to think so—I don't miss the way she subtly puffs out her chest, further displaying her very generous bust framed by the neckline of her soft-magenta gown.

While I've always been well-endowed in that department like my mother, by comparison, I somehow seem flat-chested. I would think her daring neckline almost indecent if I were actually familiar with the courtly customs and fashions of the capital. But, Ryland doesn't spare them, or the lady herself, a single glance. Either because he's uncomfortable by her obvious display of cleavage or has seen so much of that before that her particular assets do not draw his particular attention.

Thankfully, Aurelia and the couple lose themselves in conversation. Having no desire to continue resisting the urge to glare, I take the opportunity to step away and further admire the room. The grandeur of it all is still baffling. It's as if I flitted away from reality and into a dream, filled with such tantalizing beauty and elegance. A gentleman's imperious chuckle, a lady's flirtatious coo, beatific smiles, clinking glasses, and stirring chatter.

From a gap in the crowds, I'm able to catch sight of the small orchestra at the far end of room, situated in the corner, each member so enraptured by their own music it's as if they're blind to the commotion before them, reminding me of the street musicians from the other evening.

"Do you have any idea how beautiful you look, little thief?" The words are murmured into the shell of my ear, Ryland's breath caressing my skin and making me shiver. I didn't see him follow me, but his sudden presence sends an electric current through my pulse.

I bow my head slightly. "Doubtful," I whisper. *Certainly so after beholding the likes of that wife and all the others that surround us, so ostentatious in their gowns and glory.* While I may have felt beautiful when I saw my reflection back at the townhouse, I don't think I merit the word in the way Ryland says it.

"You're right. That was a wholly inadequate word," he murmurs, voice low. "Breathtaking, ravishing...bewitching." Facing his devious smile, I find his eyes alight with hunger. My lips part in startlement, and he catches the movement, eyes dropping to them.

I break my stare from the sight, looking down bashfully, only to find Ryland's fisted hands flexing, as if in restraint. The sudden musings of what might happen if he weren't exercising self-control cross my mind. Where his hands might reach...where I would want them to...

"There's King Rhidian." His words interrupt all sinful thoughts as he nods his head toward the stone dais at the other end of the room where a stoic gentleman sits on the grand throne. The king is fairly young, maybe in his early thirties, or perhaps younger. Handsome, too, at least from what I can gauge at this distance. He has black cropped hair, a short, trimmed beard and a pale complexion that alludes to much time spent indoors.

There's no throne beside him as it's common knowledge the king is in the market for a queen. Whether he wishes to find one or not is another question entirely. "So, is the ball tonight to help the King find a wife?"

"I'm sure he considers every occasion an opportunity to hunt a wife. As far as I'm concerned, he's welcome to all here but one." Ryland says this with a pointed look. My heart warms, and yet I can't help but scoff a laugh.

"Right, because the king of arguably the greatest empire in the world would be so tempted by a small-town convict."

I feel the light brush of Ryland's knuckles against mine, as if he can't help but touch me. "You are truly blind to yourself. Any king, *any man*, is unworthy." All levity in his tone from before is completely gone, replaced by an intensity that has my body winding tight.

"If no man is worthy, then does that mean I'm to spend the rest of my days alone? How fulfilling that sounds." *And not far off from what it would've been before I met Ryland.*

"I never said alone," he corrects, his fingers shifting to entwine with mine.

I once again turn to meet his gaze, and the tenderness in it steals my breath. That bright blue, so vivid, often renders me lost in its beauty. But his eyes suddenly drift beyond my shoulder, hardening into sapphire slits. I turn around, following his gaze, but my short stature has my stare only meeting the back of the guests' heads. "Wait here, I won't be long."

I frown at the abrupt interruption, more than a little deflated that the moment was ruined, but Ryland raises my hand

and places a soft kiss atop it before dipping his head and turning away, stealing all the warmth within me. I try to watch where he goes, to see who he's going to meet, and, by the look on his face, he's not eager, but I quickly lose him amongst the crowd, his figure swallowed by dancing couples and skirts of silk and satin.

Standing alone amidst the throng of couples and guests, my nerves spark to life. I'm not exactly enthralled with the idea of forcing conversation with strangers. Without allowing myself the chance to contemplate the decision, I head in the direction Ryland went, choosing to satiate my curiosity as opposed to dwelling in my socially anxious state. Threading through the sea of people, I berate myself for breaking Ryland's request. *But, really, how could he expect me to stand around awkwardly for who knows how long? With no one to talk to, I'd look lonely and pathetic.* Besides, I'm not intending to ask questions. I'm simply hoping to make an educational discovery, like I did at the artifacts shop.

Eventually, I spot a familiar shade of blonde hair along the outskirts of the room, looking rather unenthused. It's a moment later that I notice with whom Ryland is speaking. A gentleman with sable skin, smooth as leather, dressed in luxurious sepia silks.

Tucking myself behind a marble column a few feet away, I remain out of sight, straining to listen to their exchange, but the chatter of the event drowns out their words. Peeking my head just slightly around the pillar, I catch sight of the two gentlemen, hoping to better get a sense of their interaction by reading their lips.

The eyes of Ryland's companion suddenly slice to mine like an arrow to a target, curiosity sparking in his gaze. "We seem to have an admirer, or, perhaps, just I do," he murmurs waggishly to Ryland, voice sinfully deep and decadent, an unfamiliar accent painting his tone.

Ryland follows his gaze, somehow neither surprised nor disappointed by my presence. In fact, I suspect there might be amusement dancing in his eyes before it hardens to ice when he glances between his companion and me. I drift toward the two men, feeling like a small mouse standing in front of two giants what with their towering heights and hulking forms.

"It's rather the other way around, my friend," Ryland returns as I arrive at his side.

"So, you are the lady's escort?" the gentleman confirms.

"Which kind are you implying?" Ryland returns with a sharp grin. The two men share the jest like two fiends while I simply die quietly of embarrassment, the only indication I haven't yet expired is the flaming warmth coloring my cheeks.

From a closer view, I'm able to fully take in Ryland's acquaintance, noting just how disturbingly handsome the man is. Flawless skin pairs with vibrant copper eyes as arresting as Aurelia's but with more orange hues. Seemingly in his early thirties, his hair is practically shaved to his scalp, adding to his smooth and polished exterior. The scent of cedarwood and something spiced fills my nose, further imbedding his aura with sharp masculinity.

A sleeveless silk shirt reveals dark brown arms, the well-defined muscles banded with golden cuffs. The rest of him is no less bedecked. Dangling from each of his ears is a razor sharp tooth from some ferocious beast, the ivory bones polished and gleaming. He boasts several gold necklaces, and his long, elegant fingers are strung with thick gold rings that span to his knuckles reminding me of armor. *Clearly, he shares Ryland's taste for jewelry.*

The man arches an amused brow, maintaining his attention on me while he enquires to Ryland, "And, are you going to introduce me to this lady of yours?"

In my periphery, I can sense the tautness of Ryland's jaw, hesitant to do exactly what his companion's asked. I want to demand why, but instead, I decide to be bold, offering my hand. "I'm Wren. It's a pleasure to meet you…" I hold the last syllable in question.

The gentleman smoothly takes my hand in his before bowing low and pressing his lips to my skin. I try not to flush from the warmth of his mouth or his alluring gaze as he looks up at me beneath dark lashes, copper eyes enough to rattle any girl's senses.

"This is Addris," Ryland supplies tersely.

"Actually, it's *Lord* Addris Nyangard. At your service, my lady." That voice alone could get plenty of women into trouble.

"Is it now?" Ryland questions dubiously.

Trying to keep the mood light, I enquire, "You aren't from Osterley?" His accent is too foreign to place him from any region in this kingdom.

"The Isles of Sevris. But I've made Kingsmar my home for a few years now," he replies, sliding his gaze to Ryland.

"Until when," Ryland demands. I want to cringe at the brusque tone but instead plaster a pleasant smile on my face.

"Until I receive my next post."

I'm not sure I understand his answer. Though, if he's an emissary perhaps he means his next location of work. "You're a diplomat?"

Ryland barks a rough grunt of amusement. "He's anything but. Tradesman and socialite would be better titles—or pain in my ass," he quips, tone erring towards prickly rather than teasing.

"And how is it you're both acquainted?" I probe, trying to learn anything I can.

Lord Nyangard opens his mouth, but Ryland cuts in quickly. "Through a mutual connection." It's a strange sight to see Ryland so flustered. He rarely shows vexation, and Addris's presence seems to flare it.

"And what sort of trade are you in?" Perhaps his answer will help me better understand his connection to Ryland.

Ryland is about to answer again, but Lord Nyangard is quicker this time, giving me the full brunt of his attention as he supplies his response. "Whatever my master wishes to invest in." His eyes hold mine as if waiting for me to understand. But I don't.

My brow quirks, confused by his choice of words. "Your master? But...slavery doesn't exist in Osterley."

Lord Nyangard flicks his stare to Ryland curiously before returning to me raising his brow secretively. "That you know of." He says it tauntingly as opposed to condemningly, as if it's an intriguing and alluring concept. Though I'm not sure why. Slavery is a disgusting notion. And yet, I get the impression he doesn't view it that way which makes me wonder for a moment if I'm once again oblivious to some inside joke.

Ryland, however, seems increasingly annoyed by the conversation, a muscle in his jaw feathering. Addris either doesn't notice or is content to ignore him, continuing his explanation. "We are all slaves to something, are we not? Everyone is run by a master of their making." I consider his words. I suppose I was a slave to my suffering. Before Ryland, I was chained to my grief and misery. And, I imagine Ryland is a slave to his past, wishing to outrun it but never able to fully lose sight.

"Little thief," Ryland begins, stealing me from my thoughts, "I'm afraid I must speak with my friend a minute longer. Aurelia, I'm sure, has plenty of guests to introduce you to." He must sense my immediate surge of nerves at the prospect for he quickly adds, "Or not."

A dismissal nonetheless. He wants me gone, which means there are, in fact, confidential matters he intends to discuss. And, from the almost hostile way he keeps glancing at Lord Nyangard, I don't think they'll be pleasant ones.

I offer a small curtsey to the lord who in turn flashes a most charming smile, his white teeth a sharp contrast to the rich darkness of his skin. "A pleasure, my lady."

As I reluctantly leave the two men in search of Aurelia, I can't help my frustration. In all my efforts to acquire answers, I only ever seem to end up with more questions.

It doesn't take me long to find Aurelia. She catches my gaze across the room before flitting to my side, her tinkling voice dancing in the air as she asks, "Where'd Ryland run off to?"

"To speak with a...friend." With the tension that was radiating from Ryland, I'm not sure the label is fitting. I nod my head toward the direction of the two males, and Aurelia stretches upward to catch a glance. She must be successful for her amber brows knit. I'm about to enquire if she knows the gentleman when she loops her arm through mine, tipping her chin to the left. My gaze drifts to where King Rhidian sits atop the dais. I have a better view now that we're slightly nearer.

"Did you know the throne was made for a Sildhe?"

Aurelia's sudden question draws my attention, and I follow her stare to the King's throne as I shake my head. "One of the Sildhe wanted to fabricate for themselves a seat of power, not an unusual desire amongst their kind. Tyrus, I believe his name was, erected the piece; solid silver. So it goes, the precious stone decorating it was mined by slaves in the mountains of Tavlar in the north—moonstone. Once the throne was completed, Tyrus ensorcelled it so that whomever sat on the throne couldn't be harmed by magic. Leave it to the Sildhe to make political ambition a cruel and lethal pursuit."

I study the imposing seat with sharper focus, noting the gleaming silver and the many cavities that hold near glowing white stones. A pale blue hue, they almost possess an inner light. Naturally, the Sildhe selected moonstone—a moon-blessed stone for a moon-blessed ruler. "How did it come into mortal possession?" I ask.

"Years passed, and Tyrus was eventually killed by a human legion, stabbed in the heart with a Drith Stone weapon. The throne then passed into mortal possession. Until, one day, a Sildhe breached Kingsmar, barging straight into the throne room and attempting to dethrone the king with magic. But, none of his spells worked. For eleven days, he tried ceaselessly. And, for eleven days, the Osterlean king remained trapped on the throne as unseating himself would forfeit the protection the magic of the throne granted him. Eventually, the Sildhe attacker was killed, and the throne has never been challenged since."

Admiring the fascinating tale, I continue to inspect the ancient relic, appreciating the unique, ethereal design. Apparently, Aurelia is as well-versed in Sildhe history as Ryland, which I suppose shouldn't surprise me.

Her cinnamon eyes are suddenly alight, and she whips her gaze to mine. "I should organize you and Ryland's introduction to the King!"

"Oh, Aurelia, no, it's fi—" I begin, my protestation cut off as she pulls away excitedly. "I'll come back for you shortly!" Like a wisp of smoke, she evaporates into the crowd. And, once more, I'm left to my own devices.

I decide to entertain myself by watching all the couples dance. Standing along the outskirts of the room, I situate myself close to the wall as I study the dancers, mesmerized by their fluid movements. They remind me of synchronized figurines in a music box, moving at the same time and pace. As if they've practiced this many times before.

It's so different from the dancing Ryland and I partook in the other night. While equally as beautiful, that dance had been wild and chaotic with no order, abstract compared to the structure of this. The dance slows to an end, and I find myself almost disheartened, wanting to watch the couples dance forever. When the other guests begin to lightly applaud, I join them, my clapping a little more passionate than the rest.

A servant offers me a glass of some bubbling alcohol a stunning shade of lavender. The floral drink fizzes in my mouth, sweet like nectar and just as smooth. I have no idea what the drink is, but I'm instantly an admirer.

"You look as though you've never tasted Rhuan wine before."

THE ETERNAL HUNT

I turn toward the mild, male voice, wondering if Aurelia has found me and brought someone to introduce. But she isn't there, only a dashing young man with beige hair and a soft smile. At my furrowed brow, he nods his head to my drink.

"Oh, that's because I haven't," I reply with a polite smile, dipping my gaze timidly.

"It's from the vineyards in Rhua. My father once imported a cask, but he refuses to open it. Saving it for a special occasion, though he's yet to deem on special enough."

It's a challenge to maintain the neutral expression on my face, to not let my puzzlement slip as I wonder why this young gentleman has approached me and with seemingly genuine intrigue.

"It's very nice," I remark...and instantly regret.

"I presume, then, that you're not from this region," he says, eyes lit with curiosity. Curiosity about me, I realize.

Surprise swells, quickly chased by pure giddiness. "No, I'm afraid not. Although, I'm beginning to wish that I was. It's a wonderful city."

A whirl of movement in my periphery briefly steals my attention as couples take to the dancefloor once more, preparing for the start of a new set. When I turn back around, I find the young man's hand extended in offering. "Would you care to dance?"

It takes twice as much effort to restrain the grin pulling at my lips. *Perhaps I do look prettier than I thought.* As I quickly ponder his offer, knowing I only have seconds to decide, I consider the part of me that wants to accept. With those kind brown eyes and his gentle manner, any lady would be lucky to receive such an offer. And, it would be the polite thing to do. Besides, I'm at a palace ball—why *wouldn't* I accept a gentleman's offer to dance?

And yet, there's a nagging part of me that swells with instantaneous guilt for even contemplating accepting. After all, the man's hand—it's not the one I wish was being offered to me.

But what if someone has already asked him*? What if he accepted? What if he's already amidst the sea of couples, some affable lady in arm?* After all, Ryland isn't one to turn down an opportunity for fun. The stinging thought has me returning the question to myself. *Why should I spoil any fun for myself?* That was the point of attending this ball in the first place. Even if Ryland just said that no man was worthy of me, this contender hardly seems awful. In fact, he's rather attractive. Dashing, really.

My hand twitches, about to accept his offer when a new hesitancy forms. I most likely won't know the dance. Doubtful it's one of the two Aurelia tried to teach me. I could take that chance, but I have too much pride to embarrass myself in front of a complete stranger. *I should just savor his offer instead of tarnishing the moment by humiliating myself with a fumbled dance.*

Firm on my decision, I open my mouth to delicately decline, wondering if I should suggest having another drink with him instead, when a familiar figure suddenly appears at my side, materializing out of thin air.

"I'm afraid she's spoken for," Ryland states, voice cool with indifference, not even bothering to look at the gentleman. "Aren't you, little love?" he asks me with a knowing look. He swiftly takes the drink from my hand, setting it on the table beside me.

I flush at his cavalier tone as well as the public use of the nickname. But, Ryland doesn't allow me the chance to respond, instead taking my hand and leading me directly toward the dance floor.

I fume, face heating with embarrassment. I turn my head, offering an apologetic look to the young man, hoping he sees my regret when Ryland abruptly spins me to face him. His arm hooks around my waist while his other hand grasps mine, extending them out to the side.

"Ryland! That was awful," I chide, ensuring my voice remains hushed despite the mortification that rings through it.

"I know," he agrees, brow furrowed in distaste. "You were going to jilt me for some murmuring fool."

"He wasn't a murmuring fool, and I was actually going to turn him down. *Politely*," I hiss. "Besides, you jilted me first."

His eyes flicker. "I suppose I deserve that. Although, I would argue I'm much better company."

Unintentionally, my glare incites a smile of amusement. His mood certainly seems to have shifted, but I can't let his poor behavior slide. After all, he ditched me to speak in secrecy with someone, and when I went to entertain myself, he humiliatingly pulled me away.

If he finds my irritation so amusing, then perhaps I should stoke his.

"I'm not so sure. You have very interesting acquaintances," I begin. Ryland lifts a brow, waiting. "He has a lovely voice—very sultry."

"Is it?" he asks with false interest.

"Very. I hope to run into him again. Perhaps he'll save me a dance later on."

Ryland's gaze darkens before a cunning smile graces his lips. "Wicked, little thing…" he drawls, voice a rolling purr. Before I can further retort, I notice the music beginning to play. It's then I'm reminded that we're situated right in the center of the dance floor. Around us, other couples prepare themselves, waiting for the music to build in tempo.

"Ryland," I whisper with pleading eyes. "I-I don't think I know this dance."

He pulls me closer until our bodies are flush. Our stance is undoubtedly too informal, but Ryland merely instructs, "Just hold on to me, and you'll be fine."

The music picks up and the dance floor swirls with movement. Ryland brings us into motion, and I do in fact hold onto him for dear life.

With Ryland supporting most of my weight, I feel like a floating feather at the mercy of the wind. We whirl and spin, swerving seamlessly amongst the other couples. I don't have to do much as Ryland carries us across the floor with swift ease, like everything else he does.

No longer the assassin on the run, in this moment, he reminds of an aristocrat; noble, resplendent and charming, all paired with that edge of princely arrogance. The rings adorning his fingers, the cruel amusement that sometimes lights his eyes. I feel as if I'm dancing with a king. Utterly unworthy of him and his attention, yet enthralled and desperate for it all the same.

And his attention is focused solely on me.

The ball, the dancers, they all blur in my vision—the only thing I can focus on are his violent blue eyes. Eyes that study my face, flitting about from my eyes to my lips, and at some moments, lowering to my chest.

As the music fills the room and my soul, I feel breathless and free. Enraptured by the moment and by him. By the fact that two weeks ago, I never could have possibly imagined being here in this moment. My burdens lift, sorrow melting away with the acute sensation that there *is* a future out there for me. That there's hope.

Suddenly, everything slows, the electric rush ebbing like ripples in water. Ryland comes to a halt, and I with him, panting softly against his chest. His lips curl into a half-smile, and all I can say is, "Thank you." For not letting me stumble, for giving me such an experience.

"I like you all flushed like this," he observes. The half-smile breaks into a full on grin.

"There you are! Come, both of you." Aurelia's shrill tone bursts our hazy moment as she suddenly appears at our sides. "It's our turn to greet the King," she urges. Ryland doesn't break his stare with me until Aurelia jostles his arm, jolting him from his stupor. "Hurry! It's rude to keep him waiting."

Ryland keeps my hand in his as we follow Aurelia through the crowds, weaving our way toward the back of the room. She gracefully walks up the dais steps before curtseying low to the King seated upon his silver throne.

Ryland and I wait at the base, watching as she and our sovereign share a few indiscernible words. With a final curtsy, she departs to the base of the dais, gesturing for us to approach.

Ryland raises my hand to help me up the steps until we're both standing before King Rhidian. My eyes scan the gleaming throne, suddenly feeling a wave of ancient power wash over me as though the throne itself is alive and sentient. Beyond the grand royal seat are two guards in silver uniforms, one, a male with olive skin and a shorn head, the other a tall, statuesque female with long blonde hair and chocolate eyes as sharp as her Cupid's bow and the blade at her hip.

My gaze quickly shifts to the male seated on the throne as he awaits our acknowledgement. I wasn't wrong. He's young and, more than that, very handsome. Neatly groomed in a pristine crimson jacket and pants that suit his pallor. Much like the structure of the palace itself, the silver crown glistening atop his head is made of sharp angles and edges, as intimidating as the ones of his face. Yet, during my study, I happen to notice that his dark brown eyes are a bit too alight, his posture mildly slumped. Less regal than what I'd witnessed earlier.

"Your Majesty, Ryland and Wren, guests of Lady Aerin," Ryland announces before bowing low.

"Your Majesty," I murmur softly, falling into a deep curtsy, forcing my legs not to wobble. I can feel the weight of the King's gaze on me, heavy like a brand. Yet, when I look up from my lowered stance, I find his eyes not on my face, but rather on my chest and the swell of my breasts. *Perhaps the fashions of Kingsmar should consider switching to higher necklines.*

"I'm happy to host any guests of Lady Aerin. It's always a pleasure to meet new faces," he murmurs, eyes glazed over. His voice is deep and melodic, although it's a little slurred. He's drunk, I realize suddenly, wondering if this is a frequent occurrence.

Even as I slowly rise, his gaze doesn't move from my chest. My teeth clench uncomfortably, the urge to raise my arm and cover my décolletage a nagging thought. But, I imagine that would be too obvious, so I remain still.

"Then perhaps it is her *face* you should address, Your Majesty," Ryland says, voice icy despite the formality.

The King's attention snaps to Ryland, as does mine, finding his gaze sharp and severe, mouth a tight line. The King glares, obviously embarrassed by being called out for his impertinence.

I knew Ryland liked to live on the edge. But I hadn't realized that he had absolutely zero sense of self-preservation.

"Your name again?" King Rhidian enquires, returning his attention to me.

"Wren, Your Majesty."

"And how long are you to reside in Kingsmar?" he asks next, seeming to ignore Ryland's presence altogether.

I flush again at having not only the King's attention but his interest. *Why would he bother to ask me, a perfect stranger, such questions? Especially when I haven't mentioned any title or position. Maybe his drinking has impaired his sense of judgment a little too much.*

"For as long as I'm here," Ryland interjects before bowing quickly and pulling me down the steps.

That's the second time he's answered on my behalf, drawing me away from a potential suitor. Not that the King *actually* was one. Nevertheless, the attention was mine to turn away or encourage. "You can't keep—"

"Careful, little love. I'm feeling rather cross at the moment, and whatever it is you're about to say is undoubtedly only going to make things worse."

I snap my mouth shut as I catch the slight flare turning his eyes that unusual icy blue. He's angry. Which means that other-like side of him is trying to show itself. While he should be admonished for his own impertinent behavior, I don't want to risk his eyes worsening and potentially bringing about his more primal persona.

Aurelia, as gracefully as any lady could, storms over to us, glaring at Ryland, and I try not to cringe. "I hope you behaved up there," she hisses under her breath, though it's quite evident she knows he did the very opposite. She follows closely behind as Ryland once again leads us through the crowds.

"I was perfectly polite," he answers casually, though his face remains set in a hard mask.

I give an unsure glance to Aurelia from across Ryland's body, and she rolls her eyes. Ryland tugs me so that I can meet his quickening pace, and we shortly lose Aurelia. He guides us out to the long terrace where there are a few couples and guests but not so many as to diminish the privacy.

"I'd have to confirm with Aurelia and her expertise, but I'm fairly certain that was not an appropriate way to address the King," I quip, trying to keep my voice level. I don't want to provoke the anger that incites those unearthly eyes, yet I can't keep my feelings to myself. He's acting so...territorial even though the whole point of a ball is to socialize and meet new people. And yet, both times I received male attention, he insulted the suitor and snatched me away before I could get a single word in.

"Really? I thought it was proper behavior for a gentleman to defend the honor of a lady," he replies smoothly, face now relaxed.

He's trying to play with me, but I won't fall for it. I stand my ground. "It is. But not in the manner you displayed, and certainly not toward *the King*!"

"I don't care if he's the king or one of the bloody gods. His eyes should be gouged out for the way he leered at you," he snaps.

My heart wants to soften for the way he's defending my honor, but his behavior was too out of line. One minute he's smug and smiling, relaxed and mild, the next, he's taut as a bowstring, unforgiving and sharp. His moods shift so quickly, I can hardly keep up.

"Aurelia said tonight was to have fun, to dance and meet people, but when I introduced myself to your friend, you couldn't get me away fast enough. But, when someone approached *me*, you dragged me away before I could even ask his name."

"Yes, those were my intentions for tonight, for you to have fun and dance—with *me*."

A flash of guilt strikes. I'd considered accepting that man's offer to dance. It's clear Ryland was under the impression that we were attending the ball together. My ensuing apology is interrupted by Ryland's easy grin. "It's no matter anymore now I have you all to myself."

Taking my hand once more, he steers us to the end of the terrace, guiding us down a set of steps that leads into the gardens. He whisks us deep into the greenery until we're hidden from view, the guests on the terrace small figures in the distance.

There's the faint gurgling of a fountain somewhere nearby, but it's too dark to see. The moon is the only source of light, and I can just make out the faint colors of the flowers surrounding us. There's a haunting beauty to our setting; the star-flecked sky above us, the cool enveloping us in the fragrant scent of roses and hydrangeas. Completely secluded, it's as if we're in our own little world.

When I turn to face Ryland, I find his gaze trained on me. My breath hitches at the intensity of his attention, his body so close to mine. He raises a hand to brush his fingers across my cheek. "Apart from our minor debate back there, is tonight to your satisfaction?"

"It has exceed all my expectations. And you, are you enjoying yourself?"

"I'm enjoying you." His fingers shift to lightly grip my chin, tilting my head.

Something shifts in the air around us, growing heavier, thicker. That strange concept of time seems to slow itself again, and my surroundings blur until all I see, smell and feel is Ryland. His ethereal beauty bathed in moonlight. I sense what's coming and this time I have no intention of pulling away.

Slowly, Ryland lowers his head until it's a mere inch from mine. My heart hammers in my chest, and I wonder if he can hear it, the yearning, desperate way it beats for him.

There's a moment's pause between us, allowing me the opportunity to pull away or protest. But I don't this time. We both want it.

For so long, I've taken only what the world has given me. For once, I'm going to take for myself. Ryland closes the distance between us, gently pressing his mouth to mine.

My entire soul blooms.

A bolt of electricity strikes my entire being the minute our lips touch. Suddenly, I feel as if I've not been alive until this very moment. The moment feels as vibrant and vitalized as the flowers around us. My heart beats twice as fast, skin tingling, pulse thudding with undiluted joy.

The softness and warmth of his lips hits me next, and my heart turns molten in my chest, heat spreading like a wildfire throughout my body. I move to meet his kiss, and the fingers on my chin tighten. After a moment, he gently pulls back, eyes dipping to my mouth as if entranced by it. His thumb brushes across my lower lip as he lets out an unsteady breath.

Drifting from my trance, I slowly bring myself back into focus, trying to recall how to breathe again. Ryland gives a pleased, almost inward smile, before offering his hand to me. "Another dance?"

Too breathless for words, I can only manage a nod.

WE DANCED ANOTHER TWO SONGS, EACH ONE AS PREcious as the last. Even Aurelia danced with me, and we giggled the entire time as she whispered gossip about various guests, discretely nodding her head to the individuals and supplying me with scandalous tales and tidbits. We drank wine and studied the artwork, greeting new faces and figures. I forgot almost every name I was told, but I smiled and curtsied.

Now, in the carriage returning to Aurelia's, I find myself dazed. In a dream-like state. My entire skin is flushed, head swimming, limbs heavy. Ryland's kiss replays in my mind over and over, and my lips tingle with the memory. It goes without saying that it was the highlight of the night. The greatest moment of my life, really.

Once we arrive, and the servants collect our cloaks, I bid Aurelia and Ryland goodnight, or rather good morning. I'm unable to hold his gaze for more than a few seconds without butterflies erupting in my stomach. Inside my room, I pause in the center, frozen in place as the events of the evening strike me with greater potency. My stomach flutters and my heart pounds wildly as I recall every searingly perfect detail. They already morph into a desperate longing to be relived. Restlessness begins to settle within, my body too wired to find sleep just yet. The magic of the night is fading away, and I'm trying to cling to it.

Perhaps possessed, maybe corrupted by an impulsive urge derived from the wine, I find myself tip-toeing to our connecting door. I suck in a deep breath before knocking softly.

It takes less than three seconds for it to open.

My mouth parts when I see Ryland, barefoot in only his pants and a deep blue robe. It's tied loosely around his waist, revealing a large section of his smooth chest.

"Restless, little love?"

I nod, and he wordlessly steps aside, allowing me entry. I've never actually been inside his room before, but I'm too distracted to take much of it in, only acknowledging the dark wood and rich blue and black tones.

Turning around to face him, my eyes instinctively land on his lips, and I lose all train of thought. Whatever I was planning to say evaporates on my tongue.

I'm no stranger to the sensation of hunger. Most of my life I've suffered its hollow ache, the throb of desperation. But this is a new brand entirely. One I'm quickly acquainting myself with as I stare at his mouth.

My body tingles, craving to feel his lips on mine again. He smiles as if well aware of my desire, and a wave of embarrassment rolls through me, breaking my haze.

"I'm sorry…I don't know why I knocked." His stare is so exquisitely intense that my thoughts fog and my tongue loosens. "I don't know what this is," I breathe, shaking my head. Delirious and vexed, I can hardly make sense of the emotions consuming me, that brought me to his room with the urge to draw him closer and breathe in his intoxicating scent. To let him devour me. It's a maddening, unfamiliar plague, incurable and insistent.

Ryland advances a step, eyes blazing. "I know *exactly* what this is," he assures me. He stops when we're an inch a part. One deep breath, and my chest would be brushing his upper abdomen. "Have you been thinking about our kiss as I have?" he asks, voice so deep my stomach tightens. I dip my head.

"And you want more?"

The question draws another rush of heat to my face, and this time I can't manage a nod. Ryland doesn't wait for an answer. He closes the distance between us, gripping the sides of my face with his large hands. Hands that are capable of impossible strength, of breaking iron, of inflicting wild and violent death. But the hands that hold my face are gentle, as if I'm made of glass.

My chest sparks at the press of his lips. What was gentle and sweet in the gardens is now something desperate and hungry. The heat of his body radiates in waves, his breathing ragged as his mouth fiercely claims mine. A gasp escapes when his tongue sweeps across mine.

Ryland slides a hand to my lower back, suddenly turning us around and backing my body until it's pressed against the door. My hands reach up to his neck, running through his loose, silky curls, savoring their feel. He groans into my mouth, and it instantly becomes the most intoxicating sound I've ever heard. The hand on my waist moves to my arm then my shoulder, greedily touching any exposed skin.

My tongue dips inside his mouth, savoring his taste, eliciting another groan from him. Ryland adjusts his stance, shifting even closer, and I suddenly feel something pressing against my thigh. I gasp, breaking the kiss.

The room is heavy with silence apart from our labored breathing. The heat of our bodies entwines between us like the raw, unfiltered need.

Ryland traces the side of my jaw, eyes smoldering as he tears his gaze from my lips. "Goodnight, little thief," he rasps.

I balk, not having expected him to conclude whatever we just started. He must see my confused disappointment, for he adds with a surety that soothes some of my worry, "All in good time." He then places one last kiss to my swollen lips, soft and sweet, before pressing his brow to mine as he seals his eyes shut for a few steadying breaths.

Our gazes never break as I slowly retreat from his room and into mine before he closes the door. The sound as it clicks shut mirrors the sound of my brain snapping into focus.

Neither of us was ready to end things, but he did. *All in good time.* Promising but vague, like almost everything else he tells me.

A few deep breaths calm me enough to manage undressing and readying myself for bed, though I have no chance of falling asleep. The air in my room still feels charged, like there's a string connecting me to Ryland and the closed door is pulling that string taut. The only release would be our nearer proximity, but I refrain from indulging.

Things just irrevocably changed between us. Only, I'm not sure if it will make things worse or better for our future.

CHAPTER 15

I DON'T SEE RYLAND FOR THE ENTIRE DAY.

He was already gone when I woke, which, to be fair, hadn't even been morning. Aurelia barely mentioned his absence, too eager to debrief the events of last night. When I'd casually enquired, she simply said that he had a meeting with a client and was unsure when he'd return.

The news left me stewing over the two possible *real* reasons for his unannounced departure. One, he was avoiding me. Avoiding last night and what transpired. I've never been naive enough to assume Ryland hasn't known the company of other women so, of course, I've considered the mortifying option that he was underwhelmed by the kiss—kisses. Unimpressed enough to have fled before noon and avoid my person altogether. Most men wouldn't show that kind of restraint or awareness to walk away. Either he was being thoughtful or wasn't impressed.

Or, two, the more hopeful answer, he genuinely had a meeting which he simply neglected to tell me about as he did with most other matters. After all, he has mentioned having jobs since we arrived, so meeting a client could very well be what he's doing. But, the timing of it feels more than a little coincidental.

HOLLIS SOPHIA

With it raining the entire day, Aurelia and I elected to remain indoors despite her having offered to take me out. The dreary weather matches my mood, which I'm sure Aurelia's noticed. If she's sensed anything is off between me and Ryland, she hasn't let on. Which is most appreciated.

So, we sit in the drawing room—a pleasant space of blended blue tones, navy walls and milky blue upholstery—each working on an embroidery project, sipping our tea as daytime quietly settles into dusk. I take a small drink from the gold-rimmed cup, the steaming brew warming my belly, before I enquire if I may ask her a question.

Aurelia nods, pulling the soft green thread upward as she continues to stitch the vines and leaves weaving throughout the elaborate floral design. "Does it…bother you at all, knowing what Ryland does?" It's felt like an unacknowledged weight in the room, knowing where he is, what he does, all without actually saying it aloud.

Aurelia's expression sobers as she ponders her answer. "It might have bothered me when I was much younger, but…Ryland has endured more than most. I think his kind of work gives him a bit of power when he's lost so much of it to the past."

Her explanation is like a gold mine of information, and I hoard each word, tucking it away for later. Suddenly, her gaze sharpens, amber eyes holding mine. She subtly leans forward as if trying to catch my attention, even though she already has it. "The Stornvahl line has been the bearer of misfortune for some time."

She's trying to tell me something without *telling* me, that much I can glean. There's empathy shining in her gaze, a spark of heedfulness. So, I let the words trickle through my conscience before I latch onto her implication. "Stornvahl… his family name?" She nods in confirmation, expression grave.

Finally. A real piece of concrete information. I'm not sure what the name will provide, what it means, if it's *supposed* to mean anything, but I'll take it. Aurelia seems to dislike Ryland's obscurity almost as much as I do, and I'm grateful for her sympathy.

A knock on the front door interrupts my plans to further probe, promptly opening and clicking shut. Both our heads lift to the sounds of soggy footsteps approaching the drawing room.

Perfect timing, I grumble inwardly. *The gods must really have it in for me for how few bones they throw me.*

Ryland, radiant as ever and completely drenched, stands in the doorway, a warm smile on his face. His eyes are brightly lit, and I recall how he once mentioned preferring rainy days to dry ones. "Don't you all look cozy."

He makes to step inside when Aurelia abruptly cuts him off with a chiding expression. "If you think I'm going to let you drip on my good Tavlarian rugs, you're sorely mistaken."

Ryland flashes her an impish smile. "Relax. I wouldn't dream of defiling your dear furniture, Relly. I simply came to deliver this before I head upstairs and dry off," he explains before reaching his arm outward. In his hand is a creamy envelope with a bronze wax seal.

Aurelia collects the mail from Ryland who offers her a wink before leaving to change. Upon returning to her seat, Aurelia finds me watching her with an arched brow, question clear. Letting out a disgruntled sigh, she pulls her lips into a frown, muttering, "He knows I hate that name."

I can't help but laugh.

"YOU HAVE A JOB THEN?" AURELIA ASKS CASUALLY, SPEARing her golden fork into the tender flesh of the strawberry cake that was served for dessert.

Ryland nods as he takes a sip from his goblet. "It'll be a quick one."

I try not to tense at the thought of what he'll be doing, to whom, how and when. If he'll be in any danger. I haven't exactly come to terms with his profession yet—haven't wanted to.

"Well, I hope it won't take place Wednesday night. We already have an engagement." Ryland and I each shoot her a perplexed look, this being the first we've heard of where we're expected to be in two days' time. "Lord Feldryn hosting a dinner party, and we've all been invited," she announces. At my further noticeable confusion, she adds, "You met him last night."

In truth, I can't recall his face from the dozens of people I was introduced to. Sensing this, Aurelia adds, "He was a close friend of King Rhidian's father, well-favored by society. His home is twice the size of mine, so it will likely be a large dinner. Over a dozen guests I'd imagine."

"Wouldn't miss it for the world," Ryland teases, eliciting an unamused eye-roll from Aurelia and a very amused smile from me.

After dinner, we retired to the library for the rest of the evening, savoring the warmth and comfort of the grand fireplace. To the sounds of the crackling logs and the pelting rain on the glass windows, we fell into an easy silence, each engrossed in the books we'd selected.

I'd known exactly what I was going to look for when we first entered the room. After several minutes spent attentively scanning the shelves, well after my two companions had already found their books, I discovered exactly what I'd been hoping to find: *The Genealogy of Kingsmar's Noble Lineage*.

It was safe to surmise that Ryland was of noble lineage since he and Aurelia were family friends. I could only hope that the Stornvahl name was mentioned within this tome.

Thankfully, no one commented on my peculiar book selection as I took my seat on the velvet sofa next to Aurelia, Ryland across us in one of the armchairs.

Reveling in the room's cozy atmosphere, I can't help but be reminded of winter evenings spent with my parents. The scent of burning kindle and dried orange peels that hung in the air as we'd all sit by the fireplace and my father read to us while my mother brushed and braided my hair. Those feelings of safety and comfort, of abundance and stability, envelop me in their loving arms, stirring the sensation that in a way I'm with family again. There's a kinship between me and Aurelia, however brief a time we've known each other. It's there in the warmth of her cinnamon eyes, the kindness bubbling behind her every thought and gesture. And, the same goes for Ryland, though ours is a relationship that runs far deeper than mere kinship.

Scouring through the yellowed, dusty pages, I try to abate the growing dread that the glossary of names won't contain the one I'm looking for. I nearly exclaim in triumph when I lock eyes with the printed letters of his surname and it's corresponding page number. Quickly flipping to it, my eyes rove over the names and history of his family ancestry.

As suspected, the Stornvahl family has been one of fortune and status, breeding a strong and healthy line that spanned generations...at least, until a little more than three-hundred years ago.

My brow furrows as I take in a gaping hole in the family tree. In the following text, I read that the last direct descendants of the Stornvahl line, a family of four, all died tragically in a fire. Their estate on the outskirts of Kingsmar burned and, in the process, felled one of Osterley's greatest families. Distant relations carried on the family name, spreading their roots further and further like a sapling to the earth until, eventually, "Stornvahl" was lost completely.

I don't see Ryland's name on the list, but, in all fairness, this record is dated by many decades. *Always the enigma. Like a lost piece of history roaming the earth*

Aurelia said that Ryland has endured a great deal in his lifetime...along with his entire bloodline. She wasn't wrong about his bloodline. Perhaps the Stornvahl name is cursed. Perhaps that's why so many relatives took their spouses' names, to be rid of the poisoned misfortune their ancestry carried.

Despite that somber bit of history, I don't find the answers I was hoping for. Nothing revealing as Aurelia had seemed to imply. I'm tempted to ask, but with Ryland's presence in the room, I keep quiet, instead flipping through the rest of the book, loosely reading about the city's other great families.

"Anything interesting in there, Wren?" The jarring interruption to the otherwise peaceful silence we've been settled in startles me upright. I meet Aurelia's expectant stare. Though her voice was mild, I find her gaze as wary as it was this afternoon when she'd shared Ryland's surname.

"Not really, not from what I've read," I reply, hoping she'll understand my meaning—and resulting disappointment.

But she doesn't latch on, changing subjects, eyes now lit with intent. "Do you know much of the Sildhe history?" she enquires with a curious glint.

"I know a little. My father used to tell me stories."

"You know, this city is where many of the battles were fought. Have you heard the legend of the Sildhes' creation?"

"Not exactly." I'm not sure where's she's taking this, but she's piqued my interest. My father only told me that the Sildhe were known as the 'moon-blessed', their magic having been sourced from the powers of the moon.

"Oh, that's such a shame! It's a really fascinating tale. Ryland tells it best." I watch Aurelia's not so subtle glance to the storyteller in question who returns her stare with a more than displeased look. Ignoring his glare, she continues, "Wren ought to know the story. After all, it plays an important role in this city's history."

"I'm sure she knows enough," he returns, eyes narrowed into sapphire slits. The tension is palpable, and I fight the urge to squirm in my seat. Though nothing is being said aloud, I know there's an entirely silent conversation taking place between them.

THE ETERNAL HUNT

After a few more seconds of heated stares, Ryland shifts his gaze to me, features softening in what almost looks like pity. He releases a heavy sigh before offering me a small smile. "Would you like to hear it?"

"Not if it bothers you," I answer earnestly.

Ryland shakes his head even though I can still sense his reluctance. Closing the book in his lap, Aurelia and I follow the motion. His face slackens in soberness, gaze boring into mine with an intensity that feels a little weighted for simple storytelling. The library falls silent again, and even the pattering of the rain settles a little as though in reverence to the imminent tale.

"This story starts with a caution: Power is its own peril. Whether held within the right or wrong hands, capable or inept, it often incites chaos, injurious and irreparable, much like the fighting that took place between mankind and the Sildhe all those years ago. But it wasn't always like that..."

Tucking my legs to the side, I better situate myself as I listen to the steady sound of Ryland's deep, rumbling voice. "Millennia ago, the gods ruled over our world, watching as our race evolved, reigning over us with quiet authority. Slowly, empires emerged, territories warred and history was gradually written; all entertainment for the ever-powerful eldritch above. Our two kinds never engaged, coexisting separately and peacefully. The divide meant amity...for a time."

A quiet flutter of intrigue rushes through me, drawing all my attention and focus to his words. "One of the immortals, Sidiah, the Goddess of Desire, made the grave error of falling in love with a mortal. She'd spent her time watching him from above, slowly succumbing to her feelings for the lonesome woodsman. Her husband, Kryus, God of War and Battle, had been too distracted by his conflicts and frays to pay her attention. The sting of his rejection cut far deeper, the great irony being that the Goddess of Desire was not desirable enough for her husband to remain at her side.

"Restless from her neglect, Sidiah carelessly ventured down to the earth to see the mortal she'd so closely studied, knowing he would submit to her beauty and charms without hesitation. Naturally, the woodsman had been entranced at first sight, awed by the unearthly being who'd graced him with a visit. He had little choice but to worship at her feet.

"The two lost themselves in each other, ignoring all sense of consequence. The other gods urged Sidiah to return to where she belonged lest she be exiled and lose her divine powers. Conflicted, Sidiah ultimately chose to return to her people and husband, abandoning her mortal beloved. But, not before imparting him with a gift: a child. Half-human, half-god, born on the moon and blessed with immortal powers.

"Embittered by Sidiah's actions, Kryus made a journey to earth and mated with a mortal woman, spiteful that his wife had defiled their union so carelessly. When the time came, he brought the human woman to the moon where she gave birth and thereafter died, leaving behind another crossbred child. And, thus, the race of the moon-blessed was born. With a new precedent set, others gods began to partake in Sidiah's misdeed, forging offspring with mortal folk. The numbers of the Sildhe grew until there were almost as many magic-welders as there were mortals.

"A new age was born, and it was peaceful for a times. Magic was woven into the world with a seamless beauty and splendor. Miracles were made real, fantastical creatures brought to life—it was a golden era. But, the Sildhe began to abuse their powers and lord over the mortals. They manipulated them with force and malice, regarding them as a lesser, inferior race, and their power grew to be nothing but a spiteful, dark magic. And, any hope for coexistence dissolved.

"Of course, the gods weren't blind to their children's misdeeds. They recognized a need for balance lest there be no mortals left to worship at their altars and sustain them with their prayers. Despite risking the welfare of their offspring, the gods created weapons to be used against the moon-blessed, sourced from the raw earth. They were stones, each imbued with a fraction of the forging god's power. Some were made into jewelry, the wearer able to veil themselves from a Sildhe's detection. Others, the rarest kind, prevented the wearer from being ensorcelled."

My thoughts flash to King Rhidian's throne and its ability to thwart enchantments, recalling the moonstones that decorated the seat.

"But, the main gift were the Drith Stones. Embedded into any weapon, they had the power to suppress the Sildhes' magic enough to have them either killed or imprisoned. However, if the Drith Stone weapon was removed from their body, the Sildhe would be revived and regain their powers. Naturally, the magic-blessed wanted the stones destroyed, a quest which only fueled tensions. And so began the age-old wars we know so well."

Indeed. The wars lasted for centuries, the humans courageously battling against those with such distinct advantages and, in the process, suffering the cruelest practices of warfare. And we very nearly lost.

I can hardly imagine living in a time so rife with danger and uncertainty, at the mercy of an enemy so omnipotent.

"However," Ryland continues, "internal fighting between the Sildhe weakened their front. Many of their kind wished to retire the conflict, preferring to use their magic for other purposes, alchemy, divination and the like. But those who coveted power and dominance remained adamant. The disagreements led to fractures and instability which, in turn, allowed the mortals to strike at their weakest points. Then, as you know, the Sethel, which means "shield" in Talaar, was created, providing an advantage for the citizens of Kingsmar. Eventually, the rest of the Sildhe scattered, dispersing themselves across the continents, veiling themselves and our memory of them. With every passing century, the Sildhe lost themselves to legend," he finishes forebodingly.

My mind tries to wrap around the dark tale, trying to grapple the fine line between legend and history. "So, there aren't any Sildhe left?"

Neither companion answers me straight away. Aurelia remains silent out of what seems expectancy for Ryland to reply, and yet, he himself appears disinterested. "There are probably a few out there, hiding from the masses."

"And, what about the stones? The Drith Stones?"

Ryland's jaw ticks, a glint of aversion in his eyes. "Nonexistent."

A chill creeps over my skin, and I stifle a shiver. *If there are no weapons left to fight against the Sildhe, what would happen if they ever came into power again?* It's a chilling thought, and I send a grateful prayer that none seem to have made their existence known. "Do you think they'll ever return?"

Ryland's grim expression combined with Aurelia's stilted silence are an answer in and of themselves. "Let us hope that they don't," is all Ryland says.

An unbidden shiver runs down my spine with a creeping bite. Seeming to notice it, Ryland's face marginally relaxes, some warmth returning to his gaze. "They're just stories, Wren. Don't worry yourself." And, yet, somehow, I find myself doing just that.

Chapter 16

After last night's unsettling story, it didn't come as much of a surprise that my dreams were haunted by visions of shadowy figures with immeasurable powers hunting mortals and torturing innocents. The terrors chased me into an early rise before the sun had even made its ascent. Donning a silk robe, I decide to venture downstairs and clear my mildly disturbed thoughts.

While the table hasn't been set for breakfast, there's coffee and tea pots waiting, the steam wafting from the elegant porcelain. I opt for the stronger of the two, the nutty, roasted scent of the coffee already invigorating me. Pouring in some cream, I can't help but emit a small delighted smile, marveling at the welcome fact that I'm for once the first one to rise. I take a tiny sip of the steaming drink, instantly wincing at the bitter taste before my attention shifts to the sound of quiet footsteps coming down the stairs. On cue, my heart proceeds to commence its regular nervous flutter at the thought of Ryland approaching. Only, it's not his figure that appears under the archway.

And it isn't Aurelia's either. Not even a servant's.

It's a man.

Although, that statement would be quite an injustice to the level of beauty this particular male possesses. He's more muse than man. With black glossy hair that's been haphazardly coiffed upward into soft, tousled peaks, and a sharp facial structure, I can't help but startle a little. Especially when he lifts his brows in soft surprise at discovering my presence, unveiling shocking teal eyes the color of a forest lake. A very lovely shade, but nothing in comparison to Ryland's magnificent blue.

"She didn't mention there was another lady in the house," he murmurs in an unexpectedly alluring voice that has my body straightening. Though I guess it shouldn't be that surprising given how attractive he is. Lethally so. If I hadn't known Ryland and his god-like beauty, I might have considered this male the most exquisite man I've ever seen.

Despite his ruffled appearance, from his lightly mussed hair to his mildly wrinkled clothes, he reeks of seduction. Maybe it's that smoldering glimmer of wickedness in his eyes, heavy and tempting as any sin, or the way his lips are perpetually set in a soft, effortless smirk. His erect, arrogant posture and the fine fabrics allude to a wealthier status, but the question isn't what he does—it's what he's doing *here*. The "she" he'd referred to was obviously Aurelia. *But who is he to her?*

"I-I'm a new acquaintance," I reply, instantly flustered by my awkward stumbling…and ogling.

He smiles, fully aware of his effect on people and consequently enjoying my blubbering. "It would appear so," he agrees, voice smooth and velvety like a purring cat.

I open my mouth to prompt an introduction when he drops into a bow, giving me a slow appraisal that has me swallowing. That look alone would undoubtedly unleash more than a few violent intentions from Ryland.

"If you ever seek the same services as the lady of this residence, my name is Asher Tomlen. I'd only be too happy to oblige." Taking one step inside the dining room, his motions swift but elegant, Asher snatches an apple from the fruit bowl on the table beside me before departing the space entirely. As if in a trance, I find myself following after him and the crisp, minty scent that trails in his wake.

THE ETERNAL HUNT

He reaches the door when I blurt, "Who are you?" Somehow, I'm far less worried about sounding impertinent since this particular fellow seems to lower my inhibitions.

The male throws me an easy grin, a gesture I'm certain has stolen many hearts, and probably broken a few as well. "I could ask you the same question, darling, but I think it's a little early for interrogations, don't you?" he replies, voice a seductive purr.

He must register my befuddled expression for he shifts to face me fully, opening his mouth to say more when another voice behind me sounds, cutting through the lulled, foggy morning quiet which has already been disturbed by this intriguing man's aura.

"You're supposed to leave *unnoticed*, you impish clod," Aurelia scolds, standing in the middle of the stairs dressed in her soft pink silk robe. Her hair is in an uncharacteristically unruly state, creamy skin flushed and mottled with what appears to be embarrassment.

The male looks to her with an expression that evokes both innocence and mirth, one I've seen Ryland wear many a time. "Rather challenging when there are unmentioned guests in the house," he returns smoothly.

Aurelia's gaze dips, noting the apple he holds in his slender fingers, fingers that seem capable of handling much more than just fruit. "Breakfast has never been included, and you know it. Tell Mara I'll be hiring someone new in future. Someone better."

The charming guest scoffs in amusement before arching an imperious brow. "Darling, that threat would only work if there *was* someone better."

It all suddenly clicks into place, embarrassingly late.

"Rest assured I will," Aurelia retorts, hand clenching into a small fist.

The imperious Asher lifts a shoulder in a casual shrug, tossing the apple in his hand. "Then consider this my tip."

With that, he brings the fruit to his mouth and takes a large bite, his sharp crunching echoing in the now silent foyer. "Although, we both know I'm worth a lot more than that," he adds smugly. "Or are the nail marks on my back just your signature?"

There's a split second of silence. Heavy, heated, deafening silence.

Faster than I thought possible, Aurelia is suddenly clutching one of her pink slippers, cinnamon eyes blazing as she flings it at Asher's head. He dodges the attack swiftly, the slipper hitting the front door with a soft thump. I'm not sure I've ever seen the lady so ruffled; even Ryland's antics haven't driven her to this level of animation.

Returning to his full height, the male gives Aurelia a taunting lift of his brows before looking to me, flashing his snow-white teeth in a dazzling grin. With a parting wink sent my way, he vanishes out the door.

Wishing I could dissolve into thin air, I stand in place, gaze reluctantly shifting to Aurelia who pinches the bridge of her nose between two dainty fingers, complexion and coloring reminding me of a beet. "He wasn't supposed to disturb anyone on his way out."

I hold back my grimace, knowing how mortified she must be feeling. "He didn't. I suppose I engaged him first."

Aurelia offers me a sympathetic look. "You're not the first victim of his charms." She shakes her head in distaste before sighing and continuing down the stairs.

She's right though. That male knows the measure of his looks and skillfully wields them to his advantage, much like Ryland. And, if the luxurious clothing he was wearing is any indication, he's clearly one of the best in his...field.

He *was* handsome...too handsome, I think. Perhaps I'm biased, but Ryland, he possesses an unparalleled beauty that I'm not sure even the gods or Sildhe could rival.

Another sigh draws my attention. "I'm sorry you had to bear witness to my shame. I'm not proud of using him...but,

I have to find pleasure in some manner or another," Aurelia admits.

I nod in feigned understanding. "So, you're not interested in something more permanent?" Aurelia would make any man a lucky one, and I can't imagine that she would truly deny herself a partner; one that would keep her company when Ryland's away.

She scrunches her tiny nose, freckles blurring into her skin. "Too complicated. Besides, I'm happy enough as I am. I only call on him every now and then. I prefer discretion, so I have him come here instead of going to the bro—"

"You don't have to explain to me," I quickly interject, raising my hands, my own cheeks crimson. "I mean, I don't judge—not at all," I say sincerely. While my words seem to soothe her a little, I can sense she's still embarrassed. All of sudden, Ryland's footsteps thud down the stairs, and we both rush into the dining room, not uttering another word on the matter.

IN THE MIDAFTERNOON, I WAS AFFORDED AN ENCOUNTER with another one of Kingsmar's unexpected and equally wonderful attractions. The destination was left a mystery when Ryland pulled me from the townhouse after breakfast. He even went so far as to cover my eyes as he led me inside a nameless building, steering me in an unknown direction. When he'd unveiled my surroundings, it was safe to say that I was stunned with shock.

He'd taken me to the city's Archers' Hall, an indoor and outdoor practice range where the most talented archers come to shoot. When I'd asked him how he'd managed to get us in, he casually mentioned being a member of the establishment and was therefore allowed to bring guests. If he was as talented with a bow as he was his blades, I had no doubt that he was a welcome member of the institution.

After providing me with a rental bow and quiver, Ryland took me to one of the indoor ranges, the soggy grounds from the previous night's heavy deluge having made outdoor shooting inconducive. I could hardly believe Ryland remembered me mentioning my love of the sport. I'd murmured about my handmade bow and my mother teaching me during our walk through the wheat field when Ryland had attacked me with a slew of queries. But, I hadn't imagined that he'd remember one small seemingly insignificant fact amongst a host of other insights into who I was. Or that he'd think to help me practice again after so long.

My eyes glistened as he steered us through the white marbled halls, the setting stark and crisp. Calming in a way, allowing one to focus on their craft with little distraction.

My fingers began to tingle with excitement, anticipation bubbling in my veins. However, as we passed the other archers coming in and out of their enclosed shooting ranges, the eagerness was rapidly subdued and promptly replaced by an attack of nerves.

Mercifully, the range Ryland brought me to was empty, leaving me alone to practice. Wholly alone it would seem, for after I was situated, Ryland announced that he would be leaving as he had business to attend to. While I'd been somewhat relieved by his advance notice of absence—I hadn't touched a bow in years and was likely a very poor shot until I reacquainted myself—my hackles raised. It felt as though, despite his seemingly pure intentions, he was trying to keep me occupied. Distracted by an activity that wouldn't have me pestering him or Aurelia with more questions about his affairs and whereabouts. It was another strategic move, and I hated him even more for the brilliance of it. Because as soon as I held the bow in my hands, my suspicions were doused with the demanding need to fire at a target, to let my soul sing with that freeing rush one feels when releasing an arrow.

Alone in the milky colored range, I reach for the quiver, about to sling it over my shoulder when I realize that there's more inside it besides arrows. There's also a leather grip for my fingers so as not to have them irritated by the string and a leather armguard. I've never used these tools before—my mother taught me to shoot in a more rustic setting. These accessories are for professionals, those trained to use the weapon not just for sport or leisure but for skill and trade.

As I'm a left-handed shot, I slide the grip over my three middle fingers on my left hand before I wrap the guard around my right forearm, recalling the purple and yellow bruises I used to acquire as a child from shooting without one.

Notching the arrow, I raise the bow, a little heavier than I'm used to, and take aim, relishing every humming sensation that courses through my veins. The peace and isolation, the stillness, the electric thrum of power and capability—it's a rush unlike any other.

But, all those sensations vanish once I fire the arrow. The first one strikes the very edge of the circular target, not even hitting the outer ring. Needless to say, I flush with humiliation, very glad indeed that I have no audience. But, I press on until my quiver's empty.

When I go to collect my first round of arrows, I can't help the splitting grin on my face. Despite my unsteady aim, the motions are still second nature. It's a relief not to have lost my love for the sport, to be just as enamored with it as I'd been all those years ago. Once again, I have Ryland to thank for it.

My time in the range is spent in quick intervals of shooting with very long breaks in between. Though I've been well-fed since staying with Aurelia, my body hasn't managed to miraculously produce bounds of muscle and stamina, so I'm easily fatigued after only a few rounds.

Once an hour's passed, Ryland comes to collect me in time for dinner. With trembling, sore arms, I follow him out of the alabaster hall, offering my sincerest gratitude. Other than my aches and pains, I feel light as a feather, exhilarated and weightless, humming with remnant joy.

And yet, as soon as I casually enquire where Ryland has been, as soon as he supplies me with a nondescript answer, I'm burdened with the familiar weight of caution. *He definitely planned to keep me occupied for the day alright.* He's keeping more secrets and telling more half-truths. My heart both fissures and mends as I study the back of his tall form as he walks ahead of me, warmed that he brought me to such a place but wounded by the chance that he only did so out of the need to distract me.

Despite all the joys of being in Kingsmar and the grand adventure these past few days have been, it's beginning to feel like Ryland is toying with my feelings, and I'm not sure just how much more of it I'm willing to take.

Aurelia hadn't exaggerated, Lord Feldryn's home is beyond extravagant. The entire foyer is constructed of rich mahogany walls and flooring, two grand pillars erected on each side of the entryway. At the bottom and top of each pillar are intricate carvings of wolf-heads with venomous eyes and vicious teeth. An intimidating space to walk into, and I can't help but wonder if that was the intent.

The dark and heavy tones of the wood cast a dimness to the lighting, reminding me of a hunting lodge. On either side of the room are two massive paintings, each of a forest scape. The one on the left depicts a group of hunters on their majestic white steeds chasing a lone fox. The other, I suppose, illustrates the end of the story, as the fox who was once running for its life lies dead with an arrow in its side. A small stream of blood is shown trickling down its fur. I think it's safe to conclude that Lord Feldryn is an avid hunter.

After collecting our cloaks and overcoats, a servant leads us up the grand staircase which is twice the width of Aurelia's and overlayed with a crimson velvet rug. Mounted upon the walls are the heads of various animals ranging from stags and wolves to rabbits and deer, and even a bear's grizzly maw. The sight of them is mildly disturbing, reminding me of the taxidermy at the artifacts shop, and I turn my head away having seen enough. While I'm fond of a bow and arrow, I'm not sure I'll ever understand the pleasure in killing harmless creatures.

Casting my gaze downward to the thick, red carpeting, images of the warm, syrupy blood of one of the poor prey from the walls might've spilled after its cruel killing flit through my mind. They're abruptly interrupted, however, when I stumble on one of the steps, nearly tearing the hem of my dress. With a quick recovery, I lift the skirts higher, feeling like an eyesore in this environment. The emerald green of my velvet gown clashes with the dark reds and browns of the interior.

Regardless of the lack of coordination, this is probably one of my favorite dresses. The shoulders are slightly elevated to add dimension to the look before tapering into form-fitted long sleeves. The front of the dress is draped vertically, giving the heavy fabric fluid movement as it falls into a simple A-line skirt. To complete the look, Aurelia lent me a necklace that pairs perfectly, a delicate golden chain with a square cut emerald that rests at the hollow of my throat. My hair is swept up and pinned into a loose twist, further accentuating the neckline of the dress.

I look the part—the elegant and demure courtesan—but feel far from it. *Always an imposter.*

We're led upstairs to the drawing room where the other guests are waiting. Lord Feldryn is situated at the doorway, providing us his full attention as we appear before him. Much like when we'd entered the ball, Ryland gathers my hand and wraps it around his arm in a confident, easy manner. As if that's where my hand belongs.

In his proximity again, his forest scent wraps around my senses, making my insides churn and my thoughts a little hazy.

"Lady Aerin, I'm delighted you were able to accept my invitation. It is always a privilege to host you," Lord Feldryn greets in a courtly tone. His voice is rough and husky, likely on account of a fondness for smoking pipes.

Aurelia flashes a beatific smile, her auburn locks, which have been piled atop her head, framing her dainty face. "I'm most pleased to be here, Lord Feldryn, as are both of my guests."

Now standing close enough, I'm vaguely able to recall our host's features from the ball. A gentleman seemingly in his late fifties with silver streaked hair and a thick, dark and scruffy beard. He's of average height and in relatively decent shape—no doubt from all the hunting he partakes in. His chocolate eyes shift to me and Ryland, and we both bow and curtsey before exchanging pleasantries. "You're both most welcome in my home."

"And such a lovely home it is," I reply warmly, hoping it isn't improper to make such a remark.

Lord Feldryn releases a humored grunt. "I prefer the comforts of my winter lodge, but I thank you nonetheless."

His gaze lifts to Ryland, and as the two shake hands, Lord Feldryn's eyes brighten with a pleased, knowing smile. "I know a hunter's hands when I feel them—which beast is your quarry? You look as though you've taken down more than just a stag."

Ryland matches the lord's grin, tilting his head with that roguish look I've come to recognize. "Whoever said it was animals?"

My heart skips a beat, gaze flicking to Ryland and that irreverent mouth of his. After a moment's pause, Lord Feldryn barks a hearty laugh, clapping his hand on Ryland's arm, delighted and entertained. Aurelia, on the other hand, looks as though she's restraining an eye roll. I'm tempted to join her.

Once the laughter fades, Ryland angles his body toward mine, as he adds, "But, actually, it's Wren here who you should speak of sport with. Though she doesn't hunt wildlife, she's a gifted archer. I'd wager she could put some of your best huntsmen to shame."

I'm very certain an unflattering shade of scarlet paints my cheeks as everyone's attention shifts to me. My gaze, however, is trained on Ryland, brandishing my own brand of daggers. He took me to the hall yesterday, but it's not as if he watched me practice and can attest to any sort of skill. Not when he'd left right away at least.

And yet, the way he just spoke, so assuredly, so genuinely…there was no deception in his tone, just a confident pride, as if he's watched me shoot a hundred times. I want to ask him how he could have so much faith in me, when Lord Feldryn turns to me again. "She could, could she?" he arches a bushy brow, eyes roving over my frame as though sizing me up as the "stiff competition" I most certainly am not. "That is something I would like to see one day."

Shaking my head bashfully, Ryland gives me a disapproving look as though both frustrated and endeared by my modesty. Mercifully, Lord Feldryn's attention is stolen by another couple waiting to be greeted. Meanwhile, the three of us step further into the drawing room, Aurelia almost instantly swept away by other guests.

I move toward the back wall to admire another large painting—this one of a hawk perched on a tree, its yellow eyes fierce and luminous—and perhaps also because I was shy of engaging with other company. *Especially after the mortifying scene that just took place.* There will be plenty of opportunities for me to force engagement during the dinner, so why endure extra socialization sooner?

My breath hitches at the sudden presence at my back, but I don't bother turning around. I've become so familiar with Ryland's aura that I'm more attuned to it.

"You've been awfully quiet, little thief," he murmurs, his warm breath caressing the shell of my ear.

"We just arrived," I reply, maintaining my gaze on the painting and *not* focusing on the deep rumble of his voice so close to my skin.

"I meant with me."

Although I haven't been exactly cold with Ryland, I haven't been friendly either. I suppose I've simply been quiet as he says. To be completely honest, I've actually been avoiding his private company altogether. After his deliberate attempt to mislead me yesterday at Archers' Hall, I was spent. Today's been worse if anything else. Even when we toured the Palace Gardens, I engaged only with Aurelia and was careful to avoid Ryland's eye. Aurelia, being the bastion of sisterhood that she is, still tried to pry stories from Ryland's tightly sealed lips, asking him to share memories of their youth. Unsurprisingly and infuriatingly, he declined. When Aurelia then opened her mouth to supply me with such stories herself, he gave her a look more foreboding and thunderous than any storm. All enjoyment of the day evaporated like chimney smoke into the sky.

It's been challenging enough to bear the weight of Ryland's evasive tendencies, but to add to it the nagging knowledge that Aurelia is also withholding information at his behest…the sting has begun to burn doubly. That blade I found in Aurelia's chair has been a perplexing piece in this growing puzzle of Ryland and his allusive world.

For so long, I've been dancing a fine line with Ryland. Some moments, I'm tiptoeing around his secrets, trying to ignore his warning signs all while helplessly slipping under his beguiling spell. On other occasions, I'm employing the tactic of a strong offense, attempting to push and prod my way through his barriers, demanding answers as I guard my wary heart. And, every time he chips further past my armor, every time he displays that heartbreaking tenderness, every adulation he offers, the noose around that fragile organ both loosens and strangles tighter. Because I know that whatever he's hiding will change things, will alter my opinion of him. It has to, for why else would he keep it from me?

Yet, I seem to be succumbing to him nonetheless. A battle between the wits and the heart—a war, I fear, that promises victory for neither side.

"Something troubling you?" The question interrupts my thoughts, and I realize I hadn't given him an answer to his implication. His tone is knowing, and yet I have no desire to have an honest conversation in this public setting.

"No," I answer, voice filled with a false surety I'm surprised I'm even capable of evoking right now.

There's a beat of silence behind me, and I nearly heave a sigh of relief.

"How much did she tell you?"

My brow scrunches as I turn around to face him. "What?"

"Aurelia. I knew it was only a matter of time before she loosened her tongue."

My heart stalls in my chest, palms growing clammy. *He knows that she's privately tried to tip me off about things.* In an effort to spare Aurelia's fidelity, I attempt to feign ignorance. "I'm not sure what you mean," I reply, furrowing my brow further as though truly vexed.

Ryland simply watches me, unimpressed, though his lips are tilted upward. "You may fool anyone else with that front, but not me."

"I—" My mind scrambles to think of a response.

"You can't expect me to believe you pulled out a book on genealogy for the fun of it, hmm?"

So he's known. All of yesterday and today, he's been aware that Aurelia attempted to help me. This is why he thinks I've been so quiet, because he thought I gleaned something about his past. Unfortunately, he couldn't be more wrong.

I huff out a nettled breath, eyes narrowing. "Fine. She told me your family name. But, spare yourself the concern; I've discovered nothing. So rest assured, your secrets are still perfectly safe." I swivel back to face the painting once more.

Ryland steps closer, facing my profile. "When the time comes, *I* would like to be the one to share with you. Is it so terrible for me to make such a request?" he asks softly.

"And yet, I think that time will never arrive. I understand you're allowed your privacy, but it's becoming immoderate how little you can share. I'm not even allowed to know about your childhood," I retort, voice laced with quiet frustration.

"Questions about my youth will unequivocally lead to questions about my present, and I've promised not to lie to you."

The same words I've heard before. What he fails to grasp is that his omissions are as wounding as any lies. And, the more I don't know, the worse I'm going to assume. "You make me feel like I'm being demanding, but really, it's reasonable. I'm just trying to understand—Aurelia gets that. Why can't you?"

"Aurelia cares about honesty, yes, but she fails to recognize the precedence of your safety, and you are safer not knowing."

I shift my narrowed gaze to his, a clash of violent blue and muted green. Two oceans swallowing my verdant lands. But I won't let them swallow me, not this time.

"Do you understand how completely vexing that is?" I demand, my patience whittling into nothing more than wisps. "How could your past cause me danger? How is it that remaining in your presence is safe for me, but knowing your history, events that *previously* transpired, is a threat? It makes no sense at all." My voice is a hopeless rasp, face creased in confusion.

Perhaps I might've let things go without Aurelia's encouragement of my investigation. But, someone else agrees that his obscurity is unnecessary and unfair. All the while, he treats me as if I might be something special, someone he could share his truths with, but, at the end of the day, he chooses not to over and over again. Because of my supposed "safety".

Ryland seems to consider his next words, working his jaw in the process. "Wren, in the fairly short yet rather intimate amount of time that we've known each other, have I not been honest in every single aspect of myself apart from my past? From the very start, have I not shared the grim reality of my work, my morals and values, my unnatural abilities," he adds with a pointed look. "And, on a few occasions, albeit omitting some specifying details, glimpses of my upbringing and background?" His eyes are sharp with sincerity, tone firm. Imploring. "Have I not made sure of your safety and welfare, guaranteed your protection every step of the way?"

I have no choice but to nod. Because any gesture otherwise would be a lie. He's done all of those things.

"Then you can understand that *because* your safety is my utmost priority, I cannot risk it by exposing you to realities that would impart you with knowledge that poses a threat to your very being. Surely you must understand that?"

The anguish in his gaze leaves me breathless as he moves even closer.

"Surely you must understand that it sits on my chest like a leaden weight, not being able to tell you? To crave your confidence and full acceptance, to have you know me wholly and completely, and not be able to? To sit with the fear that your perception of me could be irrevocably altered the minute you learn everything, that you might turn me away after?"

His gaze bores down on me with an intensity that seems unmerited for the short time that we've known each other. I don't really understand it, can barely comprehend it let alone examine the mirroring reflection of my own feelings for him. I'm fairly certain, though I've tried to tamp that part of me, that I often look at Ryland with very nearly the same degree of emotion.

"You have no concept of the battles that I've been fighting, no idea of my duress. Your deservingness of honesty and yet the shackles of my secrecy—it's all driving me mad." His heavy stare continues to ensnare mine in its ceaseless hold, and my heart unwillingly aches for him. For his struggles, his admissions, his pain. "And, in my fevered state, I'm so tempted to slip, to infect you with my truths. Were it anyone else, I might have succumbed sooner. But I've kept up these walls, made my defenses unbreachable purely because of how much I care about you, Wren. How much you mean to me."

I hadn't fathomed that any of his omissions would affect him like this. Had no concept of the pain it's inflicted on him.

That he's wanted me to know this desperately. While I've been worried that my opinion of him might change after knowing, I hadn't thought that he might be worrying the same. Perhaps my sole greed for answers has blinded me to the selfishness of my requests. In it, I've ignored the struggles Ryland has faced in result of his inability to do so.

"Ryland..." I breathe, at a total loss. For words. For an answer. For my feelings.

His eyes fall closed as he looses a pained groan. "Don't."

"Don't what?"

"I love the way you say my name. You can't disarm me like that now," he rasps, revealing those dark, blazing irises again.

My lips part, mind swimming as his admissions swirl around in my skull, trying to gauge where I now stand. "I—"

"Ryland, Wren—there's someone I'd like to introduce you to." For the first time since knowing her, Aurelia's voice is a very unwelcome interruption.

I nearly gasp from the abrupt reminder that we're not alone, the private haze of our intense conversation clearing instantly. Just before I turn around, Ryland's mouth hovers at the shell of my ear, voice a gentle caress. "Don't give up on me yet, little thief. *Please*." His lips brush across my cheek, ever so slightly, my skin singing in his wake, before I greet Aurelia and her companions. Erecting a mask of social civility on my face, its hold feels as fragile as the current state of my heart. One second away from crumbling to pieces.

I PLACE A STEAMING BITE OF ROAST PORK IN MY MOUTH, the succulent juices flooding my tastebuds as soon as I start to chew.

"My husband and I just passed through Atherton last month actually. We dined with your new lord and a few other families. It's a shame you hadn't been there or else you might have joined us," Lady Willum remarks, a kind smile painting her face.

As it turned out, Ryland and I were seated apart from each other at the dining table—both a mercy and a cruelty. I was allowed the necessary time to recover from my flustered state and yet deprived of the opportunity to finish to our vital conversation. Of course, Ryland had picked a public place to reveal all those vulnerabilities to me, leaving me no chance to have him elaborate or for me to respond. Instead, we were swept up into the social assembly, one I was suddenly desperate to depart.

I shouldn't be all that surprised. Ryland never plays fair.

To make matters worse, I'm not seated near Aurelia either. Completely isolated from my companions, I've been forced to survive on my own for the duration of the dinner. Which sounds rather spoiled, but being so completely out of my element with people who are so far beyond my status makes engaging that much more of a challenge. Not to mention, with my soured mood, a seat next to Aurelia would've spared me half my social obligations.

In the long table that seats the total dozen guests, including Lord Feldryn, I'm seated in the second chair from the left. One chair over, is Lady Svar, who is currently engaged in conversation with our host at the head of the table. She's an elderly woman bedecked in jewels from her ears to her fingers which clink together every time she moves or shifts. I'm surprised her posture is so straight with how many diamonds she's wearing around her neck. They must weigh a collective ton.

Despite having been in no mood to converse when I'd first sat down, still reeling after speaking with Ryland, the old crone had initiated our introduction. She'd eyed me down the bridge of her sharp nose, dipping her head in what I assumed was approval before repeating my name aloud. Only, she'd called me "Rem", which I'd attempted correcting, but she just ended up saying it the same way. Then, she'd decided to add the title "Lady" to it. I gave up after that.

I'd tried to engage her with a few simple pleasantries, deciding it was best to distract myself since Ryland's nowhere in my vicinity, but her cold and abrupt answers tipped me off that she had no interest in my company either. The feeling was mutual.

To my right is Lady Willum, the young, new wife of Lord Willum, a handsome man with blonde hair and a matching mustache, who's seated beside Aurelia further down our side of the table. It's been relatively easy to converse with her, and I'm grateful for her docile nature. But, it seems I'm treading on dangerous ground after what she's just said. If I were the kind of wealthy socialite I'm posing as, I *would* have been invited to a dinner like the one she mentioned.

"A shame, indeed. I believe I was already here in Kingsmar," I reply absently, as if I couldn't be bothered to remember. That my life is so busy, it's difficult to keep track of my packed schedule, full to the brim of social affairs.

Lady Willum opens her mouth, likely on the verge of more questions, but I continue speaking. "You'll have heard that our previous lord recently passed away, and I was desperate to escape the gloom. He was a beloved man after all."

Her dark brows furrow in sympathy, brown eyes tender, and I once again note just how beautiful she is. The gown of violet silk offsets her dark hair and smooth, chocolate skin. I've noticed, however, that she's fairly tall for a woman. Even sitting down, I have to tilt my head to look at her. She's charming nonetheless, a certain aura about her that radiates the vibrancy and joy only a new bride could emit.

"Oh, how dreadful. His successor seemed rather austere."

An understatement. Lord Cornelius was drastically different than Lord Eggar which makes me wonder how the latter could've chosen Cornelius as his replacement. Thoughts of Atherton spur my curiosity as to its state since my unexpected departure. *How many other death sentences have been ordered? How many other people's lives have been irreversibly ruined?*

"So, how long have you been acquainted with Lady Aurelia and Ryland?" Lady Willum enquires, a welcome attempt to divert from the "somber" subject. The latter's name incites a sharp pricking in my chest, our recent conversation having set me on edge.

I take a drink from my glass of wine, buying myself time to think of an answer. It's slightly more bitter than the ones I've had at Aurelia's, but I drink it nonetheless, taking advantage of every luxury I'm offered. As I sip, my eyes flit about the dining room, observing the space. More mahogany walls, crimson rugs and hunting paraphernalia. I find the décor to be a little too rich and heavy, akin to the feeling after one eats too much. There's something more balanced about Aurelia's interior style and furnishings. My tastes align far better with hers it would seem.

"Lady Aurelia and I are fairly new acquaintances. Ryland introduced us not too long ago. And him...I've known for some time now," I reply as casually as possible. It's not a total lie. I don't know the exact number of days since I met Ryland. It feels like an eternity.

She nods. "He's very charming."

"That he is," I agree, both our attentions shifting to the male on the opposite side of the table. He's several chairs down, currently laughing at something a gentleman beside him said, and the sound makes my stomach flutter, fingers fidgeting with the napkin in my lap.

Sensing my stare, Ryland cuts his gaze to mine, blues eyes piercing even from a distance. His expression both stiffens and softens at once, and I hardly know where I stand with him anymore. The male is an infuriating puzzle that I cannot seem to solve and yet cannot seem to give up on.

I'm not sure how long our gazes remain locked, but it's long enough for Lady Willum to repeat my name for my attention. "I'm sorry?" I say, quickly turning to face her.

There's a faint, knowing smile on her lips. And, while part of me has enough faith in Lady Willum that, if we were someplace else, I could admit to her my affection for Ryland and she might make a good confidante, I keep quiet.

I trust Aurelia even more, enough to be completely honest. Despite her close relationship with Ryland, I know she would treat my feelings with true consideration and compassion. But, I haven't approached her yet on the subject. Mainly because I haven't yet admitted to myself the depth of my feelings. Besides, if I ever did reveal to her my sentiments, I'm not sure how she would react. Would she be happy that her brother-like friend kissed me? She wouldn't be insensitive, but would she be genuinely supportive of it? I wouldn't be able to stand it if she lied about her true thoughts in an effort to be polite.

"I was asking if you had any other suitors of interest," she explains patiently. It's not lost on me her use of the word "other".

In my periphery, I can sense Ryland's attention on us, and I'm cautious with my response, that remarkable hearing of his no doubt tracking my every word. "Um…not that I know of—I mean, I-I haven't been looking for any," I answer, the most awkward I've been all evening. "There's been so much to preoccupy me since I've arrived here. In Kingsmar."

I hear a familiar soft chuckle across the table and, as subtly as I can, send a glare his way. It only seems to amuse him more. I'm at least relieved to see that his spirits have lifted, the intensity of our discussion, of his distress, having unsettled me deeply. It eases something inside me to see him somewhat returned to his usual smug and insufferable self.

Lady Willum lowers her head so that her words are for me alone. "You know, when I first met Arthur, I wasn't quite sure of his feelings towards me. There were so many other women who were desperate for his attention and tried to steal him away whenever we were together. I feared that perhaps he would be easily tempted by them. So, when he proposed...I was rather hesitant," she admits softly.

I can tell this isn't something she typically shares with people, and I appreciate her honesty. *Perhaps I could invite her to tea one day. I'm sure Aurelia would help me arrange it—even better if she joined us.*

"What made you accept then?" I ask curiously.

She smiles fondly. "The way he looked at me. As though he truly saw me. He never turned me away, whether I was sad or joyful, vexed or hurt. Even others noticed. They would tell me that he looked at me like a man in love. Completely devoted. One day, I realized they were right, and that I often returned the very same gaze."

I smile with her, leaning forward slightly to catch a glimpse of her betrothed down the table. With that neatly groomed hair and those warm, hazel eyes, and kind, welcoming smile, I can see why he was so sought after. But, it seems that didn't matter to him at all, for he had his sights set only on one.

"It's similar to how he stares at you." My gaze flicks back to Lady Willum, and there's that knowing look in her eyes as she glances to where Ryland sits. I hope my blush isn't visible.

I can't help but wonder if she's right. *Does the way Ryland look at me convey "completely devoted" as Lord Willum's?* I'm not sure.

I instantly scold myself for the lie. I've never been looked at by someone the way Ryland does me. As if he really sees me beyond any façade that I may present. Into the depths of my very soul. As if he were bonded with me deeper than flesh. It's the same look he gave me just before we were seated for dinner.

Ryland saw me for everything I was when we first met, lost and alone. Broken and afraid. But he didn't turn away. Instead, he wanted to give to me, show me the world and offer luxuries I could've never imagined. All while embracing who I am, encouraging me to be myself.

Warmth floods my chest at the same time self-loathing gnaws at my stomach. He's been plagued with so much guilt, so much pain, and all because he wishes to maintain *my* welfare. Meanwhile, all I've done is continuously pester and probe him. I may despise the situation, despise our circumstances, but I would despise a divide between us even more.

Ryland asked me not to give up on him. After all he's done for me, it's the least I can do. He's vowed to tell me. He's vowed to keep me safe. I have no right to contest him any further.

Perhaps there's reason to hope. Even though hope has never gotten me very far in the past. Even though I know it to be a dangerous, capricious little thing. My fears may be substantiated but my hope, it seems, has only a mind to flourish.

Chapter 17

MY CONDITION UPON DEPARTING THE DINNER PARTY was far more battered than I'd imagined, having almost nothing to do with my forced socializing and almost everything to do with the male sitting across me now.

Though the carriage ride has been a fairly smooth journey, quiet and placid, I keep catching Ryland looking at me. As if I were miles away from him. As if he can't quite reach me but is desperate to. But, I don't have the energy to consider the implications, not with the weight of exhaustion that tugs on my every limb and the roiling in my stomach as it churns uncomfortably. I'm not sure if the queasiness is remnant from my conversation with Ryland or from something I ate. Nevertheless, with every small bump and jolt of the carriage as it trots down the stone-laden midnight streets, my state only seems to worsen.

Likely noting my rigid posture and fisted hands, Ryland asks softly, "Are you alright?"

I manage a quick nod, keeping my gaze forward, imagining lying in my soft, warm bed—with *zero* movement. "Just a little tired." After further contemplation however, I'm not sure a warm bed sounds so appealing after all. The nausea in my stomach has overheated my skin, and my head has begun to ache, the muscles straining behind my eyes. The fabric of my dress feels too thick and heavy, oppressive to the point where I'm itching to claw it off.

Thankfully, the carriage halts, and I nearly pounce across Ryland to reach for the door. But I refrain, allowing him to open it for Aurelia to depart first. As soon as my feet touch solid ground, I let the cool air wash over my face, hoping it will serve as a balm to my sudden affliction. It barely refreshes. In fact, the swift movement of exiting the carriage has only increased my nausea, and a rush of lightheadedness takes over.

As I slowly start to ascend the few steps to reach the front door, knowing I need to lie down immediately, the motion suddenly sets off an acute throbbing in my head. I wince, halting mid-step as I clutch my temple. My vision starts to blur, colors and shapes forming one hazy scene.

And then, the whole world suddenly tilts on its axis. My legs buckle, the ground rushing up to swallow me.

"Wren!" I hear Aurelia gasp. But, I have neither the swiftness nor strength to brace for the impending impact, my mind sluggish and reflexes stifled.

I wait for the collision. It never comes.

Ryland's steely arms catch me before I hit the ground, his handing cupping the entire back of my head. A worried expression settles into view as he hovers above me, blurred around the edges. "Wren?" His voice is urgent, laced with a sharp panic that makes my nerves flare.

I'm about to answer, brain trying to muster the capacity to formulate thoughts into words. Just when I think my mouth will be able to function properly, it isn't words that escape my lips.

It's blood.

The dark red substance gathers in my mouth before I begin to choke, spattering it on the ground as I shift my head to face the stones. It burns up my throat, the metallic taste bitter, and my stomach starts to cramp, muscles seizing with an insufferable pain.

What's happening to me?

In a flash, Ryland scoops me into his arms, the swift motion nearly inducing another heave, and hurries up the steps into the townhouse. My eyes, sealed shut to avoid throwing up, leave me blind to my surroundings. I can tell by the change in light that we've made it inside. The warmth of the townhouse envelops me like a soft blanket, and I feel a small sense of ease at being someplace familiar.

"You don't think—" Aurelia begins, voice trailing close behind.

Ryland's sharp reply cuts her off. "Poison."

The word strikes like a bolt of lightning, and fear shudders through me.

Poison. But how? Why? And by whom?

I'm about to ask those very questions, but more blood spurts out of my mouth, spilling onto the luxurious carpet as Ryland rushes me up the stairs. "I-I'm sorry," I manage to get out, voice broken, eyes flickering open to convey my guilt.

Flashes of colors, of dark green and pomegranate, of honey blonde and electric blue, smear like paints in my vision. I can hardly make sense of all the shades and shapes. A whimper escapes as another stronger wave of stomach cramps and dizziness consumes me.

"It's alright, my love. You're going to be alright," Ryland soothes. Though his voice is gentle, his body and grip are as stiff and firm as granite. From the worry I glimpse in his gaze, I understand just how dire the situation is, that my chances right now aren't looking very good. The symptoms are attacking me all too quickly.

My eyes fall closed again in the hopes of evading the dizziness. I feel myself gently laid on a bed, my bed from what I can tell. After a minute of being settled, I manage to crack my eyes open which are now blurred with tears, finding Ryland standing before me as Aurelia helps remove my slippers.

Ryland's thumb swipes the blood from my lips, fingers tracing across my skin. I can't tell if I'm the one trembling or him. "She's burning up," he says to Aurelia.

Indeed, it feels like my skin is on fire, raw and angry. I imagine how I must look—flushed, reddened and damp with sweat. A flickering flame on the verge of burning out.

I surge forward, coughing up more blood. Despite trying to cover my mouth with my hand to collect it, it slips through my fingers and drips onto my lap. A forceful shudder racks through me when I behold its alarming shade.

Black.

"W-what's happening?" I quiver, voice managing to cooperate for the moment.

"I think it's vastaral leaf," Aurelia's grim voice sounds as she studies my eyes with a clinical gaze. I'm not sure what she sees in them, but her head dips in confirmation.

I slowly ease back onto the propped pillows, dizziness overwhelming, trying to recall where I've heard that name before. It's like trying to look through cloudy water, but I manage to pull the memory. It was when my father took me woodchopping one day when I was little, in need of materials for his next commission. We'd ventured into a new part of Stone Wood as he was searching for a particular kind of tree.

I'd been wandering around the bushes while he'd swung his axe, stumbling upon an especially intriguing plant growing at the base of a maple tree. The leaves had sharp points, their tops glossy and smooth, distinctive only by the faint yellow freckling on their surface. Having equated the small spots to the sun's kisses, I'd gleefully plucked a leaf to show my father my discovery, recalling how grave his face suddenly became. He'd snatched the leaf and tossed it to the ground, taking my hand and wiping it on his shirt to remove any of the plant's residue. Then he'd knelt in front of me, his tone dropping to that paternal resonance.

That's vastaral leaf, Wrenley. It's a poisonous plant and very dangerous. If a person ingests it, it will kill them. You never *go near that plant again.*

My naive, seven year-old mind had tried to process the severity of his words, but the question I ended up asking was, *What about the animals?*

It doesn't harm them. Their bodies are different than ours, so you must never go near that plant, do you understand? I'd nodded fervently, thoroughly spooked, having never come across the lethal plant again—until now.

"She needs havick root," Ryland grits out.

I lose focus as the room begins to shift again, managing to catch a glimpse of Ryland's face, cold and unforgiving as ice. And his eyes…perhaps it's just my delirium, but they seem to be flickering to that glowing light-blue.

New fear starts to consume me. Fear that he might depart, might try to seek whomever did this, and that I might be left without his warming, grounding presence as I succumb to the poison. "Don't leave me," I beg, voice so breathless I can barely hear myself.

His face contorts, eyes warring with confliction of whether to stay or go. The irises start to flare brighter. "Stay with her," Aurelia commands. "I need to get the root." Whether or not she's aware of the change in Ryland's eyes, I can't tell. But, I hear the door open and close, and my head begins to throb more fiercely.

"Ry-ryl—" his name barely escapes my lips, and I hate that my mouth will not comply. I want to apologize, to tell him how sorry I am for my disregard, for my carelessness earlier. I want to tell him that I in fact care *very much*—too much. That I seem to want him despite any secrecy or evasion.

"I'm here," he reassures. "I'm here, my love." His hand returns to cup my cheek, the coolness of his rings soothing my heated flesh the slightest bit. It makes me realize just how high my temperature must be, for usually, their sharp frost against my skin is a biting surprise, not a welcome reprieve. "You'll be alright," he promises.

I cling to those words. With my life, I cling to them.

Ryland vowed that he'd never lie to me. So, I must believe him. Even as blackness starts to crowd my vision, I cling to his words.

I cling to him.

WHILE MY BODY MAY HAVE SURRENDERED TO THE poison, my mind still possesses the will to fight. To battle oblivion and its indomitable force, fearing that if I don't try and break through its entombing clutches, I may never resurface. I may never wake up.

As I claw and tear at the haze of my stupor, hushed murmuring, slowed and slurred to my fatigued ears, bleeds into my subconscious, familiar voices with names I can't manage to recall.

"…It's too much of a coincidence. He knows you're here…"

"…said they could malfunction…my location must be coming through…"

"…Where will you go? You…"

"—have to think…she remains in peril even if…"

I strain to bring myself into focus, to latch onto those voices and have them pull me to the surface. But, their words slowly ebb away, oblivion gaining the upper hand before it strikes me with another blow, so strong, I have no choice other than to submit.

I'M CHOKING, SOMEONE FORCING WINE DOWN MY THROAT as I lay on the cold, stone floor. Somehow, I know that the drink is poisoned, but the shadowed figure is pinning me in place, shoving the liquid down my throat. I try to cough and spit it out, but they've poured so much that it's futile. I can already feel it burning my insides, feel my body slowly starting to perish.

My gaze shifts to the side, latching onto Ryland's motionless form as he lies beside me. His skin is so violently pale, eyes glazed and vacant that I cry out, hand reaching for him desperately.

He doesn't move.

The sight of his lifeless frame is too much, my entire body thrashing violently. Then, a knife is lodged into my heart—

"Wren...*Wren*."

My eyes fly open as I launch forward taking in short, desperate breaths. My skin is clammy, and my cheeks are wet with tears. Damp and disoriented, I find Ryland sitting on the edge of my bed, one of his hands holding mine.

"It's okay," he says calmly, soothingly. "You were having a night terror. You're alright."

That's what it felt like. Pure, undiluted terror. As consciousness slowly starts to trickle back into my system, I can feel some of the fear starting to fade, quickly replaced with the suffocating weight of sickness. My body feels drained and weak, throat raw, stomach muscles tight and aching. I look down to find myself in a white nightshift. Memories of black blood and terrifying dizziness suddenly flash through my mind.

My gaze shifts to Ryland. "Wh-what—" My throat catches, raw and tender.

He cuts me off quickly. "Aurelia gave you a remedy. You're weak from the poison's effects, but you'll be alright. You just need to rest."

I didn't die. I survived.

It takes me a few moments to process the information before my next thought forms. "How did she get it in time?"

He presents me with a much needed glass of water, helping me drink. "She had some here."

"Aurelia had the cure *here*?" I ask in between sips.

Ryland's expression remains guarded, and he simply holds my gaze, his silence telling. He won't answer, but I'm too fatigued to argue. "How long was I asleep?"

"Four hours."

From his wrinkled clothes, strained eyes and rigid posture, I can tell he's been here with me the duration. It's pitch black outside the window; dawn must still be a few hours away.

"Who…" I can't even finish the question, still processing the fact that I was poisoned in the first place. That it wasn't a poison to simply incapacitate but to kill.

Ryland's face tightens, eyes blazing with nothing but sheer, ruthless menace. "I'll find out." The lethal promise in those three words sends a shiver down my spine.

He'll find out—and end them.

There's no point in asking *why* I was poisoned given that we haven't the faintest idea. "Do you think it was someone from the dinner?" I enquire instead, trying to go over all the attendees, imagining who would want me dead. But, I hardly know any of them. None of it makes sense. Lady Svar may have been venomous, but capable of murder, I think not. I believe her malevolence is limited to withering looks and embittered grumblings.

Ryland shakes his head. "None of them had any motives against you. Someone else must've slipped it in your drink."

The wine, I realize with aching clarity. I remember that there'd been an odd taste to it. I'd chalked it up to being a particularly old bottle or something, but apparently it had been tainted with poison.

"Where's Aurelia?"

Ryland pulls the bed linens further up my frame, fussing like a worried mother. "I told her I'd watch over you. She went to get some sleep."

Fuzzy glimmers of their voices dance over my memory, a conversation that took place. As quickly as the vague shape of a memory surfaces, it fades away, lost to my subconscious.

What's not lost on me though is the fact that the two both saved me tonight. Aurelia knew the poison and Ryland the antidote. Another reason to be eternally indebted to them. Otherwise, I would've been left to die, choking on my own blood as my organs failed me. The reminder of that gruesome image has me glancing again at my change in clothes, recalling the state I must've left the previous garment in, how similar stains have probably ruined Aurelia's furnishings.

I frown into my lap. "I'm sorry about the carpet and the dress," I mumble, thinking about how much of my blood soiled them. It won't be easy to get out, if at all.

"I hope you're joking," The words escape clenched teeth.

Of course I'm not joking. That carpet and dress are undoubtedly worth a fortune, and now they're ruined. My brow wrinkles, and I realize how heavy and glassy my eyes are.

"As if I give *a solitary fuck* about a carpet and dress," Ryland growls.

"They're worth more than my life. Literally," I add before coughing away a scratch in my throat.

"If you say one more word about the fucking carpet and dress instead of focusing on yourself…" He can't even finish the threat his body is so tense.

I'm too tired to argue with him and, in my frail state, I find his fury unnerving. "I don't understand why you're so angry."

His livid eyes meet mine, as if stunned. "Angry? You think I'm angry? That word is *nothing* compared to what I am right now."

"But I don't understand why you sound so upset with me? *I* almost died."

"Exactly, I almost lost you again. And, the fact that you're more worried about two pieces of meaningless fabric is infuriating." The harshness of his words and sharpness of his tone strike me like unforgiving blows. I'm beginning to wish I was still asleep. My eyes sting with fresh tears. I'm already in a delicate state and seeing him so angered makes me feel worse.

Reading the hurt on my face, Ryland's expression softens. "I'm sorry," he breathes, voice full of remorse. His hands cup the sides of my face, thumbs tenderly brushing away my tears. The touch is so soft and gentle, providing the most comfort I've felt all night. He leans in and presses a long kiss to my forehead, lips moving against my skin as he murmurs another apology.

When he pulls away, his gaze is soft yet intense. Somehow more intense than it was when he was angry moments ago. There's a lingering panic in his eyes, a hint of what he must have endured earlier. He looks to my lap. "You have to understand…I'm an assassin because death sustains me." His eyes lift to mine, and the sheer ruinous pain in them steals my breath. Those deep blue irises simmer. "But your death… would *destroy me.*"

"How?" I demand. "You still hardly know me, and I you. How could I affect you that much?"

He shakes his head. "I know you far more than you think, Wrenley Hawthe. And, while I may not know everything, I intend to. I intend to learn *all* of you. Mind. Body. Soul."

I want to ask him why, want to hear him say more, but my body is so, so tired. It's a fight just to keep my eyes open. And, I want to be fully awake for this conversation. There's a chance that I'm so drowsy right now, I might not even remember this the next time I wake.

"You know you have the habit of saying these sort of things at the worst possible times," I murmur, remembering that night at the inn.

A faint smile graces his lips, one that says I've amused him. I think it's become one of my favorite smiles of his. "My apologies, little thief."

"I would like to discuss this again. Preferably when I'm not recovering from being poisoned."

Another smile before he nods. "I'm not going anywhere."

Something in those words acts as a trigger, and a rush of worry surges through me in response. As though somehow the opposite is true. As though he's supposed to leave, though I can't recall or make sense of the premonition.

Ryland presses the softest kiss to my lips, a light brush. My heart races. When he starts to pull away, likely to return to the position he was in when I woke, I latch onto his arm, holding him still. He meets my gaze. "Will you lay with me?"

Ryland watches me for a long moment before he nods, rising to move to the other side of the bed to join me atop the covers. His arms wrap around me, pulling me close to him with a gentle grip, conscious of my frailty. Immediately, his warmth envelops me like a cocoon, and I realize how much I missed this, laying with him. When he'd held me close under the canopy of Lyrewood Forest all those nights on the road. The way he cradled me in his arms at the inn, as if I was the most precious thing in his world.

It's the same feeling now. So incredibly right. And yet, the thought of falling asleep, of perhaps falling into another night terror, of losing the sense of comfort he instills within me, has me tensing with worry. But Ryland begins to stroke my hair, a soothing cure to my sudden fear. As darkness, a gentle one very much unlike the one that had claimed me from the poison, wraps me in its soft embrace, I hear Ryland murmur against my hair, "Rest, little love."

I follow his gentle command.

CHAPTER 18

I AWAKE TO AN EMPTY BED, THE COLD SHEETS ALERTING ME to Ryland's absence. Slowly, wincing through layers of soreness, I ease myself upright. The bright light streams in through the window, and my sensitive eyes squint. Despite my stiff and aching limbs, pounding head and all-consuming fatigue, my body feels far better than it did last night on the brink of death.

I don't think I'll ever forget the unforgiving rush of the poison, how it nearly took me out in the span of minutes.

It takes more energy than I thought it would to rise from the bed and don my mauve-silk robe. Carefully, I manage to make my way downstairs, hoping to find Ryland. Instead, I stumble upon Aurelia in the drawing room, stirring a teacup. When she notices me, her eyes widen. "Oh, you're awake! I was just coming to bring this to you," she explains before extending the cup of tea. From the scent alone, I know it's an herbal brew.

I ease myself onto the ivory settee while she sits across from me in a soft, robin's egg blue chair. It's an effort not to cringe at the bitter taste from my first sip, but I remind myself that it will help with my recovery.

"How do you feel?"

"Better. A little weak and sore, but whatever you gave me helped immensely. Thank you." My voice is frail, but I hope it conveys at least half the sincerity I feel.

"You don't need to thank me. I'm just sorry that it ever happened."

"Do you have any idea who could've been behind this?"

Aurelia reaches for a separate tea pot and pours herself a cup. I get the feeling her gaze is deliberately averted from mine. "Not exactly," she murmurs.

Not exactly? So she has a hunch. I open my mouth to ask, but she continues. "You need to be careful with yourself, Wren. Your body is very fragile right now, and you need to rest today. Well, what's left of today." She notices my puzzled look and adds, "It's half past four."

It takes me longer than normal to process her words. I guess my brain isn't functioning properly either. "I slept for over twelve hours?" I ask in disbelief.

Aurelia nods sympathetically. "Sleep is crucial for healing. Your body suffered a vicious attack."

The day is already gone. No wonder Ryland wasn't there when I woke. The reminder of his absence has me enquiring where he is. I expect Aurelia to say in the library or his room, but she instead replies, "He had a job to do. And he also wanted to try and find out who did this."

Another abnormally long pause from me as I process. "But...he didn't say goodbye." He left to complete two incredibly dangerous tasks, all without a parting word to me.

Aurelia quirks her brow with a peal of laughter. "I think he didn't want to wake you. Not when he'll return tonight."

She acts as though my worried tone is wholly unnecessary, and yet panic starts to tighten my chest. He left to do his job, to fulfill the contract with a client—to kill someone. Perhaps *two* someones if he's successful in finding the culprit for my poisoning. *And he didn't say goodbye.*

What if something happens? What if it all goes wrong? I would never see him again. Never would be able to finish the conversation he started last night. Never be able to tell him how *I* feel. I'm still not sure why, but I've been carrying that sensation of pressure in my chest, the feeling that Ryland will leave permanently. Though I haven't surmised a reasonable logic, the feeling is there all the same, implanting an irrational, urgent fear in my stomach since I woke.

Sensing my panic, Aurelia steps forward and takes one of my hands. "Wren, you needn't worry. He'll be back soon, I promise." Her expression falls into something more grave. "In fact, he intends for us all to have a discussion upon his return."

"About?"

She glances downward. "Many things, which I've been sworn not to inform you of until he arrives."

If I had the energy, I might produce a scowl. *Many things like my attempted murder? Or how Aurelia knows of poisonous plants and their antidotes? About Ryland's past?*

With her lips sealed, Aurelia shifts into a nursemaid once more, forcing me to eat some toast and drink more of that horrid tea which I wonder isn't itself a poison. When she wasn't in my company, and even sometimes when she was, I spent the entire evening pacing in my room, the library or the drawing room, awaiting the anointed and yet seemingly distant hour of Ryland's return.

I'm not sure which matter I found more concerning during my nervous treading, Ryland's prolonged absence or the fact that my soul seems only to find ease when in his presence. *But how is it that I can feel so calm and settled by someone whom I know nothing about? Who remains so evasive and obscure? Why is my connection to a walking mystery so strong and undeniable?* As the sun's light faded and a steady rain began to fall, I still hadn't arrived at any answers.

In between periods of rest, my body has been strained and antsy all evening, my mind unable to be put at ease. Aurelia's tried several times to console me, but it never helps. I know the stress isn't exactly helping my recovery, but I also know that I won't truly rest until Ryland returns safe and sound.

It's near midnight when I hear the front door open and close. My heart stops beating for a second. "You're back," I hear Aurelia say before I'm bounding out of the library where

I find Ryland standing in front of the doorway, tall and dark in a black cloak and hood. Like night and shadows given form.

His eyes instantly lock with mine right before I throw myself into him, arms wrapping around his waist and holding tightly. Despite my force, he doesn't stumble back an inch, his broad frame steady and solid. Ryland holds me with equal force while Aurelia enquires from behind me, "Did you find him?"

"His staff said he's away on business. I sent a note for him to visit as soon as he returns," he replies, voice less than pleasant.

I'm not sure who they're referring to, but I'm too wrapped up in Ryland's return to bother asking. Breathing in his woodsy scent, I can hear the amusement in Aurelia's voice as she says, "I'll go make you something to eat."

I don't let go, not one bit. I cling to him like life, even as I feel a chuckle rumble through his chest. "I'm glad to know I was well-missed," he murmurs warmly before pulling back and taking my chin between his thumb and finger, forcing me to meet his now serious gaze. "Are you well?"

I lose myself in those blue eyes, consumed with the thought that I might not have seen them again. "I was worried," I manage to get out.

He chuckles again. "What on earth for?"

"Aurelia told me what you went to do. You didn't even say goodbye. What if something happened, Ryland?"

"I didn't say goodbye because you needed to rest, and I knew I'd be back very soon. Nothing would've kept me from returning to you, little thief. I told you, I'm very good at what I do."

I guess that means he was successful tonight. Someone died at his hand. I suppress a shudder, trying to ignore the grim thought. I suppose then that the person he'd referred to as "away on business" was a suspect for my attack last night.

Ryland gives me a pleased smile. "You're concern is heartwarming though."

257

I try to give him a smile in return, but I don't fully master it. "Aurelia said you wanted us all to talk?"

His smile fades as he offers a grim nod. The expression signals what he intends to reveal, and my heart stutters in my chest. I can hardly believe it. Though I have no guarantee how much he plans to share, I at least know I'll be unlocking some truths. Despite my apprehension, frightened of what I may learn, I steel myself in preparation. We've been heading to this point for a while now, and I don't want any more hesitations or delays.

Ryland releases my chin with a final brush as he says, "Let me quickly eat and change. Then we'll talk. Go rest upstairs until then."

Reluctant to leave his side, I ultimately avoid debating and agree to his suggestion. But, before I can take my first step, Ryland cups the side of my face and presses a quick kiss to my brow.

I head upstairs, trying to gather my now dazed thoughts. I decide to wait in his room, knowing I'll be too restless in my bed where I've already spent so much of the day. Perhaps when Ryland arrives to change, he'll begin his explanations sooner. Stepping inside the darkened space and closing the door behind me, I'm immediately enveloped by his intoxicating scent which blends with the smokiness of the crackling fire heating the room.

As I wait, my mind races with the imaginings of what he intends to reveal. Does Aurelia know all of it or is she equally as unaware? I wonder if they're talking right now, if he's prefacing her or refuses to share until we're all gathered. My heart hammers in my chest, stomach twisting with nerves.

The bond that we've developed over this short amount of time—it's indescribable. The pull that I feel towards him. But, I can't help but wonder if that's all about to change. Will his reality lead to a harsh, immediate severing of the connection between us or a slow, painful unraveling? Or maybe, just maybe, his admittances won't be so horrific, won't ruin our chances. Perhaps my opinion of him won't be so skewed, and we—

A shadow emerges in front of me with the blinding speed of a serpent. Thoughts, sounds, reactions have no chance of intervening, not when I'm struck in the chest with a blinding blow that knocks me off my feet.

I crash onto Ryland's bed, roughly hitting the mattress, gaze flying to the large form suddenly looming over me. A male, but I'm unable to note any distinct details before I see the knife in his meaty hand hovering above me. A raw scream tears from my throat just before he slams the weapon down. I take a split second to roll to the side just before I hear the blade pierce the mattress.

Shoving my body backward, I scurry away frantically, falling off the other side of the bed and slamming onto the wooden floor. My head pounds, bones and limbs protesting any movement, but I manage to shuffle backward in retreat.

Gasping as I hit the wall, there's no more distance to create between me and the assailant. My eyes scan around wildly, looking for something, anything, to use as a weapon as the man saunters toward me.

There's nothing within reach. Even if there were, I doubt I'd manage to fend him off. The blow knocked all the stamina I'd built up today, and I'm too weak to recover quickly enough.

With a single hand, the man grips the front of my throat, hauling me off the floor and up along the wall until my feet are dangling desperately for the ground. I thrash and buck, clawing at his hand, but my efforts are in vain. I'm too weak to employ Ryland's maneuver—I won't be so lucky this time. Pinned by his unforgiving grip, my eyes bulge, face reddening as he chokes me mercilessly. My lungs spasm in my chest, limbs tingling from the loss of air as my vision starts to blacken.

The door bursts open, Ryland rushing inside, blade already in hand. For a split second, his eyes lock with mine, glowing violently. Faster than my fading vision can catch, he sends a blade flying, my attacker suddenly hissing and drawing back abruptly. I collapse to the floor again, desperately sucking in air, heart beating erratically as I try to keep conscious.

As the attacker removes the dagger from his shoulder, Ryland spares another moment to take me in, huddled on the floor, small and terror-stricken. His eyes seem to burn brighter.

My body instinctively wants to curl away from the sight, from the unnaturalness of those eyes, but I'm spared their weight as Ryland turns to face the assailant, and I watch as recognition flickers in his expression.

"Reaver," he growls.

The man reveals a delighted smile as he studies Ryland, palming the now bloodied dagger in his hand. Brown, straggly hair hangs to his shoulders, brushing the edges of his worn, umber leathers. While there's a similar flawlessness to his features like Ryland and Aurelia, there's an overall raggedness to him. Something more fiendish and brutal; a rough stone where Ryland is a polished jewel. As though he spends far more time amidst copses, caves and creatures than civilization.

"It's been an age, boy. I see you've been busy," he grunts, nodding his head to me.

The words unleash another rumble from Ryland's throat that sounds more animal than man. "Still sending out lowlives, is he?"

The man sneers. "You know he's the impatient sort, but he trusts me to get the job done. Of course, I hadn't expected it to be so fun. Finding out you had a little friend made the job even more entertaining. Picturing your rage after the poison killed her was a lovely thought," he reminisces fondly before his gaze shifts to me, flickering with annoyance. "Though I suppose I needed something stronger."

My blood chills as his words settle. *It was him. He'd poisoned me.*

My entire body trembles. It's one thing to know that someone wants you dead. It's another experience entirely to see the face of your attempted killer. Obviously, he's an enemy of

Ryland, and he was willing to kill me, an innocent, to get to him. I wonder if he's connected to those men we ran into in Lyrewood or is he a different foe altogether?

"I dare you to look at her one more time." Ryland's warning cuts through my stunned silence, voice a searing hiss.

The man chuckles, facing Ryland once more, somehow unaffected by his injury. "You can make this easier on yourself if you comply, Ryland. He's waiting for you." Reaver then reaches a hand behind his back before pulling out a pair of iron cuffs almost identical to the ones the ruffians had carried. The ones with the strange markings. And yet, not so strange anymore. For I now recognize those markings—at least, where they come from.

Talaar.

"I'll spare her if you don't put up a fight," he adds with an oily smile. "Of course, after I've left a mark or two."

"Lay another hand on her, and I'll peel the skin off your bones, strip by bloody strip." The sickening threat is followed by a vicious smirk. "And we both know I can do it." Even the attacker's eyes dim a little at the gruesome picture.

Ryland tucks a casual hand in his pocket, tone now conversational. "As you're well aware, I'm not overly fond of in-person meetings, so I think I'll send a message instead."

Reaver's eyes narrow at Ryland, and he raises the dirtied blade, his blood gleaming in the firelight. But, he isn't quick enough.

A thin dagger lodges in his stomach with a soft squelching sound. He grunts, and Ryland appears before him to remove the blade. But, Ryland's expression seems irritated as opposed to satisfied as he looks at the wound, brow mildly slanted. The golden blade is lost to his flesh, the lavender handle jutting out from his leathers.

It's then that my gaze drifts to the doorway where Aurelia now stands, hand extended, breathing heavily with fierce eyes. Fierce, *glowing* eyes, a bright, buttery shade of yellow. Like liquid sunlight.

She's like him. *She's like him...*

My attacker drops to his knees, dagger clattering to the floor as he clutches his abdomen. Ryland stands above him, a vengeful executioner ready to unshackle his restraints. His fingers twitch, body still primed for violence. "I had it under control," he growls.

"I've just as much reason to loathe him as you," Aurelia bites, her voice unrecognizable.

Ignoring her justification, Ryland continues to stare down at his victim as he directs, "Take Wren downstairs."

Wordlessly, Aurelia steps inside, bending down to help me up before guiding my shaking frame across the room to the doorway. I hesitate at the threshold, trying to look back at Ryland, my body instinctively unwilling to leave him.

"He needs to finish the job, Wren," Aurelia says quietly, towing me into the hall. My gaze latches onto hers, and I flinch at the near-blinding yellow. She looks away in shame before gently leading me downstairs into the library.

I remain silent, hopelessly attempting to process everything that just happened, all that was said, all that I've seen. Even Aurelia doesn't speak to me, seeming to sense my inner turmoil. Her eyes have dimmed to their usual shade of rich amber, but her expression is focused, as if she's devising strategies and plans in that sophisticated brain of hers. I doubt she'd answer any of my questions anyway.

She knew the man, too. He was just as much her enemy as Ryland's. But how is she tied into all of this? She's like Ryland, but is it only her eyes that glow or does she also possess the unnatural abilities of heightened strength and speed, the expedited healing? She'd thrown the blade into his stomach with perfect aim. Had it been another one of her daggers like the one I'd found in the library? Have these attacks in her home occurred before? With weapons and cures for poison stashed about the place, I suppose the answer is evident.

I remember Reaver mentioning that someone wanted to see Ryland. Is this person a client of his? But then why would

Aurelia be involved in that? My mind races with endless questions all swirling inside me like a brewing storm. I feel like I might explode.

Time passes in a way that feels like several hours when I'm sure it's only been one. Every now and then, I think I hear a muffled scream or a soft thud. Trying to ignore the sounds, to not imagine what's occurring just upstairs is an effort that occupies my thoughts for most of the duration.

When Ryland suddenly appears in the doorway, face a morbid mask of simmering hostility, Aurelia and I both slowly rise from our seats to face him. His entire body is locked, jaw clenched, but his eyes are no longer glowing. Which means the threat has been dealt with.

"Is he…" Aurelia begins carefully.

"Dead," Ryland confirms, voice lethally quiet.

I shiver, knowing how long it took Ryland to kill him, how much he prolonged it. I knew he would make the end for whomever poisoned me a painful one, but I'd never imagined something so drawn out.

"The body's been disposed of."

He left? How did I not hear him exit and re-enter the house?

"It will only serve to raise his ire," Aurelia warns, both reluctant and resigned. I presume this is the "he" the attacker had mentioned.

"I know what my message will do." Ryland's voice is cold as ice. In his left hand, he grasps the intruder's unusual iron cuffs. I'm not sure why Ryland would've wanted to keep them, but even Aurelia's gaze drifts to them with a palpable disgust.

When Rylands meets my stare, I can see the faint glow in his eyes flickering back to life along with the depth of his violence, still churning like a tempest. The weight of that gaze is too much for me to handle. All of this is too much.

I break his stare only to shake my head in confusion. "I don't understand what just happened. Any of it. But I know that this is all wrong, that this isn't normal." I swallow back the lump in my throat, trying to keep my voice steady even though it shakes despite my efforts. "I need you to explain to me what's going on."

Silence greets me for several agonizing moments.

"Ryland, she's seen so much now," Aurelia implores. "She deserves to know all of it. It's pointless trying to hide it any longer."

Ryland lets out a heavy breath before taking a step toward me, face etched in remorse.

"Perhaps you should sit down," Aurelia offers, gesturing to the settee. But I can't. My body is too tense, chest full of knots. I've waited for these answers for so long that I can hardly believe I'm about to hear them. My entire frame goes very, very still, and I scarcely breathe, fearful that any sudden shift might have Ryland change his mind. His eyes evoke reluctance, and in the blue depths, I can see the soft glimmer of fear.

Finally, he begins to speak, voice low and hoarse. "You're right. I'm not normal, and I haven't been for a very long time."

He's trying to preface me, to ease me into the harsh reality, the complex and tangled web that is Ryland Stornvahl. But it does little to prepare me for the next words that leave his lips.

"I'm immortal."

My heart stops beating. For an immeasurable amount of time, everything within me just…ceases.

Any illusion of ignorance, any semblance of naivety shatters irrevocably. I can feel the shards of my blindness crumbling, each fragment of blissful oblivion falling from within reach. My world begins to shift from its once grounded and sane axis. I realize that I wasn't ready, that I'd never be ready for this.

Ryland continues to speak, expression morose. "I have been for over three hundred years. Since the night I was killed and brought back to life. The very night the same fate befell Aurelia."

Stunned, stupefied, blaring silence roars in my ears.

Immortal.

Immortal.

Ryland was killed. Which makes him…dead. He's not living. And he's been this way for more than three centuries.

Things slowly begin to piece themselves together, memories and facts suddenly making sense. The unnatural, flawless beauty, the abnormal strength and energy, the speeded healing, the extreme emotions—he's not human.

He never was.

I can feel my mouth part, tears burning my eyes. He's *dead*. Yet I've felt his heart beat…

My attention suddenly shifts to his mentioning of Aurelia, and I turn to face her. She returns my gaze with a grim expression. Of admittance and guilt. She's immortal too. Which explains her own glowing eyes.

All this time, I'd thought Ryland possessed all the secrets. I'd only begun to suspect that there was more to Aurelia's story but not that she too had an equally dark and intricate past.

It's been the pair of them this entire time.

"What I told you before was true. I *was* born and raised just outside the city, with my parents and younger brother. My father was the patriarch of the Stornvahl line, and we lived in the family estate that had housed generations of Stornvahls before us. Aurelia and her family were our neighbors. We grew up together."

So, there'd been some truth to their explanations before. They've truly known each other since their youth. But now, I realize just how long ago their youth was.

"Unlike most lords of Kingsmar who aim to serve the monarchy as advisors, strategists or politicians, my father was a philanthropist. But, his real passion was history, specifically the history of magic and the Sildhe. He dedicated all his spare time to it, collecting ancient texts and relics, searching for anyone who studied sorcery like him."

Ryland's expression twists, eyes shadowed as he loses himself to his haunted past. "He eventually met someone, a wealthy historian from the Southern Continent who'd made his way through Osterley trading priceless historical objects. My father was introduced to him in Kingsmar and was so enraptured by the breadth of his knowledge that he brought him to our home.

"But Raigar was no historian. He was a Sildhe—as ancient as the earth itself and infinitely more lethal."

A Sildhe.

"As soon as I saw him, I knew there was something wrong, but my father wouldn't listen. Completely blind to the Sildhe's duplicity, my father showed him his trove of relics, wanting to make a deal. But Raigar didn't come to trade. He'd come with one sole intent: to collect an object my father had no idea he possessed. A Drith Stone."

The Drith Stones. I remember Ryland mentioning them in the story the other night. A weapon with which the gods provided the mortals to create a balance of power. To ensure there was a method to impair the magic of their half-breed children.

"For centuries, it had been Raigar's mission to destroy the stones, ensuring there were none left to threaten the Sildhe. My father had no knowledge of the true nature of the stone in his collection. He'd bought it at an auction in Kingsmar where it was said to be a rare stone used in healing rituals found on the banks of the Breyr River. As soon as Raigar laid eyes on it, he unveiled his true form. I'd never seen anything like it. It was real magic, the kind you heard of only in stories and legends. That's when I realized just how dangerous he was.

"I'd sent my brother to go hide in the cellar—"

Aurelia cuts in, drawing my attention. I'd almost forgotten she was here. "She should know my part in this too." Ryland's silence is her cue to proceed. Aurelia holds my gaze, those amber eyes suddenly so dull and lifeless. "Unlike Ryland's, my family wasn't very kind. My mother spent all her time instructing me on how to be the most eligible lady in society, trying to marry me off to the wealthiest bidder. I often spent my time at Ryland's home with him and his brother, hiding from her.

"And my father, he wasn't a good man. He was selfish and cared very little for his family. He'd lock himself in his study counting his gold and jewels for days on end, neglecting his wife and only child. But, when he'd heard that Ryland's father was bringing a wealthy tradesman to his home, that brought him out of his hole.

"He'd made me and my mother go with him that night, wanting to present a beautiful, successful family in the hopes of also making a favorable trade. Even my mother was hoping to make a deal, practically peddling me to the mysterious, wealthy visitor. We'd joined everyone in his father's collection room…" Her voice trails off, eyes glassy with tears as she looks to Ryland, waiting for him to continue.

"We were like lambs for slaughter. Raigar took the stone and anything else he deemed useful. Then, he killed my father right in front of us. Used his power to smash one of the relics against his head. He died instantly. The rest of us all tried to flee, but Raigar killed Aurelia's father at the entrance, severing his head with a snap of his fingers. Then, my mother…" Ryland doesn't dare describe her demise, and I'm certain that I don't wish him to.

"The three of us managed to make it outside. I was trying to help Aurelia and her mother escape before going back for my brother. I wanted to lure the Sildhe out of the house, but we were hardly able to see in the dark, and we couldn't run fast enough. He'd suddenly appeared, blocking our path… smiling. He held Aurelia and I frozen in place while he made us watch as he ripped out her mother's heart. Then he…" He hesitates for the first time and, in my periphery, I catch Aurelia giving him a nod of grim encouragement.

"He suffocated Aurelia to death." My gasp is the only sound in the momentary silence. "I watched her die next to me." The devastation on his face looks as fresh as it was from the night he's describing. "I tried to fight him. Every time he knocked me down, I'd manage to get back up again. But, he'd just look at me laugh...

"I don't remember much after that. I think he slit my throat with his magic. All I can recall is lying on my stomach, blood pooling around me." The tears silently stream down my face, my mind unable to visualize such a sickening sight. Refusing to.

"I died. And then, I awoke, and everything felt different. My mind, my body. I knew something wasn't right, and I started to remember things. Raigar was gone at that point, Aurelia and her mother's corpses the only people in sight. Eventually, I turned around and watched as my house was engulfed in flames. I didn't know what had happened to me or where he was, but all I could do was run to my brother who was still inside."

Ryland's face falls, and it's the most heartbreaking thing I've ever seen.

"I was too late. Half of the house had already collapsed. Everyone that had been inside that night—my brother, the servants—were all dead. The story that Raigar spread was that a house fire killed everyone. And, for three-hundred years, no one has suspected otherwise."

My eyes flare as a dawning realization strikes. The Stornvahl family history in the genealogy book—the one in which the last family of the direct line had all died in a tragic fire—that was Ryland and his family. While the records were accurate in that the house had burned, it's missing a crucial detail: the family had been dead well before any flames were alight.

Aurelia really had tried help me when she shared Ryland's surname. All the information I needed had been right in front of me. It's a strange coincidence that we both lost our homes to a fire. Ryland said that he understood what it's like to lose everything, to have it taken from you. I realize now just how much he'd truly meant that. Literally and figuratively. His home was burned to nothing but cinders and ashes, his family mercilessly killed in front of him. We both had to watch it happen, knowing our loved ones were inside and that there was nothing we could do. We both suffered that crushing weight of helplessness.

The understanding splinters something in my chest. Even then, having barely known each other, we'd bonded in an acute and undefinable way. And I hadn't even known it.

Ryland shakes his head bitterly. "I'd held on to the hope that my brother might have survived if he'd been underground, but he never made it to the cellar. Aurelia eventually found me, the only other person to have woken, and we grieved together. We had no idea what had become of us, but we didn't care. We buried her mother and the other bodies. At some point, we'd fallen asleep, and when we woke, we found ourselves captive in a fortress in the woods somewhere with Raigar standing over us. He explained what we were, how he'd brought us back to life, why he'd done it. He'd seen potential in us, that we could prove useful to him. He'd created a new race, and we were just new members to his growing ranks.

"For three months, we were trapped with him. Until, one day, Raigar left and took me with him, leaving Aurelia behind. Having seen less potential in her use for his plans, he decided to let her go, and she was free to leave, a very rare act of mercy from him. Raigar kept me for a year, bound me to him with his magic and forcing me to do his dirty work. Over time, I met more of his creations like Reaver, many of whom were used like myself for missions or tasks.

"One day, I managed to escape, and thus began our game of cat and mouse. Raigar and I have been playing it all these decades. I run, and he hunts. Has his slaves seek me out. He only ever looks for me when he requires my services. Otherwise, he allows me to live my life. That is, with his shadow chasing after me, forever keeping me on a string. He enjoys offering the illusion of freedom. I've only ever been re-captured four times, and each time he kept me trapped in his fortress for months." Ryland's gaze clears a little, sharpening with focus.

"It's been a little over a decade since I saw him last. But he's demanding my return again."

It takes me a moment to complete the calculation, but I eventually sort it out. I was only a small child the last time he saw the Sildhe. Ryland was the same man that he is now. I manage to swallow back some of my abhorrence.

"I ignored his messages, which is why he sent those men we encountered in Lyrewood and why he sent Reaver. They're all to ensure I return to him. Your poisoning was just an added attempt to remove any distractions that would keep me away."

My mind spins. It reminds me of the circles we danced in when Ryland and I joined the dancers in the street that night. His story swirls around in an endless loop, the information a torrent of overwhelming madness. How could one person process all of this? How am I expected to take it all in?

My heart pounds against my chest, beating so fast I wonder if it'll burn out. It's all just too much to accept. Despite the occasional oddity I noticed, Ryland seemed so relatively normal. Yet, all this time, he's carried this kind of past. It feels as if I've known an entirely different person from the one he's just described. And that's because I didn't know him. I didn't know the real Ryland. I knew the charming assassin who kept his secrets like a pirate does his treasure. There were signs, warnings that there was something darker within, but they weren't clear enough to help me realize the extent of his truths. I never could've imagined the depth of his past. Accepting his lethal lifestyle was already challenging enough, but this...

"Wren?"

The sound of my name on his lips brings me back to the present. My glassy eyes meet his, and the honesty and sorrow on his face is too much for me to bear.

"You're...dead?" The words are barely a whisper, a broken question of desperation. It's certainly low in the rank of important questions I should be asking, but it's what escapes first.

The pain in his face is answer enough. I can feel the new round of tears in my eyes spilling over and no doubt he can see them.

"I-I'm so sorry, for both of you. I..." I lose my voice, stomach fighting a wave of nausea. Ryland takes a step toward me, and I reflexively inch back. He raises his hands, palms outward, but I shake my head. I need a minute to process this. Knowing whatever else I say will be as inadequate as the pitiful apology I just gave, I decide it's best for me to remove myself from the room.

Without another word, I flee up the stairs in a desperate search for air. I take another flight of stairs and another until I reach the rooftop. Shutting the door behind me, I let the exposure of the elements rush through me. The crisp, damp air, the pattering of the rain, the comforting darkness of night.

The ledge above the rooftop door shields me from the rain, only a light mist washing over my skin. But I relish the refreshing sensation, helping cool my overheated body. After a few minutes pass, I find that I'm no calmer than I was before. My head aches and my heart weeps, recalling every detail of Ryland's story.

I cringe as I hear the door creak open. I'm not ready to face him, to face the countless truths he told. Truths *I* asked for.

Footsteps stop just behind me, his dark shadow looming. "I've felt your heart beat," I whisper helplessly. Whether the words are spoken to him or myself, I'm not quite sure.

"I'm not mortal like you, but I *am* living in a sense." His soft tone carries over the drumming of the rain.

"You can never die?"

"No, I can die. By very few methods, but I can," he answers.

"And, you were killed," I murmur, the thought causing my chest to tighten in a noose-like hold.

"I was," he replies solemnly.

And now he's immortal. Frozen in time. "So, w-what are you then?"

"Even I'm not quite sure. But Raigar calls us the Astarith—the unending. We're certainly not as powerful as the Sildhe, we've no magic. But we're immortal, with unnatural strength and abilities. The glowing eyes are our biggest giveaway."

A million more questions course through my mind, but I fear I'm in no state to process the answers. The hurt is still too strong. I whirl around to face him. "And you've known, all this time, you knew you'd live forever, and yet…all the things you said to me?" The pain in my voice is a mirror of the pain on my face.

"Wren," he begins, voice strained.

"Why bring me? Why bother with me at all? What was the point?"

He takes another step until my neck has to crane to look at him. "I lost everything that night. My home, my family, myself. All control, all power, was in his hands and has been ever since. I had absolutely nothing. So, whenever I was able to escape, I was desperate for those two things. I'd trained to become an assassin because it helped me channel my rage, gave me skills and a purpose. Gave me a semblance of power where I didn't feel so helpless. It helped me release a fraction of my rage and vengeance. I'd thought it was enough to sustain me." His jaw flexes. "But, as the decades went by, I wasn't fulfilled. So I gave myself into the chase with Raigar. The hunt, it gave me a distraction, a small way to retaliate. Even then, my existence remains a pitiful one."

His eyes bore into my own with a fierceness I can hardly manage to behold, the world around us a hazy blur of smudged and shiny midnight. "And then I saw you that day. I'll never forget the moment I laid eyes on you. It was like I'd been struck in my chest. You were burdened by so much hardship and pain, but you weren't broken." A soft smile graces his lips. "You were made of iron strength and, beneath it, full of so much light. I'd never seen anything more beautiful. And you were walking to your death.

"I knew I was going to save you, that part was easy. It was trying to figure out a way for you to stay with me after that I was worried about. But you did..." The last words are laced with quiet awe. "Eternity had become so dull, and suddenly, every day felt like a gift again. I awoke feeling no longer weighed by my burdens but excited for each new day, excited to spend them with you. Every moment in your presence, every second you are with me, I feel full, more fulfilled than I've ever been in my entire life. I've begun to forget my pain and started to *desire* a future. I realize that I've found my true purpose."

I shake my head, the words building such hope in my heart, only to have reality smash it apart like a hammer to glass. "But, you'll live forever. We could never—"

Ryland takes the sides of my face in both his large, warm hands. "*Nothing* is going to keep me from you. I told you before that the only person who could separate us would be you, and I meant every word. Even then, I'm not sure I could stay away. Wherever you go, I will follow. I am bound to you, Wrenley. My life is yours. And, when your last day comes, we will greet the gods together."

I don't even want to begin dissecting the terror those words instill within me. I can't fathom a day where Ryland might not exist, a world without his infectious smiles and teasing voice.

He brushes my tears away with an aching gentleness. "I realize that all that I went through, all of my suffering all these centuries, it was to lead me to this, to you. Meeting you has been like meeting my other half. I saw you and felt an instant sense of completeness. It was a little startling, to be honest. And yet, it was electrifying. Like I'd truly been a walking corpse, and your existence breathed life into me." His thumb brushes over my lips. "I love you, little thief."

The words are a spark to my weighted soul, flaring warm, brilliant light inside. But Ryland's lips pull into a frown, dimming that spark. "I don't expect you to love me back. I know I have many proclivities that would repel most. You've already been so generous with me, trusting me with your safety and welfare."

My trembling hands reach up to rest on the center of his chest over his beating heart. His eyes close at the contact as if my touch is as much a balm to him as his is to me. When his gaze returns to mine, I speak, ready to reveal my own truths.

"I hadn't thought I could suffer any more pain in my life after I'd lost everything. And yet, since we met, I've been so afraid. That you'd leave me one day. That I'd be alone again. No matter what you said, no matter the promises you made, I thought you'd disappear. And it terrified me because I'd realized that, despite how little we've known each other, how little I knew you, I was already yours. That I'm in love with you and have been. It seems no matter what you do or say, no matter how scared I am, how uncertain, my feelings for you don't change."

Ryland's eyes flare with breathtaking hope. His lips find mine, and the warmth of them seeps through my entire body. I can feel this kiss in my very soul, igniting flames so bright and pure, I feel I could light the sky.

Whatever his past, whatever his present or future, I cannot alter my feelings for him. He's branded himself so deeply within me, I can't stand the idea of being apart. I'm petrified—of all that I've learned, of what we may have to face. But, what's more terrifying and unbearable is the thought of a future without him.

I can no longer ignore that fact that there's something that feels so momentous about the day we met. Like my life had been on a certain course and, the moment our paths crossed, it completely shifted. If we were to part ways, I wouldn't really be rid of him. He'd forever remain within my mind, like an ink stain upon flesh. Permanently etched into my soul.

My arms wrap around his neck, and one of his hands slides across my back, pulling me flush against him. The surrealness, the madness, of the moment washes over me, and I let myself speak the words I've held within for so long. "I love you, Ryland." I whisper the admission against his mouth.

His arm tightens, and his lips move more fervently before he breaks away to hold my gaze. "There is more I need to tell you, more you need to understand."

I nod, because I have countless more questions to ask. But I withhold them. There will be time later for more answers. For now, I just want to enjoy him.

Foreheads pressed together, we take a breath and savor the moment. "You are the sun to my moon, and I will forever chase your light." He leans in to kiss away my tears, his tongue gently soaking up each drop before returning to my lips, worshiping them as if they alone were the god he prays to.

The murmured words are a breeze that fans the flames ablaze in my heart.

Ryland is like the moon, cold and isolated, surrounded by darkness. Trapped within its confines, he tries to pursue the light and find a better fate but is never able to outrun his shadows.

It's in this moment that I make a vow to myself. As long as I am with him, I will do anything in my power to chase those shadows away. If I am his sun, then I will cast my light on him, always and forever.

AN IMMEASURABLE AMOUNT OF TIME PASSES, BUT Ryland eventually leads us back inside. As we make our way down the stairs, I ask, "Will we be safe here tonight?"

He nods as he pulls us back into the drawing room. "For tonight."

As we step through the doorway, Aurelia's gaze instantly locks on our entwined hands. She rises from her seat, expression hopeful. "Are you two..." she begins, waiting for a response. Ryland reveals a not-so-subtle smirk before offering a nod.

Aurelia releases a giddy squeal before scurrying toward me, pulling me in a cheerful embrace. "Finally! Oh, I'm so thrilled for you both!"

I guess she knew *exactly* how Ryland felt all this time. Somehow, my appreciation for her is greater than ever. That she'd refrained from saying anything, allowing me to come to a decision on my own without any influence. How she tried to help me piece together some of his mysteries so I wouldn't fall for a lie, all while not explicitly sharing his secrets and defying his trust. She was a true friend, to us both.

She pulls back, grinning brilliantly. "He may be an arrogant prick, but you won't find a better man. And I know your happiness means everything to him."

My eyes moisten a bit, touched by her words. "You knew?" I ask, wanting to hear it confirmed.

"He's like a brother to me. Of course I know when he's utterly besotted. I knew it from the moment you both arrived. Besides, it's not as if he tried to hide it," she says with a knowing look pointed at Ryland.

The male gives an unabashed grin. "An impossible feat."

A flush of embarrassment hits. I suppose I was a tad oblivious. Looking back, Ryland made his advances fairly clear. I was just too afraid to trust his words when I knew so little. But knowing everything now, it's like the wall I'd erected between us has been torn down, the bond burning bright now that there are no barriers.

I give Aurelia a grateful smile which she returns. "It's a relief that you know everything now. We can discuss things openly from now on." I nod in agreement.

"With that said, I think we all should continue our conversation. I'm sure Wren still has much to ask," Ryland suggests.

"I'll go make us some tea. It's going to be a long night." Aurelia dashes away as Ryland and I take a seat on the settee. I let out a breath, trying to still my racing mind. Aurelia's right. It's going to be a *very* long night.

I can feel the gaze of the immortal with silky blonde hair and deep blue eyes trained on me, and I turn to meet his stare. He watches me with such sincere intent and tenderness, I find myself unable to move for several moments. He lifts a hand to trace his fingers across my jaw, the touch featherlight.

Looking into Ryland's flawless face, the unnatural beauty of it...I recognize how inhuman he truly is. That he's always looked that way. But it's hard to fathom just how old he is. How long he's lived. How fleeting my lifespan must seem in comparison. How much knowledge he's acquired, how much of the world he's seen, all the things he's done. And despite all that he's experienced, those years were tainted with suffering. To have lived for centuries running and hiding, constantly looking over his shoulder, that isn't living at all. That is to endure.

Gentle fingers tuck the strands of hair behind my ear before they travel to my throat, brushing across the skin carefully, gaze sharpening with menace. I realize what he's staring at—bruises from Reaver's brutal hold when he'd choked me. I can only hope that they'll fade along with the entire memory of his attack.

"I'm never letting you go now," he says softly. I lean in to rest my brow against his chest, the steady rhythm of his heart soothing. After a moment, he cups the side of my face, lifting it to meet his gaze. The cool bite of his rings seeps into my skin. "You understand that?" His voice is deadly serious. As if I don't truly understand the gravity of his statement. And perhaps he's right. The depth in his eyes—he's warning me. That he doesn't intend to ever leave me, and that if I don't want that to be the case, I need to say so now. Otherwise, there's no going back.

I nod slowly, understanding every implication. I want all of him, immortal, tragic past and all. *Is it brash and likely naive?*

Yes. But, right now, the thought of not being with Ryland is too impossible to fathom.

His fingers tighten their hold on my face as he presses his lips to mine, sealing my decision. Heat pools in my belly, but he breaks away as we hear Aurelia's soft footsteps before she re-enters the room, tea tray in hand.

Time for my interrogation. "So," I begin, "the man tonight was another…Astarith? Am I saying that correctly?"

Aurelia nods as she seats herself across from us, pouring everyone a steaming cup of tea. Mercifully, it isn't that herbal concoction. She grimaces with a nod. "His name is—*was* Reaver. He was one of Raigar's more dispensable pawns, tasked with hunting Ryland over the years. He was always a demented brute." Ryland's expression remains hard as stone.

"And how did he find you? How did the other men from Lyrewood?"

Ryland sighs. "Some decades ago, I'd come here to pay Aurelia a visit, as I always do every few years. During my stay, I went to a certain oddities shop owned by an even odder fellow," Ryland explains with a pointed look in my direction.

"Mr. Maleck's shop," I realize to which he nods. It all makes sense now. The quirky old man had seemed to know Ryland, recognized him but had said that it'd been many years ago. Decades apparently.

"It was there that I found a specific object within his horde, one that proved extremely useful. A veiling ring." He lifts his right hand, pointing to a familiar ring on his middle finger. The same one he'd been staring at that day in Lyrewood, the one with the amber stone. This all explains why Ryland knew so much of the Sildhe history and the Sethel, why he can speak and understand Talaar. How he knew of the markings in the tunnels of Atherton during our escape.

"Like the Drith Stones, they're extremely rare. They were used during the Sildhe Wars for mortal spies. Whoever wears one is able to go undetected by a Sildhe's preternatural senses.

As long as they're not within visual proximity to the Sildhe, their presence will remain unknown, no matter where they are in the world. It's how I was able to prolong the hunt, why I remained out of Raigar's reach for such an extended period. But, to ensure he didn't know the ring was in my possession, I'd stashed it someplace safe and paid him a brief visit about ten years ago. Raigar would destroy the ring if he knew I had one. It was never a solution to ending my servitude, but it has at least delayed my returns."

His brow knits in vexation. "But something seems to be wrong with it, a malfunction of sorts. His men found us in Lyrewood, then Reaver. It's part of the reason I went to visit Errol the other day. I wanted to ask him if the power in these rings can diminish overtime. Apparently, it's possible." That explains then why all these servants of Raigar keep finding Ryland so easily. "And now that Reaver's dead, Raigar will soon find out."

"And send others," Aurelia adds gravely.

"What does he do with you, when he calls you back?" I ask.

Ryland shrugs as he sits back. "Capture and confine me. Send me out on missions to imprison others, steal items, kill people. He likes to own his creations," he mutters off-handedly. "But, I'm not sure why he wants me so urgently this time. I believe he's planning something. I just don't know what it is. He's never fully revealed his schemes to me, only alluded that I've a part to play in them."

The casualness of his tone does nothing to deter the panic from settling inside me. "But why *you*?"

"Raigar...particularly enjoys my suffering. Anything that causes me pain delights him."

"He's a sadist," Aurelia spits.

"He enjoys our game. I'm a challenge for him. Where his other servants are willing and obedient, appreciative of their immortal nature, I challenge his authority. In his sick, twisted way, he thinks we have some sort of bond," Ryland finishes with a bitter edge.

"So why doesn't he ever collect you himself? Wouldn't it be easier for him with all his power?"

"Yes, but Raigar is like any pretentious leader—indolent and vain. He doesn't often partake in his own errands, not when he has others to do them for him. Besides, he can't come now given that we're shielded by the Sethel." *Right, because we're in Kingsmar.* I wonder if that had been Ryland's plan all along, his reasoning for selecting Kingsmar as our destination.

I look to Aurelia in realization. "And that's why you stay here."

She nods, tracing the rim of her teacup with a slender finger. "I rarely leave. I just feel…safer staying within the borders." I can hardly blame her.

"But, if you're also immortal and rarely leave here, how has anyone not said anything about you?"

Her lips pull into a guilty smile. "They have, but it's sort of become an unspoken acceptance. Since I've made myself such a generous benefactor to the city, the community…lets it slide. I ensured I became an invaluable asset when I decided to stay. They know I mean them no harm."

I nod before returning my attention to Ryland. "So, you're only choice is to hide and run?"

"Not exactly," he begins cautiously. "There might be a way to deal with him."

"The Drith Stones?"

His face instantly hardens as he shakes his head. "Raigar destroyed all of them. The last stone was the one my father possessed."

My heart aches for Ryland as I try to fathom that sort of pain and frustration. His father having unknowingly possessed the one item that could've killed the person that ruined his life. That same item which Raigar took and destroyed himself. But Ryland said he may know of another option, and my chest sparks with hope. Eyes widening, awaiting his explanation, Ryland frowns. "I'm afraid this too I cannot share. With Raigar, I want you to know as little as possible. Already just knowing of his existence is dangerous enough."

Aurelia nods in agreement. "He's right, this time, Wren. It's safer if you're unaware." My skin chills, imagining just how lethal this Sildhe is let alone the fact that they even exist at all.

Ryland rests a hand atop mine which are clasped in my lap. "But I want to be able to help," I implore.

The meaningful look on his face warms my skin. "For now, this is all I can share."

Once again, Ryland's asking me to trust him. Given my reservations, I should hesitate. But my guard falls far too easily when it comes to him. I trust Ryland and have done so for longer than I'd care to admit. I may not know him well still, may not have known him long enough, but I've always felt safe with him. He's finally revealed his secrets, and I can't exactly be angry at him for not sharing all this with me before. They weren't just his secrets alone.

"In order for me to see if my theory is viable, we need to remain in the city," Ryland adds.

Aurelia's lips tug downward. "But staying here is no longer an option. He'll send more Astarith. And as happy as I am to host you, people will start noticing violent outbursts in a residential street."

Ryland nods in agreement. If Raigar and his men have found us here, more will follow, and I don't wish to risk Aurelia's safety. It wouldn't be fair to her, and I know Ryland feels the same.

"I could ask some of my friends to host you," she offers.

Ryland shakes his head as he reaches for my teacup, proceeding to add a spoonful of honey to it. "Still easy for him to locate us with my ring not working properly. I don't want to endanger innocents like that. Besides, I already know where we're going to go."

Aurelia and I watch him with furrowed looks as he swirls the small spoon in my cup back and forth. If I didn't know better, I'd say he's enjoying our puzzlement, the dramatic silence he's left us with hanging in the air. How he's able to shift to scheming so quickly while I'm still processing the singular bit of information that the two of them will live forever is vexing to say the least.

"The Assassin's Guild."

"*The Guild*?" Aurelia asks dubiously.

"My old home," Ryland sighs fondly. I recall him mentioning that was where he'd trained. "I still know many of the members well. They'll let us stay. What place is safer than a fortress filled with dozens of the best trained killers?" The diabolical smile that splits his lips is a sharp contrast to the delicate china in his hand as he pours milk into my tea.

"But, would they welcome me?" I'm certainly no assassin, and I highly doubt they'll let just *anyone* into their society. And, it's not as though Ryland could simply smuggle me in.

He passes me my cup, and I take a sip, surprised to find it's made just to my liking. I'm not sure how he learned how I like my tea, but it warms my insides to know that he does.

"There's a way for you to join me, which we'll discuss later. Besides, if I tell them I'll be continuing your training there, they might warm to the idea of having you around." Suffusing the urge to laugh at the word "training" given that I'm essentially hopeless in terms of combat, I nod, still unsure of this plan.

"It'll be a different environment though, not Aurelia's level of fussing. I mean, most of the members are extremely wealthy from their work and possess a taste for finer things, but they're killers at their core. They're nasty when they wish to be, so we'll have to fend for ourselves," he explains.

I give him a knowing look. "I'm quite used to that." His expression softens in understanding.

"Are you sure, Ryland? Surrounded by all those manipulative, savage killers?" Aurelia questions.

"You and I both know that some of them happen to be the most refined people in this city," he replies. "It's not ideal, but it's one of the safest options for us. If anyone attacks us, every single member will be on high alert. In this case, we'll have strength in numbers. And it's just while I wait to receive my answers."

Aurelia nods reluctantly. "I'll organize a messenger to provide contact between us while you're there."

"Good. The Guild will offer resources and connections, but I still might need some of yours."

"So, the public is aware of the Guild's existence? It's not operating under some sort of front?" I interject confusedly.

"*Aware?*" Ryland snorts. "Half of its funded by the palace. Who do you think hires us? The Guild only accepts the best, and only the wealthy and elite can afford us. The Crown occasionally needs a discrete way to tie up loose ends or remove any ill-favored adversaries. Politics can be cutthroat in more ways than one. They'd rather have it out in the open where they can keep a close eye on its operations as opposed to it being under cloak and dagger." I roll my eyes at his jest, allowing this new information to sink in.

A guild of assassins that everyone is aware of... A home full of the most lethal and ruthless people who have no moral compass, no mercy and no weaknesses. And Ryland lived there at one point, trained with them. It was a home to him.

"But, you were trained centuries ago. How do you still know the people there? Are some of them like you?" I enquire, wondering if I'll be meeting more immortals.

"No, those I trained with have long since died. But I return there every so often to reestablish myself within the Guild. It's always good to have a place to stay, to have contacts."

So, this is where we're headed. I'll have to prepare myself mentally for this. If I felt out of place coming to Kingsmar, then I can only imagine how isolating it will be to live in a community of trained killers.

"When will you leave? Today?" Aurelia asks.

Ryland looks to me for a moment, gaze thoughtful in consideration. Calculation. "Tomorrow morning. We'll be fine to stay one more night." A wave of relief washes over me. At least I'll have a little more time to prepare myself.

"So, that's your plan then?" Aurelia confirms.

"For now, that's our plan," Ryland replies with enough confidence that I settle in my seat a little more. He takes a sip of his tea, and Aurelia and I watch him, both amazed by his unaffectedness. We lock gazes, sharing a look of bewilderment before regarding once again the male in front of us. While Ryland and Aurelia are the same species, it's clear that he's another breed entirely.

Chapter 19

We spent the rest of the night—or early morning—going over various matters such as transportation and packing. The discussion shifted to Aurelia and Ryland reviewing some finer details as I'd begun to slump in the settee, fatigue settling over me like a blanket. I hadn't meant to fall asleep, but after I'd laid myself down, head resting on Ryland's lap as he stroked my hair, it was a losing battle.

When I woke at sunrise, we all ate a quick breakfast before Aurelia towed me upstairs while Ryland left to run an errand. She helped me pack a few "essentials" as she'd called them—spare nightdresses and undergarments, samples of hair oils and lotions—as she'd insisted they wouldn't have such things there. She recommended bringing only a few pieces of clothing given that they'd have their own dress code I'd have to follow.

I'd bathed and dressed myself in a simple silk dress of midnight blue before Ryland returned home long after, requesting my presence in the library. I figured it must be about the method with which I'll be able to enter the Guild, so, for once, I'm not riddled with uncertainty as I step into the room. Ryland elects to stand, and I do the same, waiting for him to explain.

His expression is set in an unreadable mask, and my body tightens in anticipation. "Once we depart tomorrow," he begins warily, "...things will be different. You see, there's a stipulation for us to be able to stay at the Guild, and we'll need to have met it before tomorrow, and I fear it might...startle you," he warns, fumbling with his words. *A rare occurrence.* In fact, I've never seen Ryland so hesitant before. His speech and manner are always nothing short of confident and charming.

Anxiously, I wait for him to continue, and he levels me with those steely blue eyes. "Will you marry me, Wren?"

I'm not sure how many times this male has stunned me to silence, but I'd say he's reached an overwhelming number at this point. All I hear is the slow, methodic ticking of the clock on the wall and my hammering pulse.

So, the Guild will only let me in if I'm married to Ryland. Spouses must be the only outsiders allowed entry.

I'm not sure how long it takes me to find use of my mouth again. "But...there's no need for you to do that," I murmur, trying to think quickly. "I can just stay here with Aurelia and—"

"I'm not letting you out of my sight." His jaw sets, eyes ablaze with wrath. "Though I loathe myself for being responsible, you've now become a target too."

"But—" I chew on my lip, debating how to phrase this. My stomach churns, hating that he's being forced into asking me this, all because he feels the need to bring me along with him. Admitting my feelings for Ryland was one thing, accepting his love, another. But to have him bind himself to me like this so soon...we've not even known each other a month.

"I...I don't think you want to do that."

He rears back as if I've just slapped him. "Why not?"

"Because..." My lips, the traitorous things, begin to tremble. "This isn't a decision you should be forced into."

"Forced?" His brow quirks. "Wren, how else can I express that I *want* this?" Ryland shakes his head, searching for a new tactic. "Perhaps I've done a poor job conveying my feelings, so allow me to elaborate." Those blue eyes glimmer like starlight. "I want this so much, it's made me selfish. I could've taken you to any other town or village, set you up in a nice home, let you fashion yourself a better life. But I didn't do that. I brought you with me, risked your safety with my past and line of work just so I could have you near...because I couldn't stand the idea of letting you go. Not when I'd only had a taste of you. You've given me all whereas I've done nothing but endanger you and risk your life."

He's wrong. So wrong. My life was already at risk since the day he met me. Without him, I wouldn't *be* here. Only knowing Ryland a few weeks, I nearly went mad after he'd left for a day. That's how deeply he's embedded himself within me. His claws are hooked that tightly around my heart. "Those instances weren't your fault," I argue.

He laughs humorlessly. "But they were. Because of me, they happened to you. Don't paint me a hero, little thief. More than anything, I want to deserve you. To be worthy of you. And, I've tried. But, in the end, I've been the source of much of your fear and pain." Another bitter shake of his head. "And yet, I still can't seem to let you go. No matter how much I know you deserve better, I cannot forsake you, cannot bring myself to do the right thing. I don't think I physically can.

"If you will let me be selfish, if you let me have you, I will offer everything I am to you, Wren." He moves to kneel before me, taking my hands in his. "You have given me a purpose to exist. What I give you in return is my sword and unyielding devotion."

Still hesitant, I stare down at his glorious face. *It's too early.* This question should come after months and months of courting, a natural progression of our feelings. Not because some establishment demands it. Somehow sensing the train of my thoughts, Ryland's face suddenly relaxes, and he gives me a rueful smile, as if I don't understand a thing. "Wren, this isn't just for the Guild. You don't know how long I've been alone, what it's like to have you now. How desperate I am for you, and have been, since I first laid eyes on you." A small smile breaks across his lips. "I'm actually a little surprised by my self-restraint. Whether it's in the name of marriage or not, I'm already bonded to you."

My glassy eyes shift, looking anywhere but his beautiful face as I contemplate, gauging his words.

"Wren, look at me." The calm demand in his tone has me complying. "I need you to listen to me very carefully," he says slowly. "I don't want to waste another single moment pretending that you aren't wholly mine. I *want* you to marry me, Wrenley Hawthe. I'm *asking* you." His eyes twinkle with that mischievous, devastating beauty. "I warned you this morning that I'm never letting you go," he says, a sly smile pulling at his lips. "You had to realize that nothing is going to throw me off."

I huff a short laugh, a small smile forming on my face. Ryland cups my cheek, a tender look in his gaze. "Will you marry me tonight?"

Despite any lingering doubts, Ryland's conviction convinces me enough to dip my head.

One second, he's still kneeling, the next, he's hauling me in his arms and spinning us around, burying his face in my neck and hair. He breaks away to kiss me firmly once before grinning brilliantly as though I've just given him the sun and moon. I smile in return, shaking my head. "Aurelia's right, you're too persuasive for your own good."

A smirk tugs at that beautiful mouth. "And I didn't even have to resort to any of my persuasive tactics." He strokes his thumb across my bottom lip, hinting at what those tactics may entail. "Perhaps I'll use some of them tonight."

My heart stutters.

Tonight. I hadn't really thought of it. I mean, I've thought several times of being with Ryland in that way. But, given that he's only just now proposed, I hadn't thought of *tonight*. Somehow, it doesn't quite scare me like I thought it would. I dip my head, face blushing as I whisper, "Perhaps I'll let you."

Stealing a glance beneath my lashes, I find his expression surprised but pleased. "We should inform Aurelia, she'll help us make the arrangements." Sensing my imminent questions, he explains, "We'll go to the church tonight to swear our vows and sign a document." His expression dampens, the light in his eyes fading. "I'd like to give you something far grander, but it's only because we have so little time. But I promise that one da—"

I press a finger to his lips. "I prefer something quiet."

Ryland's face softens before he presses his brow to mine. "You can't possibly imagine how long I've waited for you."

I smile softly, lost in the depths of his eyes, his words offering a new perspective. He's right. I truly can't imagine how long he's waited to find someone. No wonder he's been so committed so quickly, never hesitated. He's waited *centuries*. I have no desire to stand in his way. If this makes him happy, makes him smile like he is right now, then I'll do anything.

He kisses me gently before he faces the doorway, an expectant look on his face. "You're not as stealthy as you think. Just join us," he calls out.

I throw him a puzzled look before Aurelia comes trudging inside with a scowl. "You know I'm just as stealthy as you," she grumbles, and I stifle a giggle as she rarely sounds so disgruntled.

Ryland glances at me and lifts his brows tauntingly as if to say: *Watch this*.

"I hope this isn't how you plan to treat me for the rest of the day since I'm giving you a wedding to attend this evening."

We both watch Aurelia as her eyes double in size. "*A wedding?*" Her voice is so high pitched, she sounds like a squeaking mouse. "Tonight?"

We both nod before Ryland explains the Guild's policy. Her shrill squeal echoes in the small library. "Leave it all to me. I'll arrange the carriages, and I know the church we'll go to. When do we need to leave?"

"In an hour."

"Then we can't waste a single minute," Aurelia says before promptly taking my hand and pulling me toward the door.

Glancing over my shoulder to Ryland, he offers me a comforting smile before saying, "I have to run another errand. I won't be long."

Aurelia stops us at the door so we can face him. "You'd better be back in time to clean yourself up," she urges with a stern look. "And don't even think about interrupting us."

Ryland raises his hands placatingly. "Wouldn't dream of it." He can't seem to stop grinning, his white teeth shining brightly. It's the last glimpse of him I get before Aurelia tugs me into the hall and up the stairs to turn me into a bride.

CHAPTER 20

DESPITE THE WHIRLWIND OF EVENTS THAT TRANSpired within the span of less than forty-height hours, it's not lost on me that this is my last evening in this townhouse. That I'll soon be parted from the comforts of Aurelia's home. It isn't necessarily the luxurious furnishings and fine clothing that I mourn. Rather it's the essence of home and a place of belonging that I'll miss most. The intimate dinners, the cozy evenings spent in the library reading books, waking in my warm bed to the sun's first rays. And, of course, Aurelia herself. After all, this house *is* Aurelia.

She made herself rather easy to love, and I'm already lamenting her absence. I've never had a sibling or a bestfriend, and I've come to think of her as something between the two. A confidante and an ally.

Aurelia's mood seems to match mine as she rhythmically brushes out the long tresses of my hair. "I'm so relieved that he told you everything," she admits, glancing at me in the mirror of my bedroom vanity. Her amber eyes are radiant, offset by the powdery blue shade of her dress. "It's nice to have someone know the truth for once. It wasn't fair having to lie to you."

"But I understand why you did. It wasn't fully your secret to tell."

Her lips pull downward as her gaze casts away. "We're sorry to have put you in any danger."

"What you both forget is that my life had been about to end when I first met Ryland. Every day since has been a gift. A second chance. I'd take the risk of other dangers over the executioner's sword to my neck any day." Though I can still sense her guilt, she relents with a nod. "Is that why you choose not to be with anyone, because it would risk their safety?"

Aurelia pauses her ministrations, lost in thought. "Not exactly. I haven't seen Raigar in centuries and don't ever plan to. It's more about my immortality. I'll live forever whereas they would just…" A cringe mars her features as she realizes that such a predicament is one I currently face. Me growing old and frail while Ryland remains eternally young. Me walking to my grave while he walks into forever. The thought still sickens stomach, but it's a problem I'm trying to put off for another day. Right now, we need to focus on the challenges that are directly ahead of us. I can worry about my impending aging and Ryland's horrifying threat of ending his life with mine another time.

Regardless, I can easily sympathize with Aurelia's rationale. She couldn't stand to fall in love with someone only to watch them wither away. So, she chooses to live and love alone.

Attempting to change subjects, I stray to a different topic of curiosity. I have limited time with Aurelia now, so I want to make the most of it. "Ryland and you said that he had a younger brother…"

Aurelia nods, face lighting with both fondness and sorrow. "Maxim." The weight that single name carries tells me that I've hit another sore subject and instantly regret it. "He was nine years younger than Ryland and completely idolized him." A soft smile crests her lips. "While Ryland was strong and cunning, determined and fierce like his father, Maxim was sweet and endearing. He worshiped the very ground Ryland walked on, always chasing after him, always looking up to him." The smile grows. "Then, he grew up and began to chase after me too." Her eyes glaze as memories play through her mind. "He'd pick me wild flowers and ask me to dance at every party. He even trained a messenger bird to start sending me notes. He was so gentle and kind, only seventeen." Her throat bobs. "He was…good."

My eyes glisten, feeling as though I know the young man, sensing the tender and sweet spirit he'd been. I only wish that he'd been spared, that he was still here to idolize his older brother and to chase after Aurelia.

A few tears slip down her porcelain cheeks, but she doesn't bother wiping them away. "Out of all the deaths from that night, Ryland and I mourned Maxim the most. We knew none of it had been our fault, and yet we'd taken the blame for his loss all the same. Ryland…" Her eyes go distant. "I've never seen someone grieve like he did. He-he'd tried to end himself shortly after it all happened. But the wounds began to heal straight away."

Horror swallows every thought and feeling. That Ryland would attempt something so drastic. I can't even fathom the thought, the pain that drove him to try and take his own life.

Aurelia finally wipes the dampness from her face, letting out a small, painful sigh. "Maxim would've made such a fine lord. And, I might have been his lady had he asked. He was the kindest man I've ever known."

My heart aches for both of them. Neither Ryland nor Aurelia deserve such tragic pasts, and it only makes my rage for the one who inflicted their suffering burn with molten heat.

"Oh, that reminds me," she suddenly says, setting down the hairbrush and stepping back, quickly diverging from the somber conversation. "I'll be back in a minute." Aurelia promptly disappears, allowing me a chance to gather my own emotions.

She's the only family Ryland has had all these centuries, and he can only visit her every so often, forced to flee from Raigar's men. He's never been allowed to stay, to settle with his one and only kin. Driven to endure his time alone, longing for what he's had to leave behind. Perhaps then, this marriage truly means more to him than I could ever understand. That it's more a gift than a sentencing.

Aurelia returns, extending her hand which holds a small vial and cork filled with tiny, round tablets. Some herbal blend, ground and formed into a chalky sphere. "For you to take. Once every month."

My wrinkled brow informs her that I've absolutely no idea what this stuff is for, and she gives me a knowing look. "Take one before *tonight*," she hints. "Though I'm fairly certain procreation is impossible for the Astarith, I figured you wouldn't want to take any chances, especially since you're mortal. It's never been an issue for me, but, just in case."

Oh.

Clearly, my brain is still overwhelmed. I hadn't even thought of the risk of a potential pregnancy or the fact that it might never be possible due to Ryland's immortality. But since I think I'm physically incapable of processing more upsetting news right now, I shove the thoughts aside and accept the vial, taking one of the pills with the tea that was brought up for us earlier.

"Thank you, Aurelia," I supply sincerely. "I owe you so much."

A roll of those amber eyes is followed by, "You owe me absolutely nothing—except not to always take Ryland's side over mine in any of our future battles," she adds with a humorous smile.

I share her grin. "You have my solemn promise. Actually, I was wondering if I could write to you when we're gone if we don't get to see each other? It's been nice, more than nice, to have a female friend."

"I hope that you do. We'll still be able to meet, not as frequently, but letters would be lovely. As wonderful as Ryland is, I know he can be quite a handful." She offers a sympathetic look. "I'll only be too happy to empathize with your plights."

FIVE AGONIZING MINUTES. THAT'S HOW LONG I WAS TOLD to wait when Aurelia left the carriage moments ago, departing with a bubbly grin.

The hour-long carriage ride to this mystery destination was another round of torture. All I know is that wherever we are, it's elevated within the city, the ride a slow but steady incline. But, since the windows were draped, I wasn't able to confirm my suspicions.

Taking deep, calming breaths, I continue this excruciating countdown. My stomach feels lodged in my throat, and my pulse hammers beneath my skin like a drum. Aurelia left to meet Ryland, who'd rode here separately, inside the church. Apparently, it was bad luck for him to see me before the ceremony. I doubt either Ryland or myself would care about such superstitions, especially given the hurried nature of this marriage, but Aurelia had been insistent.

When I finally reach the final few seconds, I take in one last breath before opening the carriage door and stepping down, trying to navigate amongst all the fabric.

Though I'd mentioned not requiring anything elaborate for my dress, Aurelia dutifully ignored my words and searched through my new wardrobe for the most appropriate piece, which was nothing less than extravagant.

I'm not sure how to describe the color—a unique blend of dusty lavender and silver, the fabric a silky, shimmery material that falls and sits like water on my skin. The gown itself is strapless, the sleeves connecting in a straight line across the bodice where they taper down to the floor like fluttering trains. The veil, which was a makeshift item from Aurelia, is a sheer silvery fabric with glittering stones along the trim. They shine and twinkle like starlight. Two diamond studs are nestled in my ears, tucked behind my hair which is curled into soft waves.

Turning around, I squint into the darkness as I take in my surroundings. Another grand stone edifice lies before me, this one slightly more demure compared to the main church near the palace. It's also half as big but a little more charming. The main spire holds a large clockface while the two spires aside host two sturdy bronze bells. The sandy-colored stone offers a welcoming facade, the wooden doors wreathed with vines and blooming flowers.

Like a tug from a string, I follow the pull drawing me toward those doors, knowing what awaits me inside.

Once I cross the threshold, the breath escapes my lungs in a soft gasp. The interior is even more breathtaking. The same sandy-stone lines the floors and walls, leading up toward a vaulted ceiling of beige wood, giving the space an intimate feel. There are only five rows of pews on each side.

Several yards ahead lies the altar, set in front of a beautiful gothic stained-glass window, the only window in the entire space, the main spectacle to admire. Shades of ruby red, citrine yellow and sapphire blue blur with the moonlight from outside, casting a warm, dreamy glow in the space. That, along with the several iron candelabras that stand along the main aisle. White flower displays rest on either side of the altar, perfuming the room with their sweet bloom. And, right in the center, standing tall and achingly beautiful, is Ryland.

Once my eyes lock with his, everything in me softens. All stress and nerves evaporate as if they never existed. Suddenly, this marriage doesn't seem like a last-minute plan but rather a long-awaited event.

Aurelia selected the perfect place. It's beyond my imaginings. I never thought something so sudden, so hasty, could turn out to be so perfect.

As I close the distance between us, which feels miles long, I can see Ryland's radiant, soft smile, his brilliant blue eyes, and golden hair shining in the moonlight. He's wearing my favorite color on him, a dark blue.

On his right is Aurelia, practically vibrating with giddiness as she offers me an encouraging smile. Eventually, I notice the priest standing behind Ryland, seeming far kinder to the one we'd encountered in the city church. The docile smile on his face eases any last doubts as I arrive at the altar.

Even with my heeled shoes, I have to drastically tilt my neck to hold Ryland's gaze, his lips pulling into one of his usual smirks before he murmurs softly, "My bride."

I give him a soft smile in return before the priest clears his throat and begins to recite a passage, commencing the ceremony. After a lovely sermon on the bond of marriage, the beauty and significance of it, the priest presents us with a marriage band, a long piece of creamy satin which has been stitched and embroidered with intricate patterns and designs. Once Ryland and I join hands, he proceeds to wrap the fabric around them, providing each of us with vows to recite. Every word I utter feels weighted, as if the words themselves are filled with magic.

Ryland's gaze never strays from mine, holding my eyes captive in their rich depths.

As our hands remain bound, the priest reaches for a goblet filled with wine, a small knife held in the other hand. He takes a drop of blood from a finger from each of our free hands before presenting us with the goblet. He explains how our joined hands symbolize our marriage of the flesh, and the drink, the marriage of our blood, and, by drinking it, our souls joining as one.

As Ryland takes his sip, rings glinting in the candlelight, I suddenly notice that it's only his right hand that wears them now. His left hand, which is bound with mine, is empty of all rings. Only one will be worn on it tonight.

I take the goblet from him, his fingers brushing against mine, supplying me with a wave of chills in the process. Taking a slow sip, I taste the strong wine, a hint of copper and salt dancing on my tongue and something inexplicably occult.

Once I return the goblet to the priest, he says a final prayer before unbinding our hands and requesting our rings.

I gape.

They must all think I'm the densest female on earth to not have even thought about rings for her wedding. But Ryland simply smiles down at me, clearly amused with my apparent distress as he swiftly reaches into his pocket and pulls out a silver band to fit one of his fingers.

He extends his left hand before me and, with trembling fingers, I place the ring he's given me on him, admiring the cool shade against his sun-kissed skin. Ryland reaches once more in his pocket, and I extend my own hand, mouth parting as I behold the magnificent ring.

A thin silver band that bends into a sharp V-shape beset with a narrow, oval diamond stretched into sharp points at the top and bottom ends. The diamond itself is larger than any I've ever seen on a ring, the value likely more than Aurelia's home itself. I have no earthly idea how he procured this jewel, but I'm quite certain that it cost an absolute fortune. Ryland slides the breathtaking band onto my finger, a perfect fit.

The amount of wealth that's now sitting on me steals my breath. The stone sparkles in the dim light, and I take a moment to adjust to its weight on my finger. It's stunning.

With the rings presented, the priest concludes the ceremony, and Ryland doesn't hesitate to step forward, bending down to press his lips softly to mine. It lasts only a moment before he pulls away, eyes blazing with such joy, I nearly reach for him again. He takes my hand instead, following the priest as the old man leads us to a table in the corner in which we sign our marriage contract where it will be added to the city's registry and safely stored.

After providing our thanks, Ryland leads us back down the aisle toward the doors, Aurelia following behind. Outside, she gives us each a tight embrace. "Words can't express how elated I am for the both of you."

I pull her in for another hug for so much wouldn't have been possible without her aide. She then looks to Ryland, and the two seem to share a conversation in silence, but the emotions are there all the same. "Thank you," Ryland finishes, eyes shining with love for the sister of bond not blood, the one who's stood by him all these years.

She nods, tears glimmering in her gaze before she shakes herself to clear them. "Well, I'll be heading off now."

I give her a furrowed brow, wondering why she's not going to leave with us, but she looks to Ryland. "The house is yours for the night. I've made other arrangements for myself. The staff has been sent away as well, so it'll just be the two of you."

My face heats as I register her meaning. Ryland's expression, however, remains completely unfazed, as if he's well aware of these arrangements—or perhaps requested them. With a small, knowing smile offered in my direction, Aurelia makes her way toward her carriage, leaving us alone.

I can feel Ryland's gaze on me, and I turn to face him and his proud smile. As if he holds the world on a string.

"Are you pleased?"

He takes my left hand, eyes studying the ring now resting on my finger. "More than you'll ever know." He pulls me with him beyond our waiting carriage, and I gasp when I see it.

I'd been facing the opposite direction when we'd arrived, too jittery with nerves at the time to have bothered looking behind me. Sitting before us is a small stone wall overlooking a complete view of Kingsmar. As I'd suspected, this church is situated on a steep elevation, providing the perfect vista.

All of Kingsmar is aglow like a burning candle flame, humming with vibrancy and light. The view illuminates just how vast the city truly is, how far it spans. The canopy of stars above light the sky, the brilliant full moon overhead, its pale yellow glow in the darkness a torch. The palace lies to the west, the striking, formidable structure an emblem of power, standing fiercely for all to behold.

Somehow, in this small amount of time, this city has become a home to me. And yet, tomorrow, we head into completely uncharted territory. The thought makes my stomach sink with dread. But, I shake the worries away, wanting to savor this night.

Ryland wraps an arm around my waist, his hand stroking up and down slowly. I rest my head on his shoulder, turning thoughtful as we stare out. "This is all so surreal. We've not even known each other a month," I murmur before tilting my head to look up at him, eyes now glassy. "Thank you for saving me that day. I guess it was worth it to steal those apples."

He shifts to face me fully, taking my chin between his fingers and tipping my head even further. "Do you remember the first words I spoke to you?"

I nod amusedly. I'll never forget. "'Have they brought me a gift?'"

He nods as well, a similar smile on his lips. "I believed it then as I believe it now. You are a gift to me from the gods. A gift more precious than any treasure the world could ever offer. One that I often question my worthiness of, and yet, one that I will never part with, will never share." His thumb sweeps over my skin. "My Aelyra," he murmurs softly. I'm not sure what the term means or when the tears began to fall, but Ryland gently brushes them away.

THE CARRIAGE RIDE BACK HOME WAS...INTERESTING, TO say the least. The very air between us had been charged and tense. With Ryland sitting beside me this time, I felt every inch of his presence, every breath and movement. The anticipation sat between us, so thick, it felt like a cloud hanging overhead.

I'd attempted distracting myself with the ring on my finger, tracing the exquisite stone, but it did little to quell my nerves. My knee kept bouncing up and down at an alarming rate, and even Ryland seemed restless, his foot occasionally tapping, fingers flexing.

Stepping into the townhouse is both a blessing and a curse, for I'm suddenly relieved of tension and doubled over with it. It's silent inside, all light removed apart from the fireplaces.

We're completely alone as Aurelia said we would be.

I turn to face Ryland, uncertain of what to do from here. An amused smile paints his lips, the one that always makes my heart flutter. Tapping a finger on my nose, he murmurs, "Nervous, little love?" Upon my nod, his smile softens into one of understanding. "Just because we married tonight doesn't mean we have to do anything," he assures me, taking hold of my chin. There's not a single line of dishonesty marring his features, no tell to belie the sincerity of his words. He means it. "Believe it or not, I can be patient," he adds playfully.

Despite his grip, I avert my gaze, casting it to the floor. "I do want to…it's just, I'm afraid I'll disappoint."

He jerks my chin slightly, forcing me to meet his firm stare. "Trust me, Wren, the last thing you could ever do is disappoint. The very sight of you is enough to bring me to my knees."

With those awe-striking words, Ryland scoops me into his arms and carries me up the stairs to his bedroom of dark blues and browns. Aurelia seems to have made preparations for this too because the interior is lit with several ivory candles, the fireplace roaring.

Ryland gently sets me down to close the door, and I stare at the bed, trying to calm my racing heart. My fingers twist with each other, body on the verge of bouncing. The sudden brush of Ryland's lips along my neck sets chills along my skin. My nerves electrify from his proximity, head instinctively tilting to give him better access.

"Did I tell you how breathtaking you are tonight?" he murmurs against my skin.

"No," I breathe, eyes fluttering closed as warmth pools in my stomach. "Did I tell you the same?"

I can feel his smirk against my skin before his hand wraps around the front of my waist, turning me to face him. My heavy lids open as soon as I catch sight of that deep blue. "You're exquisite," he says softly.

Silvery lavender pools at my feet as Ryland slowly removes my veil. His eyes hold mine as he pauses, expression wary, the question clear in his eyes. I nod for him to continue, ready to cross this line.

More than ready.

He reaches further behind me and begins to undo the buttons of my dress, never breaking our gazes. When he starts to tug the dress down, I reflexively lift my arms to stop him. He freezes in place, expression puzzled until I reach for his jacket to help him out of it. *If I'm going to be undressed, he's going to have to join me.* Unlike me, Ryland holds no apprehensions. He even helps remove his shirt, revealing a torso as sculpted and carved as any marble statue. Every ripple and divot, every curve and line—a work of art I'd like to one day take the time to just sit and admire.

Ryland takes a step forward, the muscles and tendons flexing with his movements so that there's only inches between us again. As though any distance is unbearable. My eyes flare a little, and Ryland smirks, wholly aware of his astonishing physique.

His biceps flex as he reaches behind me once more, slowly pulling the fabric of my dress, letting it slide down my body and exposing my entirely bare figure. Ryland's gaze darkens, lips parting as his eyes roam over me, leaving not one part of me unclaimed. I feel every inch of his gaze on me, warming my skin with a searing heat.

"Even more perfect than I imagined," he murmurs, voice a deep, sensual rumble.

My heart flutters at the realization that he's fantasized about this. About me. Perhaps like I have, during that quiet time of night when all is still and silent, when forbidden fantasies are made a reality even for the most fleeting or lingering of moments. On some nights, I reveled in that special hour, visualizing a moment like this, Ryland watching me with that hungry gaze, his lips on mine as he whispers sweet words into my ear. Those daydreams all pale in comparison to the reality of right now.

The air around us is a heavy, suffocating haze until all I'm breathing in is him. This remarkable man. One who's suffered so many variations of pain and misery, who tries to chase his shadows away and yet still bears their black veil. Who ruthlessly protects and mercilessly plunders. The very same man who kept a stranger warm during cold, windy nights, who brought me to dance beneath the stars, who lulled my racing mind during a thunderstorm. The man who took a starving girl and fed her with life.

Ryland's fingertips softly brush up the skin of my hips, causing me to shiver and warm at the same time. Then, he lowers his mouth to mine.

I open for him immediately, and his hum of satisfaction travels down my entire body, settling low in my stomach. He lets out another sound as his tongue slips inside my mouth as he tastes me. My arms wind around his neck, running through his hair. And, as my chest brushes his, I let out a soft sound of my own. Ryland only pulls me closer until our bodies are fully flush, the heat of his skin melding into mine.

Our kisses melt into something hungrier, but Ryland breaks away after a few moments, nibbling on my bottom lip.

"You've not done this before?"

I nod, and the muscles in his jaw tick.

"I don't want it to hurt for you, so we're going to need to get you comfortable first," he explains, already a little breathless. If I didn't know any better, I'd say there are stars in his eyes, twinkling and shimmering within the midnight blue.

My face heats, unsure of what exactly he means. Registering my confusion, Ryland cups the side of my face and lowers his head in front of mine. "Trust me," he implores softly.

My answer is to lean in and place a soft kiss on his mouth. In many ways, trusting Ryland was never a choice. Though I'd lied to myself on several occasions, told myself it was a conscious decision—that I hadn't yet decided to fully put my faith in him—I'd already unknowingly done so. All my trust has belonged to him for longer than I ever allowed myself to realize. All his secrecy and deceptions were not enough to keep me grounded and sensible. The more time I spent in his presence, the further I fell under his spell, the further I strayed from the path of common sense. So, trusting him now isn't a question or a choice. It's my reality.

Ryland claims my mouth with a ferocity that steals all breath, his tongue tangling with mine as he devours my very soul, only for him to rip away, leaving the flesh of my lips swollen and tender as he lowers himself to the floor. Settling on his knees, one hand clutching my hip, the other reaches for my chest as Ryland drags a finger around the curve of my breast. My breathing shortens as his finger draws circles smaller and smaller until he brushes over the peak. I bite my now sore lip.

His mouth starts to travel up my stomach, placing slow, savoring kisses along my flesh, tasting and exploring every inch of me. His teeth nip along my breast, and my hand reaches out to hold onto his shoulder from the overwhelming assault.

When his mouths closes over the sensitive peak, I release a quiet gasp, a rush of warmth washing over me. He takes his time, worshipping each breast until I'm flushed all over, skin buzzing with sensation, a dampness starting to form between my legs.

Eventually, Ryland rises, mouth ravishing mine thoroughly as he towers over me once more. I'm so drunk from his kiss that I don't notice one of his hands moving. Not until I feel him slowly slide it between my thighs.

A finger brushes against me, and I suck in a sharp breath, the dampness spreading as he strokes it back and forth. My heart hammers in my chest as my legs start to tremble. Every nerve ending inside comes to life, his touch awakening a part of me I hadn't known was left slumbering.

My soft breaths and his labored ones are the only sounds in the room, my soul thrumming as he teases the sensitive flesh. My eyes widen as he begins to push a finger inside me, and a whimper escapes as my frame instantly stiffens.

"Relax, my love," Ryland says soothingly. "You have to relax."

I take in a deep breath, closing my eyes and willing my muscles to loosen. After a few moments, Ryland pushes a bit further, and is greeted with less resistance. He loosens a groan when he reaches my end, and I let out a breath before he retracts his finger and reinserts it over ang again, the foreign sensation too much and not enough all at once.

I pull Ryland closer, clutching his arm with one hand and his shoulder with the other, widening my stance to give him better access.

"Gods, you're so small," he breathes, his rough voice skating over my heated skin.

After a few strokes, he adds another finger. My body strains as it tries to accommodate them both, standing on the tips of my toes, barely supporting myself. "That's it," Ryland encourages, kissing along my neck, helping ease some of the remaining tension. He curves his fingers, suddenly hitting a spot that makes my legs shake and a moan escape. He maintains a rhythmic pace, and my breathing quickens, grip on him tightening as a coiling pleasure starts to settle low in my stomach. My forehead drops to his chest, entire body now trembling.

"Hold onto me," Ryland instructs, and I do just that.

With that maddening pace, the muscles in my core tighten. My body is aflame with that liquid heat pooling inside me, winding and building with sensation. To what end, I'm not sure. But it feels too good to question the destination.

Ryland suddenly presses his thumb on the apex of my thighs, rubbing in small circles. My entire body locks as a force of pleasure crashes over me, lighting every cell in my being, blinding all other sensations. The force leaves me a trembling, panting mess in his arms.

Ryland holds me steady as my body shakes with tremors. My brain slowly comes back into focus, recovering from whatever that just was. He places featherlight kisses over my face as he withdraws his fingers before lifting me up, helping wrap my weak legs around his waist. His eyes are bright and slightly wild. Gaze holding mine, he brings those two fingers to his lips and wraps his mouth around them. I watch, completely dazed and bewildered as he closes his eyes, humming at my taste. The sight has my stomach tightening all over again.

Ryland removes them after a moment, a smug smile pulling at the corners of his mouth as he licks his lips. "Are you ready for more?"

I'm not sure what else could surpass whatever he just did, but I nod anyway. Because I *do* want more. Of him, of his touch. I want more of the indescribable pleasure he just gave me.

Ryland leads us to his bed, bending over to gently lay me atop it before stepping back to remove his pants and boots. I wait, averting my gaze as I try to calm my still thundering heart.

I look up when I feel him crawl over my body, his mouth returning to mine eagerly. Just the taste of him is enough to drive me mad. Kissing Ryland is a pleasure in and of itself, an activity I could do for hours on end. But my attention is stolen from his mouth when something brushes against my abdomen, and I gasp in realization.

It's...*large*.

Too large. Without even looking, I know that there's no way it will fit. He was right—I'm so small. *Too* small. But Ryland doesn't seem as concerned as he reaches a hand down to part my legs before he settles his weight between them. I can feel my essence spreading down my thighs, making it easier for him to align himself at my entrance. Once again, his eyes lock with mine, awaiting any protest. Instead, I supply him with another encouraging nod.

Slowly, he pushes himself inside.

I try not to tense up like before, but it's a challenge. Despite Ryland having tried to prepare me, this invasion is different. I hadn't realized how big he'd be, how much the stretch might burn. And he's barely moved inside me yet. I think he's only made it all of two inches.

"I'll stop if it's too much." He eyes me cautiously, fearful of causing me pain.

I shake my head. "Don't stop." In this moment, I've never felt closer to him.

Very slowly, he pushes in further, and I force myself to steady my breathing, hands gripping his neck and back.

An immeasurable amount of time later, after several pauses and exerted breaths, Ryland reaches his end, and I'm struck by the full sensation of him inside me. My body tenses a little, but my reaction only makes him groan. "Are you alright?" he asks, raising his head to look down at me, brow furrowed in concern. I nod softly, afraid to shift and cause any discomfort. I feel so very full, filled in a way I've never experienced before. But I'm adjusting to it with every passing second.

"Are you?"

He lets out an amused breath, shaking his head. "You're ruining me as we speak." In truth, his voice is a little shaky, gaze awe-filled. But, before I can savor the expression, his lips meet mine. Then his hips begin to move, slowly gliding in and out.

The burn starts to dissipate with each motion, morphing into something molten and fluttering in my core. Ryland's pace remains even, but the rush of sensations has me starting to writhe beneath him, desperate for more. The muscles of his back work beneath my hands, the warmth of his skin surging into mine. His woodsy scent envelops me like a cloud, drowning me in everything that is him.

Gradually, I can feel myself building towards that pinnacle again. My hands desperately run through his silky hair, our bodies glistening as they mold themselves together.

Ryland's face suddenly hovers over mine, and I startle to find his eyes glowing that glacial blue. He slows his movements, looking down at me with those unearthly irises. Glowing because of the consuming emotion he's experiencing. I realize just what that emotion is, for it shines within the luminous glow brighter than any flame or star—love.

His gaze shudders in realization and guilt. Afraid of my reaction, of frightening me, he closes his eyes. But nothing about this male could discourage me. He's thrown almost every obstacle and deterrent my way, and I've overlooked nearly every single one of them. I want him no matter what he does or has done, no matter what or who he is.

Cupping the side of his face, I bring his lips to mine. "I love you—*all* of you," I whisper, and his body racks with a shudder. Those radiant eyes open once more to hold mine, the flames of their emotion a fire I would happily burn in. They are, like everything else with Ryland, exquisitely intense.

There were no stolen glances and bashful smiles drawn out over months or years. It was all within a span of mere weeks, thrown together by chance as we were thrust into a whirlwind of danger and adventure. The brevity of our time together has had no impact on the depth of our love. Even with his secrets and evasions, I fell hard. I fell so deeply, so suddenly, I think I lost part of my soul in the process. A part that molded into something new. Something that was built for him. He became my breath and beat. My other half. How it happened so quickly, how he's become so irreplaceable to me, how he became *mine*, remains a mystery. The answer must lay with the gods.

Ryland shifts his angle, causing my muscles to tense around him, and he releases a moan, eyes falling closed. So, I do it again, clenching around him. This time, his eyes fly open, full of caution. "If you keep doing that, I won't last much longer," he warns, voice roughened. But I do just that, relishing in seeing him so undone.

Slamming his lips to mine, stealing all breath and focus, he drives into me with more force. A force I'm wholly unprepared for. My body is completely at his mercy, accepting his every stroke. With another slight adjustment to his angle, he hits that spot inside me, and my vision blurs. Staring up into his face, those glowing eyes, my pleasure soars.

Suddenly, I'm leaping off that precipice, his name on my lips as I cry out. This time, when I squeeze around him, it's not intentional. Ryland grunts and shudders as a warmth spills into me. His face buries in my neck as we both pant, trying to collect ourselves, piece each other back together. Eventually, he lifts his head, gently stroking back the damp hair from my face before kissing my brow. "You're like a dream..." he murmurs.

I want to reply that it's highly doubtful given my current state—face flushed, skin sweaty, lips raw and swollen. But I don't argue, seeing the overwhelming adoration simmering in his now dimmed eyes.

Slowly, Ryland removes himself from me, and I find myself too exhausted to move. My eyes are heavy, barely able to keep open as he pulls back the sheets, helping cover me before joining me at my side and pulling me into his chest. I press my lips to his smooth skin, and he hums, the sound reverberating against my mouth.

I'm too tired to meet his gaze, to gauge his expression as to whether tonight was everything he'd hoped for, whether he's feeling as shattered and irrevocably altered as I am. That everything he just fragmented and broke within me was remelded to fit with his own pieces. That I'm no longer myself, but completely his. That we are one.

✟

HOLLIS SOPHIA

APART FROM THE CRACKLING FIRE ACROSS THE ROOM, I wake to darkness. The several candles have all since burned out, alluding to a late hour. And yet, I find the other side of the bed empty. Sitting up, I wince at the soreness already attacking my body. I squint into the dim space, searching for Ryland's tall form. But he isn't here. Rising from the bed, legs a little weak, I reach for a blanket from one of the chairs and wrap it around my body. Barefoot, I creep out of the bedroom and slip downstairs.

I find the drawing room empty apart from another fire roaring with life. The breakfast room and library are vacant too. Trying to maintain my composure, to not assume the worst case scenario—that my performance was subpar enough to have him flee the house—I carefully continue my search, pulling the blanket tighter as a draft washes over my skin.

Padding down the hallway, I notice a faint light emanating from where I think the kitchen is, and relief settles in. Slowly, I push open the door, finding Ryland standing by the counter, a glass of water in hand. He has on a pair of loose cotton pants slung low on his hips.

I can't help but stare at the smooth expanse of his back, the rippling muscles and broad shoulders; how I felt those muscles work beneath my hands mere hours ago. But said muscles are currently strained with tension, head bowed as his other hand grips the edge of the countertop in a firm hold. I'm instantly wary, worried he's come to his senses, realized that the marriage was a mistake and already regrets it.

He inhales softly, head lifting, and I know he's sensed my presence. All concerns melt away when I see the instant relief and warmth that floods his expression as he turns around to face me. I suppose something else must have been troubling him, and I'm about to ask when he extends the glass of water to me. "I was bringing one up for you." Another empty glass sits on the counter beside him.

I cross the distance to accept it, drinking half as he watches me with sharp focus. He takes the glass from my hand, eyes bright, and I can't help but ask, "Aren't you tired?"

"Not quite. I don't require the same amount of rest as mortals," he explains simply.

Indeed, Ryland was always up before me every morning during our journey to Kingsmar, always active and doing something. I, on the other hand, would rise with heavy lids and sluggish thoughts.

"Aren't you exhausted from...?"

He smiles at my modesty. "I think you're forgetting about one of the perks of being an Astarith," he lifts his brows in a playful taunt, "increased stamina."

A frown pulls at my lips. "So...you weren't...satisfied?"

"Yes, and no." I open my mouth, likely to supply an apology, but he continues. "You see, now that I've tasted you, I don't think I'll ever truly be satisfied. I could go another ten rounds with you and still be left wanting more. You satisfied the part of me that craved to know your touch, the feel of you wrapped around me. And now, you've unlocked something far more dangerous." His eyes glint with wicked delight—and warning. "Obsession." His face softens a fraction. "I just didn't want to wear you out tonight."

So I didn't disappoint. I can't deny what a relief it is to hear it, though I suppose I'll have to work on my own stamina. I take a step toward him, and his eyes track the movement. "But I want you to." His brows flick up, surprised by my boldness. "This is our one, private night together. Just the two of us. We'll be moving tomorrow, or today, to a place surrounded by people." It's hard keeping track of time in such a state. "I want to enjoy this moment being wholly and utterly alone."

Ryland contemplates for only a second. A single second before he pounces.

Taking my face in both his hands, his mouth crashes against mine. Suddenly, he's backing us out of the kitchen and down the hall. Light returns to my vision, and I realize we're in the drawing room.

Ryland lowers himself into one of the armchairs, pulling me to stand between his legs. He tugs on my blanket until it drops to the floor. His gaze rakes over me with a scorching heat before lifting to hold my stare. The shock of those deep blue eyes, the intensity burning within them, makes my mouth go dry.

"You're magnificent, wife." The deep rumble of his voice sends shivers down my spine. His hands hook around my waist as he yanks me closer, mouth descending on my breasts. Needing to be closer, I rest my knees on each side of his thighs so that I'm straddling his lap, hands gripping his shoulders, feeling the muscles work beneath. Ryland kisses up my throat as I reach between us for his pants.

"Eager are we?" he asks, voice a delicious purr.

"For you, always," I breathe. He releases a soft groan, my words seeming to spur his desire. Helping lower his pants, I lift myself as he adjusts our positioning.

His eyes lock with mine, a glint of a question in them. My answer is to lower myself onto his length. My confidence is abruptly cut short as my harsh gasp fills the quiet room. This angle is far more brutal than the last, the stretch instilling a sharp sting.

Ryland hisses out a breath as I try to work myself down his length. "*Fuck*," he growls in a strangled moan, head tipping back against the chair, eyes closed, mouth parted in pleasure. The grip on my hips tightens, and a whimper escapes as I keep sinking lower. Trying to keep a clear head, to push past the discomfort, I somehow make it to his end, allowing myself to take a breath. Unsure of how to proceed, I look to Ryland whose gaze has returned to my face, nodding in confirmation. "Up," he breathes.

I follow his command, slowly rising up his length before I sink back down, relishing in the feel of him, every burning, blinding sensation. Ryland's head tips back once more, and his exposed neck draws my attention. I close my lips around the heated skin as I continue to ease myself up and down, soaking in this fever dream we seem to have entered.

But, after a few labored minutes, my pace begins to slow, energy pitifully dwindling. Sensing this, Ryland grabs the side of my face, taking control. His gaze bores into mine, imprisoning. "I've wanted you like this from the day I met you," he grits out, thrusting up and into me.

My eyes flutter closed from the pleasure, but his hand wraps around my throat in a possessive hold, demanding my attention. "*Every. Fucking. Day.*" His grip tightens. "I close my eyes, and I see your face. Those eyes. Those lips." His thumb presses against my lower lip, rubbing over it.

I mean to respond, to tell him I've suffered the same affliction, but I'm incapable of words, answering only by clutching his golden locks.

Ryland suddenly shifts his position, and I whimper. "*Gods!*"

"You can pray to them all you like, little love, but they can't help you right now. In this moment—in this lifetime—you're mine." His words incite a shudder that runs through my entire body, and I manage to muster a new wave of vigor. Trying to match his pace, I meet him thrust for thrust, my nails digging into the flesh of his neck and shoulders.

It feels like I'm flying, soaring up toward the sky untethered. Completely detached from earth and reality. I've never felt so much bliss feeling so utterly lost. Because somehow, I know Ryland will catch me. That he'll always be there.

With his sharp, steady pace, it doesn't take long until I'm clenching around him as euphoria consumes me, his name a chant on my lips. Ryland curses as he too finds his pleasure, slowly ceasing his movements until we slump into the chair, a warm and sticky tangle. As my head rests on his shoulder, his hand rubbing up and down my back soothingly, I find myself once again fighting a weighted exhaustion and losing to it.

CHAPTER 21

THE CHIRPING OF BIRDS WAKES ME THIS TIME, AND I groggily open my eyes. The warmth of Ryland's skin seeps into my cheek, the steady beat of his heart thrumming softly. My muscles relax in ease. Flashes of last night flit through my mind with aching clarity. I must've fallen asleep in Ryland's arms downstairs after our second round, and he carried me up here. *So much for demonstrating my capable stamina.*

Tilting my head in his direction, I find his gaze trained on me. "You're radiant," he murmurs in a sleep-roughened voice. I breathe out a dubious laugh, shaking my head as I reach to adjust the covers when a soft glinting catches my attention.

The diamond on my finger glimmers in the morning light, sparkling like the most dazzling star. "We're married," I whisper in disbelief.

In a way, it feels wrong to wear the ring. As though it's out of place on my person. With Aurelia's fanciful clothes and jewels on last night, it was excusable. But now, on my bare form, just me, it doesn't seem right. Like I'm not fit to wear something so exceptionally stunning.

Ryland nods, taking my hand in his as he too admires the ring. "It was a family heirloom," he explains. "There were a few items I was able to salvage after the fire."

The faint edge of somberness in his tone has me leaning in to bury my face in his neck. "It's beautiful." Despite the doubts about my worthiness of wearing such a piece, I feel honored to wear it given the sentimental value it holds for him.

"More so on you," he replies.

Stealing another few moments of the perfect peace we're lying in, I pull back, wincing as the light penetrates my gaze again. The brightness makes me wonder just how late it is. "When do we need to leave?" I ask, realizing the answer is probably "sometime ago".

"We should start preparing now. The sooner the better."

I sit up, racked with guilt. "I'm sorry I slept in."

Ryland sits up beside me, tucking a piece of hair back in its disheveled place. "I'm sorry I wore you out." A kiss on my shoulder. "Actually, I'm not."

He rises, striding toward his dresser. My eyes catch on his very exposed backside, staring for longer than is probably wise. The powerful muscles of his thighs flex with each step, further displaying just how lethal his body is. A body that could overpower mine in less than a second if he wanted.

After rummaging through his drawers and procuring some clothes, he turns to face me. I hadn't had the opportunity to notice his length last night, but now, in the broad daylight...I'm not even sure how it was able to fit inside me. A medical mystery if ever there was one. I quickly avert my gaze, and Ryland smirks as if keenly aware of my train of thought.

"I suggest we bathe and dress separately. If we do it together, I doubt I'll be letting us leave for another several hours," he explains, eyes darkening as his gaze travels over me sitting in his bed, only covered by the thin sheet.

I nod in understanding before reaching for a blanket and proceeding to wrap it around me. Shuffling to the end of the bed, I lower my feet to the floor before pushing off to stand. My legs instantly buckle, and I have to clamp a hand onto the mattress for support as my legs shake in violent tremors. The muscles ache and twitch, and I look to Ryland with wide eyes.

He simply chuckles. "Weak, little love?"

I nod. Heat flushes my skin along with a large dose of embarrassment. *How ridiculous I must look. Unable to walk, my trembling legs no better than a newborn fawn's.*

Ryland's smile only grows as he strides toward me before scooping me into his arms and walking me to my room. Once in my bathing room, he carefully sets me down, and I have to grip his arms for support. He smiles down at me softly. "It'll pass."

"But will it happen again?" I question, trying to imagine having trouble walking like this more than once. *How would I ever go out in public?*

His grin is nothing short of cruel. "I'll make sure of it."

My cheeks burn as I watch Ryland's gaze sharpen. His nostrils flare a little, eyes wandering across my face down to the bit of cleavage exposed from the blanket, to my hands gripping his bare skin and then where our bodies are pressed closely together. I know what he's contemplating, can *feel* against my stomach how ready he is to act on his urges right now. I'm not quite sure that I'd protest even despite my wobbling legs, even despite feeling raw and tender this morning.

In a flash, he takes my face in his hands and pulls me in for a searing kiss. When he releases me, his eyes rove over my face once more, jaw clenching before he draws away altogether and exits the room. My eyes immediately drift to the mirror as I examine myself. Tired eyes, lips now swollen again, hair mussed…in other words, looking completely ravaged.

I savor every second I spend in the quick bath that I take, knowing it will be my last for some time. Utilizing several of Aurelia's luxurious salves and soaps, I scrub my skin thoroughly before washing my hair.

Once clean, I don the clothes Aurelia's laid out for me; a cotton, russet skirt and a black blouse with billowing sleeves and a corseted-bodice. Modest, comfortable, nothing to allude to a life of wealth and luxury. A neutral canvas in which to enter the Assassin's Guild. The only thing that is sure to stand out is my ring.

I lace up my boots before brushing out my wet hair, making my way downstairs to where I hear voices. My pace doubles in speed when I detect Aurelia's dainty tone drifting from the dining room. Bounding inside, I find her standing beside the table with Ryland who's also in fresh clothes, golden hair dampened over his brow. My gaze locks with Aurelia's, and we both share a smile before I embrace her in a tight hold. "You came back."

"Of course. We hadn't said a proper goodbye. Besides, we still have to review a few matters," she explains, pulling back to regard me and Ryland. "I arrived with some of the staff, and they're preparing breakfast now. You can't leave without a little food."

We take our seats as a maid pours us tea and coffee, and I can't help as my gaze keeps flicking to Ryland. The deep blue of his shirt in combination with his black trousers and darkened hair is a distraction I shouldn't let affect me so easily. And yet, every time I behold his magnificent beauty, my stomach flutters in response.

I'd been naive to think that last night would take some of the edge off between us. It's only fanned the flames. Just looking at him has my heart tumbling, fingers itching to trace the contours of his face, to feel his lips on mine. Sensing my stare, Ryland's gaze shifts to mine, lips pulling at the corners. Quickly looking away, I reach for my cup, covering my mouth as I yawn.

"So, I trust you both had a...pleasant evening?" Aurelia enquires, watching me amusedly. I shoot her a mortified glare to which she simply smiles in delight, completely unruffled. Ryland shares her grin, evidently quite pleased with how little sleep I had.

"I'm not sure any word could quite capture what last night was, but sure, let's go with *pleasant*," he replies, voice heavy with implication.

I smack a hand over my brow. "I can see why you two have stayed such close friends after so many years. You're incorrigible" I grumble, causing both of them to laugh.

As we eat a rather rushed breakfast, we run over last minute details. Aurelia will have our bags sent to the Guild as Ryland apparently has a stop for us to make before we reach our destination.

Excusing myself from the table to wash my hands before we leave, I make my way toward the stairs when a knock sounds at the front door. A maid swiftly arrives, greeting the guest. A familiar voice sounds, murmuring to the maid before she allows him entry, and I pause on the third step. Tall and regal, an umber-skinned figure strides into the entryway like a shadow until I'm peering into copper eyes.

Lord Nyangard.

His gaze holds mine, a small furrow in his brow before he seems to recall propriety and dips into a bow as he addresses me, voice smooth and rich as honey. "My lady."

My mouth opens, confusion written plainly across my features, when the entryway suddenly becomes engulfed in chaos. I'm not sure how Ryland arrived so quickly or how he became only centimeters away from Lord Nyangard's form. All I know is he strikes a brutal punch across the unexpecting lord's face who stumbles, expression etched in bewilderment as Ryland prepares for another blow. Addris blocks it this time, instinct leading him to attempt a punch of his own.

But Ryland is faster, rage fueling his fight as his eyes come sparking to life. He pummels Addris once more, knocking him against the nearest wall before ramming his forearm against the man's windpipe, sharply cutting off his air supply. Ryland's other hand grips a dagger, pressing it against Addris's abdomen. The male has no choice but to submit.

Aurelia rushes in, standing beneath the dining room archway looking as perplexed as I am. "Don't you dare shed any blood on those floors! Sort your affairs with a modicum of civility, will you?"

I'm not sure if Ryland hears her, not when he shoves his arm even further against the lord's throat. About to intercede myself to diffuse the tension, my breath catches. Copper eyes suddenly flicker with an orange luminescence.

Another Astarith.

"You were working with Reaver," Ryland snarls.

Addris's eyes widen before they cut to me, some emotion I can't discern welling within them. He looks back at Ryland, shaking his head firmly.

"*Don't* lie. You helped poison her." The accusation is a vengeful growl.

Shock trickles through my system. *Addris worked with Reaver to help poison me.* No wonder Ryland seemed tense when I'd approached him and the mysterious male at the ball. It all makes sense now. I was meeting another servant of Raigar, and Ryland didn't want my identity exposed. It was his biggest fear, and I all but pushed myself onto the lord—and ended up paying the price for it.

Lord Addris struggles, mouth opening. "Let...me...explain," he rasps.

Ryland's icy-glowing eyes narrow, fighting with his bloodlust. He studies the Astarith, glancing at his slack form, noting how he hasn't tried to fight Ryland's hold, and loosens the pressure slightly.

Addris takes the opportunity, ensuring his words are spoken slowly and clearly. "Reaver came to me, asking for the poison and Feldryn's address. He never mentioned who the victim would be—only that it was connected to Raigar's orders." He shifts his gaze to me once more, rusty irises sincere. "I had no idea it was going to be used against you, my lady. For that, you have my sincerest regret and apology."

"And your sudden departure?" Ryland questions, still unconvinced.

"Business took me to Willesden. I just returned this morning and received your message. I came straight away."

"If I find out you were involved—"

"I swear to you, my friend. You would've had my warning." His words are full of truth. I can hear it, and I know Ryland can too because he releases his hold, taking a step back and allowing Addris to regain his composure. After several deep breaths, the male asks, "Reaver?"

"Dead."

No remorse or guilt shadows Addris's features at the news. Instead, there's almost a tilt to his full lips. "And Raigar?"

Ryland's face locks. "I'm handling the situation."

He cuts his friend a dubious look. "Because that's so easily done." Ryland doesn't share his humor, still seething.

The entryway settles into a heavy silence as Addris's expression sobers, running his fingers along his jaw as he considers Ryland. The same armor-like rings adorn them, though the rest of his attire is more subdued than it had been at the ball, merely a rich brown jacket and pants.

"I won't pretend to know the nature of whatever game you're playing with him this time, but I'm willing to help should you need it." A peace offering. A reestablishment of the seemingly tenuous alliance they had before.

"I very well may," Ryland warns.

"Thank you, Lord Nyangard," I insert, hoping to further strengthen the tentative peace that's been formed.

Ryland snorts. "Please, that title is about as genuine as the gold he wears." The man in question shares Ryland's amused expression in contrast to the severely confused one on my own.

Ryland explains, "Addris and I have known each other for centuries. He also works for Raigar, though his line of work is different to mine. Raigar moves him around different cities every few decades where he establishes himself as a lord of trade, accumulating wealth and status."

I'm about to ask what goods he trades in when Addris answers for me. "Drugs and poisons are my specialty, among other commodities…including gold, which *is* very much genuine," he adds with a pointed look to Ryland. "One would expect no less from Kingsmar's wealthiest merchant."

"Top ten at best," Ryland corrects.

While the two insist on continuing their juvenile banter, I'm more focused on contemplating the implications of Addris's black-market dealings. It certainly explains how he possessed Lord Feldryn's address as well as my poison. At that, another puzzle piece clicks into place as I look to Aurelia. "The cure."

She nods. "Addris is my supplier, though *my* connection with him is purely professional." There's a slight edge of aversion in her tone as though she wishes to associate with the immortal as much as a social scandal. Likely because of his connection to Raigar. I can't really blame her.

My mind is still reeling at the unexpected discovery of another Astarith. *How many are there?* I suppose the imposing beauty should've tipped me off, but there's something so calming about his aura and manner, so steadying. It's difficult to imagine him dealing in illegal trade in the service of another, though he'd said as much at the ball. His words had been another hint sitting in right in front of me.

Addris removes himself from the wall, approaching me in two graceful strides before taking my hand in his and offering another bow. His spicy scent drifts over me, warm, copper eyes holding mine. "I hope this misunderstanding hasn't altered your impression of me," he murmurs against my skin, making my cheeks heat.

"You'll kindly remove your mouth from her hand—unless you actually came here for a brawl." Ryland's warning cuts through the air, drawing a smirk from Addris before he steps back.

Feeling a little flushed, I fold my hands together, the movement catching Addris's eye before he arches a dark brow. "It would seem congratulations are in order," he offers, eyeing my wedding ring. "You've been busy since I left." His gaze shifts to Ryland as he inhales, head cocking to the side as a knowing look passes over his face. "Especially busy last night,

I think." I'm not sure how he knows what transpired last night by scenting the air alone, but he obviously does, bringing a fresh wave of heat to my face.

"Any wedding gifts can be sent to this address," Ryland replies smoothly, not a hint of shame painting his tone.

Addris grunts in amusement. "Noted."

Another lapse of silence ensues, and Ryland glances at the clock. I know he's itching to leave. Sensing this, Addris dips his head to each of us. "Should you require my aid, you know where to find me," he says to Ryland who offers a nod of his own.

Once gone, Aurelia turns to Ryland, wary. "Do you trust him?"

"The only ones I trust are the people in this room. But, he's never betrayed me before. He's loyal to Raigar, but Addris also plays his own games."

With no more time to spare, Ryland swiftly retreats to his room to procure his weapons while Aurelia helps me into my black cloak, the same as Ryland's. When he returns, I find him practically covered in blades, reminding me of our days in the wild. From the daggers strapped around his thighs and waist to the sword sheathed along his back, he truly looks like the seasoned assassin he is.

I turn to Aurelia, expression hopefully conveying at least some meaningful measure of my endless gratitude. Her eyes glisten as she pulls me into one last embrace. "I look forward to receiving your letters. Feel free to grumble about him as much as you like."

"I'm sure you're not referring to the person who took pain-staking efforts to ensure that not a single drop of blood soiled your precious furniture when I delt with our intruder the other night," Ryland adds dubiously.

We both give him an irksome look before she steps away and wraps her arms around his waist, all jesting aside. "Call on me with whatever you need. Take care of her…and yourself. We've survived this many centuries; I expect the same for a good many more," she demands, a few tears slipping. "And try not to be too much of a smug prick."

Ryland looks down at her fondly, gaze lit with warmth. "The first two requests I shall happily oblige. As for the second..." he lifts his brows, "I make no promises."

With a roll of her amber eyes, Aurelia steps aside, allowing us to reach the door. After one last parting glance, we head outside, the late morning breeze ruffling my hair and caressing my skin. I look back to the beautiful townhouse, saying a silent farewell. Like Ryland once offered it, this home became a place of refuge, of safety and comfort. I'm saddened to be leaving it so soon.

Taking my hand in his, Ryland steals my attention as he looks down at me, expression softening in understanding of what I'm feeling—the sorrow for what we're leaving behind, the apprehension for where we're headed, the fear and uncertainty of our current path. In usual Ryland fashion, he offers me a wink. A reassurance that we'll be alright.

"So, are you going to tell me where we're stopping first?" I ask as we make our way into the bustling city streets.

"I want to pay a visit to Errol and check for updates on something."

"Something, meaning your theory on a way to end...you know who?" I confirm, voice dropping to a whisper for the last few words.

Ryland's deep chuckle sounds. "You needn't fear saying his name. It won't summon his presence or anything," he explains with mirth. "And yes, that's the plan."

Recalling the artifacts shop and the treasure trove of curious oddities inside, I'm reminded of another peculiar oddity that I've come across since meeting Ryland. "What were those cuffs Reaver carried? The markings were Talaar, right?"

"Yes. Another one of Raigar's creations, specifically for the Astarith. Iron is of little deterrence to us, as you already know," he explains, referring to our prison escape. *As if I could forget witnessing such a remarkable display of strength.* The way he so effortlessly snapped the chain without a single grunt or expression of exertion. "But, with those markings, they're spelled to keep us bound. They dull our strength, similar to the Drith Stones' effects on the Sildhe. If cuffed, we're far more susceptible to capture." His eyes narrow in satisfaction. "And now, we possess two pairs."

"Two?" I only saw Reaver carrying the one, but maybe there were more on his person that Ryland discovered when dealing with the attacker.

"The men in Lyrewood had a pair as well." I'd almost forgotten, but he's right. Those men possessed the same cuffs. "I took them before we left," Ryland explains. I must not have seen him, which makes sense given in that particular moment, I'd essentially been unresponsive. The aftermath of that massacre still remains a bit of blur; how we ventured to the inn, how Ryland procured a room for us.

Shaking off the horrid memories, I return my attention to Ryland. "Are we bringing them with us?"

"I left one with Aurelia. It's wisest to divvy them up. If either of us requires a pair, we'll each have access. Gives us an edge." Perhaps I'll sleep a little easier knowing that if ever we come across another one of Ryland and Aurelia's kind, we have the means to incapacitate them. To an extent, at least.

We reach Errol Maleck's shop within half an hour's time, the reclusive fellow once again lost to the disarray of his cluttered shop. As we trudge through the endless depths of the store, weaving our way around the myriad objects, I can't help but ask, "So, you last visited this place decades ago?"

Ryland's gaze is filled with amusement, knowing his answer will shock me. "Almost five if I'm not mistaken. But, it feels like a lot less."

My mouth goes dry. Fifty years...my parents hadn't even been *born* then, let alone me. The unsettling information reminds me how little I've adjusted to the fact of just how old

Ryland is. His spirit is so youthful and vibrant, and yet, he's also incredibly wise, packed full of knowledge and experience. A walking contradiction.

"And, you're centuries old?" I confirm, unable to prevent the awe from my voice.

He looks down at me with a quirked brow. "Why? Is our age difference bothering you?" he teases.

"No," I lie quickly. "Just trying to figure out what's older, you or the objects in here." He throws me a rueful look before tapping the tip of my nose playfully with the same hand that now bears a new silver band around his ring finger. The sight of it has me slowing my steps, the severity of the situation hitting me. Ryland notices my faltering and turns to face me with a concerned look.

I take in a steadying breath. "Are you sure you wish to do this, take me with you?" He continues to watch me with puzzled features. "We've established that you're centuries old. You really want to bind yourself with someone as young as me? You said you get bored easily, what if that happens with us?"

His expression tightens, eyes narrowing as he takes another step toward me until there's only inches between us. "You don't understand. It's *because* I'm so old that I know exactly what I want. I've had centuries to see the world, to taste everything it has to offer, to meet people from all different places. And, never in all those years, those centuries, have I ever felt anything like I do when I'm with you.

"My love for you is not some fleeting fever that will fade. It's a permanent presence, embedded beneath my skin. Embedded in my soul." His brow creases. "It's me who should be worried about *you*, and I am. You may feel this way about me now, but, in a few years, when I've shown you more of the world, you may find you wish to explore it with others."

Now, he's the one who doesn't understand. He couldn't be more wrong. In fact, I can't think of a more disturbing and awful thought than that. Me moving on with someone else. It's laughable. Impossible. Insulting.

I shake my head, about to explain just that, when he cuts me off, cupping the side of my face. "You own me, little thief. Whether you're aware of it or not." His mouth breaks into a grin. "Would it sound too soppy if I said that you stole my heart?"

I smile with him, huffing a breath of amusement. "Well, yes. But I wouldn't mind hearing it anyway."

With a soft kiss to my brow, he pulls away, taking my hand once more as we work deeper into the shop. "Maleck? Are you in here?"

"Hello?" We follow the faint voice's trail until we find the old man standing on a rickety ladder as he tries to place a thick tome atop a precarious pile of others on a high-reaching shelf. Ryland comes to his aid, taking the book from his hands and placing it on the stack, tall enough to reach it on his own. Honestly, his height is unsettling.

The old man murmurs his thanks as he slowly lowers himself from the ladder, finally taking the two of us in. Recognition flickers in his eyes. "Ah, yes. Mr....?"

"Ryland will do," my *husband*—I'll have to get used to that—replies politely.

Errol nods before his eyes settle on something. "My congratulations," he offers, and I realize his gaze is on my wedding ring. I guess the ring draws even more attention than I thought. I shouldn't be all that surprised as Mr. Maleck's appreciation for old, priceless items has been honed to an expert level.

"Which is why I'm here. In order to keep my wife safe, I need my order to arrive as soon as possible. Have you any updates?" Ryland asks.

Mr. Maleck fiddles with his spectacles before wiping his hands on his apron. "I'm afraid the shipment was delayed. The vessel stopped in Hethro after Hesgeth. I would expect it to arrive within two weeks."

Ryland's face tightens, the delay a clear nuisance, but I'm more focused on what the old man just said. *Hesgeth, Hethro...*

The shipment is coming all the way from Kharia, a region in the Southern Continent. *But what on earth could be coming from there that Ryland needs so desperately?*

"The Sildhe you're after, he's far from the city?"

My brows practically raise to my hairline. "He knows?" I ask Ryland.

Mr. Maleck smiles at me, releasing a throaty chuckle. "It's not so difficult to put one and two together after the questions the boy has asked. Besides, I know Sildhe magic when I see it." He gives Ryland an appraising look, as though he were an object himself to be studied. "Fifty odd years is a long time to remain so well-preserved," he muses knowingly. He isn't wrong. "Then, of course, after enquiring about—"

"*That* part will remain a private matter," Ryland cuts in. I can't help my frown as I'm reminded of the last time I was here when I wasn't allowed to know anything.

The shop owner watches me carefully, and I sense his gaze is assessing. "Very well. As I said, return in two weeks and, hopefully, I'll have your delivery."

I know it's the very opposite of what Ryland was hoping to hear, but he nods his thanks anyway, turning to depart when Mr. Maleck's gaze flicks briefly to me once more before he suddenly adds, "I'm afraid I require the first installment of payment, Mr. Ryland."

We both follow him to the counter we'd stood near during our last visit while he rummages in a back room, returning with a scroll of parchment. After rolling it out along the countertop's surface, his eyes lift to mine. Once the document is fully unraveled, Ryland takes a step forward to read the contract of purchase when Mr. Maleck's hand suddenly jerks, the clumsy error of an old man. The parchment slips off the table, fluttering to the floor. Right at my feet.

As I retrieve the document, I can't help it as my eyes latch onto some of the writing.

Item of Acquisition: *Book of Hessan*
Source: *The Twelve Pillars Library of Hesgeth*

My eyes widen in both confusion and interest as I offer the paper to Ryland, but his gaze isn't on me. It's currently trained on the old man, a dark glower that even I might tremble from were it aimed at me.

I suddenly understand the reason for his glaring as Errol Maleck watches me with a knowing stare. An unexpected ally; I'm grateful for his assistance.

"It's safer for her not to know," Ryland says to him sharply, though not as cutting as I know he could be.

Mr. Maleck's gaze remains on me as he replies, "Ignorance is one's greatest enemy. If she knows half your reality, she should know the rest."

"I think that's my decision to make," Ryland counters, the muscle in his jaw feathering.

While I feel a little guilty for going against Ryland's wishes, I can't help but appreciate Mr. Maleck's assistance. He knew I was curious, knew that I wanted to know. And I agree with him. Ignorance is a threat to me, especially now that I'm joining Ryland as he hides from Raigar's men, buying himself as much time as possible. I should understand what exactly we're risking our lives for, waiting around in this city like walking targets.

Ryland releases a heavy sigh, pinching the bridge of his nose as his eyes fall closed.

"The Book of Hessan," he begins, relenting this final battle of secrecy and satiating my curiosity once and for all, "is a volume about the Sildhe. Their history, attributes and creations. It was written by one of their kind who'd decided to document their species, Hessan, son of Thalas, the God of Knowledge and Strategy." It makes sense that Hessan was the one to write the book, given his direct lineage. Being son of the God of Knowledge would have certainly made him an accurate source.

Mr. Maleck pushes his glasses up the bridge of his nose as he adds, "The book is the only one of its kind, though duplicates were made. But, those often omitted pieces of information, details previous kings and rulers did not wish for the public to have access to. The book that Mr. Ryland has ordered is the original work that has been stored in The Twelve Pillars Library, one of the oldest and most sacred houses of historical documents and manuscripts."

I look to Ryland. "And you're hoping to see if there's another method to destroy a Sildhe?"

He nods grimly. "Supposedly, it lists all the Sildhes' strengths and weaknesses. If there's any other way to kill one of their kind, it will be in Hessan's book."

"And you weren't able to access the book before now?" I'm fairly certain that Ryland would've looked into this sooner since his desire to see Raigar dead has haunted him for so many centuries.

A dip of his head. "No one knew of the book's whereabouts for over a century, and it was genuinely accepted that it had been lost or destroyed. I'd only heard of its existence a few decades after meeting Raigar, a slip of the tongue on his part. One of Osterley's kings ordered it's relocation to Hesgeth. He felt it was better to erase the memory of the Sildhe after the wars.

"As it goes, the ship that had been carrying it was lost at sea, and the book passed into legend. It was only after visiting Errol last week that I was made aware of its survival."

That explains the spark of hope I'd seen in his gaze that day we first came to the shop. He'd finally received a sliver of good news. "And how did you know that the book still existed?" I ask Errol.

"We collectors keep sharp eyes and open ears on all the continents' greatest treasures."

"But, how is it the library relinquished the book if it was ordered to remain in Hesgeth?"

The old man's lips pull in a slightly mischievous smile. "I happen to have a contact within the library. For a decent price, he occasionally helps me...smuggle certain items from their archives. Understanding the dire nature of Mr. Ryland's circumstances, I was able to persuade my contact to assist me in procuring this particular relic. I'm not so foolish as to think this matter isn't bigger and graver than us three." It seems we owe more to Mr. Maleck than I realized.

"Thank you," I offer sincerely. He doesn't have to help us. He could have turned Ryland away knowing the risks of associating with someone like him. But he didn't.

Ryland reaches for the quill on the desk, bowing over the parchment to sign. I try not I balk as I notice the staggering price listed at the bottom of the page. This is just the *first* installment. Mr. Maleck's friend must be risking a great deal if that's only half the total sum. But, Ryland scratches out the written number, writing a new total, twice the original amount. "I'll pay the other half when I see you next."

The old man mutters his agreement, not having noticed Ryland's price adjustment since he's currently scanning through some of the shelves, searching for something.

I take a step toward Ryland, giving his hand a grateful squeeze. I know he's truly appreciative of Mr. Maleck's help, understands the risks he's taking. He brushes his thumb across the back of my hand in response before we both shift our gazes to Errol who shuffles toward us, moving in front of the counter. As the old man is only slightly taller than me, Ryland towers over him, making him seem even more frail. His small eyes hold mine as he extends an enclosed hand toward me, opening his fingers to reveal a tiny charm.

"A talisman of protection. The symbol represents—"

"Rhasha," I murmur in realization. The Goddess of Aegis. I recognize the charm's symbol, the tiny, iron shield with a four-point star engraved in the center representing safety. Errol nods, pushing his hand forward for me to take the gift. Holding the man's gaze, I see it stirring in his eyes, the concern. He knows just how fragile I am compared to Ryland, the threat I face staying at his side.

Gently, I approach the shop owner, offering a small embrace as I murmur my thanks. I wouldn't go so far as to say he bristles with discomfort, but I do notice his face going a little pink. I catch Ryland's grateful expression before I bend down, attaching the charm to one of my boot laces and knotting it securely. Hopefully, Rhasha will look out for me and Ryland by proxy. Surely the Goddess of Protection would not fail us. Not after everything we've already been through.

After parting with Errol Maleck, promising to return in two weeks, Ryland and I depart the shop. We're greeted by a foreboding silver sky which motivates us to set off before it starts to pour as the thick and heavy clouds suggest is imminent. Ryland takes my hand in his as he leads us through the empty streets, taking us down a back-route.

"So we're headed to the Guild now?" A sharp nod. "Where we'll wait for the next two weeks until your order arrives at Maleck's?" Another nod. "Then we'll see if there's another way to—"

"Still as methodical as when I first met you, hmm?" Ryland murmurs from beside me, amusement lacing his tone.

I lift my shoulder in a small shrug. "A tree never grows different leaves. Besides, while you may be more reckless, you're just as calculati—" The air whooshes from my lungs as Ryland suddenly pulls us down a side street, slamming me against a stone wall. I gasp as he grips my face with both hands, lips pulled in a wolfish grin before he seals his mouth to mine.

Just the first touch of his lips has my heart thundering in my chest. Stretching up on my toes to try and reach him, I loop my arms around his neck, running my hands through his waves, savoring his warmth. He tilts my head for better access as his tongue tangles with mine, releasing a groan that settles deep within my core. Sliding a hand to the back of my neck, his fingers knot in my hair, holding me close as his mouth devours mine.

I suddenly wish we were back at Aurelia's, sprawled in his bed instead of this exposed side-street.

His lips work down my neck, kissing along my cleavage as my hands grip the edges of his cloak. "Ryland," I breathe, voice filled with both lust and warning.

"Say my name like that again, and you'll be screaming it in minutes."

His words send a shiver through me as I debate whether I should actually defy his warning. Ultimately, I push him back far enough to hold my stare. I have no interest in potentially having a public audience for *that*.

"Shouldn't we keep going?"

While his eyes simmer with desire, his lips flatten into a harsh line before he nods in concession, taking a reproachful step back. Gathering my hand once more, he returns to leading us down the side streets and alleys, weaving through the stone buildings and apartments.

Still recovering from the fever of our kiss, I don't notice when Ryland suddenly halts in place, body brimming with tension. I stumble into his rigid back, steadying myself before I open my mouth to ask what's wrong. Flashes of red slice into my vision, stealing my attention as a briny, metallic scent filters through my nose. My hand flies over my mouth as a horrified gasp escapes.

Painted on the wall ahead of us, in crude and thick writing, is a message. Before my eyes can actually read it, my stomach twists with a sickening realization that the paint is not paint at all. It's blood.

And I know the source.

Lying on the ground by the wall is the corpse of a middle-aged man, two slices along each wrist where the blood has dried and crusted. A bucket lies on its side next to the body, a pool of crimson marring the stone ground. My face blanches, and it's a fight not to let the eggs and toast I had for breakfast make a reappearance.

Trying to make sense of this, my stomach suddenly sinks with dread as I recognize the wording on the wall. Talaar. It dawns on me then, the true author of the writing.

Raigar.

A message for Ryland, one that only he would understand.

If I hadn't believed in the Sildhe's omnipotence before, there can be no doubting it now. *That he can truly detect Ryland's location, before we even knew which route we'd be taking to the Guild...*

"What does it say?" I manage to ask, voice a weak rasp.

Ryland's gaze remains trained on the writing as he answers me, voice unsettlingly grim. "'You have chosen to ignore my many summons, so I shall write your orders instead.'" My heart tightens in my chest, pulse throbbing beneath my skin as I wait for him to finish. "'Find the method to destroy that which denies me entry.'"

Ryland works his jaw, teeth clenched so tightly, I imagine they must ache.

A range of emotions rush through my system, one of the being relief. Relief that Raigar seems to have put a pause on demanding Ryland's return. The sensation is quickly washed away, however, by an overwhelming sense of wariness about this new mission. Ryland remains stiff as stone, eyes narrowed in calculation. His detached tone carries with the cool breeze.

"He wants me to learn how to destroy the Sethel. He wants entry into Kingsmar." The hint of surprise in his voice tells me that even he didn't expect this.

"Why?"

Ryland releases a cold huff of laughter as he rubs his jaw, seeming to come to a realization. "Why does any ruler wish to reign from the land's greatest city? The ultimate symbol of power. Easy access to wealth and supplies, proximity to ports and trade routes."

"He wants to rule," I conclude.

"I shouldn't really be surprised. When it comes down to it, Raigar's like any man with a little cunning and lot of greed. I just didn't expect he would make this kind of move now."

The fluttering of dread in my stomach morphs into a full on storm as his words resonate fully. Raigar wants access to the capital. He wants to rule Osterley. I wouldn't be surprised if he intends to dispose of our current sovereign, and probably a good many other individuals deemed hindrances. If the Sethel is destroyed and Raigar can finally enter Kingsmar, there's nothing stopping him from taking the throne. The Sildhe throne with its protective magic that would make him invincible.

And now, Ryland's tasked with the job of figuring out how to put him on that path, how to destroy the Sethel—the last hurdle.

Our sense of urgency had been well-established before, but now, we're really under the clock. We need to access that book to discover another method to kill a Sildhe. *If there even is one.* Then, we need to procure whatever is required to do so, which could be located anywhere, if that something even exists, all before Raigar grows impatient enough to check on Ryland's progress with this new task. My head spins with the impossibility of it all.

Ryland turns to face me, expression set in resolve. "Our plans don't change. We still go to the Guild and wait for the book."

"But—"

"Remember, Raigar is immortal like me. Which means our perception of time is different to yours. A few weeks will feel like only a few days for him, a few hours. He knows to give me enough time to solve this."

"Then, do we even need to leave Aurelia's anymore?"

He nods. "Just because he's given me new orders doesn't mean he won't still place obstacles in my path for entertainment. We'll be safest in the Guild—*you'll* be safest."

I swallow as I realize what obstacles he's referring to: more attackers. Or worse.

"It seems Edwyl is looking out for us," he murmurs with a glance to the sky.

I reel back. "*Luck?*" He thinks the God of Luck and Fortune is on our side right now? I might laugh if I weren't so distressed.

"I'm willing to bet the answer to Raigar's question about how to destroy the Sethel can also be found in the Book of Hessan."

I'm not sure how he's able to recover so quickly from the shock we've just been landed. To recover from it and have his wheels already spinning with plans, jumping straight into strategy.

With a final glance at the wall, Ryland once again gathers my hand in his, leading us away from the bloody message the approaching rain will soon wash away, erasing all traces of the sorcerer's work. Despite Ryland's assurance that we have more time than I think, I can't help the pressing sense of urgency that sits on my chest.

Ryland's blue eyes are fierce as he swiftly moves us along the streets back into the populated thoroughfare. "We'll get through this," he reassures me.

"Alive or dead is what my concern is," I mutter, voice distant as my thoughts whirl into a muddled torrent.

"I told you back in Stone Wood to have a little faith, remember? I'm asking the same of you now," he replies. I stare into those dark eyes, into the conviction and promise that lurks in their depths. He's going to find a way. He's going to protect me. He's going to do whatever it takes. I know Ryland is capable of anything he sets his mind to. His determination and dedication, his cunning and cleverness, his loyalty and care, are what have helped him survive this long. I know that he'll never concede.

As we make our way to the Assassin's Guild, a den of wolves where we'll likely have to spend as much time protecting ourselves as we will using them to protect us, I send a quick prayer to Edwyl to spare us from harm. To ensure that the Book of Hessan is a fruitful acquisition. That it will give us what we need to keep Raigar at bay and Kingsmar protected—and Ryland and me safe. While I don't exactly feel confident that my plea will be answered, I can't help but force myself to place some credence in the god's influence.

After all, we're going to need all the luck he can spare.

CHAPTER 22

THE SILVERN, SULKING SKY UNLEASHES HER GRIEF upon the streets of Kingsmar in a merciless downpour. We departed the Historic District moments before she began her weeping, making our way east toward the ominous compound that we now approach. Our new home for the foreseeable future: The Assassin's Guild.

The slate clouds overhead only increase the intimidation the Guild's buildings and expansive grounds impose. Enclosed by iron fencing, I'm just able to make out the elegant, stately facade of limestone and wrought iron windows. The streets around its perimeter are relatively empty apart from mine and Ryland's sopping forms as we trudge through the deluge. It would seem that the public is neither oblivious nor blind to the nature of residents that inhabit the elegant estate. They simply know to steer well clear of it.

Squinting through the torrent, my gaze drifts over the three-floored structure reminiscent of the countless grand homes we passed when we first arrived in the city. It's secluded enough to create some semblance of privacy whilst still being centrally located.

Perpendicular to the main building, on the right side, is another structure, made of red-brick. Half as large, the smaller edifice boasts a hall of outdoor archways on either end, one which connects to the main house, the other to a small side entrance that intercepts the fencing.

There's a grander gate to our left which also allows entry to the limestone grounds, but I imagine that entrance is used for carriages given its wide berth. I'm certain there are plenty of other hidden entrances and exits, secret tunnels and halls designed to allow for undetected travel, ones I'll likely discover during our stay here. But, it's toward the side entrance along the fence where Ryland leads us, hand clasped around mine as I cling to the flickers of warmth emanating from his palm. The last thing I need is to catch a cold.

Standing before the black gate, Ryland reaches for the dangling rope and proceeds to tug on the bell. Peering through the fence, I note the soft glow of lights from the windows evoking an inviting warmth, beckoning my shivering figure into its tempting embrace. In many ways, the premise looks charming and welcoming, the exterior in complete contrast with the brutal and severe prison I'd had in mind. But, I remind myself that I shall find no comfort or care inside, for some of the most lethal and sadistic killers reside within those walls. A home of butchers and brutes.

"It looks so ordinary," I murmur.

Ryland lowers his gaze to mine, mirth alighting his features. "Were you expecting spiked heads and limbs littering the ground?"

Unwilling to admit to having had precisely such imaginings, I reply, "I definitely wasn't expecting this." But, I suppose, much like the assassins themselves, the establishment is dressed in a disguise. A front of civility and gentility.

A blurred figure makes their way across the grounds toward us, a wisp of shadow trailing through the pale-stoned surroundings. Halting before the iron wicket, the figure's dark eyes narrow in suspicion. "We don't house asylum seekers," he bites, manner most unwelcome. He wears black leathers and no cloak, unperturbed by the inclement weather.

Ryland returns the stare with that unruffled expression of his, a half-smirk toying at his lips. "And what about a colleague?"

Our greeter's eyes relax a fraction, and he inches closer. "Name," he demands.

"You might know me as the Wraith. The Master certainly will."

The man's expression suddenly sobers, brows inching upward as recognition etches into the planes of his face. Clearly, the name means something here, something worth remembering. Once again, I'm reminded of just how little I know about my husband, even now.

"Who's she?" the man questions next, evidently doubting all possibilities of me possessing any lethality. Apparently, I don't carry the look of an assassin. But, after a brief glance at my slight stature, drenched clothes, trembling frame, and hand which clutches Ryland's like a lifeline, I can't exactly blame his assumption. I possess none of the effortless virulence Ryland emits like an intoxicating scent.

"My accomplice," Ryland returns with a wink, voice carrying over the pelting rain. Unamused, the man opens the gate for us. Crossing the threshold, I inhale a steadying breath, awaiting some sort of palpable shift in the air. Ryland swiftly pulls us under the protection of the covered hall, and our clothes drip along the stone floor.

I lift to remove my hood, fingers just having hooked around the soaked fabric, when I'm roughly yanked to the side. Ryland shoves himself in front of me as a cutting force of air slices past my face. My heart skips a beat, and I gasp as a pointed crack sounds beside me. Lungs seized painfully, I shift my gaze, catching sight of the shining dagger only inches from my temple, the blade lodged in the thin crevice of grout between the bricks.

Whipping my attention forward, I watch as our greeter nods at Ryland in approval. Dazed, I realize that the maneuver wasn't meant as a threat but a test. For Ryland. To see if he was skilled enough to truly be a member; if he had the telltale reflexes and speed.

Apparently, he passed.

I hadn't seen the man move, hadn't heard him reach for a weapon, hadn't even seen one on him. But Ryland was prepared for this, only a flicker of rage whetting his gaze as opposed to the frosty glow to which I've become accustom. He knew what to expect, what we were walking into. I thought I did too, but my heart thuds in tandem with the singular warning that blares in my head—we've just stepped into a place of danger, the magnitude of which I've clearly already underestimated. It reestablishes the fact that I can't lower my guard here. Not ever. Despite Ryland's previous assurances, I'm not so sure we'll be safe staying in this place after all.

The man tips his lips at me in a half-grin, a sign of both welcome and warning. As if he's sensed the line of my thinking and agrees with it. My stomach knits itself in knots as I study the sadistic glimmer in his dark eyes, the sharp edge of indifference to suffering and fear, the mask of cruelty and violence firmly intact. A mask I know Ryland has no qualms sporting. One he'll likely be wearing for the duration of our stay here.

Sensing my evident discomfort, the assassin's smile grows, the warmth from Ryland's hand suddenly melting away into an icy dread that now paints my chilled flesh, unease stabbing through my insides like the dagger that rests beside my skull. There's no turning back.

This lamb has just walked into a den of wolves. And they're hungry.

"Welcome," the figure intones, "to the Assassin's Guild."

Author Bio

Hollis has been writing since she could first hold a pen, a passion she has carried throughout her life. When she isn't scribbling stories, Hollis has a successful career in Public Relations and Strategic Communications and works as a freelance consultant for author marketing strategies. Originally from the United States, she resides in London and can often be found wandering its historic streets, visiting her favorite museums and perusing one too many bookstores. An avid traveler, Hollis finds inspiration from all her adventures abroad. She is the author of *The Eternal Hunt*, her debut novel and the first installment of The Moon-Blessed series.

Instagram: @author_hollis.sophia

www.ingramcontent.com/pod-product-compliance
Ingram Content Group UK Ltd.
Pitfield, Milton Keynes, MK11 3LW, UK
UKHW041943230426
12048UKWH00008B/98